American Folk Music and Musicians Series

Series Editor: Ralph Lee Smith
1. *Wasn't That a Time!: Firsthand Accounts of the Folk Music Revival,* edited by Ronald D. Cohen. 1995, paperback edition, 2002.
2. *Appalachian Dulcimer Traditions,* by Ralph Lee Smith. 1997, paperback edition, 2001.

Series Editors: Ralph Lee Smith and Ronald D. Cohen
3. *Ballad of an American: The Autobiography of Earl Robinson,* by Earl Robinson with Eric A. Gordon. 1998.
4. *American Folk Music and Left-Wing Politics, 1927–1957,* by Richard A. Reuss with JoAnne C. Reuss. 2000.
6. *The Hammered Dulcimer: A History,* by Paul M. Gifford. 2001.

Series Editors: Ronald D. Cohen and Ed Kahn
5. *The Unbroken Circle: Tradition and Innovation in the Music of Ry Cooder and Taj Majal,* by Fred Metting. 2001.
7. *The Formative Dylan: Transmission and Stylistic Influences, 1961–1963,* by Todd Harvey. 2001.

Series Editor: Ronald D. Cohen
8. *Exploring Roots Music: Twenty Years of the* JEMF *Quarterly,* edited by Nolan Porterfield. 2004.

Exploring Roots Music

Twenty Years of the JEMF Quarterly

Edited by
Nolan Porterfield

*American Folk Music and
Musicians Series, No. 8*

The Scarecrow Press, Inc.
Lanham, Maryland, and Oxford
2004

SCARECROW PRESS, INC.

Published in the United States of America
by Scarecrow Press, Inc.
A wholly owned subsidary of
The Rowman & Littlefield Publishing Group, Inc.
4501 Forbes Boulevard, Suite 200, Lanham, Maryland 20706
www.scarecrowpress.com

PO Box 317
Oxford
OX2 9RU, UK

Publication of this work was supported by a grant from the Arhoolie
Foundation and the Fund for Labor Culture & History.

British Library Cataloguing in Publication Information Available

Library of Congress Cataloging-in-Publication Data

Exploring roots music : twenty years of the JEMF quarterly / Edited by
Nolan Porterfield.
    p. cm.— (American folk music and musicians series ; no. 8)
    Includes bibliographical references and index.
    ISBN 0-8108-4893-7 (pbk. : alk. paper)
    1. Country music—History and criticism. 2. Country music—
Periodicals—History. 3. JEMF quarterly. 4. John Edwards Memorial
Foundation. I. Porterfield, Nolan. II. Series: American folk music and
musicians ; no. 8.
ML3524 .E9 2004
781.642'05—dc22

                                                 2003015349

Contents

Foreword   viii
Ronald D. Cohen

Introduction   ix
Nolan Porterfield

Folklore: A Sub-Discipline of Media Studies?   1
Ed Kahn

Scopes and Evolution in Hillbilly Songs   7
Norm Cohen

Commercial Music Graphics #9: Sheet Music Covers   15
Archie Green

Grass Roots Commercialism   19
William Henry Koon

Between Two Cultures: One Viewer's Response to
"Earl Scruggs: His Family and Friends"   27
David E. Whisnant

The WLS National Barn Dance Story: The Early Years   34
George C. Biggar

"I'm a Record Man": Uncle Art Satherley Reminisces   45
Norm Cohen

The Life of Alfred G. Karnes   52
Donald Lee Nelson

International Relations, Dr. Brinkley, and Hillbilly Music   58
  Ed Kahn

"Henry Clay Beattie": Once a Folksong   78
  Norm Cohen

John "Knocky" Parker: A Case Study of White and Black
Musical Interaction   86
  John Solomon Otto and Augustus M. Burns

"We Made Our Name in the Days of Radio":
A Look at the Career of Wilma Lee and Stoney Cooper   94
  Robert Cogswell

WNAX: Country Music on a Rural Radio Station,
1927–1955   118
  Bernard C. Hagerty

Woodhull's Old Tyme Masters: A Hillbilly Band in the
Northern Tradition   127
  Simon J. Bronner

Roots of the Country Yodel: Notes toward a Life History   135
  Robert Coltman

Riley Puckett: "King of the Hillbillies"   143
  Norm Cohen

Folk and Hillbilly Music: Further Thoughts on
Their Relations   157
  Anne Cohen and Norm Cohen

Commercial Music Graphics #44: John Held Jr.:
Jazz Age and Gilded Age   169
  Archie Green

Buell Kazee   183
  Loyal Jones

Columbia Records and Old-Time Music   199
  Charles Wolfe

Popular Music and the Fiddler   218
  Gene Wiggins

Country Music in Italy: A Matter of Controversy   237
  Fabrizio Salmoni

The Rise and Decline of the Standard Transcription
Company   248
  Linda L. Painter

Early Knoxville Radio (1921–1941): WNOX and the
"Midday Merry Go-Round"   259
  Willie J. Smyth

Ethnic Country Music on Superior's South Shore   272
  James P. Leary

Commercial Music Graphics #64: Farewell, Tony   289
  Archie Green

"Wreck on the Highway": Rhetoric and Religion in a
Country Song   300
  Tony Hilfer

Index   310

About the Editor   332

Foreword

Nolan Porterfield's editing of twenty-seven seminal articles from the *John Edwards Memorial Foundation Quarterly* significantly expands the breadth and depth of the American Folk Music and Musicians series, launched by Ralph Lee Smith. This volume was initially suggested by my former co-editor, Ed Kahn, whose death in 2002 cut short a life of significant vernacular music scholarship. Indeed, Ed contributed an essay to the first book in the series, "Wasn't That a Time!" (1995, now available in paperback), and it is a most fitting tribute to his scholarly reach and research that the current volume begins with his thoughtful piece "Folklore: A Sub-Discipline of Media Studies?" and also includes his later essay, entitled "International Relations, Dr. Brinkley, and Hillbilly Music." Ed was one of the JEMF founders and served in a significant capacity through its rocky early years.

This book series last issued Todd Harvey's *The Formative Dylan* and will soon publish David Bonner's detailed history of Young People's Records/Children's Record Guild, further demonstrating the flexible definition of folk music that has been our hallmark. Additional titles are in the works, but more are definitely welcomed, as the series continues its thoughtful growth.

Ronald D. Cohen
Series Editor

Introduction

Although it existed in one form or another for some twenty years (1965–1985) and provided the first public forum for the serious scholarly study of country music and other vernacular forms, the *JEMF Quarterly* never became well known, even in academic circles. As its last editor put it, "The name still inevitably elicits a 'J-E-M-what?' response from the uninitiated." Be that as it may, the *JEMF Quarterly* was the right thing at the right time to perform a role of vast importance to the study of our common culture: awakening the nation to the significance of country music, charting its origins and evolution, and providing a platform for research and opinions on the subject.

The history of country music—not unlike other forms of popular culture—is filled with irony, discrepancy, and anomaly. To those who understand this, it should come as no surprise that the pioneer scholar of American country music was a young Australian who never set foot in the United States.

John Kenneth Fielder Edwards was born July 22, 1932, in Sydney, New South Wales. He discovered American country music as a teenager when a friend at school urged him to tune in the local radio station in Newcastle to hear a Carter Family song. This single event, according to Edwards's mother, made a deep impression on him and, in fact, "greatly changed the pattern of John's life." Almost instantly, it seems, he recognized the music's intrinsic value and appeal—those ineffable qualities which attract yet so often elude scholarly definition—and set out at once to find more records and information about them. It was a search that would occupy him for the rest of his short life.

Edwards's family lived comfortably but modestly; like most young collectors, and more than a few older ones, he found his early ambitions thwarted by lack of funds. His first careful purchases were made with what he could save from a meager weekly allowance, but he had moral support as well as extra pennies here and there from his mother and grandmother (who bought him a guitar and paid for lessons when he was fourteen). Soon he had a core collection of several hundred records, assembled from Australian pressings of U.S. masters and discs he found at junk stores or on auction lists put out by American collectors. As his holdings grew he started what was to become a voluminous correspondence—eventually totaling hundreds of letters—directed to other collectors, to record companies and artists, to retired sidemen and minor functionaries, indeed to anyone who might offer a scrap of information or a clue to the whereabouts of some forgotten artist or undocumented recording session. Although others had tried similar methods from time to time, few pursued the quest with such zeal and with such overwhelming results. It was largely through Edwards's efforts that contact was made with dozens of old-time artists who had faded into obscurity (many of whom, it was felt, ignored inquiries from scholars in the United States but answered Edwards because they were flattered by the attentions of someone in faraway Australia). Within a few years, he had located such important early figures as Cliff and Bill Carlisle, Buell Kazee, Gid Tanner, and Goebel Reeves. Later there was correspondence with Sara Carter (who called him "Our John in Australia"), Gene Autry, Wilf Carter, Jimmie Rodgers's wife, Carrie, and Dorsey Dixon, composer of the classic "Wreck on the Highway." When Dixon learned that the last record Edwards had played on his phonograph was the Dixon Brothers' "Not Turning Backward," he composed a tribute song, "Our Johnny," included in the 1965 album *Babies in the Mill* (Testament T-3301). "Our Johnny will always be listening to the music and songs that he loved," Dixon sang.

After finishing school at sixteen, Edwards went to work for the New South Wales Public Service's Department of Transport—his first and only job. Some years later, after he had begun corresponding with American collectors, there was a move among them to bring him to the United States with a university scholarship to study American folklore, but for whatever reasons, he was reluctant to come. Meanwhile, his real enthusiasm, amounting almost to an obsession, continued to be the collecting of country music records by American artists and exploring the then-unknown territory behind them—the lives and careers of those who recorded them, when and where they were recorded, and by what corporate entity. In most cases, this was "mail order" research—seeking to locate some old-time artist, he reached his objective by poring over old record catalogs, folios, and advertising brochures, then simply writing to the postmaster in whatever out-of-the-way hamlet where the person had last been reported. From this barrage of correspondence, and with the help of a few record company executives who were sympathetic—Helen Chmura at Columbia, Brad McCuen at RCA, Milt Gabler at Decca— Edwards began to organize a systematic archive of artist biographies and discographies. In time, this material proved to be even more valuable than his record collection itself.

To disseminate his findings, Edwards turned to the only medium open to him, the few helter-skelter fan magazines and amateur publications, such as *Country and Western Spotlight, Disc Collector,* and *Caravan,* put together by other devotees of early country music and old records. Simultaneously, he shared his work by mail with other collectors around the world and provided valuable information about his methods that allowed them to undertake similar research on their own. Gene Earle, an engineer for ITT then living in New Jersey, relates how, in the early stages of his collecting efforts, he wrote to Edwards asking for a numerical list of recordings by Cliff Carlisle. Edwards's reply was, essentially, "Do it yourself," with a skeleton discography and detailed instructions on how to complete it. "Thus," says Earle, "I learned the technique of discographical research." Earle went on to produce the first discographies of Carlisle, Tom Darby and Jimmie Tarleton, and Bill Cox and Cliff Hobbs. Edwards's enthusiasm was catching; his love of early traditional American folk music and his dedication to researching its history, despite the handicap of great distance, inspired dozens of American scholars who continued his work. Bill Malone's assessment makes the case: "The independent research carried on by men like Edwards, oblivious of whether their work was academically respectable or not, laid the groundwork for full-scale scholarly treatment in the future."

Edwards's activities, including ambitious plans for writing a history of early country music, were cut short by his untimely death in an automobile accident near Parramatta, Australia, as he was returning home from a party on Christmas Eve, 1960. He was twenty-eight.

From adolescence on, Edwards had demonstrated a keen mind and a wide range of interests. In addition to his growing involvement in old-time country music, he loved the outback and spent many hours bushwalking, bike riding, and, later, traveling by car into the country. He was an accomplished artist with a particular bent for drawing maps and locating places not identified on official charts (after his death, this work led to the naming of a mountain after him—Mount Edwards on the south coast of New South Wales). As roster officer for buses and trams with the Department of Transport he became especially interested in trams; a member of the Electric Traction Society, he led a doomed effort to prevent the tramway system from being replaced by buses.

On the personal side, Edwards seems to have been good-natured but fiercely independent and displayed an unusually far-ranging intellect for one who was largely self-taught after high school. He read Chaucer while listening to Jimmie Rodgers and knew several foreign languages. In late 1960 he had enrolled in night classes in folklore at Sydney University but died before the term began. Archie Green thinks that a few years later, he might have been in the vanguard of the hippie movement; he seems to have both cherished and resented his place as an outsider in his native culture. He never married and was still living with his parents when he died. He was a heavy smoker and a serious drinker (which probably contributed to the accident which ended his life).

In October 1958, some fourteen months before his death, Edwards had taken the somewhat unusual step, for someone so young, of making out a will, in which he specified that his collection should not be "given, sold, or made available in any way to anyone outside the U.S.A." Further, he named Gene Earle to take over "all the discs, tapes, dubs, files, photos, and all printed matter relative to my collecting interests," with the intention that they should be used to further the serious study of "genuine country or hillbilly music," from what Edwards considered the "Golden Age," 1924–1939. He was an outspoken critic of the country music of his own time, calling it "pop with a pseudo-western flavor." One can easily imagine what he would make of the Nashville Sound or what passes for "country music" on commercial radio today.

The first stipulation, directing that the collection go only to someone in the United States, was probably in part a reflection of the fact that his work had attracted little interest in Australia; he was, in fact, often laughed at by his countrymen. As someone with strong opinions and great confidence in the value of what he was doing, he did not take such snubs lightly. Further, he had developed close ties (via mail, of course) with various American collectors—Archie Green and Ed Kahn, in addition to Gene Earle and others—who appreciated his efforts and ranked him foremost among early collectors of "hillbilly" music. It would also appear that the United States would be the logical place for Edwards's collection, exclusively comprised of a fundamental element of our native identity. But as a writer for the *Los Angeles Times* so appropriately put it:

> If John Edwards had searched for an area of American culture that was resistant to scholarship, with the possible exception of the Mafia, he could not have found anything tougher than the country and western music field.

He should have also remembered that all countries are blind to their own culture to a greater or lesser extent. The choice of the United States as the repository for his collection was not wise.

The first indication of this problem came when U.S. Customs declared that anyone "importing" the Edwards's collection would have to pay a duty on its assessed value. Said the *Times* writer, "Only the United States would levy a tax on a priceless chunk of its own culture." Eventually U.S. Customs relented when a home was found for the collection at an educational institution, but the road to that destination was not an easy one.

THE JOHN EDWARDS MEMORIAL FOUNDATION

Following John Edwards's death, Gene Earle circulated Edwards's will among other collectors in the United States and sought support for finding a permanent location for the collection, where it would be accessible to the public and serve to commemorate Edwards's pioneering work. He was soon joined in this effort by Ed Kahn, then a graduate student at UCLA, Fred Hoeptner, a Los Angeles engineer, D. K. Wilgus, folklorist at Western Kentucky University, and Archie Green, who at that time was librarian for the Institute of Labor and Industrial Relations at the University of Illinois.

These five—Earle, Kahn, Hoeptner, Wilgus, and Green—became a self-appointed "Board of Advisors," engaged in plans for a nonprofit corporation to be named the John Edwards Memorial Foundation, and the search for a home for Edwards's collection. It seemed logical to all concerned that some major university in the South would be the ideal place for such an archive and would be eager to have it. Early consideration was given to Vanderbilt University, the University of Texas, and the University of North Carolina, only to learn, as Ed Kahn put it, "that country music at that time still was not an acceptable area of study." Academia had no use for such lowlife carrying on; perverse as it now seems, in the early 1960s there was no serious program for the study of regional vernacular culture—certainly none that could have accommodated the Edwards collection—in any major southern university.

There were at the time only three universities in the United States with active folklore programs: the University of Pennsylvania, Indiana University, and the University of California at Los Angeles. UCLA became the logical choice; by the time Wilgus moved from Kentucky to join the UCLA faculty in1963, Earle had accepted a job with Hughes Aircraft in

In 1964 the JEMF had received a $5,000 grant from the Newport Folk Foundation; this money was used to hire a part-time secretary/office manager to underwrite the services of Archie Green as consultant, and to develop a filing system and archiving procedures for JEMF's unique collection of discographic and biographical files, song folios, fan publications, pictures, and other paper materials. Early on, the foundation had begun making available to the public a series of reprints of scholarly articles originally published in academic journals, and to that was added, in 1969, the parallel "JEMF Special Series" of miscellaneous materials and publications. The two series eventually comprised some fifty titles.

Even more ambitious was a project involving a series of record reissues, which, in the words of Norm Cohen, "would span all phases of hillbilly music in a set of carefully planned and meticulously annotated LP albums." The first of these—*The Carter Family on Border Radio* (*JEMF*, 101)—was announced in mid-1972; eight more LPs were eventually added before rights to the series were transferred to Chris Strachwitz's Arhoolie Records in 1983.

In 1967, a longtime fan of western music, Ken Griffis, learned of the JEMF's existence through an item in the *Los Angeles Times* and called Ed Kahn to volunteer his help. From this came the Friends of the JEMF, devoted to raising funds for the foundation. I see from my membership card that the number of dues-paying Friends had reached 442 by the time I became a member in December 1969. In addition to his other efforts, Griffis put together four benefit concerts in the 1970s, the most successful of which raised more than $20,000 that paid off the JEMF's debts and enabled it to remain in the black for several years. Another early and enthusiastic supporter was the late John Hartford, who also donated to the JEMF proceeds from his concerts.

With the renewal of interest in folk and other forms of vernacular music in the late 1960s, the JEMF flourished. In those turbulent but exciting times—Vietnam, antiwar demonstrations, flower children, rock 'n roll psychedelia—it became a major attraction for UCLA's graduate folklore program, drawing numbers of talented students from across the country.

THE *JEMF QUARTERLY*

Long after the fact, Norm Cohen and Ed Kahn adopted a sort of Alphonse-and-Gaston routine regarding the origins of the *JEMF Quarterly*. (Cohen: "Eventually the idea of a regular publication came up. Ed proposed that we co-edit the new publication"; Kahn: "Norm came up

Norm Cohen, 1973

with the idea to begin the *Quarterly*.") That seems merely indicative of the spirit that prevailed from the beginning: to hell with the credit, let's get something done.

What they did initially was to produce an eleven-page mimeographed *JEMF Newsletter*, dated October 1965, that contained precisely three items: (1) a detailed report from Gene Earle on the substantial progress of the foundation since moving into its new quarters in Bunche Hall; (2) a one-page account of a new series of radio programs on Los Angeles's KPFK-FM featuring records from the JEMF collection and hosted by Barry Hansen (later nationally known as "Dr. Demento"); and (3) an abstract of Bill Malone's doctoral dissertation at the University of Texas, "A History of Commercial Country Music in the United States, 1920–1924," which became the groundbreaking "bible" of country music scholarship, *Country Music, U.S.A.*

Editors Cohen and Kahn cautiously announced that the *JEMF Newsletter* would appear "several times a year at irregular intervals" more or less as a house organ, containing reports of the foundation; news of works-in-progress; notes and queries; bibliographic and discographical data; reprints of material from ephemeral sources; and correspondence. It would act, in other words, as a kind of clearinghouse for the growing numbers of professional and amateur scholars with a serious interest in the study of "American folk music" (broadly defined).

This format prevailed, more or less intact, for the next three years, during which time the newsletter grew from eleven to forty-five pages and more. From the beginning it depended heavily on the hard work and ded-

Ed Kahn, 1967

ication of volunteers and one or two part-time people who were actually remunerated. Early on, staffers even sold hot dogs at local music contests to raise money for postage, which was inadequately provided by the initial subscription price—$1.00 for ten issues. The rate was increased to $2.50 with issue no. 5. Membership in the Friends of the JEMF, announced in January 1968, was $5.00, which included a subscription to the newsletter. (Subscriptions became $7.50 with no. 29 [spring 1975] of the *JEMF Quarterly* and rose steadily throughout the inflationary 1970s. The rate was $12.00 when the publication eventually folded.)

Issue no. 6 (June 1967) is distinguished for having inaugurated Archie Green's "Commercial Music Graphics" series, which became the publication's longest-running feature and, according to Norm Cohen, "perhaps its most significant contribution to music scholarship." There were eventually sixty-eight installments, one in every issue from then on. (A possible exception is nos. 65/67, which, instead of a graphics article, contained Green's lengthy review of the Smithsonian collection of classic country music, with many illustrations.) The indefatigable Green, nationally known for having spearheaded the successful drive to establish the American Folk Life Center at the Library of Congress, served as a major guide and protector of the JEMF until the bitter end. His powers of persuasion led a colleague to describe him as "one of the great lobbyists of our time."

As time passed, the scope of the newsletter began to broaden, showing slight but significant interest in forms of commercial music apart from "hillbilly." Abstracts of dissertations on jazz and race recordings were published, and the first original article (other than Green's graphics series) appeared in issue no. 10—a biblio-discography of the "Whitehouse Blues"/"McKinley"/"Cannonball Blues" song complex, written by Neil Rosenberg.

By and large, however, the newsletter remained primarily focused on internal activities of the foundation and listings of materials from its archives. But encouraged by the interest and support it generated, in early 1969 Editor Norm Cohen took the great leap. (Ed Kahn had left in 1967 to do fieldwork in Nepal.) With issue no. 13 (spring 1969), the *JEMF Newsletter* became the *JEMF Quarterly,* forty-four lithographed pages in magazine format with a stiff, wrap-around cover. The content was still in typewriter font, but pictures were now routinely incorporated, in place of the single, specially prepared "graphics" page that had been collated and stapled into the newsletter. The publication's "mission statement" was expanded from the various terms used to describe hillbilly string band music to include articles on "race," "blues," "rhythm & blues," "soul," "rock & roll," "folk rock," and "rock." Readers were encouraged to submit original articles, and where the newsletter had advised, "Please address communications to . . .," the masthead now said, "Please address manuscripts and other communications to. . . ." It was a significant new direction for the fledgling publication.

The transformation took time. Early issues of the *JEMF Quarterly* were not much thicker than the *JEMF Newsletter,* and many submissions were by eager but inexperienced graduate students and equally enthusiastic amateurs who did not write very well. On the other hand, to its great credit, and with telling results, the *JEMF Quarterly* encouraged input from "our friends outside the academic institutions" and strove to avoid the elitism of many scholarly publications.

For some time the focus was on history, biography, and discography. Theoretical articles and features on content, psychology, or social context were rare. In a famously scathing review of *Stars of Country Music* (Bill Malone and Judith McCulloh, eds.; Univ. of Illinois Press), William Henry Koon decried the "Look! I Discovered, Still Living, the Mediocre Brothers!" school of country music writing. Koon was not entirely right—raw historical data is a necessary precursor to analysis and evaluation—but his cool assessment of "the peripheral, the casual, the slovenly, the 'legend' ridden, and the just plain poorly done" struck more than a few nerves and surely had considerable, if subconscious, impact on those who were then researching and writing about country music. It was still a new field, with unplowed ground, and there were scarcely enough good writers and scholars to go around. The *JEMF Quarterly* had to take what it could get; even so, it published most of the pioneers who went on to write books about country music and make a name for themselves in that area: Charles Wolfe, Ivan Tribe, Gene Wiggins, Loyal Jones, Wayne W. Daniel, Ken Griffis, W. K. McNeil, and many others. Their reward for an article in the *JEMF Quarterly* was little more than two copies of the journal, and for the academics, a modest item to add to their papers for promotion or tenure.

In early 1973, the *JEMF Quarterly* took notice of new publications that had joined the field. The Country Music Foundation *News Letter,* begun in 1970, had become *The Journal of Country Music (JCM)* in 1971; in London that same year, *Old Time Music (OTM),* edited by Tony Russell, began quarterly publication. Noting that *JCM* covered current and recent aspects of country music and *OTM* specialized in the artists and music of the 1920s and 1930s, the *JEMF Quarterly* called for its contributors to broaden their interests into other areas of commercially recorded and published folk music that were not receiving much attention in print. These included foreign-language U.S. recordings, rural and ethnic humorists, and turn-of-the-century banjo and fiddle music. The *JEMF Quarterly* took heat from some faithful readers who objected to what they perceived as a radical shift away from the "real" country music of the 1920s and 1930s. It was, they felt, a betrayal of the aims and interests of John Edwards himself. The editor stuck to his guns, offering evidence that Edwards had not confined his collecting and research to the so-called Golden Age of hillbilly music—among his records were ample numbers by blues, jazz, and pop artists; he wrote a bio-discography of Frank Crumit; and his discography of the Carter Family followed their career into the 1950s.

By the mid-1970s, the *JEMF Quarterly* was regularly publishing issues of fifty pages and more. Along the way, it added increasing numbers of book and record reviews and "bibliographic notes," all invaluable in helping readers keep up with what was happening in the field. Interest in material of greater scope and depth than the history of the Mediocre Brothers is indicated by such titles as "International Relations, Dr. Brinkley, and Hillbilly Music" (Ed Kahn), "Country Music in Italy" (Fabrizio Salmoni), and "'Wreck on the Highway': Rhetoric and Religion in a Country Song" (Tony Hilfer).

The period from 1978 to 1982 may be thought of as the *JEMF Quarterly*'s heyday. During that time it carried articles on an increasingly diverse range of topics, including Chuck Berry; country music in the North; "Cosmic Cowboys and Cosmetic Politics"; Bessie Smith; and "Cohen on the Telelphone," as well as several seminal pieces on early country radio. Articles tended to be longer, more in-depth, and better written; there were fewer "preliminary" discographies, sketchy biographies, and "Notes toward a Study of ——." In 1979 Patricia Atkinson Wells became associate editor; four issues later (no. 59), she was joined by Linda L. Painter. With no. 63, Painter became the sole editor on the masthead, although Norm Cohen remained a steady presence, writing many of the book and record reviews, as he had done all along, and performing other editorial tasks.

Those out in subscriber land detected the first real sign of trouble in early 1982, when the spring issue (no. 65) was delayed and then combined with no. 66, without comment from the editor. Only persons close to the scene knew that this was merely a reflection of the precarious situation of the JEMF itself. There had been warnings as early as 1978, when no. 49 of the *JEMF Quarterly* reported on the annual meeting of JEMF advisors and directors (an account probably overlooked by most of the readership). The language of the report was a bit vague, but what was clear was that, even after fourteen years, the relationship between the JEMF and UCLA had never been formalized, and the specter of "actively moving the JEMF to some other site" first raised its ugly head, although the board considered that a last resort and, in hopes of resolving the problem, appointed a committee to work with the UCLA administration.

The *JEMF Quarterly* carried no further word of the situation until the fall/winter 1982 issues (nos. 67/68), which were also combined. Norm Cohen, as executive secretary of the parent organization, took a page headed "JEMF Changes Status" to quietly announce the rather startling news that the physical assets of the archive were being sold to the University of North Carolina. In making the announcement, Cohen tried, as he said, "to avoid the tone of either defeatism or triumph," but he was clearly disappointed. The JEMF, despite the high hopes, dedication, and hard work of its founders and others had never quite established a secure financial base. At UCLA it always struggled to maintain a status even lower than that of a stepchild, consigned to a far, far corner of a cold hearth. For a brief time it seemed to have gotten to its feet, only to be done in by cash flow, ambitious but costly projects, and rob-Peter-to-pay-Paul bookkeeping schemes.

Along with the archive's move to North Carolina came a name change, for legal reasons: "John Edwards Memorial Foundation" became "John Edwards Memorial Forum." The *JEMF Quarterly* would remain at UCLA; Wayland Hand had retired, but the new director of the Folklore and Mythology Center was, in Cohen's words, "anxious to continue some relationship with JEMF." That "some relationship" didn't show a lot of enthusiasm on the director's part; it was as limp and vague as the old arrangement.

At the same time, Cohen rightly called attention to the JEMF's achievements over two decades:

> We have led the way, in both printed and recorded media, toward the acceptance of country music and its related folk-derived forms as a subject of serious study at American educational institutions. In a more intangible way, we have been partly responsible for the contemporary country music industry's realization that it had an obligation to foster the study of, and respect for, the music to which it owes its existence. And as it has become apparent that country music's acceptance is nearly complete, we have turned our attention to other aspects of American vernacular music (e.g., folk-rock, gospel, and ethnic music) and music-related culture to pursue the same goals.

The *JEMF Quarterly,* said Cohen, would continue "as a magazine that straddles the gap between the scholarly and the popular orientations, with the object of its attention being all forms of American vernacular music. ... Whether such a venture will be financially feasible remains to be seen."

Within a year it had proved to be neither financially feasible nor physically possible, lacking ready access to the archive or serious institutional support. Six more issues—some with as many as sixty or more pages—were published at UCLA, but the gap between cover date and actual publication steadily widened, stretching out through the late 1980s. The seventh, dated fall/winter 1984, was another combined issue but with only the single number (74) and appeared in late 1987. It was published by the Center for Popular Music at Middle Tennessee State University, Murfreesboro, and carried an unsigned "Editorial," ostensibly by Norm Cohen, once again listed as editor. The editorial explained that Paul Wells, former JEMF advisor and employee, now director of the Center for Popular Music, had agreed to undertake "publication of the final issues of the JEMFQ in its present format"—a cautious way of indicating that the *JEMF Quarterly*'s days were numbered. Irony of ironies, just as the publication was going on life support, it was being printed on better paper, with computerized typography and improved reproduction of graphics.

The next issue, spring/summer 1985 (nos. 75/76) didn't appear until May 1989. Only the long delay betrayed the true state of affairs; otherwise, it was a plump (seventy pages), healthy offering, with eight substantial articles on diverse topics, a lengthy book review essay (again by Norm Cohen), and a lively exchange in the letters column. Another editorial, however, announced the forthcoming "last *JEMF Quarterly*." It would be succeeded, we were told, by a semi-annual publication entitled *American Vernacular Music,* and the masthead carried detailed instructions about style and subject matter for those interested in submitting articles to the new journal. Sadly, *American Vernacular Music* sank without a trace before it ever reached the press.

The last *JEMF Quarterly,* dated fall/winter 1985 and originally scheduled for the fall of 1989, finally appeared a year later—"With this issue, we lay to rest the name *JEMF Quarterly.*" At the suggestion of Archie Green, it carried a series of articles reflecting on the JEMF's history and achievements and, perhaps fittingly, obituaries for Wayland Hand and D. K. Wilgus. It was the end of an era.

When the John Edwards archive—now known as the John Edwards Memorial Collection—reached the University of North Carolina at

Chapel Hill in April 1983, it was greeted with enthusiasm and considerable fanfare. For some time, however, it languished, unpacked, in a locked room in the basement of the Undergraduate Library. In late 1986, it was combined, on paper at least, with the UNC Folklore Archives to create the entity now known as the Southern Folklore Collection (SFC) and placed under the administrative control of the Manuscripts Department in the university's library system. A few months later, the SFC found a permanent home in the newly renovated Wilson Library, a building for special collections at UNC.

As time passed, however, the JEMF (as "Foundation" or as "Forum") steadily shrank from view. For scholars and others distant from its home location, the *JEMF Quarterly* had always been the JEMF's most visible and vital function; without that public voice, it became just another archive within an archive, valuable to the University of North Carolina but far removed from its former coterie of enthusiastic editors, scholars, and camp followers.

The last hurrah came in early 2002 with the publication of *Country Music Sources: A Biblio-Discography of Commercially Recorded Traditional Music*. This monumental work, begun and nurtured for years by the late Guthrie T. ("Gus") Meade, was almost finished at the time of his sudden death in 1991 at the age of only fifty-eight. A close friend, the noted discographer and collector Dick Spottswood, volunteered to bring the manuscript up-to-date and put it in final form, with the assistance of Meade's son, Douglas. The John Edwards Memorial Forum offered the Southern Folklore Collection the last dollars in its coffers to see the book into print, after which the JEMF ceased to exist as a legal or physical entity. Edwards's collection, of course, remains within the SFC at the University of North Carolina. I like to think that John Edwards's ghost walks those halls, serene and happy with the knowledge that his work continues to aid and inspire new generations of scholars, historians, and plain ordinary people who love the music of their native culture.

THIS VOLUME

Reading through the complete run of the *JEMF Quarterly* is something of an education. Perhaps I should say "re-education"; I read every issue from cover to cover when it appeared but digested and retained only a fraction. There is much to be learned and relearned not merely from articles in the *JEMF Quarterly* but also from letters, book and record reviews, and other ephemera. Names, dates, and facts, once disconnected and unfamiliar, now fall into place, and it is not only interesting but instructive to look back and see the beginnings of studies that turned into books, how opinions were formed, and what topics held the interest of scholars and writers who were operating essentially in a new field of study two decades ago and more.

Hence the impulse to want to reprint everything. But taken out of context, letters and reviews lose most of their value, and many projects which never got beyond the "preliminary" or "notes toward" stage now seem irrelevant, when in fact they do have certain significance as negative results, always an important part of scholarly investigation. Reality must be faced, however: no publisher or reader is really interested in twelve (or however many) volumes of the *JEMF Quarterly*. Decisions have to be made.

It would be easier if this section could be headed "Principles of Selection," but, alas, the "principles" are vague, subjective, problematic, miasmic, and sometimes, it might seem, mutually exclusive. I suspect that no one familiar with the publication will be entirely happy with the results. I'm certainly not.

First, this volume was not conceived of as a "best of" anthology, although quality was a primary consideration. We certainly wanted to use only good stuff. "Representative" is perhaps a better term: seminal articles along with those which demonstrate the range and diversity of the publication over time. But add the quality factor, and mutual exclusivity immediately sets in. Who determines "seminal," and what to do with an otherwise valuable piece on ethnic music that is poorly written? Deciding on arrangement was a simpler matter; printing the articles in chronological order seemed both easy and logical, and it might also allow the reader to gain some insight into the development of the journal. (In the interests of design, the three items from Archie Green's graphics series are spaced early, middle, and late, without regard to the place of the issue in which they appeared; for various reasons, some illustrations which accompanied the originals have been deleted.) We hoped that the ultimate selections would be both interesting and informative, and given other priorities, we sought articles that have as much relevance today as when they were published, some as many as thirty years ago. (Note that the first-person plural pronoun in this paragraph is not the editorial "we." Ron Cohen generously acted as a sounding board and offered wise counsel; valuable input also came from Archie Green, Norm Cohen, Gene Earle, and Chris Strachwitz. Thus I think of this as "our" project, but of course all responsibility for bad calls, errors, and omissions is mine.)

At the outset, we boldly asserted that only one piece per given author would be included—and quickly had to give that up. The work of Ed Kahn and Norm Cohen was simply so pervasive, strong, and valuable that it would defeat our overall purpose to limit them to only one title. Only three entries from Archie Green's graphics series is certainly inadequate, but, again, considerations of space and reproduction ruled.

It is easier to say what was excluded: articles judged too brief, superficial, or badly written, as well as features with a short shelf life, notably letters and reviews. In some ways this is a shame, because letters and reviews—especially negative reviews—were often lively and interesting. (Readers tended to complain about negative reviews, not necessarily to defend the victim but to assert that if the *Quarterly* couldn't say something nice, it shouldn't say anything—an understandable but wrongheaded notion.) A fairly easy call was the exclusion of articles or topics that later became books or were otherwise superseded by later scholarship. Still, it was only with great reluctance that we passed up such items as the delightful two-part "Recollections of Merle Travis" (nos. 54 and 55), on the grounds that much of the same material is available elsewhere.

We also had to take into consideration accompanying "apparatuses"— endnotes, headnotes, discographies, pictures, graphs, and so on—which would unduly complicate the process of transferring material from the original to book form. One article on bluegrass illustrates the problem. It contained markers for eleven endnotes in the first paragraph; the complete set of notes took up three pages. In light of our priorities concerning style, readability, and space, this seemed excessive. Similarly, time and changes in technology took its toll: Dave Evans contributed a fine article in no. 50, "Field Recording with the Phonograph Record in Mind," but improvements in recording equipment and, especially, the passing of the LP rendered much of it obsolescent.

Finally, consider the numbers. I estimate that the *JEMF Quarterly* published some 240 articles over its twenty-year span. Of those, ninety-one were initially selected; then the list was pared to fifty, which produced a manuscript about twice as long as could comfortably fit into a decent and feasible volume. By the time the final decisions had to be made, we were long past mourning for those articles which didn't make the cut.

A word or two about editing: wherever possible, we have printed the original article intact. In a few cases I have done minor editing to remove or amend references to material now dated. Almost entirely, pictures or other graphics accompanying the article (and references to them) have been deleted because we have no access to the originals, thus rendering reproduction inadvisable or impossible. For a variety of reasons, we decided not to include discographies, both stand-alone and those accompanying articles. Many were preliminary, incomplete, or prone to error. The *JEMF Quarterly*'s early discographical work was invaluable at the time, but it has now been superseded by comprehensive, definitive works on the subject, notably Gus Meade's *Country Music Sources* and Tony Russell's *Country Music Records: A Discography, 1921–1942* (Oxford University Press).

If those who assembled the *JEMF Quarterly* followed a style sheet, there's little evidence of it; block quotes were sometimes indented, sometimes printed in italic; some sections had headers, some did not. Documentation form varied widely from issue to issue. Given the conditions under which the magazine was produced, the marvel is that the editing was reasonably consistent over the years. I have attempted to correct those occasional typographical errors that later caused Norm Cohen to wince, unnecessarily, long after the fact. Otherwise, I've made little effort to regularize form and style; the articles are reprinted as they appeared in the original. Some were preceded by headnotes; most were not. Where those headnotes provide pertinent information today, we have retained them without regard for consistency throughout the volume.

In general, articles which hold up best are those dealing with a subject enclosed in a past which was distant from the time of writing, and they are most easily read today without regard for timeliness. But we have also included pieces about people, events, and topics contemporaneous with publication, some of which may seem "open-ended" or confusing unless the reader bears in mind that they were written as long ago as thirty years. We believe that their historical value alone justifies inclusion, but most are as relevant today as when they were written.

The *JEMF Quarterly* strived, under the circumstances, to be as comprehensive, informative, and carefully documented as possible. That was the spirit which created and motivated the publication. It is my fond hope and firm belief that you will see that spirit at work in this book.

Nolan Porterfield

SOURCES

Information for this introduction came from various articles on John Edwards in the *Ralph Stanley International Fan Club Journal,* 3, no.1 (n.d.); Bill Malone,

Country Music, U.S.A. (Austin: University of Texas Press, 1968), 355; various articles in *JEMF Quarterly,* nos. 77/78 (fall/winter 1985); Norm Cohen, "The John Edwards Memorial Foundation: Its History and Significance," in *Sounds of the South,* ed. Daniel W. Patterson (Durham, N.C.: Duke University Press, 1991), 113–126; telephone conversations with Norm Cohen, Archie Green, Gene Earle, and Chris Strachwitz.

(The complete run of the JEMF Newsletter/Quarterly, *ISSN 0021-3632, is available from University Microfilms, Ann Arbor, Michigan, www.umi.com.)*

Ed Kahn

Folklore: A Sub-Discipline of Media Studies?

Folklorists traditionally have been concerned with a wide range of materials as well as with a variety of approaches to the subject matter. Studies have focused on text as well as style and form as well as function. But central to much of folklore scholarship has been an interest in folk process. Folk process when applied to an individual item becomes a case study; folk process when applied to several items of any genre leads to broader generalizations about the nature of the folk process itself. In this paper I shall focus upon questions involving folk process in an attempt to see how folklore studies might move into the twentieth century.

Folklore scholarship dealing with folk process traditionally focused on older items that have been handed down for some time. The emphasis has been on items that have been transmitted in the simplest way: by word of mouth for verbal folklore. Generally, folklorists have tended to avoid items that can be demonstrated to have non-folk origin. Also they have shied away from items that have case histories in which simple folk transmission has taken a secondary role to more complex forms of transmission. But this insistence on folk origin and folk transmission has caused the discipline many problems and promises many more.

In the area of folksong, it has long been tacitly recognized that we cannot insist upon an unhindered oral tradition. In this century, folksong—at least in the English-speaking world—has been heavily influenced by numerous devices of mass media, such as phonograph, radio,

1

and television. To ignore these influences is to ignore the development of most folksongs in the twentieth century. In an earlier period, the same kind of influence was felt from print. Once we commit ourselves to study the process of traditional items, we must inevitably come to terms with the role of mass media in the transmission of these items if we are to deal with such material in a highly industrialized complex society.

Let us illustrate this point briefly by reference to the American ballad, "The Wreck of the Old Ninety-Seven" (Laws G2). In addition to the historical data dealing with a wreck that occurred on September 27, 1903, at White Oak Mountain, just north of Danville, Virginia, we must also delve in great detail into the annals of the commercial music industry. Dispute over the authorship of this ballad eventually led to an appeal to the Supreme Court. So to study properly the process involved in this ballad we will be called upon to go far from what we have conventionally defined as our field. We must refer to court records and corporate files as well as the more conventional folklore data. To evaluate this data, we will require an understanding of the business practices of the music industry in the 1920s. To account for the popularity of the ballad across the United States we will be forced to consider the marketing practices of the companies which offered recordings of the ballad. Where were sales concentrated? How do the recovered texts and tunes of the ballad relate to the numerous commercial recordings? By delving into company histories and trying to fully understand the corporate structure of the music industry, we might be able more fully to answer such questions. We will also be forced to examine broadcasting policies of radio stations. Did stations play the recordings of the ballad? Were live performances frequent? These kinds of questions will be dealt with only through extensive interviews and examinations of station histories and broadcasting regulations.

Folklorists concerned with the dynamics of folk process have always tried to learn as much as they could about the transmission of folklore. As print became a real factor in folklore, the folklorist enlarged his model to take this into account. Now he is being called upon once again to enlarge his model, but the new dimension is a good deal more complex than the old. Folklore in a highly industrialized society is seldom a simple word-of-mouth transmission. Increasingly there is an intermediary between the transmitter and receiver of folklore that must be taken into account. In the simple model of person-to-person transmission, the major factors were the attitudes and tastes of both the transmitter and receiver. A folktale that gained currency obviously said something of interest to both teller and listener. In a traditional setting, balladry could be analyzed in terms of the aesthetics of the performer and the aesthetics of the audience. But with the introduction of the mass media into the process, whole new dimensions must be taken into account. Now, for the first time, we have an intermediary level between transmitter and receiver of folklore: namely the mass media industry.

In order to understand this more complex model, we must devote a good deal of attention to this intermediary level, for it will inevitably have a strong influence upon the material. In a sense the industry serves as a filter and ultimately determines what is offered and the style of presentation. As an example of this influence, we can look briefly at the change that took place when commercial recording became a factor in traditional music. In the days before recorded traditional performances, a musician developed his aesthetics in terms of a first-person audience. He made music that both satisfied himself and pleased his audience. The best musicians were rewarded by eager listeners. We can begin to see the traditional performer's aesthetics in relation to the aesthetics of his audience. If there were not some agreement, his success as a musician would be slight. His regional style was also the predominant musical style to which the audience had been exposed. But with the introduction of a sound recording as an intermediary factor, the entire model changed. Suddenly the musician had no relationship to his audience other than sales figures. There was little or no feedback. It was virtually impossible for him to perceive his audience's aesthetic response. He did not even know whether a customer bought the record for the first or the second side. Furthermore, the widespread mass audience represented a diversity of aesthetics about which the musician could know little because his training had been in the single aesthetic of a region. In addition to these changes, the musician's emphasis shifted from pleasing the small audience to trying to anticipate what the recording executives wanted. In effect, the audience became the record company rather than an expanded listening public. So in order to understand the nature of the filtering process which the industry provided, we must understand the factors that were guiding the industry in its choice of material. More often than not these forces were stated in business rather than aesthetic terms. We are just now beginning to recognize that the formal corporate structure of a mass media industry has a strong influence upon the output provided. For example, in the United States a major record company cannot afford to release a record with limited appeal because there are so many distributors that the required inventory might exceed anticipated sales. In Japan, on the other hand, affiliate companies can afford to release relatively obscure material with a limited market because there are so few distributors throughout the country that a large initial inventory is not required.[1]

With such pressures—of which we know far too little—operating within the mass media industries, we must be aware that the nature of folklore is going to be increasingly shaped by those industries. It is clear to anyone working with traditional music that rural music today is being strongly influenced by commercial country and popular music. Older styles are dying out to be replaced by more contemporary styles learned from radio, phonograph, television and personal appearances of professional entertainers. Like it or not, traditional music is being heavily influenced by a new brand of music being presented to a mass audience. Regional styles are being supplanted by a national and even international style. The folklorist interested in folk process has no choice but to become more familiar with the inner workings of the media industries if he hopes to understand the dynamics of change.

While the process of transmission is much more complex when we deal with mass media rather than person-to-person transmission, there are great similarities between the two. The folk process is essentially the same in either case. Although the complexity of the situation is in sharp contrast to the simpler person-to-person transmission, we can perhaps begin to find answers to many of the questions about folk process that have until now eluded us. When we examine traditions that are born, transmitted and developed through the aid of mass media, we have in many ways a laboratory condition. The rate of change is much greater when mass media are involved. While we try to build up enough good case studies of traditional materials, we generally lack adequate data to begin to make valid generalizations.

In folk process studies involving media, we can often get more details to help us draw conclusions and furthermore we can see traditions throughout their entire life cycle. Joke cycles, for instance, which begin on a person-to-person level are from time to time picked up by television and given a wider audience as well as an expanded currency on the folk level. After the cycles run their course in a matter of weeks, months, or television seasons they will drop from popular currency. With enough adequate case studies of these kinds of cycles we can hope to begin to make valid generalizations. With these conclusions we can then begin to examine some of the traditional person-to-person case studies and look for expanded generalizations. Not only will we gain additional insight about the folk process, but we will also see clearly the role of media in

shaping tradition. It is precisely the contrast between traditional folk process studies and the more complex media folk process studies that will give us insight into the role of mass media not only in folklore, but in society in general.

Admittedly the model for studying folk process when mass media are involved is a good deal more complex than in the case of person-to-person folk process. If we master the more complex model, then we can regard conventional folk process as merely a special case of media process studies: that in which there is no intermediary between transmitter and receiver.

The folklorist is in a unique position to make a special contribution to media studies and at the same time broaden his own horizons. The processes involved in media transmission and in the transmission of folklore are so similar that the folklorist can begin to make comments upon a continuum of processes ranging from the simple person-to-person transmission of traditional folklore to the highly complex passing of material from business firm to business firm without its ever filtering down to a popular level of participation. Between these two extremes lie a wide variety of different combinations. With the insight the folklorist has gained through a long history of detailed folk process studies, he is now prepared to begin to expand his model to include the newer more complex forms. He will undoubtedly add new insight to media studies and at the same time prepare himself to deal with the reality that folklore is indeed influenced by mass media of communication.

(An earlier version of this paper was read on April 19, 1969, at the seventeenth annual meeting of the California Folklore Society held at Northridge, California.)

NOTE

1. See my "Folksong on Records" in *Western Folklore,* 27 (1968): 224–228.

Norm Cohen

Scopes and Evolution in Hillbilly Songs

In mid-October 1970, John Thomas Scopes, then a resident of Shreve-port, La., died of cancer at the age of seventy. Forty-five years ago, Scopes and the little Tennessee town of Dayton had been at the center of world attention when the then young high school biology teacher was on trial for violating Tennessee state law by teaching evolution.[1] Much has been written about that trial and its bizarre features: nevertheless Scopes' recent passing provides an occasion for commenting on an aspect of the trial that has practically escaped notice, namely, the several hillbilly songs that were recorded in the wake of the litigation and that offer an interesting example of the attitudes of the southern mountain folk toward evolution, the Bible and related matters.[2] In this brief article I offer transcriptions of several hillbilly recordings, including only enough general historical background as is necessary to appreciate the events under discussion.

The 1920s in this country, in the aftermath of the Great War, were a period of great social upheaval and unrest: violent race riots, repressive measures against radicals, the growth of such products of intolerance as the KKK and the prohibition movement, and the isolationism evidenced in the rejection of the League of Nations and the World Court character-ized the spirit of the times. William Jennings Bryan, in earlier years the thrice-unsuccessful Democratic presidential candidate, was now the leader of the Fundamentalist Party, a religious-political movement one of whose aims was the suppression of the teaching of science, and in par-

7

ticular of the theory of evolution. Bills were introduced in almost every southern state legislature to prohibit the teaching of Darwin's theory. On March 21, 1925, Tennessee's governor signed into law the Butler bill, which made it unlawful "to teach any theory that denies the story of the Divine Creation of man as taught in the Bible, and to teach instead that man has descended from a lower order of animals."

John Scopes, the science teacher and football coach at the Dayton high school, expressed bewilderment to his engineer friend, George W. Rappelyea, that the state should supply him with a textbook that presented the theory of evolution but make it unlawful for him to teach it. Rappelyea suggested that he swear out a warrant against Scopes for violating the state law in order to test the constitutionality of the law. This was done on May 5, and two days later Scopes was arrested. Within a week, the American Civil Liberties Union in New York announced that they would defend Scopes, and subsequently appointed counsel, including Clarence Darrow. William Jennings Bryan announced he would join the prosecution.

On July 10 the trial began, and continued until July 21. During the trial Darrow, who was widely believed to be an agnostic, brought Bryan to the stand to testify as an expert witness on the Bible, in the course of which he elicited from Bryan the statement that the Bible is to be believed verbatim. Although Darrow had brought to Dayton numerous religious authorities to testify on the Bible and to argue that there were other ways to interpret its meaning, Judge Raulston did not allow them to testify. He contended that the trial was not to determine the constitutionality of the law, but simply whether or not Scopes had violated it. Darrow and the others agreed that there was no sense contesting Scopes' guilt on that count, and on July 21 Scopes was found guilty and the minimum fine of $100 was imposed. On July 26, Bryan died in his sleep in his hotel in Dayton. The following year the Tennessee Supreme Court heard the appeal case, eventually upholding the constitutionality of the Butler Act but reversing the conviction on a technicality. The Butler Act remained in effect until a few years ago.

On July 10, the day the trial began, Vernon Dalhart recorded Carson J. Robison's composition, "The John T. Scopes Trial," for Columbia. Although Robison's text avoids a direct assertion of Scopes' guilt, its author was sufficiently familiar with southern attitudes and mores to know that the sentiments he expressed would find ready acceptance throughout the South. The recording was released before the end of July, and in the next two months Dalhart recorded the song for three other companies. The text of the song follows:

All the folks in Tennessee are as faithful as can be,
And they know the Bible teaches what is right;
They believe in God above and his great undying love,
And they know they are protected by his might.

Then to Dayton came a man with his new ideas so grand,
And he said, "We came from monkeys long ago";
But in teaching his belief Mr. Scopes found only grief,
For they would not let their old religion go,

Cho: You may find a new belief, it will only bring you grief,
For a house that's built on sand is sure to fall;
And wherever you may turn there's a lesson you will learn
That the old religion's better after all.

Then the folks throughout the land saw his house was built on sand,
And they said, "We will not listen anymore";
So they told him he was wrong and it wasn't very long,
'Til he found that he was barred from every door.

Oh, you must not doubt the word that is written by the Lord,
For if you do your house will surely fall;
And Mr. Scopes will learn that wherever he may turn
The old religion's better after all. (Repeat Cho.)

Although Robison forecast correctly the local attitude toward the trial, he could not foresee Bryan's sudden death. Consequently, another song was required, which Dalhart recorded for Columbia on August 10, and then later for two other companies. The song, "Bryan's Last Fight," was a generous eulogy of the silver-tongued orator and his fundamentalist views:

Listen now all you good people, and a story I will tell,
About a man named Mr. Bryan, a man that we all loved so well.

He believed the Bible's teaching, and he stood for what was right,
He was strong in his convictions and for them he'd always fight.

Cho: Now he's gone way up in heaven, where he'll find an open door,
But the lesson that he taught us, it will live forever more.

When the good folks had their trouble down in Dayton far away,
Mr. Bryan went to help them and he worked both night and day.

There he fought for what was righteous and the battle it was won,
Then the Lord called him to heaven for his work on earth was done.

Cho: If you want to go to heaven when your work on earth is thru
You must believe as Mr. Bryan, you will fail unless you do.

On August 7, 1925, Charles O. Oaks, a blind minstrel from Richmond, Kentucky, recorded two songs about the Scopes trial: one was Robison's "John T. Scopes Trial," but the other was his own composition, "The Death of William Jennings Bryan." Oaks, born around 1870 or possibly earlier, wrote several songs dealing with local incidents or accidents. Two of his early broadsides were published in the *Journal of American Folklore* in 1909. One of these dealt with a murder in Knox County, Kentucky, and the other with a 1904 wreck on the Southern Railroad near New Market, Tennessee. Oaks attended Virginia School for the Blind, where in 1921 he met Lester MacFarland and Robert Gardner, with whom he later sang and recorded. Between August 3 and August 7 he recorded two dozen songs for Vocalion, including the two items dealing with the Scopes trial. His other songs were mostly sentimental numbers dealing with alcohol, orphanage, mother, and infidelity.

His song about Bryan, although expressing the same point of view as Robison's two compositions, differed in an important way from them. Whereas Oaks minced no words in praising Bryan and roundly condemning his adversaries in the strongest terms, Robison's pieces had no harsh words for anyone. This was characteristic of all of Carson Robison's pieces—there was little adverse criticism except when couched in a humorous vein. Perhaps this characteristic was partly responsible for his popularity, whereas the more outspoken songs by Oaks and Charles Nabell, given below, were evidently soon forgotten. The text of Oaks' "Death of William J. Bryan" follows:

William Jennings Bryan is dead, he died one Sabbath day,
So peacefully was the king of sleep, his spirit passed away;
He was at Dayton, Tennessee, defending our dear Lord,
And soon after his work was finished he went to his reward.

He fought the evolutionists and infidel men, fools,
Who are trying to ruin the minds of children in our schools;

By teaching we came from monkeys, and other things absurd,
Denying the works of our Savior and God's own holy word.

He was a natural born'd orator, his voice was rich and grand,
A writer and a statesman too, the greatest in the land;
Three times he ran for President, but capitalists wouldn't let him
win,
Because he was a friend to the poor and to the working man.

He was a father good and kind, a son loyal and true,
A great and mighty man was he, a hero through and through;
His wife, his children and his kin all mourned his sudden end,
The nation bows with them in mourning a loss of a noble friend.

He will be missed throughout the land, his speeches often read,
His mem'ry will live in our hearts while he's among the dead;
He's gone to his eternal home, forever he's at rest,
His name will here be loved and cherished, his works forever blest.

Of the life and career of Charles Nabell nothing is known, save that he
recorded a handful of songs for Okeh thrice in St. Louis. As in the case
of Oaks, most of the tunes he put on wax were sentimental songs about
mother and home, although there were also a few cowboy songs. At his
last session, very late in October 1925, he recorded the song incorrectly
titled on the record label "Scope's Trial," which he accompanied with his
own guitar playing.

Of all the songs recorded about the Scopes affair, Nabell's was richest
in details of the trial, although its author (probably Nabell himself) was
overzealous in crediting Bryan with all the glory. For example, in his second stanza Nabell recounts the objections Darrow raised on the third day
of the trial to opening court with a prayer, but then credits Bryan with
quashing the objection. Actually, the argument over the prayer was
between Darrow and Judge Raulston alone, with Bryan playing no part
in it. Nabell's "Scope's Trial" was as follows:

Down in Dayton Tennessee a famous trial was held,
John Scopes taught evolution and a prisoner was held;
The papers told the story and it traveled far and wide,
'Til at last the whole creation knowed John Scopes was to be tried,
Bill Bryan wired the sheriff, "Tell the folks I'll soon be there,
If Darrow aims to fight this case, it must be fair and square."

All the leaders of religion convoked from far and near,
Said they, "We know Bill Bryan, boys, and need not have a fear."

Now the courtroom it was crowded, the case came up for trial,
From every state the people came, they travelled many a mile;
Then old judge Raulston took his place with twelve good men and true,
To keep the faith and mete out justice when the trial was through.
The usual prayer each day was said though Darrow did object,
For old Bill Bryan stood right up religion to protect;
Now Darrow made a forceful plea, for win this case he must,
But Bryan again was on his feet, said he, "In God we trust."

A plea of guilty then was made and Evolution fell,
The news was broadcast through the land all godless folks to tell;
Bill Bryan was a hero, by the nation he was loved,
He kept the faith within his soul 'til called by Him above.
Now the death of Jennings Bryan caused sadness in our land,
He gave his life for sacred faith, he nobly made his stand;
He's sleeping now in Arlington where other heroes lie,
Though God has called him, in our hearts he'll never never die.

Although contemporary commentators on the trial varied in their interpretation of what was the real issue underlying the events at Dayton, to people of a fundamentalist persuasion it was clear that it was the Bible that was on trial. This viewpoint is suggested in some of the above songs, but it is expressed more clearly in an unpublished song written by Rev. Andrew Jenkins. Blind Andy, born in Jenkinsburg, Georgia, in 1885, lived his life in the Atlanta area, where he composed some 800 songs, secular and sacred. Many of his topical ballads, such as "The Death of Floyd Collins," have become firmly fixed in folk tradition. Jenkins was a religious man, who saw the hand of God everywhere, and even his secular ballads were often vehicles for homily. The opening lines of his song, "Evolution—Bryan's Last Great Fight," suggest a personification of the antagonists in the trial—evolution and the Bible—reminiscent of medieval morality plays. The first two verses follow:

There was a case not long ago in sunny Tennessee,
The Bible then on trial there must vindicated be,
The evolution was its foe, it could not understand
How in those pages white as snow we find the fate of man.

Oh, who will go and end this fight, oh, who will be the man,
To face the learned and mighty foe, and for the Bible stand?

I see a man though old in years, a mighty man is he,
Amid the nation's sighs and tears, he starts for Tennessee—
And when he reached old Dayton-town, he faced the foe for, said he,
"I'll never turn the Bible down, 'tis good enough for me."
Yes, Bryan went to end the fight, there was no greater man
To face the learned and mighty foe, and for the Bible stand.[3]

Uncle Dave Macon, one of the most popular and prolific of the hillbilly entertainers of the 1920s and '30s, recorded numerous songs of topical significance. Uncle Dave was a deeply religious man, who included
many sacred songs in his repertoire, attended church and even preached
a sermon or two. His first recording session after the Scopes trial was in
April 1926, and at that time he recorded his own piece, "The Bible's
True." Although admittedly it contains no direct reference to the Scopes
trial, it is appropriate for inclusion in this brief survey:

Spoken: Now I don't believe in evolution or revolution, but when it
comes to the good old Bible from Genesis to Revelations, I'm right
there.
Evolution teaches man came from a monkey,
I don't believe no such a thing in the days of a week of Sundays.

Cho: For the Bible's true, yes I believe it,
I've seen enough and I can prove it,
What you say, what you say, it's bound to be that way.

God made the world and everything that's in it,
He made man perfect and the monkey wasn't in it.

I'm no evolutionist that wants the world to see,
There can't no man from anywhere, boys, make a monkey out of me.

God made the world and then he made man,
Woman for his helpmate, beat that if you can.

We conclude this discussion with another song similar in spirit to
Uncle Dave's commentary on evolution. In 1928, four male members of
the Gentry Family recorded a half dozen songs for Victor in Nashville.

The first item in their offering was "You Can't Make a Monkey Out of Me":

Many theories are spent on the origin of Man,
Some can trace our name to the family tree;
But for me, I'm content with the blessed Bible plan,
And you can't make a monkey out of me.

Cho: You can't make a monkey out of me, oh no,
You can't make a monkey out of me, no, no;
I am human through and through, all my aunts and uncles too
And you can't make a monkey out of me.
(Repeat)

Some believe that the earth started from a little spark,
But they can't tell whence came the spark, you see;
Many folks had been burnt prior to old Noah's ark,
And you can't make a monkey out of me.

Cho: If a man ever came from a monkey as some say,
They'd be coming now, and would ever be
But mankind is the same in all ages as today,
And you can't make a monkey out of me,

Cho: No, you can't make me out of a monkey.

NOTES

1. For general information on the Scopes trial, see any of the following: Ray Ginger, *Six Days or Forever? Tennessee v John Thomas Scopes* (Boston: Beacon Press, 1958); Sheldon Norman Grebstein, *Monkey Trial* (Boston: Houghton Mifflin Co., 1960); Fay Cooper Cole, "A Witness at the Scopes Trial," in *Scientific American* (January 1959), 121.

2. The only previous commentary on any of the hillbilly songs on the Scopes trial was a brief unsigned article in *Caravan*, no. 16 (April–May 1959) that included a transcription of Dalhart's recording of "The John T. Scopes Trial."

3. This song, a copy of which was made available to me by D. K Wilgus, was transcribed by Jenkins's daughter, Irene Futrelle Spain.

Archie Green

Commercial Music Graphics #9: Sheet Music Covers

The practice of pictorially identifying a song by hand illumination precedes the technology of printing. After the period of Gutenberg and Caxton, it became common to decorate song texts on cheap broadsides with crude woodcuts. Examples of such decorations can be seen in Leslie Shepard's *The Broadside Ballad* (1962). When inexpensive music sheets were first printed, it seemed natural to add graphic designs to covers, continuing the illustrated broadside tradition and adding sales appeal to the songs by attractive packaging.

Sheet music collectors Harry Dichter and Elliott Shapiro have suggested that the earliest known piece of illustrated sheet music in the United States was the "Federal March," printed about 1788. It is found in their book, *Early American Sheet Music* (1941), plate 3. Because our nation was an agrarian society in its formative years, many of the present-day visual symbols closely associated with country-western music, such as log cabins, rustic fiddlers, and plow-boys, were in use by music publishers well before the Civil War. For example, two pieces of antebellum sheet music which anticipated contemporary country graphics were "Westward Ho," published in Philadelphia in 1839 and "The California Pioneers," San Francisco, 1852. These romantic representations of frontier life are reproduced in Lester S. Levy's *Grace Notes in American History* (1967), pages 50 and 54.

One of the many unexplored areas in American folk and popular culture studies is that of the sheet music collection labeled "old-time" or "hillbilly." To my knowledge, no one has ever prepared a checklist of sheet music by the pioneer recording artists who opened the old-time field for Okeh and other firms in the mid-1920s. Nor has anyone reproduced more than a handful of these particular items.

Three excellent examples of sheet music in this genre were used in *The Country Music Who's Who* (1966), Part 8, pages 9, 13, 16. Editor Thurston Moore selected "You Will Never Miss Your Mother until She Is Gone" by Fiddlin' John Carson, "The Wreck on the Southern Old 97" by Henry Whitter, and "My Blue Ridge Mountain Home" by Carson J. Robison. These pieces, significantly, did not show the artists as comic rubes. Instead Carson and Whitter were dressed in suits appropriate for country men visiting the city for important matters. The "Blue Ridge" item, which could well have been graced by a cabin in the pines, featured a photograph of Robison and Vernon Dalhart in expensive overcoats and fedoras. One wonders today whether or not the Triangle Music Publishing Company was consciously stressing the urbanity and prosperity of Robison and Dalhart in 1927 when it offered "My Blue Ridge Mountain Home" to consumers.

"In the Jailhouse Now," the piece of sheet music reproduced here (p. 17), is obviously non-rural in design and appeal. I have chosen it deliberately because it poses several difficult problems for country music fans who are frequently torn between their affection for old-time values and their desire to hold modernity's cheer and comfort.

It is unlikely that any reader of the *JEMF Quarterly* need be reminded of the career of Jimmie Rodgers, the now-canonized railroader who made his first disc in 1927 and died of tuberculosis in 1933 at the age of 35. Three widely disseminated portraits shape the Rodgers image: a wistful "Singing Brakeman" in a striped railroader's cap, a casual cowboy in a huge white Stetson, a jaunty popular entertainer in rakish straw hat. It can currently be heard on a reissue disc, *The Short but Brilliant Life of Jimmie Rodgers* (RCA Victor LPM 2634). [Ed. note: also on Rounder CD 1056 and Bear Family BCD 15540–1.] This song was recorded at Rodgers' third session and at a time when he was first emerging into national popularity. Evidently, Rodgers' rendition was a notable success, as it was followed, in 1930, by "In the Jailhouse Now No. 2" (Victor 22523). Like many of Rodgers' compositions, this humorous jail song had roots in Negro tradition. (One early version that preceded Rodgers' recording was made by Blind Blake in ca. November 1927 [Paramount 12565.])

Ralph S. Peer, Rodgers' mentor, twice copyrighted "In the Jailhouse Now": March 24, 1928, and June 11, 1928. It was this latter form, arranged by Art Addoms, that Peer issued in sheet music form under the imprint of one of his New York firms, the United Publishing Company. It can be seen from the sheet music cover that by mid-1928 Rodgers was already nicknamed "America's Blue Yodeler," but he was not yet identified visually as a country performer.

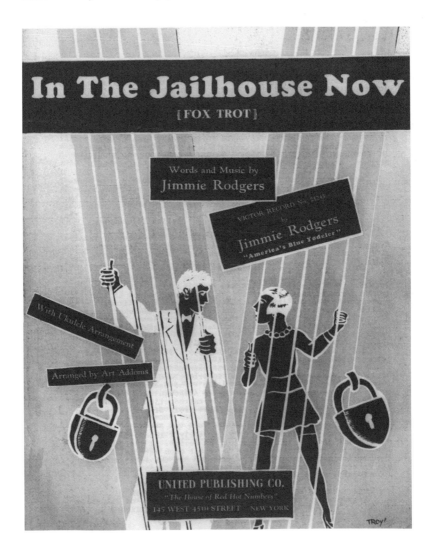

It is readily apparent that the appeal of this particular item of sheet music was directed at an urban audience more accustomed to "red hot" fox trots than to barn dances. "In the Jailhouse Now" was originally printed in bright red and blue colors in standard sheet music size: 9 inches by 12 inches. The background of the cover was blue and the jailhouse red. Although this contrast is lost in our present black-on-white reproduction, the tone of the "jazz age" is retained by the short dress of the flapper and her sheik boyfriend's bellbottoms. (I am grateful to Eugene Earle for making available this particular sheet music cover.)

Spring 1971

William Henry Koon

Grass Roots Commercialism

Starday Records of Nashville, Tennessee, has contributed much to the history of modern country music. When this small independent company first began operation, its output was restricted to the classic definition of 1950s hillbilly recordings. Later it tried to appeal to a more sophisticated audience and still later switched allegiance once more from a self-imposed traditionalism to the current Nashville product. However, by following its career, one can reconstruct some attitudes and influences that show well the state of the industry and tradition-based music during the 1960s.[1]

The independent record company is rare in this age of conglomerates. Of them, firms such as Canaan Records, which specialized in gospel music, or Wayne Raney's Rimrock, which also produced gospel records as well as custom pressings for the performer with a limited audience, are the rule. Starday decided to go about the whole matter differently. Beginning with LP records somewhat modestly, they released a series of country, old-time music, bluegrass, and western music. (As opposed to "country and western," western records are best exemplified by two rather divergent styles: western swing, a very popular music of the 1940s; and "campfire" songs in the style of the Sons of the Pioneers.) In addition, the catalog was fleshed out with gospel music of two types: the gospel quartet type (although frequently a quintet) which has bloomed throughout the South as an offshoot of the earlier shout traditions, but now highly stylized and theatricalized; and bluegrass gospel, which places an equal importance on musical performance and content.

Starday issued new or extensive recordings of the following artists: Carl Story, Bill Clifton, Moon Mullican, Stringbean, the Phipps Family, the Duke of Paducah, the Lewis Family, Chubby Wise, Red Ellis and the Huron Valley Boys, the Crook Brothers, the Kentucky Travelers, Smiley Burnette, Bill and Earl Bolick, Lulu Belle and Scotty, Buddy Starcher, Alex Campbell, the Lonesome Pine Fiddlers, Robert Lunn, Lew Childre, Bashful Brother Oswald, Curly Fox and Texas Ruby, Molly O'Day, Rod Brasefield, Cowboy Copas, the Willis Brothers, Pee Wee King and Red Stewart, Montana Slim, Leon McAuliff, Johnny Bond. Many Starday artists have recorded for other companies: Jimmie Skinner, Clyde Moody, Hylo Brown, Ernest "Pop" Stoneman, Wayne Raney, Charlie Monroe, and the Stanley Brothers.

There is a pattern in the choice of artists. First, none was a big-time artist at the time of the Starday recordings; many were remnants of a fickle past, such as the Blue Sky Boys, whose honeyed harmonies had been swept away with the onslaught of the plugged-in honky-tonk paeans to loneliness and drinking; and Lulu Belle and Scotty, who had been big-time performers on Chicago's WLS before retiring.

However, recapturing the past can be a nasty business. Trying to create a major market for material by such artists as Smiley Burnette and the Duke of Paducah was part of an economic death wish. The general problem of keeping before the public a performer whose exposure is now limited and dependent on the uncertain remembrances of an older public is tantamount to disaster. Such a performer was Wayne Raney. Although Raney was at one time a most popular performer and personality over WCKY Cincinnati, after the station switched its all-night high-powered old-time country and gospel programming to one of more recent vintage, he was all but forgotten. However, some of the Starday artists gave frequent performances at which they sold their recordings along with songbooks and autographed pictures. In this way, Carl Story, the Lewis Family, and Arthur "Guitar" Smith could expect to gain a financial reward by selling their own records. This practice of selling one's own records at performances is not uncommon, because the artist is able to get a bigger slice of the economic cake, gain more exposure, and get his records, otherwise next to unobtainable, before a buying public. But many of the Starday artists were not before a record-buying public, having slipped into the studio for a last chance at recorded fame and fortune before dropping back into obscurity. In this category were the Blue Sky Boys, who played an occasional folk festival before resuming their full-time jobs, or Sam and Kirk McGee, who mostly played on station breaks at the Grand Ole Opry. Some other performers, such as the Phipps Family and Fiddling Arthur Smith, were discovered by folk music companies and were released to an urban audience. Some, such as Arthur "Guitar" Smith, had been recorded by major companies. Smith was a prominent regional artist in North Carolina, and when his national popularity waned, he probably saw the advantage in releasing his material, recorded in his own Charlotte studio, through Starday. Some performers, such as Stringbean, who came to the Opry in 1942, had never been recorded.

All of Starday's advertising says "since 1952," but their first LP was released in about 1959.[1] They have since issued about 342 regular LPs as well as EPs, special editions (such as the four-volume histories of gospel music), and special pressings for their own record club and others. The Starday firm is not restricted to issuing records; they are, according to the 1967 Country Music edition of *Billboard,* also in the business of publishing, custom pressing, waterfront real estate, registered quarterhorses, radio-TV mail order, the record club, tobacco, and Angus cattle. Not all material stems from Starday's own lists: they also purchased material from King, Mercury, Rem, and Rimrock recording companies. In addition, their recordings are available in a wide configuration of labels abroad and at home, including Realm, Melodisc, Stateside, and London in Great Britain; Netherland's Starday, Japanese London; and Nashville, Palace, and Diplomat here in the U.S.

Starday's avowed purpose in its 1965 catalog was: "Superiority through Specialization: Bluegrass, Country, Sacred, Western, Old Time Featuring Stars and Guests of the Grand Ole Opry." By 1966, the tune had changed somewhat, for the categories enumerated had then shrunk to include only "Country and Gospel." There was good reason also, for during the two years preceding, Starday had dumped many of its old-time and bluegrass recordings at low prices to supermarkets and discount stores. The records were commonly available for 79 to 88 cents; this was three to four years before the great "mono" dumping of 1968–69. What happened evidently can be reconstructed as follows. Beginning about 1961 there was a great folk music boom that swept in a lot of wheat with the chaff, and Starday looked around and saw that it was good. But by the time the recordings had been released, the demand for bluegrass and old-time music had abated.

Starday's involvement with commercial folk music can be reconstructed by an examination of catalogs and liner notes in determining the type of music Starday released. The greatest activity in the company's history was between 1962 and 1965. During that time 34 bluegrass LPs, 27 old-time LPs, 18 LPs of specialty and humor material, and 31 LPs of religious music—much of it bluegrass—came into the catalog. During the same time only 64 C & W LPs were listed. Then what caused the later switch to the "countrypolitan" sound? Don Pierce, Starday's president, offered two explanations in the March and June 1967 issues of *Bluegrass Unlimited*. At first he wrote:

"For awhile I felt that the college and the more sophisticated city trade would create a boom for Bluegrass music sales. It sure didn't happen that way for us. The people that bought Bluegrass by mail order from Jimmie Skinner, Wayne Raney, Starday and other sources seemed to identify Bluegrass with so called "Beatniks," "Draft Dodgers," "Civil rights demonstrators," and the like including subversives, homosexuals, pill and dope takers, and, as a result, Bluegrass sales to the country music market took one hell of a beating."

Perhaps more germane to the actual problem was Pierce's reply to a letter from Neil Rosenberg:

> I believe I may have gotten Bluegrass music mixed up with certain aspects of the Folk Music Movement. I do know that my sales of Bluegrass albums declined drastically at about the same time that Bluegrass got heavily mixed up with the Folk Music Movement. Whether one was the cause of the other, I can't be sure. Our mail order sale of Bluegrass was greatly diminished when WCKY stopped programming Country Music.

Clearly, Starday moved into the field too late for the commercial success Pierce envisaged. Thus the dwindling of the fad for folk music in the open market, and the violent shift in the programming of WCKY drew the curtain on Starday's "Golden Era."

At the same time, Starday was making a few enemies by some rather deceptive packaging. For instance, one number by Ralph Stanley, taken from Mercury master number YW 14804, was released under six different titles, none of which echoed the original title, "Daybreak in Dixie." The titles were "Ralph's Banjo Special," "Pickin the Five String," "Banjo in the Hills," "Fire on the Strings," "Banjo in the Mountains," and "Banjo in the Bluegrass." Also, some albums, such as SLP 201, were deceptive: the album cover states that it is by the Stanley Brothers, but on the reverse side in small print is revealed the fact that five other artists are included, and that only six of the twelve cuts are by the Stanleys. Starday also attempted to capitalize on the new-found fame of some stars such as Rodger Miller and Glen Campbell. An album and tape release of a demonstration tape that Campbell had cut years earlier took a court case in 1969 to stop. Also, the company frequently included selections in more than one album, such as the Stanley Brothers example.

When the 1966 catalog was published, gone was most of the old-time and bluegrass music. Of the 42 new LPs issued that year, only one was bluegrass—Charlie Monroe, who, strangely until that time, had not recorded with full bluegrass instrumentation. (The earlier jackets always proclaimed "with 5-string banjo bluegrass style," even if the banjo player played in a different style. In fact, one cover photograph, used in the Kentucky Travelers LP as well as several other LPs for bluegrass, shows a banjo picker distinctly frailing.) In addition to one old-time LP, Lulu Belle and Scotty, there were four other reissue or gospel LPs that could qualify as bluegrass or traditional music; so instead of a catalog composed of two-thirds traditional material, the fraction had sunk to about 12 percent. By 1967, the traditional and bluegrass material was gone, with several exceptions, and the warehouse was filling up with mono copies of traditional artists.

During the brief period of 1962–65 some startlingly good examples of American folksong were presented and perhaps re-entered oral tradition. Such songs as "Ragged But Right," "Cyclone at Ryecove," "Motherless Children," "Little Birdie," "20 Cent Cotton and 90 Cent Meat," "Stern Old Bachelor," "Cacklin' Hen," "Corey," "Just Before the Battle Mother," "Oh, Death," "Red Cockin' Chair"; also "Nobody's Business," "Suicide Blues," "Roll on Buddy," "The Prisoner's Song," "Walking in Jerusalem," "Little Girl and the Dreadful Snake," "Death of Abraham Lincoln," "Sinking of the Titanic," "Handsome Molly," "Mary of the Wild Moor," "Cocaine Blues," "Spanish Flandang," and literally hundreds of ballads, love songs, reels, breakdowns, and other dance tunes. I say "re-entered," for the recordings, not available as a rule in northern places, were basically for a country audience. So it is entirely probable that the collector today can retrace some source to an electronically devised rendering which began with Starday studios.

The country record consumer was at this time undergoing rapid changes in taste and temperament. Country singers were beginning to sound like pop singers, and in fact many were crossing the border to use pop material, while other pop singers, such as Ray Charles, were scouring country songs for material to make into pop-country hits. Long-established stars such as Eddy Arnold were turning to pop arrangements, and Victor's number-one Nashville man, Chet Atkins, was busy filling up backgrounds with horns, strings, and the Anita Kerr singers. So the Starday output was going against the grain of the then-changing country idea of itself, which was going "uptown." To shore up its idea of what country music should be and let the public in on what they had to offer, Starday released a number of "Sampler" albums at $1.98. The sampler technique was widely used during the '50s to promote the smaller company or the specialized output of a large company. Of particular interest, Starday released *Grassroots! Real Old Time Recordings* (SLP 292), *Unforgettable Country Instrumentals* (SLP 277), *The Wonderful World of Gospel and Sacred Music* (SLP 255), *Bluegrass Sampler* (SLP 183), and five other samplers with either old-time, or bluegrass, or both.

So what Starday attempted was to compete with the major recording and distributing companies, albeit in a novel way: first, they appealed to an audience for unsophisticated country material, evidenced by the title of one of their first releases: "Hillbilly Hit Parade." This aspect of the business was kept constant throughout by releases of George Jones and Cowboy Copas as well as pretenders to a larger country such as Frankie Miller and Justin Tubb. Second, they appealed to the vast market in the South and other lands for both gospel and sacred music by a wide variety of performers, most notably the Lewis Family, and Sunshine Boys, and Carl Story. Third, they recorded some performers whose styles were extremely out of vogue, such as the Willis Brothers with their western sound. Starday's faith in such groups paid off, for the Willis Brothers eventually had two hit singles, one of which was a truck driving song. But within this same category was the large index of old-time and traditional music in which Starday's catalog excelled; this excellence was based in part on a neo-romantic concept of what the buyer of country music really wanted. These bluegrass and old time songs were also issued to coincide, if belatedly, with the folksong revival of the early '60s, although this part of the business was later renounced. Then there were the samplers to entice people into the vaguely unrespectable field of country music and its various aspects—from straight country to bluegrass and rural humor. To survive in the highly competitive recording industry, Starday resorted to some rather questionable tactics, such as the reissue and anthology albums, but all in all, the company is to be commended for surviving at all. It has continued to survive by bending with the tastes and changes of the times. For instance, in its catalog today are numerous truck driving songs; also still further attempts to raise some artists from the undead such as Guy Mitchell, George Morgan, and Snooky Lanson.

Since the line was extensive, many albums were not available in the run-of-the-mill record stores, so it is fair to assume that many of them were pressed, issued, and stood waiting for sales which never came. These discs, some of which now bring $11.00 to $15.00 in rare record lists, met an ignoble fate; they were all ground up for reuse between 1968 and 1969. Hundreds of boxes were fed to the crushing machine in October of 1969, and the formerly full warehouse shelves were almost empty. It would seem the story would end on a sad note.

But in 1968 Starday and King Records of Cincinnati were united, and a part of the ball game was begun again. Many King LPs that had gone out of print suddenly rose like Lazarus from the dead. Material by the Stanley Brothers, Reno and Smiley, and the Brown's Ferry Four came back. Also, with the release of "Bonnie and Clyde," several LPs were released by Starday covering earlier bluegrass material. In addition, in 1970 Moon Mullican was once again available on a Nashville release, which is Starday's budget line. But to add to the discographer's problem, so was some earlier Stanley Brothers material originally recorded for King. The mixing continued.

The old Stardays are gone. I don't believe the company kept even a sample of each. But they are part of a legacy of more than a hundred LPs which have slipped into obscurity, at least for the time being. Since all of the earlier recordings were monaural only, their last chance of survival was in 1968. Perhaps a few still exist, dirty and worn, in isolated record stores of the South. Periodically one turns up as a reissue.

Starday's attempt at achieving a populist reaction in a highly competitive field should deserve perhaps nothing more than a footnote, if that, to the rather turbulent era of the sixties. However, Starday attempted to capture a taste that was essentially dead, and in doing so showed the folklorist the deep traditional roots of some performers of the Nashville sound. These remarks are not restricted to Stringbean and his "coon" songs of the nineteenth century or the beautifully antiquated songs and sounds of the Phipps Family, but include such performers as the Willis Brothers, who if seen on the Opry would never reveal a hint of songs that would interest the folklorist. But as D. K. Wilgus pointed out in his *JAF* article (1965) "Current Hillbilly Recordings," the Willis Brothers recorded (for a mass audience) "Roving Gambler," "Black Jack Davie," "Old Chisolm Trail," and "Jack of Diamonds." With such songs by performers who are "straight country" as opposed to those "urbanly revived," we see that the contribution of Starday records is not merely one of popular culture, although that too is important, but also a rich and fertile field that folklorists should be harvesting.

More importantly, Starday's vast offerings and their multiple issues (which were sometimes made available on 99-cent drug store lines such as Celebrity and Design) show us that collecting and study can be done elsewhere than in "them thar hills." Folklore is all around us. With the first recording of Fiddling Eck Robertson in 1922, a small leak in the dike occurred. Now we must realize that what we do see is water indeed, and that what Starday issued was a flood.

NOTE

1. According to *Disc Collector* (no. 14, p. 34), Starday Records was started in 1952 by Jack Starnes, Jr., of Beaumont, Texas, and Harold W. Daily of Houston. About six months after the introduction of the label, Don Pierce, formerly with Four Star Records, became a partner and acquired one-third ownership in Starday. The center of operation then moved to Los Angeles. In 1957, by which time Starday had become established as a major country music label, Mercury approached Pierce and Daily (Starnes had sold his interest in the company in 1954) to take over the Starday catalog. An agreement was reached, and Pierce moved Starday operations to Madison, Tenn. For the next eighteen months, most Starday masters were released under the Mercury-Starday label. Early in 1958 the Mercury-Starday association was discontinued. Pierce and Daily divided up the Starday catalog and Pierce took over complete control of the Starday label.

David E. Whisnant

Between Two Cultures: One Viewer's Response to "Earl Scruggs: His Family and Friends"

In view of some of its subject matter, National Educational Television's (NET) "Earl Scruggs: His Family and Friends" was a bit inaccurately titled. At one level, it simply documents Scruggs' well-known development as a musician: learning his three-finger picking style in the Flint Hill Community amid the red clay fields of Cleveland County, North Carolina; playing on local radio shows with the Morris brothers over WSPA in Spartanburg; a stint with Bill Monroe; later fame on the Grand Ole Opry; and recently an enormous following among young, disaffected, largely urban college students.

Much of the material was familiar, but the program also juxtaposed images we all expected with others that came as something of a shock: Scruggs with Bill Monroe backstage at the Opry in Nashville, and Scruggs playing in a trio with his son Randy and a Moog synthesizer; Scruggs in a jam session with Doc and Merle Watson, and Scruggs playing banjo with the Byrds; Scruggs with his long-haired sons on the platform of an anti-war rally. It is more than a musical odyssey, it appears; Earl Scruggs' recent activities involve, whether he intends it or not, some of the major current ambivalences, tensions, and changes in American culture. But more of that later; first the "new sound" itself.

Quite honestly, I did not find it very appealing. It is an experiment, to be sure, so that one needn't make any final judgment. It may turn out to be an intermediate point on the way to a really viable new tradition. In any case, it seems not to work very well thus far, and the fact that it doesn't could have something to do with the inherent incompatibility of the instruments and styles. The natural brilliance and clarity of the banjo played Scruggs style can easily be heard against the relative mellowness of other acoustical instruments, but against drums and heavily amplified electric guitars it cannot. If groups such as the Byrds prove willing to adapt their own playing to the limitations and possibilities of the banjo, however, the new sound may become more appealing.

There are risks involved in experiments of this kind, but they are undoubtedly worth taking: We will do ourselves and folk music a disservice if we take the position of some recent record reviewers in *Bluegrass Unlimited* (see July 1970 issue, p. 27) who view dimly indeed just such experiments as Scruggs'. Their attitude is puristic: Bluegrass is only and always this, this, and this; it is not, and must never be, that. But surely Bluegrass itself has not been a static tradition, even if it has been fairly stable during its relatively brief existence. If the tradition is alive, if it represents a continuing effort by a significant number of people to cast their understanding of human experience into a particular form, if it fulfills some relatively invariant human needs, then we should have no fear in trusting it to preserve its own integrity. We need erect no aesthetic tariff barriers. It might be well to recall that when Doc Watson was discovered, he was playing electric guitar in a band at a VFW post in Boone, North Carolina. As long as the human need is there, the form will continue to exist; when the need disappears, no mechanisms of preservation will keep the form alive.

I am not suggesting that Bluegrass developed simply as a response to the felt needs of masses of people. One can hardly be unaware that it has to some extent been both a public relations gimmick for certain manufacturers (Martha White Flour and others) and a product of the Nashville country music industry. Hence it is possible, in the case of Earl Scruggs, that some public relations and marketing experts have simply seen which way the ideological wind is blowing, and are changing his image so as to maintain "product loyalty." But I doubt that such considerations are determinative.

If one proceeds, then, on the assumption that Earl Scruggs is doing what he is doing for at least some significant reasons of his own, and that we are therefore seeing in his present activities an instance of real cultural change, and not a technocratic illusion, what aspects of "Earl Scruggs: His Family and Friends" invite special attention?

Scruggs' apparent willingness to trust both himself and his music was the most hopeful sign I observed in the entire ninety minutes. He appears to be open to new possibilities for his own music that may derive from the advent of new instruments, musical forms, and sensibilities. He also admits that, for all its vitality, there was (is) a certain static quality in Bluegrass, although such a splendid recording as he made with Doc Watson (*Strictly Instrumental,* Columbia CS 9443) suggests that the tradition, even without opting for the sounds of hard rock, is far from devoid of new possibilities.

In the meantime, Scruggs seems confident that if for the time being he doesn't want to continue to play "Cumberland Gap" and "Earl's Breakdown" over and over again to the exclusion of all else, neither he nor the Bluegrass tradition will suffer irreparable harm. He says he doesn't know where it all leads, but he apparently isn't anxious about it. If it is fun for the moment to play in a trio with Randy and a Moog synthesizer, then why not? The Moog synthesizer does represent a danger of a sort, as anyone who has read Jacques Ellull's *The Technological Society* well knows, but the fact remains that we can still make incremental decisions about machines, and choosing to say yes in one instance does not necessarily prevent us from saying no in the future.

But to focus solely on the question of changes in musical materials, instruments, and styles is to miss some important aspects of the NET program, because Scruggs' musical odyssey appears to be to an extent related to a concurrent quest for a new ideology, values, and life-style. One does not have to maintain that Scruggs has been to any significant degree radicalized (a radical with a nine-passenger wagon and a split-level in a posh suburb?) to sense that changes in which he is apparently involved tend implicitly toward radicalization. To the extent that they do, they are of course in tension with both his own past and the Bluegrass musical tradition. There was something poignant and pleasing, but also tragic, in the scene in which Scruggs teamed up again with the Morris Brothers with whom he played years ago. It evoked a sense of the enormous, but frustrated and largely sublimated and distorted, vitality of the culture that produced Earl Scruggs, and which still thinks of him as its own: the Flint Hill community of Cleveland County, which in some essential respects is typical of vast segments of American society.

I have often driven the back roads of Cleveland County with my father. It is a beautiful, but also ruined and desolate country: red clay, broom sage, scrub pine, asphalt-shingled houses, country churches, and unscreened auto junkyards predominate. It is the domain of Tom Wolfe's "good old boys," and stock car races on quarter-mile dirt tracks every Sunday afternoon. Exactly the sort of country where the Morris Brothers have to seek security for their old age not in their music, but, by running an auto body shop, straightening the fenders of the ubiquitous Fords and Chevrolets raced up and down the black tops by all the good old boys. An unsettling question presents itself: why do we continually bequeath to our children these ruined forms and corrupted possibilities? When will we be able to sing *because* of, rather than despite, what we are as a culture?

Part of the answer lies, I think, in the NET program's sequences on Earl's son Randy, then a student at Madison High School near Nashville. Skillful editing of the film juxtaposed Randy's precocious guitar playing on the steps of the school building with scenes, thoroughly familiar, of activities inside: an end-of-the-day announcement over the public address system, asking seniors to stop by the principal's office to pick up a copy of J. Edgar Hoover's *Masters of Deceit;* a student calmly reporting the school's arbitrary rules about dress, beards, and hair length; a principal blandly reporting that the school's only real problem is absenteeism. "The kids just don't want to come," it seems. Why? And what does it have to do with Randy and Earl Scruggs, or the condition of Cleveland County, or the Morris Brothers' body shop? Or, for that matter, with *Masters of Deceit?*

Edgar J. Friedenberg's *Coming of Age in America* (1965), a study of attitude and value formation in American high schools, is subtitled "Growth and Acquiescence." Adolescents, Friedenberg says, "are among the last social groups in the world to be given the full nineteenth-century colonial treatment." Those school teachers and administrators who provide the treatment "all begin, like a Colonial Office, with the assumption that the long-term interests of their clientele are consistent with the present interest of their sponsor." Since the social and ideological control demanded by the sponsor are nearly absolute, therefore, the high school student learns quickly to "expect no provision for his need to give in to his feelings, or to swing out in his own style, or to creep off and pull himself together."

We refuse to trust certain aspects of human nature, it appears: man's need for joy, pleasure, and ecstasy; his capacity to learn from his own experience without formal instruction; his delight in openness and surprise. But perversely we choose to trust efficient mechanisms of all sorts—educational, industrial, commercial, political and otherwise. Dumbly we have watched for generations as various efficient combinations of fear, distrust, avarice, insensitivity, and cynicism have laid to waste the American landscape, distorted its institutions, and blighted the physical and spiritual lives of its children. The Moog synthesizer is an innocuous toy beside the mechanisms of distortion and suppression (such as the public schools) which operate so freely—and at public expense—in our culture.

One direction in which suppression and authoritarian control lead is toward the acquiescence Friedenberg describes: the school "alters individuals: their values, their sense of personal worth. . . . [It] endorses and supports the values and behavior of certain segments of the population, providing their members with the credentials . . . needed for the next stage of their journey, while instilling in others a sense of inferiority [Randy, said the principal, was a "slightly below average" student] and warning the rest of society against them as troublesome and untrustworthy."

Another less probable but more hopeful response than the usual acquiescence in the face of such a system is rebellion—a policy of noncooperation or active resistance. On the official ledgers of school systems, such a response may register only as an "attendance problem." But outside the sterile corridors of Madison High School it may take the form of Randy's playing his guitar on the steps, of long hair and beads and communal living, of the violence born of frustration and despair, or— more recently and more hopefully—of a quiet but intense search for viable alternatives in education, vocation, and value systems.

The mentality that apparently controls Madison High School also underlies many of the more pervasive distortions and aberrations of our culture. It is as if a line ran from the front door of Madison High School to the door of the Morris Brothers' body shop, and it is that line that Randy Scruggs early in life (and perhaps his father belatedly) may be questioning whether to walk any further. Part of the significance of Earl Scruggs' quest, it seems to me, lies in its being conducted along the boundary between his own past and his sons' future. To the extent that this is so, it is an act not of desperation, I would guess, but of courage and trust. For Randy and Gary Scruggs to experiment with new musical forms, adopt new life-styles, and protest the war is one thing; for their father even to consider doing so requires quite a different order of strength and integrity, since it is at variance with most of his own past experience and with the culture that produces him and provided the basis for his career and his music.

Cleveland County, after all, gave nearly fifty percent of its total vote in the 1968 Presidential election to George Wallace. Audiences at the

Grand Ole Opry are as WASPish as can be found anywhere. "Okie from Muskogee" is no joke to them: long hair, protest, and deviant ideology are anathema. Love it or leave it. Back our boys in Vietnam. Support your local police. If we are to find a "new America," most of this view of reality, and values implicit in it, say young radicals, will have to go.

Most, but not all. Kenneth Keniston's *Young Radicals: Notes on Committed Youth* (New York, 1968) makes the somewhat surprising observation that although young radicals reject their parents' "formal values"—allegiance to the institutional church, political and economic ideology, social status, career—they characteristically feel a strong continuity with such "core" values as honesty, compassion, integrity, and the like. These remain as a cherished link with the viable elements of the past. No doubt this is true of those who tend toward radicalism late in life as well. If it is, there is perhaps as much persistence and continuity as disjunction and change in what Earl Scruggs is presently doing. Indeed the most promising sign on the NET program, musically speaking, was Scruggs playing not with the Byrds or the Moog synthesizer, but with Joan Baez, who long ago learned that there are few things more radical in our culture than the reassertion of our core values—moral, musical, and ideological.

George C. Biggar

The WLS National Barn Dance Story: The Early Years

George Biggar joined the Sears-Roebuck Station WLS Staff, May 1, 1924, becoming Farm and Market Editor. From August 1925 until July 1929, he was producer-announcer for Sears-Roebuck & Co. Farm, Home and Musical Programs for varying periods at WFAA, Dallas, WSB, Atlanta, and KMBC, Kansas City. Returning to WLS, then operated by Prairie Farmer Publishing Co., in July 1929, he became Continuity Editor-Writer, and then served as Program Director during most of the period from April 1930 to September 1938. At that time he joined WLW, Cincinnati, to organize farm service programs and the country and western WLW Boone County Jamboree. After management jobs for WIBC, Indianapolis, and KCRG, Cedar Rapids, Iowa, he returned to WLS, November 1948, to remain for five years as Director of the WLS National Barn Dance in the Eighth Street Theatre. In November 1953, he became part owner, manager and president of WLBK, DeKalb, Illinois, until retirement September 1, 1965. He is justly credited with introducing several prominent country & western acts to radio and with developing their talent.

It was on Saturday night, April 19, 1924, that the cowbells rang out and from a small Hotel Sherman studio an old-time breakdown went on the air to usher in the first National Barn Dance on WLS, the Sears-Roebuck Station, Chicago, just one week old. The pioneer radio program of its type, it became the twentieth-century equivalent of the barn dances, barn warmin's and huskin' bees that provided lively get-togethers in the days when our prairies were newly settled. Destined to live for thirty-six years, it was to make Saturday nights happier in rural and city homes throughout the nation and Canada by reviving the songs and music of the previous seventy-five years and by introducing traditional folk and country music to millions. The program also was to develop many great performers in the Country and Western fields.

Although no record of the names of participants in that first National Barn Dance is available, I feel certain that Tommy Dandurand of Kankakee, Illinois, was the first old-time fiddler—also that Jesse Doolittle accompanied with his banjo to "make the rafters ring" for the first time in "the old hayloft." As a listener that night, I remember that a request went out for a square dance caller and the announcer soon reported: "Tom Owen, a hospital worker, telephoned that he used to call dances down home in Missouri and he'll be right over." There were too few old-time entertainers to be found to fill four hours every Saturday night, so it was not surprising that occasional ten-minute pickups were made from Maurie Sherman's Orchestra in the Hotel Sherman Inn.

THE WLS BARN DANCE ORCHESTRA

Others who joined Tommy Dandurand in his "WLS Barn Dance Orchestra," which recorded for the Sears label under that name, included Rube Tronson, fiddler; Claudia Parker, guitarist; Ralph Whitlock, pianist; and Ed Goodreau, caller. Personalities that were soon popularized on the Barn Dance in 1924–25 were "The Girl with a Million Friends"—Grace Wilson—a versatile singer of sentimental songs from vaudeville who was a barn dance star until 1960; Ford and Glenn, who became the Midwest's most popular harmony team; Walter Peterson with his "double-barreled shotgun" (harmonica-guitar); Cecil and Esther Ward, Hawaiian guitar team; Tom Corwine, barnyard animal imitator from a Chautauqua circuit; Bob Hendry, Scottish balladist; and staff organist Ralph Waldo Emerson.

Traditional country dances and toe-tickling harmonica-guitar medleys were interspersed with heart songs and popular sweet and novelty numbers which brought nostalgic memories of hay-rides and country "sociables" to thousands. It is doubtful if southern folk songs or cowboy ballads were sung, as very few Midwesterners of that day were familiar with them. Young people, urban and rural alike, had for years played and sung the contemporary "June Moon" and "Old Mill Stream" melodies of their day around the old parlor piano or organ and played the same pop records on wind-up phonographs.

Who was responsible for originating the WLS National Barn Dance? I've heard the names of several who were given the credit but I'll always rely on the information I received in a letter from Edgar L. Bill, WLS Manager, 1924–31. He wrote: "No, I cannot claim that I created and planned the National Barn Dance. The truth is that it just grew up and here is how it happened. We started WLS with a large variety of entertainment programs. We would try anything once to see what our listeners thought about it. We had religious programs and services on Sunday. We featured high-brow music on one night; dance bands on another; then programs featuring large choruses. Other nights, we'd have variety or we might have a radio play. When it came to Saturday night, it was quite natural to book in old-time music, including old-time fiddling, banjo and guitar music and cowboy songs. We leaned toward the homey, old-time familiar tunes because we were a farm station primarily."

Mr. Bill also related how he spent the early part of that Saturday night checking on Ford Rush and Glenn Rowell in a North side theatre. "I hired them that night," he said. "Then we went into a radio shop to pick up WLS. We could tell that the Barn Dance was going 'great guns' with a lot of enthused listeners wiring in. When we got back to the studio, we counted more than 250 telegrams. That was the answer to Saturday night on WLS from then on. All hands thought up ideas for the program. You see, the enthusiasm of the listeners really started the program which proved to be a spontaneous type of thing. You could tell by listening that everyone in the studio was enjoying himself."

There were some "doubting Thomases" who questioned whether it was "dignified" and "in good taste" for Sears-Roebuck Co. to sponsor a radio station which offered listeners such a program as the Barn Dance. They changed their minds when they saw the large volume of telegrams, letters, and cards from both rural and city people in many states and Canada. It was obvious that the response came from the "mass audience" which patronized the W-orld's L-argest S-tore.

GEORGE D. HAY BECOMES CHIEF ANNOUNCER

About mid-May 1924, George D. Hay, "The Solemn Old Judge," was employed by Mr. Bill as WLS Chief Announcer. A native of Attica, Ind., he had been a Memphis Commercial Appeal reporter as well as a late night announcer on WMC with his "Hushpuckana" steamboat whistle as a trademark. At WLS, he adopted a train whistle and became the "engineer" of "The WLS Un-Limited," speeding over the air lanes. Because of George's distinctive style and showmanship as master of ceremonies of the National Barn Dance and other shows—coupled with his unusual station signature "W-L-S-the Sears-ROEbuck Station, Chi-CAW-go," "The Judge" won the 1924–25 Most Popular Announcers' Contest of the Radio Digest by vote of the readers. In the fall of 1925, he joined the new Nashville station, WSM, where he continued his rise to still greater fame as originator and pilot of the Grand Ole Opry.

What was radio like then? For one thing, it wasn't very easy to create a "good time" barn dance atmosphere in a studio with heavy drapes deadening the sound. There were over 500 broadcasting stations and almost all personnel on new broadcasters like WLS were getting their first experience "on the job." Most listeners had to depend on headsets with earphones. The big "morning glory" speakers were costly and often delivered inferior quality. Battery-operated receiving sets were not to be replaced by plug-in all-electric receivers until about 1927. Listening was mainly an evening diversion. The limited daytime schedule consisted principally of weather, farm talks, market reports and homemakers' programs. Adequate local and national news coverage by radio was several years away. So were attractive salaries, for commercial radio was practically unknown. Less than 10 percent of Illinois farm homes had radios in 1924 but the number increased to 50 percent by 1930, according to Prairie Farmer surveys. The Federal Radio Commission receiving set estimate was 4 million in 1924; 6 million or 30 percent of all homes in 1927; and 23 million or about 66 percent of all households in 1936.

CHUBBY PARKER INTRODUCES SONGS
FROM THE PRAIRIE

When Chubby Parker became a barn dance "regular" in 1925, picking his little five-string banjo and singing quaint songs of the prairie like "I Am a Stern Old Bachelor" and "Little Old Sod Shanty on the Claim," he scored immediately as the station's first real folk singer. His rendition of "Nickety Nackety Now Now Now," based on an old Scottish ballad, soon became as well known as the singer. Chubby recorded several of his favorites under the Sears-Roebuck label.

In 1926, Bill O'Connor of Chanute, Kansas, who had studied law and been admitted to the bar, added Irish melodies to the musical fare in "the old hayloft," while popular and comedy barber shop harmonies by the

Maple City Four so pleased WLS listeners that this LaPorte, Indiana, foursome was identified with the station until the mid-1950s. O'Connor later sang on WLS Morning Devotions and the little Brown Church of the Air for several years.

Southern mountain folk ballads won their rightful place on the WLS National Barn Dance when Bradley Kincaid became a member of the cast in 1926, as "The Kentucky Mountain Boy with his 'Houn' Dog Guitar." He had entered the Chicago YMCA College after taking work at Berea College, Kentucky, planning to become a "Y" secretary. The WLS musical director booked the YMCA College Quartet for a program and found that Bradley played guitar and sang mountain ballads. An "audition" program on the air brought excellent listener response and regular Saturday night Barn Dance bookings.

The Kentucky Mountain Boy was soon acknowledged as the first successful artist in his field and besides thousands of orders for his song books along with exceptionally heavy fan mail, he was much in demand at theaters throughout the Middle West. His records under the Sears label moved well, also. "Of worldly possessions my wife and I had exactly $412.00 when we boarded the train for Chicago," said Bradley in an interview. "Four years later our worldly possessions consisted of twin daughters, a new Packard and more than $10,000 in the bank."

The 1927–28 period brought John Brown, another Kansas native, into the hayloft crew as staff piano accompanist. He was a popular choice in this assignment through all the years of the Barn Dance. Eddie Allen, former Galesburg, Illinois, railroad man, joined the program as a harmonica player, later assisting for years in handling studio guest reception.

Claude Moye of Gallatin County, Illinois, was hired as a country singing personality with his own guitar-harmonica accompaniment. He was soon dubbed "Pie Plant Pete" with his "Two Cylinder Cob-Crusher," adding plenty of life and rhythm to the show.

PRAIRIE FARMER BUYS WLS
FROM SEARS-ROEBUCK & CO.

On October 1, 1928, ownership and operation of WLS were assumed by *Prairie Farmer,* America's Oldest Farm Paper (since 1841), which had purchased 51 percent control from Sears, whose executives had offered the station to the farm paper so that its extensive service to farm families might be continued. Although the WLS staff saw few changes at that time, it is notable that a sales manager and staff were employed to make it possible for *Prairie Farmer* to sustain the station. All WLS offices and studios were moved during 1929 to Prairie Farmer, 1230 W. Washington Blvd., from Hotel Sherman. Big Studio A became the new home of the National Barn Dance with a Little Theatre capable of accommodating around 200 guests. The Audience Theatre at the hotel had seated only 100.

Luther Ossenbrink, the young Knobnoster, Missouri, man who had gained valuable experience on Sears programs on KMBC, Kansas City, for nearly two years as "Arkie—the Arkansas Woodchopper"—joined the old hayloft crew in the fall of 1929. He was to be called "Mr. Barn Dance Himself" until 1960. Trulan Wilder and Merle Housh, the comedy and country music-making "Hiram and Henry" team, were employed from WIBW, Topeka, Kansas, while from Walkerton, Indiana, Harry brought in his old-time and folk songs as "Dynamite Jim."

As a result of the sale of WLS control to *Prairie Farmer,* Sears took part of its payment in station time, especially for a morning program for homemakers. In 1930, Oklahoma's Gene Autry, who had worked at other stations, including WJJD, Chicago, was employed by Sears and the American Record Corporation to promote his records on a daily WLS spot and to make National Barn Dance appearances. He made early recording history with his "Silver-Haired Daddy of Mine"—one of the first million sellers in the country field.

Gene's salary at that time was $35.00 weekly, approximately the same as most of the WLS artists, individually, were making. It was considered a good living wage in those early depression years. It was quite a contrast to the $1,500 plus traveling expenses that WLS paid Gene as a guest star at the Illinois State Fair on the National Barn Dance a few years later! To augment his radio salary, he was booked for numerous personal appearances in theaters and county fairs with Smiley Burnette, comic and accordion soloist, who had been working for WDZ, Tuscola, Illinois, on their country staff. Smiley appeared occasionally with Gene on the National Barn Dance, later going to Hollywood with him.

JOHN LAIR BRINGS IN THE
CUMBERLAND RIDGE RUNNERS

In 1930, the first southern folk music singing and playing group was engaged for the WLS staff when John Lair, a native of Mount Vernon, Kentucky, brought in the versatile Cumberland Ridge Runners, which he had organized from that area. Members were Karl Davis and Hartford Taylor (to be known on records and on WLS also as the Renfro Valley Boys); Homer (Slim) Miller, comedian and old-time fiddler; Gene Ruppe, five-string banjo player; and Doc Hopkins, ballad singer. Hugh Cross of Oliver Springs, Tennessee, was a soloist with the act for several months and, in 1931, "Ramblin' Red" Foley, Berea, Kentucky, became part of the group. He was a WLS favorite for many years through World War II, with time out when he starred on *Plantation Party* from Mutual and on NBC's *Avalon Time,* originating from WLW, Cincinnati. Linda Parker, "The Little Sunbonnet Girl," was a folk balladist with the Ridge Runners until her death about two years later.

One of the first National Barn Dance half-hour commercials was a successful series for Aladdin Mantle Lamps built by John Lair, who narrated an attention-compelling musical half hour reminiscing about the old days in Renfro Valley. This was the rural community just north of Mt. Vernon where the Lair family lived for years. In about 1938 John established the village of Renfro Valley with a big red barn in which to hold radio barn dance shows, a historical rural museum, and several typical country stores. The Renfro Valley Barn Dance programs continue today.

In 1930, following Federal Radio Commission and court hearings in Washington, WLS was ordered to share 870 kilocycles frequency equally with WENR, Chicago. The time-sharing arrangement gave WLS all Saturday night to midnight and all weekday time from early morning sign-on until 3:30 p.m. This made the National Barn Dance, Saturdays from 7:00 to midnight, easily the dominant program on WLS—the climax of every week's schedule. More and stronger country acts were necessary to improve the Barn Dance. There was no way to hold the better acts and individuals except by paying them a living weekly wage and using them on more programs. Thus, while Sears-Roebuck & Co. had used country talent only on Saturday nights, *Prairie Farmer* judiciously scheduled the acts from the Barn Dance from 5:00 to 8:00 a.m. where they were on revenue-producing spot participation programs or were sponsored on fifteen- or thirty-minute programs. Barn Dance acts were also spotted on the top farm audience noon-time program, Dinnerbell Time, five noons weekly, as well as on occasional afternoon programs. As a result, the country entertainers had almost daily air exposure to build them up. This fact, coupled with promotional spots tying the acts in with the next National Barn Dance program, gave the Saturday night show prime promotion.

Under farm paper ownership, all WLS programs and entertainers received radio page publicity in each issue of *Prairie Farmer,* published every other Saturday. With its 400,000 or more circulation in Illinois, Indiana, Wisconsin, and Michigan, such constant publicity was of immense value to the WLS National Barn Dance, as the station's feature program.

Additionally, every November from 1929 to 1956, the WLS Family Album was published. It was an 8 x 11 book of from forty to fifty pages featuring photos of the WLS entertainers, and other *Prairie Farmer*–WLS key personnel, often with their families. The National Barn Dance was usually given the best "break" in the book with a double-page spread of the cast.

THE BARN DANCE MOVES INTO
THE EIGHTH STREET THEATRE

Bookings of the National Barn Dance in theatres and schools were numerous and successful starting about 1926. Bradley Kincaid, for instance, earned from $150 to $500 per day, playing on percentages with theatres. Unit shows with an average of three barn dance acts, booked by the WLS Artists Bureau, played theatres on percentages, grossing from $1,000 to $2,500 a day.

The first real tests of the pulling power of the entire WLS National Barn Dance cast were in the International Amphitheatre in the Chicago Stock Yards, October 25 and November 15, 1930. With a nominal admission price, it was recorded that 10,000 attended the October 25 Saturday night broadcast and about as many were turned away. The broadcast in the amphitheatre on November 15 was a charity performance—the proceeds to help to finance the WLS Soup Kitchen on West Madison Street—a project of the depression. Another 10,000 are reported to have attended. In early August 1931, the entire National Barn Dance was moved to the Illinois State Fair grandstand in Springfield; this big stage and air performance of five hours playing to 15,922 paid admissions.

With a six month's backlog of free ticket requests for the Saturday night broadcasts from *Prairie Farmer*'s Studio A, station executives decided to rent Chicago's "jinx" house, the Eighth Street Theatre, at Eighth and Wabash, for two Saturday nights starting March 19, 1932. An admission charge of 50 cents for adults and 25 cents for children was made to cover expenses. Two broadcasts of two hours were easily sold out on each of the two nights.

The result was a contract with the 1,200-seat Eighth Street Theatre to continue the Saturday night broadcasts indefinitely. Prices of admission were raised, of course, for economic reasons. The Barn Dance—with the exception of one year when the U.S. Army took over the theater, necessitating a move to the Civic Theater—remained in the Eighth Street Theatre over twenty-five years, until August 31, 1957. There were 2,617,000 paid admissions to see these Saturday night broadcasts.

During A Century of Progress in 1933—the Chicago World's Fair— all attendance records were broken when the entire National Barn Dance cast was engaged to present a special Farmer's Week performance in the Hall of States. An estimated 30,000 witnessed the show and as a result, the Fair management engaged the Barn Dance for four more Wednesday night performances in the Court of the States.

The National Barn Dance from the stage of the Eighth Street Theatre was primarily divided into half-hour programs—each unit period being built around a "star" with about three other acts—singles, team, trio or instrumental-vocal unit. Each program, usually sponsored, was carefully routined in advance to insure proper pacing. During a typical Saturday evening, about twenty entertainment units—singles or larger—appeared during the evening—for a total of between forty and fifty people. There were always two sets of square dancers of eight members each, with callers. The entertainers were always paid—the weekly average for each through the years being $60.00. This figure was the country musicians' union scale. Those employed only for the Saturday night program averaged approximately $20.00—the "spot" Musicians' Union and AFRA scale for many of the broadcasts.

The broadcast performances in the Eighth Street Theatre provided the best "testing ground" imaginable for untried but promising talent. If program executives agreed that an act "showed something" in an audition, one or two appearances before the theater audiences helped in arriving at a final hiring decision.

The impetus given to the Barn Dance by the theater project made it necessary to add new talent, when available. In 1931—Mac and Bob (McFarland and Gardner); the Three Little Maids—Lucille, Evelyn, and Eva Overstake; Hoosier Sod-Busters double harmonica-guitar team; and Lonnie Glosson, harmonica blues artist, were added.

The year 1932 saw Georgie Goebel introduced at age 13 to the Barn Dance audience as "The Little Cowboy." That same year, Myrtle Cooper, southern-reared and renamed "Lulu Belle," started her career; Max Terhune, "the Hoosier Mimic," joined the cast from the Weaver Bros. and Elviry vaudeville act; and Malcolm Claire, an actor, started his "Spareribs" blackface monologs.

In 1933, Louise Massey and the Westerners joined the Barn Dance from KMBC, Kansas City; Milly and Dolly Good, "The Girls of the Golden West," reported in from KMOX, St. Louis; while Clayton McMichen and his Wildcats with Slim Bryant, Bert Layne, and Jack Dunigan were hired. The same year brought the Prairie Ramblers and Patsy Montana, the Hoosier Hot Shots, and former vaudeville star Pat Barrett, who started his career as comedian-singer "Uncle Ezra." Scotty Wiseman, to be teamed with Lulu Belle, started in 1933, too. Other individuals and acts that were very prominent on the National Barn Dance were Pat Buttram, Alabama country humorist; Eddie and Jimmy Dean, Texas singing team; Henry Burr (featured on the network hour many years for his ballads of the previous century); 1935: Christine, the Little Swiss Miss yodeler; 1936: Lily Mae Ledford, five-string banjo player-singer from Berea, Kentucky; Sunshine Sue and the Rock Creek Rangers—a family country act from Iowa; 1937: The DeZurik Sisters, yodeling sister team from northern Minnesota; the Kentucky Girls, Jo and Alma Taylor, Glasgow, Kentucky; 1943: Connie and Bonnie Linder, Nebraska farm girl twins; 1945: Rex Allen, the Arizona Cowboy, who became a Republic picture star in 1949; 1946 (or thereabouts): the Sage Riders, headed by Dolph Hemitt, with Donald "Red" Blanchard, who had been an early member of Rube Tronson's Texas Cowboys, a 1929–33 act; 1949: Capt. Stubby and the Buccaneers, Indiana-originated novelty and sweet and comedy singing-instrumental five; and Bob Atcher, western ballad singer; 1951: Beaver Valley Sweethearts—Conna and Colleen Wilson, from Beaver Valley, western Pennsylvania, and Homer and Jethro, who were with the Barn Dance for several years.

THE NBC ALKA SELTZER NATIONAL BARN DANCE

The biggest national break for the Barn Dance was the full hour sponsored on the network—the NBC-WLS Alka-Seltzer National Barn Dance from September 30, 1933, to April 28, 1946. One result of network popularity was the Paramount picture, "National Barn Dance," which premiered at the Eighth Street Theatre, October 14, 1944.

From February 21 to November 14, 1949, WLS Barn Dance personalities were featured on the ABC-TV Barn Dance from Chicago's Civic Theater. During 1949–50, Phillips 66 sponsored a thirty-minute portion of the National Barn Dance from the Eighth Street Theatre.

With ownership of WLS going to ABC-Paramount Theaters on May 1, 1960, which brought a definitely modern program format to WLS, the final broadcast from the *Prairie Farmer* Studio was on April 31, 1960. Thus ended the WLS National Barn Dance after over twenty-six years as an outstanding program built around America's traditional and country music.

The National Barn Dance, which was built on the successful vaudeville formula with an abundance of "sighs, cries and belly-laughs," just as are all other top country shows, appealed to a great cross-section of the public. Surveys indicated that from 50 to 60 percent of those who attended the programs in the Eighth Street Theatre were from outside of the Chicago metropolitan area. One survey brought out the fact that there were 122 various occupations represented by one night's audience.

STATEMENT OF POLICY IN CHOOSING TALENT

"WLS talent is chosen on the basis of sincerity, friendliness and genuineness as much as for entertaining ability. We have sought to find and to develop those entertainers who have the common touch; those people whose performance is representative of the best in the American tradition in its appeal to the average American home.

"In preparing and presenting our radio programs—the executives, artists and our entire staff should bear in mind the listener—the home—the family—should have first consideration." (From the WLS FCC Clear Channel Hearing Exhibit, 1945–47)

Norm Cohen

"I'm a Record Man": Uncle Art Satherley Reminisces

The country music industry paid homage to one of its pioneer recording men in 1971 when it elected Arthur Edward Satherley to the Country Music Hall of Fame. Officially in retirement since 1952 after three and a half decades in the record business, Uncle Art could relate a wealth of facts and anecdotes concerning every aspect of the industry in which he was so prominent. Gene Earle and Norm Cohen interviewed Uncle Art twice (December 23, 1970, and June 12, 1971, to tape some of his reminiscences of his long career in the country music industry. The following material is drawn from those interviews; for further biographical information the reader is referred to Ed Kahn's "Pioneer Recording Man: Uncle Art Satherley" (1972 *Country Music Who's Who*), an article based on Kahn's own interviews with Satherley during 1969. In assembling the following the author is grateful to Lisa Feldman for transcribing one of the interview tapes.

Born in Bristol, England, in 1889, Uncle Art grew up with a longing to see the cowboys and Indians of America, and in 1913 booked steamship passage to the New World to realize his desire. He came directly to Wisconsin, which he thought would bring him near the Indians and cowboys, and almost immediately was offered a job with the Wisconsin Chair Company in Port Washington, grading lumber. Wisconsin and the surrounding area being nearly 90 percent German, his Oxford accent was considered something of a novelty, and he attributes his quick hire to that fact.

Art Satherley (center) with Norm Cohen, Ken Griffis, and Gene Earle, 1971

Satherley worked for several years in various positions in the furniture business, both for the Wisconsin Chair Company and for the Wisconsin Cabinet and Panel Company, a subdivision of the former outfit that had been bought out by Thomas A. Edison to make cabinets for his own phonographs. In about 1918, the Wisconsin Chair Company decided to go into the phonograph business and Satherley was asked to come back to Port Washington to work for them, starting at the bottom of the business. His first assignment was to handle the technical aspects of making the shellac discs, and he still has in his possession a small black notebook full of formulas for the materials used in making the shellac, the earliest dated in 1918.

Satherley next spent some years selling records. Because established dealers already had exclusive franchises with Columbia or Victor, they could not distribute for the new Paramount label, and the company's salesmen had to devise other means of reaching the buying market. Uncle Art recalls he had no trouble selling as many discs as he could carry at county fairs and similar events, but a more effective means was necessary. As Uncle Art remembers, it was his idea to advertise in the important black newspapers, such as the *Chicago Defender,* the *Norfolk Journal & Guide,* and the *Baltimore Courier.* These ads (those in the *Defender* cost $1,000 each) asked for agents, who could buy ten or more records from the company for 45¢ each and then sell them for 75¢ or more, whatever they could get—up to $3 and $4 apiece. "It was so new for the people of America, both black and white, to be able to buy what they understood and what they wanted, that we quickly had several thousand people buying records daily." Within a year they had a thousand dealers competing with Columbia and Victor. Records were sold at house parties; they were sold in established urban ghettoes like Philadelphia and Washington, as well as throughout the South.

Uncle Art sold records for Paramount from Nova Scotia to the Florida Keys. He recalls that the two biggest sellers were Ma Rainey and Blind Lemon Jefferson, and they sold almost everywhere. Blind Blake sold well, but only in the South. At the time he was with Paramount, their hillbilly records accounted for only a fraction of the sales that the race music brought in. Even among the artists of the other companies, such as Stoneman, or Puckett, there was none who did as well as Ma Rainey and Blind Lemon.

Uncle Art soon began to supervise the making of recordings as well as selling them. He was responsible for the blues material, while Art Laibly recorded mostly hillbilly music. He recalls Ma Rainey, who called him her "white baby," with affection, and notes with amusement the time when he stood behind Blind Lemon during a recording session and whispered the words of a song in his ear. According to Uncle Art, the Wisconsin Chair Co. occasionally hired writers to write songs for their artists, and this seems to have been the case with Blind Lemon on at least one session.

One of the first hit recordings that Uncle Art had supervised was "My Lord's Gonna Move This Wicked Race" (Paramount 12035), made in 1923 in New York by the Norfolk Jubilee Quartet. He had paid the members of the group $100 apiece for eight or twelve numbers plus the train fare from Norfolk, Va., to New York. When they returned, he always gave them a gift—"either a hard hat, which they loved in those days, or else a bunch of neckties and collars, which they bought on the Bowery for about four for a buck. . . . We treated them like we would like to be

treated. . . . I did not do this the way a Southerner would go about recording. . . . I had a different idea, because I didn't know what a Negro was
when I came to America. I knew what a Kaffir was, and a Hottentot and
a Zulu—part of the British Empire. But I didn't know about our own here,
you know. But I quickly came to understand that they were American-
ized and spoke the same tongue as we do." When recording black artists,

> I didn't just say, "Sing this and go out and have a drink somewhere." I
> spent my time in that studio getting them ready for the people of the world.
> . . . When I spoke to those Negroes, I would talk to them, I would tell them
> something about my background as an immigrant. I would tell them what
> we had to expect. Then when I found that I had these Negroes in a feeling,
> I would ask, "Before we sing this spiritual . . . which one of you have lost
> a loved one in the last year or so?" And one would step forward. Then I
> would say to the fellow that had some preaching experience, "Just say a
> little short prayer before we start preaching." This was not an act on my
> part. It was the simplicity of a simplicity to be an honest man, to give them
> what they wanted back. And the only way to get it back was to get what
> they felt in their souls. How many recording men know that? . . . It's all a
> study. You just don't go in like animals and talk to people, whether they're
> white, black, pink, or any color. You just have to know their life a little bit,
> and they have to know that you're not going to hurt them, too.

While Satherley was in charge of the Paramount studios in New York
and Port Washington, he supervised recordings for the Grey Gull Company, an outfit owned by a banker named Shaw in Boston. They purchased or leased Paramount masters for their label.

In about 1929, Uncle Art left Paramount to work for QRS, a piano roll
manufacturer that expressed an interest in getting into the record business. The only executive Uncle Art recalls with QRS at the time was a
Max Courtlander. Many of QRS's recordings were actually made in the
Queens, New York, studios of the Starr Piano Co. (Gennett). However,
Uncle Art soon found out that the QRS people were not seriously interested in phonograph recordings per se, but were only trying to build up a
company for financial motives, planning to sell it as soon as its stocks had
risen high enough; he then left QRS to work for the Plaza Music Co. The
people at QRS were mostly metropolitan men; they didn't understand
country people (white or black) and didn't feel like putting too much
effort into the recording business. After QRS quit the record business,
they sold many masters to Paramount; some may have been sold directly
to Grey Gull. This network of interrelationships explains the long-

unknown source of Gene Autry's 1929 Grey Gull recordings. They were originally made by Gennett for QRS, and then sold to Grey Gull either directly or through Paramount.

In August 1929 Plaza Music and some other companies were merged into a new unit, the American Record Corp., and it was while he was with this company that Uncle Art began making field trips to the South to record country music, both black and white. For over two decades he recorded some of the most popular hillbilly and blues artists of the day. Uncle Art still has in his possession his notebooks, in which he has listed, alphabetically by artist, all the recordings that he supervised from 1932 through mid-1951. Among the artists whose recordings he supervised regularly were Roy Acuff, the Allen Brothers, Gene Autry, Big Bill Broonzy, the Carlisle Brothers, Leroy Carr, Blind Boy Fuller, Memphis Minnie, Bob Wills, and Clarence Williams.

Uncle Art recalled in detail the steps involved in the physical manufacture of a record. The original wax master was made of beeswax and stearic acid. These wax masters were made in Connecticut by a man named Matthews; all steel needles were also made there. The masters were made plain, with a hole, and shipped in fitted tin cans packed with cotton. They were refrigerated until required for use, at which time one fellow would scrape the master with a razor blade until the surface was like a mirror. Then the masters would be put in a warming cabinet until they had warmed up to the appropriate temperature. The styli were also warmed, because they were made of diamond or sapphire and were very brittle. In general, they never played back a wax master, except occasionally to hear how they were doing. These masters were immediately reshaved and re-used. Three wax masters representing three successive takes were made. They were all sent to New York or Chicago for processing. When Uncle Art returned from a month or six weeks of recording, he'd have three or four hundred test pressings waiting for him. His next task would be to listen to them all and make his catalog selections.

The entire process involved fine work, and one had to be an expert to do it properly. Uncle Art recalled many a session when he had to turn the crank to pull up the weights to drive the turntable. Those weights were 100 pound blocks of concrete or iron. Occasionally, "we'd be in the middle of a recording and the rope would snap and, man, it would come down—you'd think the entire building was gone."

Each wax master was copper plated in a copper sulfate bath. When the plating was completed, the master was removed from the baths and the copper was stripped away. Then the wax man would take the wax master, repolish it with his razor blade, and ready it for use again. The copper master was dipped in graphite and used to obtain a mother. Generally several mothers were made from a single master; and from each mother many stampers could be made. Thus, for a popular record, twenty or thirty stampers would be made, and as many presses could be put to work at one time. A good stamper was usable for four to six hundred pressings. The copper masters were kept in a vault. A large company like Victor or Columbia probably had 100 tons of copper tied up in masters, Uncle Art stated. Each one was treated at least once annually with a certain type of silicone to make sure the grooves were preserved.

Although there were early artists who were very popular, such as Mac and Bob, and Vernon Dalhart, Uncle Art sees Gene Autry's recording of "That Silver Haired Daddy of Mine" as really opening up the field of hillbilly music; and much of the credit for the success of Autry and the recording goes, in Uncle Art's opinion, to a handful of people at Sears, Roebuck Co. who encouraged the WLS Barn Dance and the distribution of records through the catalog. Thanks to the Sears outlet, ARC's money, and the fact that America was right for it at the moment, Autry's recording became an overnight hit. Uncle Art, whose own role in Autry's initial successes should not be underestimated, was also instrumental in forwarding Autry's film career; it was he who suggested to Herbert G. Yates of Consolidated Films, Inc., that they film Autry. Yates at first demurred, but Satherley persisted; finally one of Yates' associates interviewed Autry in Chicago, and soon he got in pictures. At first, Gene had a rough time with the horses—Uncle Art himself having had more riding experience during his service in Britain as a cavalryman. Another offshoot of Autry's early popularity was the tremendous sales of his song folios. M. M. Cole followed the artists of the WLS Barn Dance closely, and published folios for all the prominent ones. Gene Autry folios sold at a rate of 2,000 per day, Uncle Art recalls.

Art Satherley is often considered an A&R man; he prefers to call himself a record man:

> Having had the experience I had in actually running a plant, I was fortunate enough to be able to talk all phases of the business. . . . An A&R man means nothing to me, unless he has the background of the industry and what it's all about. A song is more than a song, a song is what the people would accept. . . . I believe that I was a full-fledged man capable of telling the world, even now, what happened when we first put music on a disc or on a cylinder.

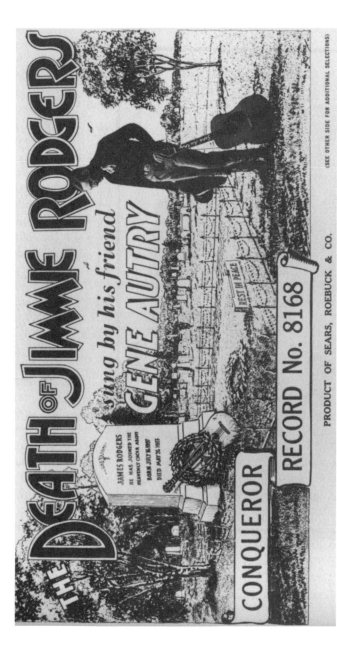

When American Recording Corp. executive Art Satherley learned of Jimmie Rodgers's death, he wired Gene Autry in Chicago to have a photograph made of himself posed as if he were looking down at a grave. The photo was quickly incorporated into artwork to promote Autry's musical tribute to "his friend," recorded less than a month after Rodgers died. It is not clear whether the two ever actually met.

Spring 1972

Donald Lee Nelson

The Life of Alfred G. Karnes

To collectors of old-time hillbilly music, Alfred G. Karnes is known as the artist on four Victor 78s of 1927–28 — all powerful renditions of religious or nostalgic songs, backed up by a distinctively emphatic guitar accompaniment. Little has been said of his life and background — a lack that is corrected in the following account by Don Nelson. The contents of this article were gleaned from a five-hour interview graciously given the author by A. G. Karnes's oldest son, Alfred James Karnes of Lancaster, Kentucky, in July 1971, and from lengthy correspondence with Rev. Oscar F. Davis of Cookeville, Tennessee. The generous assistance of numerous other ministers and long-time citizens of the Corbin/Crab Orchard/Lancaster area is also acknowledged.

Alfred Grant Karnes, gospel singer, composer, multi-instrumental musician, Methodist minister, farmer, barber, sailor, Baptist minister, patent medicine manufacturer, instrument maker, and evangelist (but not necessarily in that order) was born on February 2, 1891, in Bedford, Virginia. His mother, Maggie Grant Karnes, died at his birth, and his father, Alexander Hamilton Karnes, left him and his two brothers, William and Maynard, in the care of an Aunt Neely and Uncle Cap Harrington.

Even as a boy Karnes had two unyielding urges: preaching and music. He recalled in later years how he would go out into a large field of daisies with a violin he had fashioned from a cigar box. Using a horsehair bow on the instrument he would play for a while and then mount a stump and preach. He left the Harrington farm when he was fourteen, having received only a third grade education, and two years later was married to a woman several years his senior. The couple had two daughters, but the marriage ended in divorce.

Karnes enlisted in the United States Navy in World War I, and served as both gunner's mate and lookout on a submarine chaser. Upon his discharge from the service he went to Jellico, Tennessee, where he entered the barbering trade. It was near there, at Gray Station, that he met Flora Etta Harris of Corbin, Kentucky. The couple was married in 1920 at London, Kentucky, and two years later the first of their seven children was born.

The barber shop of the post Great War days was a social gathering place where quartette singing was just as in vogue as it had been during the "Gay Nineties." It was with such groups that the rich Karnes voice received its first general exposure. Shortly his skill with violin and banjo, combined with his movingly powerful tones, placed him in demand at local gatherings. He often recalled "singing until I could see the sun come up." It was probably here that his fondness for the particular song earned him the nickname "Red Wing."

Although born in Virginia, a state rich in heritage and grandeur, Karnes always considered himself to be a Kentuckian. Upon moving there permanently after his marriage, his fascination with the Bluegrass state increased, and in spite of future sojourns from its borders, he was never to remain away any great length of time.

A calling for the ministry, which he had always felt, finally overpowered the young barber, and by 1925 he was graduated as a Methodist minister from the Clear Creek Mountain Preacher's Bible School. Some months later Dr. Kelly of the Clear Creek School and a firm Baptist asked Reverend Karnes to debate the merits of the two sects; Kelly converted his recent pupil to the Baptist persuasion. Upon hearing this, Mrs. Karnes, a devout Methodist from birth, threatened to join the Holiness Church in protest. She did not, however, and eventually embraced her husband's newly adopted faith.

The Karneses, who were then living near Corbin, underwent the frequent troubles of a mountain minister's family. Although rural communities were made very distant by the bad roads of the day, the faithful in the isolated regions of eastern Kentucky should not, Brother Karnes felt, suffer the privation of religious solitude. He therefore pastored as many as four churches in as many widely separated communities at one time, devoting a quarter of his energies and time to each. That he was able to maintain this rigorous schedule in addition to his duties as head of a growing family is tribute to the depth of his convictions.

During his time in Corbin he became acquainted with Ben W. Davis, a local druggist, and brother of Reverend Oscar F. Davis, a minister with whom he had been ordained in the North Corbin Church. Karnes introduced his "Relax Rub," an external compound for the relieving of muscle tensions and soreness to the apothecary Davis. The mixture was a successful seller, and old-timers in the area still attest glowingly to its powers.

Just how Alfred G. Karnes and the Victor Talking Machine Company got together is not known; perhaps a local citizen, or group of citizens, impressed with his musical prowess, arranged for him to travel to Bristol, Tennessee, in July of 1927 for an audition. Rather than bring a violin or banjo, Karnes took a $375 Gibson harp-guitar on which to accompany himself. It was on this double-necked instrument that Karnes produced the distinctive sound of his bass runs. On July 29 he cut six sides, five of which were released by the Victor Company. "Called to the Foreign Field," his own composition and most popular song, was among those he recorded that day. Another Corbinite, banjoist B. F. Shelton, recorded on the same day. Doubtless they knew each other, but what connection there was in their both recording for Victor that day is not known.

Certain serious students of music suggest that Karnes also appeared, sans credit, on recordings done three days previously by Ernest Phipps and his Holiness Quartet. Phipps, also from the general Corbin area, was a Holiness preacher. Although Karnes had no vocal part on the Phipps recordings, the sound of a harp-guitar strummed in his particular style is evident.

Reverend Davis writes of a 1925 incident which gives support to Karnes's musical acumen. They had gone together to conduct morning services in a neighboring community, when "At the close of the service we were taken to a home nearby for dinner. While enjoying a conversation on a shady lawn while the dinner was being prepared, a member of the family brought out of the house an old harp of some kind. It had been there many years and idle for lack of anyone to play it. It was handed to Brother Karnes. After removing some of the dust from it with his handkerchief, he began to tune it, and he did not tune it with another instrument. I gazed with amazement while he tuned the strings. Finally I said, 'How can you tell when a string is in tune or out of tune? I can't tell the difference.' He was slow to answer, and finally said, 'I can't recall the day, even early in life that I could not tell when a string was in tune or out of tune. God gave me something that He did not give you."

In October 1928 Karnes retraced his steps to Bristol for a final recording session with Victor. He placed four sides on wax on the 28th, and returned the following day for three final songs. Only three of the seven numbers were released, and the recording career of Alfred C. Karnes was ended. The Phipps group also recorded at that session, and quite conceivably Karnes appeared anonymously with them.

As he left Tennessee for home, his harp-guitar nearly cost him his life. As he was returning along the James River with the instrument in the back seat of his car, he approached a ferry boat landing in order to ford the water. Two carloads of men in large Buicks spotted the guitar, and seeing it in the possession of a lone man, decided to rob him. The three cars, Karnes's 1928 Chevrolet and the two Buicks, were ferried across at the same time. On the other side one of the Buicks pulled ahead of Karnes's auto on the dirt road that wound and twisted high above the river, while the other stayed behind. Coming around one particular turn, Karnes saw the lead Buick pulled sideways across the road, blocking him. He swerved his auto around the obstacle and accelerated. The hoodlums gave chase with their more powerful but less maneuverable cars. Figuring he could not outrun them, Karnes pulled into the garage of a small lodge and closed the door just as his pursuers roared past. Not long afterwards the men cruised back, apparently figuring their prey had pulled off onto a side road. When they finally left the vicinity Karnes continued on his journey in safety.

He continued his ministerial duties, including establishing churches at Turkeytown, Kentucky, and Jacktown, Ohio. In addition, he visited many prisons and jails to hold services for inmates, gaining many conversions.

With the election of Franklin Roosevelt came the reevaluation of certain governmental pensions to war-wounded servicemen. Karnes had been receiving $18.00 per month, with which he was buying a home for his family at Roundstone, near Renfro Valley. What the nature of his disability was is not known, but the pension was stopped. The family faced a housing crisis, and Reverend Karnes took temporary leave of his loved ones with the assertion that "I'm going to get a home." He located the ideal spot on six acres of land at Crab Orchard. Parishioners cut wood and built a home for their new minister and his family. It was taken over on the "squatter's rights" doctrine, and remained his residence for many years. His children still remember working to clear the land, and the story-and-a-half house of which they were so proud.

At this time Alfred Karnes reached the apex of his life, both musically and professionally. He had formed a family band, consisting of his sons Alfred J. (called James) on guitar, Claude on bass (which A. G. himself made), Tom on guitar, Jack on mandocello (a bass mandolin), and daughter Doris on regular mandolin. Karnes himself played the violin—in a manner likened, by those who heard him, to Slim Miller. (This is apparently the supreme compliment a Kentuckian can give to a violinist.) Doris Karnes was such an accomplished musician that the Finley Davidson Company of Middletown, Ohio, presented her with a Gibson mandolin.

The family gave four "courthouse steps" concerts every Sunday. They would travel early in the morning to Mount Vernon, then on to Broadhead, back home for lunch, and at 1:30 to Lancaster, and finally to Stanford. A neighbor of James Karnes recalls the Lancaster gatherings: "When they came in front of the courthouse there were only a few people around, but by the time they had done three or four songs the square was so full of people you could hardly drive through." A service station owner in the same town, who had been then a small boy, remembered, "I've seen old men who'd never been in church in their lives, sometimes so crippled they could hardly walk, but they'd come to hear 'em." The theme of the family band was "This Is My Day, My Happy Day," and was one of their most requested offerings.

Only once after taking up the ministry did Alfred Karnes return to the barber's trade, and then for only a short time. The reason is unknown, but after a futile attempt at haircutting he told his wife, "It's no use, I can't make it as a barber." This, in spite of the fact that he is remembered as a good barber.

Karnes had a gift for painting that those who have viewed his works call "genuine," but only three of his works are known to exist. He painted "The Gateway Home," his childhood impression of the Blue Ridge Mountains of his native Virginia, on a plywood canvas. He also painted Washington's home at Mount Vernon from a snapshot. His only other work was one done of his Virginia home, which he had made as a boy.

Although the majority of his musical material was religious in nature, he was fond of playing such fiddle tunes as "Eighth of January" and "Wednesday Night Waltz." He enjoyed doing the Charleston, and kept himself in fine physical condition by strenuous gymnastics. At fifty years of age he was still able to kip to his feet and ride a bicycle on one wheel. He pastored Gilbert's Creek Church, a house of worship from colonial times, and at the Ottawa Baptist Church, renowned in the area for its outstanding choir.

In 1944 his beloved wife passed away, and the strain, along with the years of hard work, began to show. He held revival meetings at Roundstone, but much of his activity had to be curtailed.

He married Beulah Hays, Flora Karnes's niece, but she died of cancer within two years. Sorrow plagued him still further when his marriage to Maggie Bollanger of Middletown, Ohio, ended in her death after little more than a year. He made one final try at wedlock, this time to a Mrs. Edwards. The couple moved to Starke, Florida, where Karnes held evangelical meetings, but the couple separated, and he returned to his Kentucky home.

In early 1957 he suffered a stroke which left him partially paralyzed. He was, after months of effort, able to walk with the support of his son James. The following year he was stricken with a second stroke, and on May 18, 1958, Alfred G. Karnes died at the age of sixty-seven. His funeral service was conducted by his friend Reverend Oscar Davis, and he is buried beside his second wife at the McHargue Church Cemetery near Lily, Kentucky.

Considering the fact that only four records credited to Alfred C. Karnes were ever released, the number of people who know of him is immense. Every person thirty-five years of age or older living in the Lancaster area has a reverent recollection of the man and the minister. That he is well respected by country and blues collectors comes as no surprise to the people who knew him. Admittedly, this region is known for its devoutly religious populace, but more citizens than just the churchgoers seem to recall the gospel singer and his family band, and though he is departed these fourteen years, the Karnes charisma remains in the memory of all who came in contact with him.

Ed Kahn

International Relations, Dr. Brinkley, and Hillbilly Music

Mass media have always developed in a helter-skelter fashion. Almost without exception new media have been developed for purposes which ultimately turned out to be secondary to their real contribution to a mass society. The phonograph was developed as a business aid; radio was developed for ship-to-shore communication which did not even involve the transmission of the human voice. Each of these devices—even when they were finally recognized as media of mass communications—struggled to gain acceptance and a wider marketplace. The result was that seldom in their early years did those who manipulated the new devices realize that their future would be in an integrated aggregate of mass entertainment industries. This development of closer cooperation between segments of the mass entertainment fields still continues today with book publishers, broadcasting enterprises, phonograph record companies, and now motion picture businesses working closely together.

In the early days of radio broadcasting the broadcasters saw the phonograph recording as direct competition. The competition was sharply felt by both sides. The broadcasters felt that they would lose their competitive advantage if they broadcast phonograph recordings, and the recording industry likewise opposed such a broadcasting format because it feared that this might reduce the sale of their product. So in those days radio prided itself on its presentation of live talent. But the small local station could hardly afford to hire talent that could approach the quality that was available on recordings. The networks, of course, provided one answer, for now the expense of a high-quality live performance could in effect be shared by the cooperating stations of the network. The development of the networks, however, tended to divide the broadcasters into network and independent stations. The networks could boast of a greater variety of offerings and emphasized that they were presenting only live broadcasts. The independents, however, had a different line of development. In the early days they relied extensively upon locally available talent. But in time they began to use more and more recordings and transcribed shows. The transcription provided a means of delaying a broadcast and even repeating it. Also, through the transcription, in the days before the introduction of tape recording, a radio show could be produced on transcription and then sent from station to station in an attempt to avoid the use of recordings, but still provide a higher level of talent than was available locally. The networks virtually prohibited any delayed broadcasting until 1948.

While the hostility of the recording and broadcasting industries toward each other was producing fragmentation and false barriers, another battle was also going on that centered around the allocation of broadcasting frequencies among neighboring countries. In the early days of broadcasting within the United States, basic decisions had to be reached concerning the allocation of the broadcast channels within the limited states. Until 1912 there was no domestic regulation of broadcasting, at which time it was placed under the jurisdiction of the Department of Commerce. In 1927 the Federal Radio Commission was established for the purpose of regulating the use of broadcast facilities. Finally, in 1934, the Federal Communications Commission was established with broader authority.

The problems of allocation of broadcast frequencies became increasingly complex as radio grew in the United States; and as neighboring countries began to develop, their demand for broadcast channels created additional problems that ultimately had to be worked out through international agreements. In 1924 an informal agreement was worked out with Canada whereby the ninety-six broadcast channels in the 55–1,500 kc range were allocated in a manner satisfactory to both countries. In 1932 the United States and Canada exchanged notes on the allocation of frequencies, providing exclusive channels for both the United States and Canada as well as certain channels that were shared by the two countries. This arrangement worked well for the two countries involved, but as other North American countries began to undergo greater industrialization, their demands for radio frequencies increased. In the U.S.-Canada agreements no provision had been made to allocate frequencies to either Mexico or Cuba. Accordingly, Mexico began to apply pressure on the United States. The instruments of pressure involved a fascinating drama in international relations in which Mexico authorized a number of radio stations to begin operating on the Mexican side of the U.S.–Mexico border. These powerful stations broadcast almost exclusively in English and were directed to an audience in the United States. For the most part, the stations were controlled by individuals whose broadcasting practices in the United States had been sufficiently questionable so that their licenses were not renewed. Mexico, as part of its pressure on the United States to provide for Mexican stations, allowed these stations to go virtually unchecked until her own demands were satisfied. These stations—powerful enough to reach every state in the Union—chose a format that gained them the widest listening audience and brought in the greatest amount of revenue. By the late 1930s the Border Stations had learned that their maximum listening audience could be obtained by the use of hillbilly and gospel music in a direct appeal to the rural English-speaking people of North America. Many of the products advertised were of questionable value, and certainly the advertising standards were far below the minimum standards set for broadcasters in the United States. The result was that these stations were commanding large audiences—perhaps greater than any single station in the United States—because they were technically Mexican stations even though they were run by and directed to United States citizens. Virtually all of the advertisers were located in the United States. Beginning in 1931, the United States applied a variety of sanctions in order to curb these operations, but with little or no lasting success until the North American Regional Broadcast Agreement (called the Havana Treaty), which guaranteed all of the countries in North America certain radio rights, was put into effect in 1941.

During the years in which this drama was unfolding, there were a number of actors. Occupying the lead role was John Romulus Brinkley, medical doctor of questionable qualifications, controversial politician, and master of the uses of broadcasting. In order for Brinkley to have the impact he had, it was necessary for him to be surrounded by many supporting personalities. The Carter Family from 1938 until 1942 made their mark in the history of border stations by broadcasting over Brinkley's XERA. From one point of view, the border stations are important because they are a clear example of broadcasters catering to the demands of a North American listening audience rather than trying to raise the standards of the audience. Via the Border Stations, hillbilly and gospel music—of which the Carter Family were leading interpreters—became a factor in the ultimate solution of a complex problem in international relations. In order to understand the significance of Border Stations and to see how the Carter Family fit into this complex facet of broadcasting history, it is appropriate to review the histories of both John Brinkley and the phenomenon of the Border Station.

Although there have been a number of publications dealing with the history of John R. Brinkley, many details of his early career are nevertheless difficult to learn. On differing occasions Brinkley claimed Tennessee, Kentucky, and North Carolina as his place of birth, but it seems probable that he was born on July 8, 1885, in Jackson County, North Carolina. In later years, Brinkley liked to recall the poverty from which he rose and point out how this accounted for his basic understanding of common people.

His schooling was rudimentary, but he read whatever he could find to read and apparently had a photographic memory. While taking mail order courses, he also took a job without pay for the Southern Railway agent at Sylva, North Carolina, in order to learn telegraphy—perhaps relating to an early interest in Edison—and bookkeeping. During the early years after his marriage in 1908, Brinkley worked as a relief agent for the Southern Railway and became a "Quaker Doctor," a spieler in a kind of medicine-vaudeville show in which he learned the hypnotic style of talking to "the whistlers, whittlers, and spitters" (Carson, p. 18) that served him so well in later years.

These years were marked by a good deal of moving around in an attempt to become a doctor. Times were hard for the Brinkleys, and the aggressive young man chose the path of least resistance in his attempt to achieve his goal. By 1908 they had arrived in Chicago, where he worked for Western Union while attending the Bennett Medical College, an eclectic institution, as well as other nonaccredited schools. Eventually he received a fraudulent medical certificate dated 1913, but probably issued in 1918. In 1912 he and his wife were in Knoxville, where he had a license to practice medicine as an "undergraduate physician." It was here that he first began to learn how to make a quick buck as an "advertising doctor."

By 1915, following divorce and a second marriage, Brinkley had obtained a diploma which allowed him to practice medicine in eight states, although the other forty states did not recognize the institution granting the degree. In early 1916 he was issued a Kansas medical license and took a job at Swift Company, where he treated minor injuries of employees and did clerical work. At some time during this period Brinkley settled in the small Kansas town of Fulton and became involved in politics for the first time, running successfully for mayor against the incumbent. After a month in the Army, he settled in the small town of Milford, Kansas, located some twelve miles by dirt road from both Junction City and Fort Riley.

Radically innovative and controversial as his career became, he began his practice in Milford modestly. For eight dollars a month he rented a drugstore and lived in one of the two back rooms. The other room served as his office, while Mrs. Brinkley tended the store, which opened on November 7, 1917. His medical practice was at first reasonably conventional, but soon a local farmer came complaining that he had not been able to have a child in the last eighteen years and wanted to know if the new doctor could do anything to increase his sexual potency. At first Brinkley told the man that this was an old problem that had no real remedy. But as the conversation continued, Brinkley thought back to his days at Swift & Company and his observations that of all the animals the goat was the healthiest. He remarked to the farmer that "You wouldn't have any trouble, if you had a pair of those buck glands in you" (quoted in Relser 1958:53). Following his initial refusal to cooperate, Brinkley agreed to acquiesce to the farmer's demands for a set of the glands, provided that the farmer not tell anyone about the operation. But soon came another farmer asking for the same treatment. In time the patient became the father of a healthy son which he named Billy in honor of the goat. It wasn't long before others came to Brinkley, learning of the earlier success.

In February of 1922, Brinkley received a query from Harry Chandler, owner of the *Los Angeles Times*. It seemed that an elderly editor of the paper was in need of Brinkley's services. A temporary thirty-day license was arranged in order for the doctor to be able to practice medicine in the state of California. Although Brinkley had developed quite a following at this early date, he had hardly begun to exploit the operation. Chandler urged the doctor never again to perform the operation for less than $500.00, and it was said that during his brief stay in the Golden State he earned in excess of $40,000.

In addition to the financial rewards the journey west brought, Brinkley was introduced to an idea that opened up a whole new world to him. In early days of radio, many of the prestige stations were operated by the newspapers. Harry Chandler was just installing KHJ as a subsidiary of the *Los Angeles Times*. Brinkley's early interest in both Edison and telegraphy led him to quickly reason that radio might help him in promoting his services. By the fall of 1923 he had sent out a form letter to his mailing list urging them to "tune in" to his new station. The station began modestly shortly after receiving its license in September of 1923. The call letters were KFKB-"Kansas First, Kansas Best"—and the initial power was two hundred and fifty watts. Although this was low, KFKB was the only station in the state at that time. In the early days both frequency and power seemed to fluctuate. The programming had no paid commercials, but Brinkley's own verbal talks occupied over half of the broadcast schedule. After Brinkley's first transmitter burned down early in 1924, plans were immediately begun for a new and more powerful one. The new facilities were impressive, with a studio that would hold a chorus of three hundred people. The programs included personal travel talks, talks to mothers on their babies, and lectures on the world's great literature by teachers from Manhattan State College. Power was gradually increased until November 1928, when KFKB began broadcasting with 5,000 watts. With his new power he boasted that from his location in the center of the United States he could be heard anywhere in continental North America. The increase in wattage was accompanied by an expansion of format. The listener could hear religious programs, news from fraternal organizations, and agricultural programs as well as a wide variety of music. The talent included cowboy singers, yodelers, and crooners, a cowboy orchestra, a twelve-piece studio orchestra, semiclassical as well as classical orchestras, rural fiddlers and old-time hillbilly bands as well as three announcers.

The new expanded format paid off. In the *Radio Digest* audience popularity poll of 1930, KFKB was voted the most popular station in the country. Financially Brinkley was equally rewarded. By 1928 he was grossing $150,000 annually from his hospital. In addition he had made a number of improvements in the community by putting in city water, bringing in electricity, and planning to pave the road to Junction City. As his popularity grew, so did his radio format, for Brinkley was firmly in command of the new medium of mass communication. From the outset his rural background and a natural instinct for drama aided him in appealing to the rural audience. His radio format mixed in liberal amounts of fundamentalist theology, joys of rejuvenation, and large doses of discussions on sex—designed to titillate but not offend the rural listeners he so well understood. Gerald Carson succinctly described the Brinkley appeal: "To keep the audience glued to its radio between long-manhood commercials, KFKB offered The Old Timers, a guitar-and-banjo ensemble; Dutch, the Boy Blues Singer; Uncle Bob Larkin and his fiddle; an accordionist; a harpist; cowboy singers, yodelers, and crooners. The McRee Sisters did novelties. Steve Love and his eleven-piece orchestra played pop music, while the doctor of magic—not medicine—sold horoscopes. The Ninth Cavalry band from Fort Riley and talented people from Manhattan and Junction City also went on the air as a part of Doc's folksy and inexpensive programming. For more serious fare, he broadcast the market news—daily prices of corn, wheat and hogs" (p. 89). In Brinkley's own talks to the people, he sensed their tastes and was able to combine the appeal of both minister and medicine man. As he spoke over his gold-plated microphone he joked, spoke with a clear Southern accent, stumbled over the big words and didn't mind for he knew that this added to his appeal and furthermore that he sounded like a doctor. Despite protests from both competitors and the American Medical Association he had a strong following among the people.

The high times he was enjoying were soon to be attacked from all sides as he entered into the first of many legal battles that were to be fought during the next twelve years. The medical profession began applying pressure for his license to be revoked at the same time as the *Kansas City Star*, which owned competing radio station WDAF, began applying pres-

Dr. J. R. Brinkley
WILL SPEAK AT
Sodens' Grove
EMPORIA, KANSAS, AT 8 P. M.,
FRIDAY, AUGUST 26TH

Dr. Brinkley will be accompanied by AMMUNITION TRAIN NO. 1, equipped with loud speakers, and Roy Faulkner, the Singing Cow Boy from Radio Stations KFKB and XER, who will entertain. Dr. Brinkley will positively appear in person and the speaking will begin promptly at 8 P. M.

sures on the FRC not to renew his broadcasting license. By the middle of April 1930, Brinkley was warning over the airwaves that if the FRC denied him his radio voice, he would take "thousands of satisfied patients" to Washington and urged all of those who would like to accompany him to let him know so he could reserve the needed Pullman cars. In the end the generous boast was reduced to an offer for a round-trip ticket for $120.00 plus meals and other incidental expenses.

Friday, June 13, 1930, brought disaster for the doctor. On that date the Federal Radio Commission refused a renewal of the KFKB license and the Kansas Supreme Court refused to grant an injunction against a hearing before the state medical board. Eventually, stalling tactics were applied in order to stay on the air until his farewell address on February 21, 1931. But before his final departure from the Kansas airwaves, Brinkley began two more ingenious schemes. He quietly began making arrangements to obtain a broadcasting license in Mexico so that he would not fall under the jurisdiction of the Federal Radio Commission, and also decided to enter politics.

After an unsuccessful campaign for the governorship of the state of Kansas, Brinkley turned his attention to the problems of his broadcasting

license. On New Year's Day of 1931, he announced to the Associated Press in El Paso, Texas, that he intended to build a 50,000-watt station in Mexico if he could get permission from the Mexican government. Three weeks later it was announced that KFKB had been sold to the Farmers' and Bankers' Insurance Company of Wichita, Kansas, for a figure reported to be $90,000. Within the month, Brinkley said his final farewell from KFKB, declaring that his leaving the air was "a blow to the doctrine of free speech" but announced his intention of building a new station at Villa Acuna, Mexico, just across the border from Del Rio, Texas.

Many of the details of Brinkley's Mexican adventure are unclear, as is much other information regarding the Border Stations. But it would appear that Brinkley was the originator of this brand of broadcasting and that in this operation, as in the other Brinkley adventures, he was once more able to turn adverse conditions to his advantage. In this case, he was able to capitalize on the long-standing disagreement between Mexico and the United States.

Details of Brinkley's dealing with Mexican authorities are obviously not available, but one report has it that he signed a twenty-year agreement with Mexico that allowed him to build a transmitter at Villa Acuna that was to be more powerful than any other commercial transmitter in the world. Carson reports that following Brinkley's visit to Mexico in January 1931, he returned with permission to build a 50,000-watt station anywhere along the Mexican border (p. 179). And U.S. towns along the border also were anxious to have Brinkley choose their community. When Del Rio's Chamber of Commerce secretary, A. C. Easterling, learned of Brinkley's search for a suitable place to relocate, he wrote and encouraged the doctor to visit Del Rio. The Chamber of Commerce guaranteed clearance of necessary permits and concessions. His license from Mexico ran some fourteen pages and allowed him to do almost anything he wished. But soon after broadcasting began, there were minor problems to be worked out in order for Brinkley to be able to continue his irritations to the United States and Canada. Mexico began to resent such a powerful station being owned by an American and saw it as another case of Yankee imperialism. Finally, the papers were legally transferred into the names of Mexicans, who then privately assigned the rights back to Brinkley.

Although the official opening of XER was slated for October 21, with celebrations spanning both sides of the border, experimental broadcasts began on October 7, 1931. There are conflicting reports of the actual power of the station in the early days, ranging from 75,000 to 100,000 watts—in either case far in excess of the maximum 50,000 watts permitted in the United States. With his signal beamed to the North, the response was fantastic. In the week of January 11–16, 1932, the 27,717 pieces of mail received came from all of the states as well as fourteen foreign countries in addition to Mexico. But Brinkley wanted still more power and early in 1932 applied for an increase beyond the 75,000 watts he was permitted. On August 18, 1932, Brinkley was granted the increase to 150,000 watts.

The format of XER followed closely that which had been so successful in Milford. Many of the same rural entertainers that had gained a following in Kansas were now heard over XER. And, of course, Brinkley himself was prominently featured. The exact method of broadcast seemed to vary, and the details are still unclear. When Brinkley opened XER he did not move his practice from Milford, but rather left the hospital and the rest of his empire in Kansas. With the legal battles he was having over his own medical license, he was doing few of the actual operations himself, preferring to leave the real work to his medical staff. Shortly after the Mexican station began broadcasting, Brinkley found himself barred from crossing the international bridge into Mexico. At that time he began making broadcasts from his studio above the J. C. Penney store in Del Rio and broadcasting by remote lines across the border to his transmitter. Soon, however, a new ruling forbade Americans from broadcasting by the use of remote line into another country, obviously an attempt to stifle Brinkley. But before long he was again broadcasting from Mexico by the use of transcription discs, a technique in which he also pioneered.

Despite the fact that Brinkley made hundreds if not thousands of transcriptions of his radio broadcasts, today we have no recordings of his voice, and must rely solely upon the few extant stenographic transcriptions of his radio broadcasts. From one early Del Rio broadcast, we get an idea of his style (quoted in Chase, pp. 77–78):

> My dear, dear friends, my patients, my many supplicants. Your letters— hundreds of them since yesterday—lie here before me, touching testimonials of your pain, your grief, the wretchedness which is visited upon the innocent. I can reply now to a few—just a few. Others I shall answer by mail. But oh, my friends, you must remember that your letters asking my advice in your physical sufferings must be accompanied by two dollars, which barely covers the cost of postage, stenographic hire, office rent and so forth. I am your friend, but not even the greatest Baron of Wall Street— Wall Street, where the untold millions of money are—could withstand the ruinous cost of helping you unless this small fee accompanies your letter.

The station was assigned a frequency of 735 kc, exactly in the middle of the normal separation of 10 kc which U.S. broadcasters maintain between neighboring frequencies. But with the power which XER had, coupled with the drift from his assigned frequency, the disturbance to U.S. broadcasters was great. On a good night, disturbance from XER was felt by stations throughout North America, including WSB, Atlanta; CKAC, Montreal; WJR, Detroit; and WON, Chicago. But by the time Brinkley had moved his hospital to Del Rio, in 1933, the Texas community was delighted with its new fame. In the midst of the depression, Brinkley's $20,000/month payroll was significant for a small town of 12,000 people. The post office was enjoying greater receipts than ever before, and hotels, rooming houses, and tourist camps were all filled. One department store estimated that Brinkley's presence was worth $1,000 a month to them. Despite the depression, Del Rio was overflowing with patients who had come to visit the Brinkley hospital, and the little town experienced few symptoms of the depression.

Brinkley's career was one of constantly playing opposites against each other for his own advantage. Despite his move to Texas, he did maintain his Kansas ties for political reasons. In 1932 he once again ran for governor, this time using XER rather than his old KFKB in a campaign that was much like that of 1930. He was beaten this time by Republican Alf Landon. Although the campaign was modeled upon his earlier attempt, there were a few significant advances in terms of the development of Border Stations. He was now using a powerful sound truck to bring the familiar radio voices of rural entertainers like Roy Faulkner, the cowboy singer who had achieved fame over KFKB and XER. Then Rev. Samuel Crookson, a Methodist minister from Milford, would eulogize Brinkley's philanthropies in Milford and, following a prayer, Brinkley would be introduced. Perhaps the most outstanding innovation of the campaign, however, was the inclusion of a transcription machine on his sound truck.

When Brinkley returned to Del Rio after his defeat by Landon, there was scarcely a semblance of broadcasting in the public interest. Commercial announcements touted a variety of goods and services such as Koran's fortune-telling scheme, the sale of stock in a gold mine, oil burner sales pitches, and a variety of standard patent medicines.

Although business was good in these years, there were troubles. Mexico's goal of pushing the United States into action was bringing about the intended results. Within two months after XER went on the air, there were movements in Washington to bring about legislation that would curb Brinkley's kind of broadcasting. For the first time, Brinkley was

attempting to originate broadcasts within the United States for the purpose of having them transmitted back into the United States from a transmitter on foreign soil. In 1932, at the International Telecommunications
Conference in Madrid, the U.S. delegation found little willingness on the
part of the Mexicans to consider the Border Station problem. The United
States then approached both Mexico and Canada about the possibility of
allocating broadcast frequencies throughout North America. Mexico
seemed to be willing to discuss the elimination of the Border Stations in
exchange for the allocation of frequencies, and called a North and Central American Regional Radio Conference to be held in Mexico City in
July of 1933. Mexico, Canada, and the United States were able to make
headway on an agreement until it was learned that Mexico would insist
upon the continuation of certain of the Border Stations on the frequencies
assigned to Mexico. Accordingly, the conference ended with no formal
signs of progress toward an agreement. But at the end of the conference
certain Mexican officials indicated that although they would not eliminate the Border Stations in an international treaty, they would be willing
as a national policy to make the Border Stations unsuccessful by requir-
ing that all continuity be in Spanish. So before the delegation left Mexico City, regulations to this end as well as new rules governing medical
programs were drawn up and assurances were given that the new regulations would be strictly enforced.

On February 24, 1934, XER was forced to stop broadcasting while
complaints concerning Brinkley's medical programs were examined. But
he was used to this kind of problem and soon found a way around the

obstacle. By early November, he was broadcasting over stations in Colorado, Kansas, and Missouri as well as XEPN, a sister Border Station in Piedras Negras, across from Eagle Pass, Texas. It is uncertain whether he used remote control from Del Rio or sent transcription discs to the other stations. During this time he also tried to extend his broadcasting holdings by purchasing XEAW at Reynosa, across from McAllen, Texas, and investing $100,000 for the rebuilding of the station. With a power of 50,000 watts, the station began broadcasting on September 7, 1935. And XER, now under the new designation XERA, was also ready to return to the air. Test broadcasts, with new equipment able to transmit 500,000 watts, began on November 17 in preparation for an official opening of December 1, 1935. The new Villa Acuna outlet was able to give the effect of one million watts directed towards the United States with the aid of the directional antenna, according to Brinkley's own court statements.

Although the intentions of the administrative officials in Mexico had been sincere in the summer of 1933, the political influence of the operators of the Border Stations had been underestimated, and the stations were able successfully to appeal to the Mexican courts with consequent restriction of the influence of the administrative officials. Brinkley was now back in business stronger than ever.

It is difficult to determine which Border Stations were being run on Brinkley's principle, but it is clear that the number of these stations increased. By 1938 there were eleven in operation, several of which were operating at power in excess of the 50,000-watt limit generally imposed in the United States, and several owned or controlled by people who had been denied renewals of radio licenses in the United States. It is almost impossible to obtain records sufficient to indicate how many of the Border Stations were using hillbilly and gospel music to further their aims, but it is clear that a number of the Border Stations at one time or another were involved in the Brinkley type of operation.

Although the meetings of 1933 had ended in failure, informal talks with Mexico were held to discuss the Border Station problem. Negotiations progressed very slowly until finally, on December 28, 1939, Mexico became the fourth country to ratify the Havana Treaty which now prepared the way for the elimination of the Border Stations.

The date on which stations throughout North America were to relocate on the broadcast band was set for March 29, 1941. At that time XERA left the air and the radio voice of John R. Brinkley was finally stifled. Brinkley's empire and health were beginning to fail. In March 1941, he entered a voluntary petition declaring bankruptcy after having transferred most of his assets into the names of his wife, son Johnny, and several trusted employees.

On September 23, 1941, the U.S. federal government arrested him on a charge of using the U.S. mail to defraud. The trial date was set for April 6, 1942, but had to be postponed because of his poor health. The court appearance was never made, for death came to the controversial figure on May 26, 1942, in San Antonio.

Now both Brinkley and the Border Station were gone, but it was only a matter of time until the format which Brinkley had established was once again heard from the Mexican side of the Rio Grande. It would seem that while the United States objected to the principle of broadcasts aimed at a U.S. audience originating in a foreign country over which it had no jurisdiction, this general consideration was less important than stifling the voice of John R. Brinkley. It is difficult to determine whether all of the Border Stations ever left the air, but certainly by 1942 Mexico had licensed XELO to broadcast to the United States from Juarez, across from El Paso. The United States had continued to protest the operation of these stations, but the conditions of the North American Regional Broadcast Agreement did not specifically prohibit broadcasting in a foreign language, and the allocation of the frequencies of stations covered by the agreement specified the location of the stations, but only by state, province, or region. Thus, there was no way of prohibiting Mexico from licensing a station to operate along the border as long as an allocation had been made for the state in which the station was located.

It would seem that the station operators were able to apply a good deal of political pressure within Mexico and that for this reason the Mexican government was unwilling to do anything really to curtail their operations. As late as 1951 the FCC was still expressing some concern about the existence of these stations, which at this date still numbered eight:

XELO, Ciudad Juarez, Chihuahua, 150,000 watts
XERF, Villa Acuna, Coahuilla, 150,000 watts
XEG, Monterrey, Nuevo Leon, 150,000 watts
XERB, Rosarito, Baja California, 50,000 watts
XEWT, Nuevo Laredo, Tamaulipas, 50,000 watts
XEAC, Tijuana, Baja California, 50,000 watts
XFFW, Tampico, Tamaulipas, 50,000 watts
XEMO, Tijuana, Baja California, 5,000 watts

Both the power and formats varied on these stations, but at least some of these outlets were only slightly changed from the Brinkley format, although the bulk of advertising was now for mail-order products of questionable value. XERF was really XERA with new call letters and reduced power. Restriction of these stations was virtually impossible as long as Mexico was unwilling to prohibit extensive broadcasting in English. In fact, Mexico certainly profited from these stations, for in the period after the Havana Treaty the pattern which evolved was for the stations to be owned by Mexicans, but then sign exclusive contracts with station representatives in the United States who sold the time to the various sponsors. Thus, while the ownership and certainly a good deal of the profit from the station were retained for Mexicans, control over the content of the broadcasts was handled almost exclusively by people in the United States. These station representatives—the Americans who virtually controlled the stations—knew their business well. Advertising time was expensive, but coverage was wide and the ads brought results. In December of 1944, XELO had 27,628 paid responses to commercials coming from forty-one states, Canada, Alaska, Hawaii, and Cuba.

In the earliest days of the Border Stations there was undoubtedly great diversity in the content and format of the broadcasts, but through time more uniformity developed as one type of presentation seemed to bring richer rewards. By the mid-1940s, the successful Brinkley format had become the standard. One reason was that from the early days in Del Rio, Brinkley had employed both Walter Wilson and Don Howard. After the end of the Brinkley era, Wilson and Howard stayed in the business, now helping to set up new stations along the old lines, because each new station that they aided meant another account for Wilson and Howard, an advertising agency and exclusive station representative.

In the mid-1930s, Howard worked for Brinkley as program director and announcer. His first exposure to hillbilly music was at the Border Stations, and while it wasn't his favorite music, he did respond to groups like the Sons of the Pioneers, the Pickard Family, the Delmore Brothers, Lew Childre, and the Carter Family. The stations tried all kinds of music, but by the mid-1930s hillbilly and gospel music had established themselves as the music that brought the greatest response from the listeners, as judged by the response to the mail-order advertisements. If popular music had brought a greater response, the station would have presented this kind of music. By 1937 or 1938 XERA realized that hillbilly music was the proper format and gradually deleted all other kinds of musical offerings.

Despite the fact that Brinkley featured his own talks for about one hour each evening over XER and later XERA, from the earliest days in Del Rio the station had time for sale for other advertisers and products. And it was through the advertisers that much of the talent that worked over XERA was obtained. Early in his Del Rio days, Brinkley brought in a group of "real hillbillies"—perhaps some people he had known in North Carolina. But the first group of professional hillbilly musicians was brought to Del Rio by Consolidated Royal Chemical Corporation and their advertising agency, located in Chicago.

A year after Brinkley's gubernatorial race of 1932, he began to use the transcription discs for his own broadcasts over XER. Although Brinkley never allowed records to be played over his Kansas station, in Del Rio right from the beginning records were used occasionally when live talent was not practical late at night. As Consolidated Royal Chemical Corporation sent groups down to Del Rio, they appeared live in their daily broadcasts. But eventually as a convenience to the performers and their announcers—also sent along from Chicago—transcriptions were made on a Presto cutter to accommodate the cast. In the early days, transcriptions were made directly from the air as the performers broadcast. Then the same show could be replayed later. A common pattern was for the musicians to do their evening show live and for the transcription to be replayed on the next morning's early show. The transcriptions included music, mistakes, and commercials. The discs were good for only five or six plays before significant distortion was audible. As the discs were not intended for syndication, but rather for the convenience of the performer, the old discs were then discarded. Although the station had so many of the discs that they had to get rid of them, few samples of these programs are preserved today. Howard remarked that: "They became very popular in Mexico—these old platters. We'd get a bunch of them ahead and some Mexican would come by and want to pick them up. They made wonderful shingles if you [were] putting them on a roof because they were this acetate outside and aluminum inside and they'd last forever. They's quite a few roofs over there shingled with them I imagine."

Although transcriptions started out at the Border Stations as a convenience to the performers, in time they became a kind of syndication as firms emerged which sold regular transcription services to stations throughout the United States. In this way the smaller stations could present "live" talent not available on commercial recordings, and still avoid the ever-increasing cost of hiring musicians exclusively for their own station. Gradually, actual live shows became less and less frequent on the Border Stations as well as the small regional stations throughout the United States. By the late 1940s commercial records were becoming increasingly important to the broadcasting industry.

The details of the business arrangements that brought the Carter Family to Texas may never be known, but by October of 1936 they, along with their announcer, Harry Steele, had been sent to Del Rio by Consolidated Royal Chemical Corporation. To determine how hillbilly music made its way into the broadcasting industry, it will be necessary to learn the motivation for firms like Consolidated Royal Chemical Corporation to send groups like the Carter Family into the broadcasting studios. Unfortunately many of the key people who might be able to tell us who made the decision to sponsor this kind of music are deceased. But we are able to piece together and speculate about the details of the Carters' association with XERA and Consolidated Royal Chemical Corporation. Business details of the Carter Family were handled almost exclusively by A. P. Carter. He worked directly with Ralph Peer, and Maybelle and Sara followed his direction. So perhaps Ralph Peer made the initial contact with Consolidated Royal. More likely, however, the arrangement was made between a representative of the Carter Family—perhaps Peer himself—and Harry O'Neill.

O'Neill was a Chicago advertising man who represented Consolidated Royal. For perhaps fifteen years O'Neill advertised the products of Consolidated Royal—Peruna, a tonic to ward off colds, and Kolor Bak, a hair tint. While the personal musical tastes of Harry O'Neill remain a mystery to us, we do know that he knew of the selling power of this kind of music. As early as 1934—and probably before that—he had hired hillbilly musicians to broadcast for Peruna and Kolor Bak. O'Neill, through his agency which represented Consolidated Royal, tried various formats to learn which sold the product. At an early date he focused exclusively upon hillbilly music in a well-worked-out format. The musicians were usually responsible for one or two half-hour programs a day. In addition to the musicians, O'Neill hired announcers who gave the commercials, introduced the musicians, and maintained the informal atmosphere that appealed to the predominantly rural audience. Unlike many other sponsors who used these same stations, Consolidated Royal did not sell its product directly over the air. Rather, they ran offers giving a small Bible or some other gift to those who sent in a boxtop. In this way they built up a mailing list and at the same time stimulated drugstore sales. Each inquiry was worth fifty cents, O'Neill figured.

O'Neill's dealings were complex, and the organization included many people. In addition to the musicians and announcers, O'Neill dealt directly with Don and Dode Baxter, his agents in Texas, who were responsible for making transcription discs of the programs. At first this was started as a convenience to performers and announcers who dreaded the early morning shows which had to be broadcast live. Harry Steele, the announcer for the Carter Family, recalls making transcription discs in the Baxters' apartment in Eagle Pass. Eventually the transcriptions became more than a convenience to early morning performers—they became a means of having the musicians give the appearance of broadcasting live over stations scattered around the country and even into Canada. Often the transcriptions contained everything except the commercials, which were either done at the time of broadcast or were sent around to the stations on yet another transcription disc.

The Carter Family's announcer, Harry Steele, had an extensive background in both radio and newspaper work before joining O'Neill in 1937 as the Carter Family's announcer.

Financial details for the Carter Family during their Texas years are hard to come by, but we can make some guesses. Harry Steele recalls that he was earning $65 a week when he went to Texas. But after a response of 25,000 boxtops in one week his salary was raised. The Pickard Family, who came to Del Rio the season before the Carters, worked for O'Neill over a number of stations for nearly a decade beginning in 1934. Although their memory is also hazy, Buss and Charley Pickard—the youngsters of the group and then in their twenties—remember earning about $65 each per week. Whatever the salary of the Carters was, it was as little as the firm hiring them was able to pay. The Carter Family, making their simple music in the same way they had done first at schoolhouses and churches in rural America and then in recording studios, were now broadcasting over the most powerful commercial radio station in the world and helping to bring about a commercial success for which they were never adequately compensated in terms of today's values.

The Carter Family had once again become part of a pattern that was responding to the change from an America marked by an agrarian, rural, and regional orientation. Although the businesses with which they came into contact were using the techniques of industrial, urban society, the Carters were unprepared for this difference in orientation and continued to respond in terms of their own rural southern values. They, like hundreds of other rural Southerners, became tools which were easily exploited by city businessmen wise to the ways of industry. Until the rural Southerners learned the rules of the new game, they were destined for continued exploitation.

SOURCE

This article was extracted, with some abridgment, from chapter 5 of Kahn's Ph.D. dissertation, *The Carter Family: A Reflection of Changes in Society* (UCLA Department of Anthropology, 1970). Although Kahn drew upon a wide variety of resources, the primary ones can be summarized as follows: the material on John H. Brinkley is taken from Clement Wood, *The Life of a Man* (Kansas City: Goshorn Publishing Co., 1934); Gerald Carson, *The Roguish World of Doctor Brinkley* (New York: Rinehart & Co.; 1960); Ansel Harlan Resler, *The Impact of John R. Brinkley on Broadcasting in the United States* (Ph.D. dissertation, Northwestern University, 1958); and Francis Chase Jr., *Sound and Fury* (New York: Harper, 1942). A useful source on the history of border radio is

Louis C. Caldwell, "Developments in Federal Regulation of Broadcasting," in Edgar A. Grunwald, ed., *Variety Radio Directory, 1938–1939* (New York: Variety, Inc., 1938). Information on the workings of the Border Stations comes from Kahn's own interviews—of Don Howard in Del Rio in 1963; with Harry Steele by telephone in 1970; Charley, Buss, and Lucille Pickard in 1968; and numerous interviews with members of the Carter Family.

Norm Cohen

"Henry Clay Beattie": Once a Folksong

In our veneration of the old British traditional ballads of the Child collection that date back to the 15th, 16th, and 17th centuries, we sometimes
overlook the fact that it is not common for a folksong to last so long in
oral tradition; far more songs disappear from human memory within two
or three generations of their origins than survive with such Gibraltar-like
solidarity. It is inevitable that songs would be lost because no collector
was present to record them for posterity while they were still alive in tradition; but probably a great many more are lost because collectors heard
the items, yet rejected them as not being folksongs. This is one inevitable
consequence of collectors relying so heavily on the various catalogs and
syllabi of folksongs to classify and identify new pieces that they come
across. There is a tendency to reject an item because it has not already
appeared in some standard reference.

Almost ten years ago, when I first heard Kelly Harrell's ballad, "Henry
Clay Beattie" (Victor V-20797; reissued on County 502), I felt certain
that this must be a traditional song, yet there was no trace of it in any published folksong collection. Had Harrell composed it himself? Was there
a true story hiding bchind the sketchy narrative of his haunting song? The
tune was surely not original, as it was used by Welling and McGhee for
their hymn, "Knocking at the Door," but this says nothing of the origin
of the words, which are given here as best I can transcribe them from Harrell's singing:

Friday as the sun was lifting,
After the sun shown clear;
Down in a cell set a prisoner,
Trembling with mercy and fear.

In came his grey headed father,
Says, "Henry this day you must die,
If (you) don't confess that you killed her,
You'll go to your doom with a lie."

In came his brother and sister,
To bid him their last farewell;
"If (you) don't confess that you killed her,
You'll spend eternity in hell."

"Yes, I confess that I killed her,
I've taken her sweet life away;
But oh, how greedy and brutish,
I was for taking her sweet life."

'Twas late on Thursday evening,
After the sun went down;
Henry Clay Beattie was saying
Farewell to his friend [?] native town.

Then Friday, as the sun was rising,
Just before the sun shown clear;
Henry Clay Beattie was dying,
In a 'lectric chair.

It didn't seem as if the singer were the composer of the song. Clear evidence of forgotten words and phrases pointed to an origin preceding by many years the date of the recording, which was on March 22, 1927, for the Victor Talking Machine Company. But the song couldn't have been more than forty years old at that time, as electrocutions had not been introduced before the late 1880s. Harrell's native state of Virginia was one of the twenty or so states that used electrocution as capital punishment, so it did suggest that the song might have been a local ballad about a local incident that Harrell learned in his youth. Harrell had been born near

Mack's Meadows, Virginia, in 1889, but lived most of his life in Fries, a textile mill town in Grayson County not far from the North Carolina border. His repertoire, as represented by his recordings, was a good sampling of 19th-century American folk song and ballads.

For several years this was all that was known to me about "Henry Clay Beattie." I did find out that Bob Cranford and A. P. Thompson of the Red Fox Chasers had recorded "Henry Clay Beattie" for the Starr Piano Company in January of 1931, but the recording had never been released; and I despaired of learning anything more from that bit of information. But then, while visiting David Freeman in New York one afternoon, I learned that a test pressing of that recording was still in existence, and that Rich Nevins had a dub of it. Nevins was kind enough to send me a copy of his dubbing, along with the information he obtained from Cranford that the song had been learned off a record—which meant Harrell's recording, since no others were released. An audition of the Cranford-Thompson performance confirmed that it must have been learned from Harrell's rendition—to which it was almost verbatim identical (save for one improvement in the second line of the first stanza, which they rendered, "After the stars shown clear"). An independent text by the two native North Carolinians would have confirmed my belief that the song must have been traditional before Harrell recorded it, but alas, no such conclusion could be drawn.

In 1967, I began corresponding with readers of *Good Old Days* in search of railroad songs. I made it a point of asking correspondents from the Virginia area if they knew anything about "Henry Clay Beattie." In May of 1968 a letter came from Mrs. Ruth Butcher of Salem, West Virginia (to whom I had sent the words to "Engine 143"), with the following information:

"I used to know the old song about the villain who had his wife shot while he drove. I only remember one, or the first verse:

Here comes Henry Clay Beattie in an automobile,
He's running so fast that you can't see the wheel;
With a ring on his finger and a gun in his hand,
He's trying to put the murder on an innocent man."

Clearly, this song had no connection with Kelly Harrell's except that they both dealt with an apparent murderer by the name of Henry Beattie. Were there two now-nearly forgotten ballads dealing with a single event? Convinced that perseverance would bring me more information about Henry Clay Beattie, I continued with my inquiries.

A year later, while visiting the Library of Congress Archive of Folk-song and digging among the Robert W. Gordon collection for railroad songs, I came across the following item, sent to Gordon in 1927 by Mary H. Russell, of Lynchburg, Virginia, one of his thousands of correspondents during the years that he edited a column, "Old Songs Men Have Sung," in *Adventure* magazine. "Most everyone in Virginia knows it," she wrote. Her text follows:

Henry Beatty
"Come on honey, let's go for a spin
You won't need a wrap, just jump right in.
No, don't take the baby, we won't go far."
With these last words, he started the car.

On a lonely road just out of town
He stopped the car and jumped to the ground.
Then he placed a gun to his young wife's head
And pulling the trigger he shot her dead.

Here comes Henry Beatty in his automobile
He is coming so fast you can't see his wheels.
With rings on his fingers and a gun in his hand
He's going to blame the murder on an innocent man.

He placed her body at his side
And sat upon it during his ride
Back to his home he cried in fear,
"A robber has shot my wifie dear!"

Oh Henry Beatty, it is a shame!
Why did you blacken your honorable name?
Bowed your parents' heads in sorrow and care,
For your lies and murder took you to the chair."

Ms. Russell's song told in considerable detail the story of the murder by Henry Clay Beattie of his wife; Kelly Harrell's song focused on the convicted Beattie in the jail cell awaiting execution; together they told a fairly complete tale. But was it accurate?

My first clue to the historical details of the Beattie murder came, also quite by accident, while looking through microfilm copies of the

Nashville Tennessean of 1911 for information on Casey Jones. A small news item on the front page of the 19 July edition caught my attention. Datelined Richmond, Virginia, it told of a Mr. H. C. Beattie reporting the murder of his wife while the two of them were out riding on the Midlothian turnpike the previous night. Beattie reported that they had been driving along happily when at about 10:45 p.m. a man appeared in the road in front of the car. Beattie brought the vehicle to a halt, and he and the pedestrian exchanged angry words. The tall, bearded man, carrying a rifle, raised the gun to his shoulder and fired a shot, hitting Mrs. Beattie in the face. Beattie leaped out of the car and struggled with the assailant, wresting the gun from his grip. The attacker ran off into the woods. Beattie threw the gun into the back seat of the car and drove to his in-laws' home, where his mother-in-law was tending to the five-week-old Henry Clay Beattie III.

A few days later, while I was crowing to D. K. Wilgus about my discovery regarding the Beattie song, he called to my attention a small book about the affair that had been gathering dust in the UCLA Library since 1942. Titled *A Full and Complete History of the Great Beattie Case— Most Highly Sensational Tragedy of the Century,* it had been published in 1911—which meant it must have been printed while Beattie's corpse was still warm, as the execution took place on November 24, 1911.

The facts, as revealed in the book and in contemporary newspaper accounts, indicated that both the Russell and Harrell songs were quite accurate in their recital of events, but there was considerably more to the tale than the ballads told. The Henry Clay Beattie murder, it turned out, was another variant on the theme of the American Tragedy—a young man murders his betrothed or wife because of his love for another woman.

Briefly told, Beattie was the son of Henry Clay Beattie Sr., a well-to-do and respected businessman. The younger Beattie began at an early age to lead a rather dissolute life, supported financially by his well-meaning father. Among his various affairs was one with Beulah Binford, not quite fourteen when they began going together in about 1907. A child was born to Binford, of which Beattie was said to be the father, but the child proved sickly and died in 1910 when only one year old. In August 1910, Beattie married Louise Owen, a friend of his childhood, and a son was born to them nine months and a week after their wedding day.

But Beattie continued his contact with Beulah Binford, and although at the trial he denied emphatically that he ever loved her, he did admit to having been with her three or four nights a week for the two weeks prior to the murder. Her diary, which came to light after the trial, revealed that, although Miss Binford had an extremely unsavory reputation for many years, her attachment to Henry Beattie was quite genuine and deeply felt. Whether Beattie really reciprocated her feelings, or whether, as he claimed in court, he was simply helping her through generosity (he paid for sending her to school before their child was born, paid for the baby's funeral, and paid for her to rent and furnish an apartment in Norfolk in March 1911) cannot be known from the public record. On the day preceding the murder, he spent much of the evening with her.

Almost immediately after the murder, there were suspicions that Beattie's story was not entirely truthful. An early clue was the puzzling inability of the bloodhounds to find any trace of a trail from the site on the highway where the murder had taken place. There were other peculiarities, such as Beattie's trousers being thoroughly blood soaked at the seat, suggesting to some that he had sat on the body as he drove back to his in-laws; but his left sleeve, the arm with which he claimed he had held up the body as he drove, was free of stains. But the most damning evidence was revealed within a few days when Henry's cousin Paul Beattie, arrested on suspicion of complicity in the crime, confessed to having purchased a shotgun on 24 June at the request of Henry and delivering it to him on the following day.

The trial commenced on the first anniversary of Beattie's wedding to Louise Owen and ended sixteen days later. On 8 September, a jury of twelve Virginia farmers conferred for fifty-eight minutes before returning with the unanimous verdict of guilty. According to the newspapers, "the twelve jurymen did not hesitate to admit to their friends that they stood in judgment not only over the cold-blooded murderer, but upon his marital infidelity as well" (*Nashville Tennessean* 9 September 1911, p. 1).

On November 24, the day of the execution (Friday, as Harrell's ballad noted), Beattie finally confessed his guilt:

> I, Henry Clay Beattie Jr., being desirous of standing right before God and man, do on this 24th day of November 1911, confess my guilt of the crime charged against me.
>
> Much that has been published concerning the details of said crime is not true, but the awful fact, without the harrowing circumstances, remains.
>
> For this action I am truly sorry, and, believing that I am at peace with God and am soon to pass into His presence, this statement is made.

Which of the "harrowing circumstances" were not true ? We will probably never know.

In retrospect, then, it seems reasonable that ballad was composed soon after the execution. Although elements of the narrative are found in older songs, they seem quite appropriate here. For example, though the parade of gray-headed father, brother, and sister, coming to visit Beattie in his cell, suggests stanzas of the ballad "Charles Guiteau," Henry did bid his father and sister goodbye on the morning of the execution. Probably they, and his brother, who also visited him at times in jail, prevailed upon him to confess before his death. The Russell song was probably also written soon after the execution. The only detail that seems false is the reference to Henry telling his wife she wouldn't need a wrap, as she was wearing her uncle's raincoat all the time she was in the car.

One trivial anecdote, the sort of detail that folklorists delight in, was recounted in the Ottenheimer book:

Maizi Green, a negro "mammy" who was nursing Mrs. Henry Clay Beattie during her illness when the baby was born, said today that one midnight about four weeks before the tragedy, as she was sleeping in the same room where Mrs. Beattie and babe were, she had a fearful dream, awakening Mrs. Beattie with a shriek.

"What is the matter, Maizi?" asked Mrs. Beattie, startled from her slumber.

"Miss Louise, I saw a man creep into this room, pass around my couch, and point a gun in your face. . . . The man put the gun in your face and pulled the trigger. Just as the gun exploded it tore into your face, and you were killed."

I learned nothing further about Henry Clay Beattie until last year, when I visited Walter "Kid" Smith in Fredericksburg, Virginia. Toward the end of our interview, I asked Walter if he knew anything of a song about Henry Clay Beattie. It was the high point of a marvelous interview when, after leaning back for a few moments, Walter sang me the following fragment, to the tune of "Casey Jones":

Yonder comes Beattie on a automobile,
Riding so fast you could just see the wheels;
With a ring on his finger and a gun on his hand,
Said "Excuse me, Ladies, I'm a rambling man."

Perhaps because of the influence on the singer's memory of the tune of "Casey Jones," the stanza as Walter Smith recalled it was as suggestive of songs of fast-living rounders as of murderers. But at any rate, I was delighted to hear, after five years, the tune to this Beattie song.

My interest in these ballads has not abated. I still hope that further searching will uncover a few other fragments—perhaps even a third, different, ballad. When other collectors know what songs to look for, it is more likely that additional variants will turn up. But the songs do not seem to be widely known, and I imagine that in another generation they will be forgotten, except through the permanent memorial of Kelly Harrell's recording. Perhaps then the descendants of Henry Clay Beattie Jr. will be allowed to forget the history of their infamous forebear.

John Solomon Otto and Augustus M. Burns

John "Knocky" Parker: A Case Study of White and Black Musical Interaction

In March 1973, Dr. John "Knocky" Parker kindly consented to an interview in his office at the University of South Florida. Though a noted ragtime and jazz pianist, he is probably best known as a former member of the Light Crust Doughboys, one of the most renowned Western Swing bands. During the interview, we primarily gathered information on the process of white and black musical interaction in the Southwest. Despite formal and customary segregation barriers, interchange of elements from the white and black musical traditions occurred directly through personal contacts in recreational situations (i.e., saloons, dances, fairs) as well as in residential, work, or religious contexts. In addition, interaction occurred indirectly through the media of piano rolls, recordings, and radio broadcasts.

EARLY MUSICAL INFLUENCES:
PERSONAL CONTACTS

John "Knocky" Parker's father was a cotton farmer at Palmer, about 30 miles from Dallas. He owned about 150 acres and took Knocky up to Dallas when he went to hire laborers. Though only four at the time, Knocky remembers playing piano at the Lone Star Saloon on "Deep Elm Street." Between 1922 and 1925, Parker played with Lemon Jefferson, Will Ezell, and others at the Lone Star. Knocky would play bass on the piano while a black man played treble and they would "cross hands." He credits Lemon Jefferson with being a major influence on his piano style. "He'd play and I'd play the same thing on the piano; my piano playing is very much like a stringed instrument. . . . Now I played then exactly the same thing I play now and they taught me this. They'd play on the guitars and I learned from this and all those other little instruments too."

MEDIA INFLUENCES: PIANO ROLLS, RECORDINGS, RADIO

Parker initially learned the piano from player piano rolls by J. R. Robinson, James Blythe, and others. These were QRS (Quality, Reliability, and Service) brand rolls. With piano rolls, he could play fast or slow and imitate the notes. Parker's father purchased them at Whittles Music Store when visiting Dallas. Hazel Booth, a saleswoman, saved rolls such as "Organ Grinder Blues" by Clarence Williams and "Seattle Hunch" by Jelly Roll Morton for Knocky. He later purchased phonograph recordings on the Paramount and Gennett labels; "Cow Cow" Davenport and Roosevelt Sykes were two of his favorite artists. "I bought mostly blacks and I didn't get many whites but I didn't really know what they were . . . and I still, really don't. It never has meant anything to me . . . and frequently from the music you could never tell."

Though his family owned a radio, he doesn't remember any black radio programs or performers in the Southwest during the interwar years. "We got the Ft. Worth and Dallas stations, primarily WBAP and WFAA '800 on the Radio Dial'—by and large hillbilly performers."

COMMERCIALIZATION OF MUSICAL TALENT

Although the Parkers lived in rural Texas, "Knocky" never attended any of the country dances or suppers—important outlets for the talents of black bluesmen. Rather, he regularly played at the dances in Dallas which were held "sort of downtown and close to Elm Street and easily within walking distance of the interurban." From the age of eight or nine on, he took the train from Palmer to Dallas. "The blacks would have me come up on the interurban and play with them on some weekends and I'd stay with them, live with them, and they taught me their mores. . . . I forgot how much they paid me. I was just a little green ignorant kid but I'd get $15 or $20 or something. It would cost me one or two dollars for the interurban and I'd stay overnight with them. . . . They were fair, absolutely, in dividing up and I would get my cut."

The dances were held at downtown juke joints—"I remember they used the word 'juke.'. . . Playing with the blacks, we had no idea there was a terminal. There was no ending until 3:00 or 4:00 and we'd begin about 8:00 or 9:00! . . . The standards were higher than you'd believe . . . everybody was doing the best he could but there was no competition because there was so much camaraderie—mutual respect." At the dances, "we played 'Jackass Blues,' 'Sitting on Top of the World,' 'I Ain't Got Nobody,' 'Deep Elm,' and they liked for me to do 'Organ Grinder Blues' and 'Wild Flow Rag' and a Bessie Smith song, 'Black Water Blues.' Though Blind Lemon was gone by this time, the people played his style and played his songs. I know we did 'Matchbox Blues'— Oh, 'Matchbox' was very popular as was 'Two White Horses.' "

Since "all those people were trying to play the guitar like Blind Lemon . . . it was just easy for me to play in the keys of A and E—it was just mother's milk to play in those keys. . . . The violins were also tuned in A and E to play blues." Though the audiences were largely blacks, "there'd be some whites there too. I remember little ole kids there. They'd get to know me and call me by my nickname. Some white girls too, strangely, would attend the Dallas dances. . . . Even white musicians would come and sit in, sometimes."

In contrasting the instruments used by white and black musicians, he noted that blacks "had more home-made and more worn-out instruments. Blacks used mainly guitars, fiddles, and basses . . . and home-made combinations of horns . . . and they would get extensions of the harmonic and melodic lines with this. Just weird things! They played all those instruments in such a weird manner."

The black musicians frequently tuned their guitars to the open chords of E and A and used small bottles or bottlenecks as slides. The basses were usually jerry-built affairs with washtubs and ropes. "The hands of those people playing that bass were like leather—great big calluses.'' Their percussion instruments included brushes and whisk brooms which they would use on "suitcases of all kinds and different sizes. They would take a suitcase to be a drum. They would use everything . . . even sticks on tubs or tin drums and play solos that would be astonishing! The drummers would have a whole assembly—even sinks! Yes, they used porcelain things . . . and pots and pans of all kinds for effect—yet brilliant."

In the 1930s, Parker played with two Western Swing bands: Blacky Simmons' Famous Blue Jackets, an unrecorded group which broadcast on KRLD; and the Light Crust Doughboys (LCDB) who recorded extensively and had a radio program on WBAP. These and other Western Swing bands reached both white and black listeners through radio broadcasts and personal appearances at fairs and tent shows. In addition, the LCDB even played at stores carrying Light Crust Flour. Thus, both personal contacts and the media fostered the cross-fertilization of black and white folk music in the Southwest. But there were other influences as well.

"Down there in the Southwest, country music and the black music came from the same roots. Now, we didn't have the New Orleans horns . . . but we all had guitars and we always had the Spanish influence. The Spanish motif is stronger in the Southwest and this comes over to the blacks a whole lot. The blacks played nice pretty little Spanish folk tunes but I can't remember which ones."

In 1936, Parker joined the Light Crust Doughboys, a jazz- and blues-influenced hillbilly band. "A lot of these members had been members of the Wanderers, a group that made some Bluebird recordings, earlier in Dallas. That was the first of the local groups there to record, and they were very close to earthy jazz. We [the LCDB] did 'Footwarmer.'" I think this was the only band outside New Orleans I heard do old 'Footwarmer.' We'd do all sorts of strange wild New Orleans tunes and old early black blues that nobody else ever does."

"Earl Hines was a big influence on us down there." In addition, "I played J. Russell Robinson tunes; we did 'Aggravatin' Papa' and 'Margie' and sometimes even the blacks would sing 'Memories of France' by J. R. Robinson. It's a pretty tune and never done by anybody. They'd do it the same way they'd do 'Nobody Knows You When You're Down and Out.'" Ragtime influenced both hillbilly and blues performers. "Every once in a while on the Carter Family radio programs you'd hear some classic ragtime that is very close to the St. Louis black ragtime. Also, "blacks liked pretty little ragtime pieces. Now, this is as close to whites as you could ever get but they liked that very much."

Knocky also noted the importance of phonograph recordings in the spread of musical ideas. Blacks regularly purchased hillbilly records, especially those by Jimmie Rodgers, the LCDB, and Bob Wills and his Texas Playboys. "The blacks did Jimmie Rodgers things but what, I can't say: 'Blue Yodel No. 1' or something?" Also, "black people bought LCDB recordings because there was always tangible evidence of close affinities . . . and we did their tunes too! We did 'Gulf Coast Blues' — and 'T.B. Blues' [a Rodgers composition]." But then "everybody bought the LCDB records and they were extremely popular on jukeboxes."

Bob Wills' records also sold to blacks primarily because of his singing style. "He would stop and interpolate lines like 'God Bless you, my little sweetheart, I long to see you' or he would just throw out any nominative or directive address . . . talk, laugh, and pour out a paean of remorse or unrequited love and this is just exactly what Robert Pete Williams is doing now." Though Bob Wills was consciously imitating the blacks he was not aping them. "He was just a country boy; well, what else had he heard?"

"Oh, we Doughboys thought those black musicians were great. Whenever we were recording in San Antonio, the radio stations would have all the bands go by. We would play little programs on the radio stations advertising the records. The radio stations would get the plugs and the announcer would speak about the records being made in San Antonio. Boots and his Buddies would go by and I can't recall the name of anybody in there but some of them were very, very good. We would have jam sessions on the radio station and we'd go in there and play together. Now, this is way back: this goes back as early now as '35 or 36 which is pretty early for a mixed group down there in Texas. But we kind of understood that this was international culture."

Though regularly appearing on the LCDB radio program and going on tours sponsored by Burrus Mills, Knocky found time to play with black musicians. "T-Bone Walker and I became a little duo down there at the Gem Hotel in Ft. Worth because we were the ones who worked best together. I was playing with the Doughboys by then and going down and playing at night with T-Bone. Ft. Worth at that time didn't have too many other wild blues pianists and I fit right in."

During the interwar years, Knocky also remembers meeting "Whistlin' " Alex Moore as well as J. T. "The Howling Wolf" Smith around the recording studios. "This Howling came up there to Ft. Worth and auditioned something." In addition, he remembers hearing the names of "Texas" Alexander, Coley Jones, and the "Black Ace" Turner.

"But I'm fifty-five now and Lord knows, some of those names were from fifty-one years ago. So often it would be like this: one person comes in and sits down and we'd play and I'd never see him again."

PERSONAL CONTACTS WITH BLACKS
IN A RELIGIOUS CONTEXT

"I played many times in black churches and played in white churches as well. The black people didn't think a thing of my being there. . . . The congregations went to those dances in Dallas and knew me and we were well known within that small group there—the devotees of Texas Blues."

ATTITUDES TO BLACK MUSICIANS

Knocky felt that the Dallas musicians were above conventional morality, and whites and blacks could work openly together playing blues. "There was not any feeling of black or white because they accepted me as black . . . and they were especially wary that I would never, never do anything wrong. They hated strong drugs and yet these musicians would drink anything, but I would drink only a little bit because I didn't like it at all and they knew that. . . . They were always very careful of me and I cannot tell you the love and respect. . . . This is not race now but just sort of an affinity among musicians. I was just a little ole kid and they liked me. They wanted me to have what they had to offer which wasn't always very much. . . . They were so flattered that I could play their music."

"I know that a lot of policemen knew that I was there as this kid from Palmer, Texas, playing piano with these blacks. Black and white policemen liked me and they knew that I was cared for and there was never any trouble. . . . They loved to listen to us and did with a great deal of praise and credit. I was never any safer in my life than down there although it was a tough spot. I didn't know how bad really.

"Sometimes, when I was little and going down there, I'd have to stay the weekend. Daddy would stay on and he'd call up some friend and go do things. I'd go to sleep in some back room that I realize now was a prostitute's room. If they had to use that room, they'd move me over somewhere else and treated me always with that loving care.

"I was their student in every essence of the word—an apprentice. I'd sit down and they saw I was doing everything and working very hard. . . . Now, if you can imagine this ten-year-old just admiring them. I would pour out my heart to them and play, play up a storm. We would just cry when we'd play because it would just be so very good, so intense and so emotional.

"The blacks taught me always a seriousness and dedication and the hardest working hours you could even imagine and the hardest keys too. This is all I know. It means nothing to me to play until I can't play anymore. That's routine—the story of my life."

"Always, in playing with other pianists . . . I'd want to feature them. The blacks have brought me up right. Whatever there is that is good in my personality or that projects to the students goes right on back to those blacks that taught me; absolutely, I am theirs. . . . That's why I got my degree to carry this on."

Yet, Knocky's experiences in the Southwest were somewhat atypical, and frequently mutual antipathy existed between white and black musicians in other areas of the South. Even at the Festival of American Folklife at Montreal in 1971, the bluegrass musicians avoided the blacks and "cut them cold." Said Knocky, "But the early hillbillies closely identified with the black musicians and today these people who are playing hillbilly music will just scorn them. This is because the late hillbilly musicians have become in essence the downtown musicians." [He cited Bill Monroe's Blue Grass Boys as an example.] "Isn't this amazing! I couldn't believe it and there we all were. . . . They were looking down on those black musicians and yet I thought they were just great . . . and here I am right in the thick of things with Bill [Williams], Bob [Lockwood] and Robert Pete.''

"The musicians from Bill Monroe's group, the older ones, had known me then because when I was there Bill Monroe's people were young and coming up. I had a little acceptance there that spread over to the newer people so they accepted me because I had been an old Doughboy in the 30s. . . . But basically, I see little racism in music."

Josh White, from an early advertisement, billed as "The Singing Christian" and "Sensation of the South."

Robert Cogswell

"We Made Our Name in the Days of Radio": A Look at the Career of Wilma Lee and Stoney Cooper

Various country music stars have been quoted as saying that their success in the music business was due to their "sincerity." Regardless when, and with whom, this cliché did originate, it reflects the common knowledge that the traditional country music audience has, in the face of numerous modernizations, long favored a performance attitude which transcends the media and assures the listener that the "grassroots" have not been forgotten. Among present-day performers perhaps none exemplifies this quality, and the underlying philosophy of entertainment, better than Wilma Lee and Stoney Cooper. Their career spans several periods in the evolution of country music, and this experience has made its mark on both their attitudes about performance and style and the way they fit into the contemporary music industry. This article will provide a brief outline of that career and some reflections on it.[1]

The conception of a traditional country music performance is, of course, relative to time. Change has been constant, not only in musical style and material, but also in such elements as stage dress, audience rapport, and means of promotion. The nature of the medium itself—be it radio, sound recording, or television—has been influential in affecting trends. Performers of successive eras have, in turn, adapted to the media in different ways. For example, the discography of commercial recordings by Wilma Lee and Stoney charts the course of their efforts in one medium which, from the standpoint of the present industry, happens to be the most dominant. It says nothing, however, about radio and personal appearances, the real bread-and-butter of their career. As Neil Rosenberg has noted in his discography of Bill Monroe, it is important to recognize the secondary nature of recordings to entertainers of this type in approaching and interpreting their discography.[2] Such consideration of the conflicting demands between media, particularly undergoing trends and industry pressures, can certainly shed light on the Wilma Lee and Stoney discography regarding the choice of some items for recording, the exclusion of others, and the paucity of recordings during specific periods. In the case of the Coopers, the discography by no means represents the entire live-performance repertory from the course of their career, and to those interested in traditional song it probably has numerous omissions, for which, unfortunately, there is no complete account. Their live-performance orientation has been influential beyond mere material, however, for it provides the basis for the musical style and professional attitude which has typified Wilma Lee and Stoney Cooper to their audience over the years. The following biographical sketch is a rough summary of their story as it was related to me.

Wilma Lee was born in Valley Head, West Virginia, on February 20, 1921, her full maiden name, Wilma Leigh Leary. She was the oldest of three girls, all of whom inherited their parents' interest in music. Singing at home was usually accompanied by a pump organ, which Wilma Lee and her mother both played. When she had mastered the pump organ, Wilma's father bought her a guitar with lessons via mail from the Chicago School of Music. The family sang from Rodeheaver's and R. E. Winsett's songbooks, among others. Their repertory of "plain country gospel songs" was developed by singing at home, but gradually they began to appear in public, initially only at church-related events: regular services, funerals, and singing conventions. Their only accompaniment was Wilma Lee's rhythm guitar, and their adaptation of songbook part-songs to this format gave the Leary Family a style within a gospel tradition at that point not yet recorded:

> SC: I would class it like the Chuck Wagon Gang. It wasn't, you know, a copy of that, but it was a whole different sound. I would say their style, like the repeats and things like that, resembled the old Chuck Wagon Gang. They done that shaped-note type singing, and that's what her father and mother read—shaped notes.

WLC: They couldn't read the regular—they had to be shaped notes.

SC: So their repeats were their strongest. This is, I think, what really sold their quintet. There was five of them. Their mother done the high part, and her dad, the real low. And he was a very, very low singer—had just a real bass voice, you know, even when he spoke fast—they had fast-moving gospel spirituals.

WLC: And we did slow ones, too—just a mixture.

Among the Leary Family's most prominent numbers were "He Will Set Your Fields On Fire"; "Blessed Jesus, Hold My Hand"; "Seeking The Lost"; "Give Me The Roses While I Live"; "Farther Along"; "Never Be Lonesome in Heaven"; and "Amazing Grace." They used primarily their own arrangements for songs, and were uninfluenced by recorded music. As Stoney explains it:

> It was its own original, because there was a family that had things sort of put together as it come natural to them. I'd say they copied no one, because there really wasn't anybody out on record then but the Carter Family that you could copy, and they didn't do that type of song, to an extent. So, theirs was their own creation of singing. It's too bad we can't get a hold of it.

The family, of course, originally did not have any professional aspirations, but their success led them into continued public appearances as the girls grew older. Jacob Leary was straightforward in overseeing the family group and was reluctant to push them into becoming full-time professionals. Their professionalism came gradually, and, as Stoney puts it, "they fell into things, they really didn't know anything about show business."

In 1938, however, first place in a local contest led the Leary Family to participate in the National Folk Festival and to a good deal of recognition. As Wilma Lee remembers it:

> Yes, they had this contest in the state of West Virginia; they had one in each state. And Mrs. Eleanor Roosevelt—Franklin Delano Roosevelt's wife—was sponsoring what they called a "National Folk Festival" in Washington, D.C, which lasted about a week. And they were gonna have a group from each state to represent the state. And all over the state they held the contests, and my family won in our little section where we grew up. And then after that, all the winners of the different contests came together. And my family won, so we went to Washington in 1938 representing the state of West Virginia. They had shows, programs, lined up for each day, you know, and we sang at different places in Washington. We'd

sing once a day. It went on a week. I can't remember now—because we weren't too old, and that's the furthest we'd ever been away from home, and all the excitement and everything—can't remember how long the shows were. But I know they took us one afternoon to the Library of Congress and recorded my family singing these old hymns the whole afternoon.[3]

As the Learys began to play a wider range of public appearances, the girls added some secular folksongs to the repertory, but Mr. and Mrs. Leary sang only on gospel numbers. Also, Wilma Lee's maternal uncle began to play fiddle with the group. When he returned to schoolteaching and stopped appearing with the family, his shoes were to be filled by young "Fiddlin' Dale" Cooper from nearby Harmon, West Virginia.

Stoney's christened name is Dale Troy Cooper, and he was born in Harmon on 16 October 1918, into a family of schoolteachers. At about twelve or thirteen he began to play guitar and some "clawhammer" style banjo, but fiddle music was what he really loved. As he comments on his background:

> Well, of course, mine is completely different from hers—not so much probably the background as far as gospel if you're speaking of what was in my home. My folks were very religious. The church was the main thing; that's where we were brought up. However, being young, I turned out to be a fiddler; I was always crazy about a fiddle. My older brother before me was a fairly good country fiddler, and he would play for the square dances. And I would see this, and it seemed like it brought people so much joy, you know. They just got an awful lot of joy out of just hearing him play that fiddle, oftentimes just by himself—no accompaniment, you know. Really, I couldn't hear that much that he played so good. But Arthur Smith was on the radio here at the Grand Ole Opry, and this was the one that I heard coming through, you see. And I thought, "Boy, if I could ever learn to play the fiddle like that. . . ." I don't play anything like him at all. But he was the one. Boy, if I didn't hear Arthur Smith, I just didn't care for the Grand Ole Opry that Saturday night—I had to wait till the next one.

Dale pursued the fiddle, and in 1937, when he graduated from high school, he was offered a job with Rusty Hiser and his Green Valley Boys. Hiser was assembling a band to play at WMMN in Fairmont, West Virginia, and the other musicians he gathered all had previous professional experience. Thus Stoney learned a lot in his first fulltime fiddling job, playing mostly background fiddle and taking a vocal part on hymns. It was on this early morning show that the Learys first heard Dale.

Rusty Hiser decided to move from WMMN to a station in Lynchburg, Virginia, a shift which proved to be the group's downfall. After several months it was apparent that ends would not meet, and the group disbanded. At this time the band consisted of Hiser on guitar, a little girl singer, a tenor banjo, a bass, Stoney, and another fiddler, a man named "Smitty" from Franklin, West Virginia, who knew some of the Arthur Smith technique which Stoney admired. In Lynchburg, Stoney also met a fiddler for another group on the station, Burk Barber (who later played for Molly O'Day and Lynn Davis). Stoney remembers Burk trying to teach him to play with a looser wrist by practicing while seated in a ladderback chair with his right elbow hooked around its right rear upright. Stoney came back to work the farm with his father and twin brother. His father died the next summer (1938), so Stoney remained around home where he was needed. He was somewhat disillusioned with the entertainment business and satisfied to wait before trying again:

> You know, it was pretty rough sledding out there; it wasn't at all like I thought it was going to be. I could see our names up in lights, and it wasn't that at all. It was really a let-down, you know. But you don't start at the top and work down; you start at the bottom and work up. But, each young man or lady, I would say, no matter how successful they've been, I don't think could ever be bigger than what your imagination could capture for you.

The Learys, at that same time, were interested in getting a new fiddler, and one in particular. As Wilma Lee remembers, their first attempt to contact him was fruitless:

> We worked his hometown. We worked, I believe it was the high school at Harmon, West Virginia. So, my dad and mother thought he'd be there that night, my dad could talk to him, you know, try to offer him a job. And we got there and kept watching, we didn't see nobody looked like they'd be "Fiddlin' Dale." So we started asking, and they said, "No, he's not here tonight." That was after the show. He didn't come. They said, "I guess he's up on one of them mountains fox-hunting somewhere."

Shortly thereafter, Stoney received a penny postcard from Jacob C. Leary asking him to come to Seneca Caverns the next Sunday, where the Leary Family was making a public appearance, and discuss the possibility of playing with them. At first, he was not particularly impressed with the offer, but decided to go anyway:

I didn't think too much about it. I thought, "Well, it's somewhere to go Sunday," and I said something to my brother about it. "Well," he said, "Let's." I don't think he wanted me to take the job, but he said, "Well, let's go see the show." Okay, we decided to go. Got over there, and up on the stage there was a couple of pretty girls, you know. And one of them was only about 12. But very, very pretty girls, and their mother and father. It looked a little more interesting than the postcard had looked, you know. So, when they come off, they offered us to go through the caverns free — and back there a dollar was a dollar, if you got anything free you gracefully accepted it and was very thankful, which was a good lesson; right today if we get anything free we're grateful. Went through the caverns, and when I got out Mr. Leary said, I'll offer you ten dollars a week, room and grub." That's the way he put it — "room and grub." He was a real pioneer type.

Perhaps somewhat influenced by the Leary girls, Stoney took the job, and his romance with Wilma Lee, and their musical career together, began to take shape by late in 1938.

Stoney added a new dimension to the Leary Family band. In addition to the standard gospel numbers and the girls' trios, Wilma Lee and Stoney's duets were strictly nongospel material. Stoney feels that because they "were a young couple and looked good together," the audiences especially enjoyed their numbers, and he gives the people of the Shenandoah Valley area a good deal of credit for their courtship and marriage. Because the duet was popular and consistently well-received throughout the territory in which the Learys appeared, Wilma Lee and Stoney's segment of the act expanded. Their repertory included a range of "heart songs, love ballads, and novelty songs," and two numbers remembered as being particularly popular were "Salty Dog" (learned off a jukebox; probably from the Morris Brothers' version) and "Paper of Pins."

Of the girls' trios, "Sparkling Blue Eyes" was a favorite. Wilma Lee's sister Gerry became the M.C. for the group, and she did the straight lines in comedy sketches with Mr. Leary, who sometimes appeared in costume. Although the routines were not polished, because of Jacob Leary's local popularity they were successful. The territory which they worked continued to be centered around Valley Head. In 1939 the Leary Family received and turned down two opportunities to reach larger audiences and promote their career; Roy Acuff encouraged them to appear on the Grand Ole Opry, and "Black Draught" extended a sizable offer for the Learys to shift locales to Chattanooga and represent their product. Stoney remembers his disappointment in Mr. Leary's conservative management of the band and reluctance to take the family away from West Virginia in pursuit of a professional career. He never questioned his judgment at the time, however, for the band maintained their success with the existing audience.

Wilma Lee and Stoney were married in 1941. In the fall of 1941 the Leary Family began to appear on WWVA in Wheeling (at that time still a 5,000-watt station). Here they continued the same kind of act and increased contacts with show-business people. In March 1942, Wilma Lee and Stoney's daughter Carol Lee was born, and the couple stopped performing entirely in order to maintain their new family. Stoney worked long hours for six months at the Vaughn Beverage Company, delivering bottled soft drinks in Wheeling. Once the baby got older, Wilma Lee grew tired of being a housewife. They decided to go back to performing, not as part of the Leary Family, but to look for a job in a radio station where they wouldn't have to make personal appearances to make ends meet.

Through an announcer friend in Wheeling who had contacts in the Midwest, Wilma Lee and Stoney got in touch with the program director for KMMJ in Grand Island, Nebraska. Their acetate audition recording pleased the station, and they got the job. In the fall of 1942 they moved to Nebraska, where they worked until the next summer. The pay was not high, but acceptable, and "you were indoors, and got to pick and sing, do what you wanted to do." They worked without a band and did about six programs a day. Also appearing on KMMJ were Ben and Jesse Mae Norman, another duet, and Stoney played fiddle on their programs as well. Wilma typed for the radio station to make extra money between programs. Meanwhile, as Stoney remembers, he got in a little hot water learning to play pool:

Now the pool hall was right down below.

WLC: You had to stay at the radio station all day. You didn't know when you were going on.

SC: It was either stay up there and type—which I couldn't do, Wilma could—and busy yourself at that, or go across the street and drink coffee till your next program, or go downstairs in the pool hall. . . . Ben Norman was fine, oh, he was good at pool. And I paid for more games for that guy, till I learned how to play pool. You know, it was 'losers pay.' One day Wilma came down after we'd stayed so long, it was about ten minutes before time to be back on that program, or one had been throwed in early. All I had accredited, they put it up on a blackboard, you know. This guy never seemed to get beat out of anybody paying his debts, 'cause his name was always on the blackboard. "Stoney Cooper—Fourteen dollars and something." Wilma come down and she saw that—oh, brother, I got a sermon. But after awhile I got to where Ben was paying some of the bills, too.

Meanwhile, the rest of the Leary Family had moved to a small station in Indianapolis, and Peggy (the middle of the girls) had married an accordionist named Bob Howell, who also performed with the family. KMMJ brought the Leary Family to Grand Island, and for several months the entire family, with the two sons-in-law, was together again. Bob wrote comedy sketches, and he and Stoney began to do "Lum and Abner" type radio routines, complete with sound effects. WIBC in Indianapolis expressed interest in hiring the entire group. Mr. Wall, the station manager, had known Stoney previously in Fairmont. Stoney had learned to play dobro (actually just a flat-top guitar with raised strings) in order to accompany Wilma Lee on several Roy Acuff numbers—"Low And Lonely, 'Wreck On The Highway,'" "Cowards Over Pearl Harbor," and "Don't Make Me Go To Bed And I'll Be Good." The last two were among the most requested in the WIBC "Mail Bag" not too long after the Leary aggregation arrived in Indianapolis in the summer of 1943. Stoney had acquired a National steel dobro by then, and the duet was given their own program. The popularity of the Acuff material and style was so strong that it influenced the basic direction of Wilma Lee and Stoney's sound—it utilized Wilma Lee's strength as a "heavy" vocal solo and allowed Stoney to play instrumental backup and sing vocal harmony.

Indianapolis was just a stay of several months, however. At that time Bob Atcher and Bonnie Blue Eyes were on WJJD in Chicago with the "Breakfast-time" and "Suppertime Frolic." Atcher was called for military service, and the duet would have to be replaced. Before his departure, Atcher and several others were flying over the Indianapolis area in an airplane, covering the story of a large Indiana flood for WJJD news. While in the area they heard Wilma Lee and Stoney's program over WIBC, and Atcher returned to Chicago with the recommendation that WJJD seek an audition from the Coopers. This they did, and Wilma Lee and Stoney were more than glad to fill the request, for WJJD was a 20,000-watt station and a considerable step up. The audition recording, which featured "Cowards Over Pearl Harbor," was quite a success. They got the job and Wilma Lee was welcomed in Chicago as "the she-Roy Acuff." The duet arrived there in the latter months of 1943, and were to stay in Chicago for a little less than a year.

At WJJD Wilma Lee and Stoney had the early morning program from 4 to 7 A.M., and therefore, they were not doing live appearances at night:

> SC: You didn't need to have personal appearances, you see; and they didn't want you to, because they wanted you back there.
>
> WLC: Well, Stoney and I, we were on from 4 o'clock in the morning till 7—three hours.
>
> SC: You couldn't chance going out and not getting back, 'cause there was a three-hour program. And what were they gonna do, play records? Unheard of!

Sharing their program was Red Belcher and his partner, Paul Groves. It was big-time radio and they enjoyed working it, but tensions between the musicians' union and the Atlas Brothers, the station owners, erupted over the issue of using recorded music, and a strike ensued which eventually forced the Coopers to leave Chicago. The union demanded that the station "double their talent" to insure that there would be no need for recorded music. The station did not comply, and the strike began. For three months Wilma Lee and Stoney went daily to the station and awaited a settlement. Stoney was forced to get a job in a Gary, Indiana, defense plant. Finally all musicians were released by the station, which decided to program recorded music. The Coopers had no choice but to return to West Virginia.

They quickly picked up a spot at Fairmont on WMMN's "Sagebrush Roundup" and fell back on their sure popularity on this territory. At the time, Stoney recalls, they had not yet developed their own savvy about the music business, and it took them a while to realize the duet's potential and become inclined to striking out with their own show. Wilma Lee's songs were much-requested—so quickly, in fact, that it became obvious that she was being confused with another strong-voiced female singer, Molly O'Day, who sang similar numbers and was heard by some of the same audience which had listened to Wilma Lee from WJJD:

> SC: So we didn't know it, and yet we should have been aware of it. But this is how things can happen, you know, when you're young. This business like, I see people that come up and get their one record overnight, then they feel they know all there is to know about it. Not true, you see more of 'em go down and they wonder what happened to 'em. It's simply because they didn't know what direction to go in. Well, there we didn't realize that we'd been on WJJD, a 20,000-watt station, that had covered all that area. And we couldn't understand why they was writin' in and wantin' us out at personal appearances. And we'd only been there a few weeks. We were

going out with the "Sagebrush Roundup," and you'd have to take the split along with everybody. And you could see the people running out to certain ones, you know. And I hope it doesn't sound like bragging, I don't ever want to feel that way, but they'd run right to us and we never did understand it. We didn't have any records; we never understood it. So finally it dawned on us. People would say, "Do that 'Hills of Roane County.'" Well, I know where that started—WJJD. Molly O'Day and Wilma, we didn't know it at that time, but they were both singing that song. And I'm sure she didn't hear us, or I'm reasonably sure. And I know we didn't hear her; she was in Louisville. And so they'd write in to WJJD and say, "Please have Molly O'Day sing 'Hills of Roane County.'"

RC: They thought she was Molly O'Day?

SC: Yes. And then it went on for a few weeks that, from Louisville would come mail to Wilma Lee because it would have Stoney Cooper attached to it. Then, they'd know, "for Wilma Lee?"—"Well, not here, they've mistook Molly for that." So the two were like that. So then it dawned on me, after they started requesting some of those songs that have possibly gotten that hot in the short time we'd been at WMMN. Wilma came to me one day and said, "You know what? I think we could take our own band out and do just as well." Well, it kind of scared me, you know, my own band. This was in '44.

The idea sank in, however, and soon they were putting together a band of their own to work personal appearances by themselves while remaining on WMMN. Floyd Kirkpatrick, an electric steel guitar player they had known in Chicago, was contacted, and he agreed to come to West Virginia. Also Ab Cole, a bass player who was to remain with Wilma Lee and Stoney for the next several years, joined the act:

SC: He was the best deal we ever made. 'Cause he was a good voice in there, third part—high or low, it didn't make any difference. And a good bass player. He had them hands that looked like he'd come out of the lumber mills. When he hit them strings, I mean he could pop 'em.

A few adjustments were made to accommodate the new format of a complete band, for Wilma Lee and Stoney were used to working "forty-five minutes to an hour" straight with only a duet. After a few shows they further expanded, and hired another musician, "Yodeling Joe" Lambert, to add more diversity to the show:

SC: Boy, he could yodel. He played guitar. It didn't add to the band any, but it was another feature. See, our shows were so big there we didn't worry about getting 'em in the first show, just the second one. So I guess we got a little top-heavy, and we thought that we should give the people more than what we were—four people. Added Joe and he was popular. They really liked him; he could tear the house down. Of course, I've always been the kind that, just so the people, just so they got what they come to see.

By late 1945 the territory had been worked out for them, and Wilma Lee and Stoney decided it was time to move on. About Christmas, 1945, the Coopers traveled westward to find a new radio job. Accompanying them in the move were Ab Cole and "Yodeling Joe." Although they'd written ahead, they found that the "Midday Merry-Go-Round" in Knoxville (which had since hired Molly O'Day) and station WLAC in Nashville did not look like good prospects. Ray Duke, a singer they'd worked with in Chicago, had sent word that he'd been quite successful at KLCN in Blytheville. There the station owner, Mr. Sudberry, liked their act and took them on—the policy here being no pay, with air time providing advertisement for personal appearances.

While in Blytheville, the Coopers' radio program was heard by a young musician in Grenada, Mississippi, who was later to become an important part of their band. The grandson of Luther "Chink" Clark, a well-known fiddler in the area, Bill Carver learned to play the steel guitar while working in the PX at Camp Biscayne, Mississippi, during the war. He also had experimented with other instruments, and, still in his teens with a young wife and baby, Bill arrived in Blytheville one day to audition for Wilma Lee and Stoney. They were especially impressed with his Bill Monroe style mandolin playing as well as his versatility on steel and other instruments, and he was hired on the spot. The mandolin added to their gospel numbers, and the steel had been missing since they had left West Virginia. Also Johnny Johnson, on rhythm guitar, joined the band for a time here. By March 1947, this territory was worked out, and another move was made.[4]

This time Wilma Lee and Stoney relocated in Asheville, North Carolina, on WWNC, where response was, at first, very good. But within three months it became apparent that the territory there was very limited:

WLC: They gave us a good deal. The reason we only stayed there three months—the station was owned by the newspaper. They said they'd give us free publicity, and they gave us a salary, so much. Well, it sounded like a real good deal. We got in there and Stoney said, "Now we'll work a month or six weeks, so people'll know who we are, before we book anything." So we went along there, what, about a month?

SC: No, it was about three weeks at the most, and in comes a postcard.

WLC: Wants us at . . .

SC: Fairview, which was about fifteen miles out of Asheville. And I debated on that, I thought, "Well?" It was the principal, and I wrote him back and told him, "Alright, we had not intended to play dates until such-and-such a time, but since his town was very close, we would." Well, we went out there, and that auditorium seated eight hundred-something people, and we had nine hundred-something in there.

WLC: In about three weeks work on the radio station—that's all the time that they'd heard us.

SC: I thought, "Good heavens, I believe we've hit paydirt, this definitely was a good move." You know, you're always leery. So another one came in over the opposite way, from Black Mountain. Went up there and had something less than eight hundred in there. And I said, "We've hit, we've really hit a strong place for us." You know, you go to certain audiences and just happen to be what they want to see. So I was thrilled to death. . . . So then the station was very happy about it, because it was drawing that well; the sponsors came on like mad. Then we were doing a date over in Marion, North Carolina. It's just over the mountain, about forty miles. Well, the station, as Wilma told you the newspaper owned the radio station, so the newspaper was giving us half-page ads free, and plugs over the station like you've never heard. And they were gonna remote control, which was rare then, from Marion back to the radio station. So we set up the afternoon to do it, and you know, there wasn't hardly anybody out there. And we'd scheduled to do the broadcast in the afternoon, you know. Oh, a couple of hundred people were out there. I thought, "Well, maybe they'll be here tonight." I'll declare, I bet we didn't have four hundred people there all day long. Was it ever a disappointment. Went back to them and they didn't understand it. And I certainly couldn't understand it from the other deals we'd played. Well, my next date was Boone, North Carolina.

WLC: Across another mountain.

SC: Went over there to play the courthouse—we used to play a lot of courthouses. So we got there, and I think eight or nine people showed up.

WLC: Not even enough to play to. Then we started asking questions, you know, to the ones that was there.

SC: And they said, "Where are you from?"

WLC: They couldn't get the station.

SC: Well, that told me pretty much what I was wanting to know.

WLC: The thing was, it set there in a valley surrounded by mountains, and as long as you played these little towns in the valley, where you packed 'em in. . . . But if you went over a mountain they couldn't get the station. See, you had no territory to work. So that's why, then, we decided to leave there.

While at WWNC, however, Wilma Lee and Stoney did get their first chance to make commercial recordings. Jim "Hobart" Stanton of Johnson City, Tennessee, who had recently started his own label, Rich-R-Tone, was servicing jukeboxes in the Asheville area when he first heard Wilma Lee and Stoney singing faintly over the radio. He followed the sound to the building adjacent to the one with the jukebox and inquired about the duet. Stanton proceeded to the WWNC studio and proposed an offer to Stoney. Rich-R-Tone was a small label and not yet on solid footing, but Stoney was, at that time, open to any chances to record. Their first session was at night at the WWNC studio, and when they left Asheville shortly thereafter, Wilma Lee and Stoney Cooper were under contract, although no records had yet been released.[5]

They considered going back to Fairmont first, but after a successful interview with Mr. Ryan at WWVA in Wheeling (by now a 50,000-watt station), they were hired on 26 July 1947. The record contract, Stoney remembers, was impressive and helped them get the job. At WWVA the entertainers were paid according to the percentage of the station's mail response addressed to them, which was calculated in units referred to as "P.I.s." Among products sold over the air were nylon hose, insurance, monuments, cosmetics, carving knives, baby chicks, and seasonal products such as seeds. By the late fall of 1947, in spite of a defective initial audition recording, the Coopers were accepted for sponsorship by Carter's pills. Their taped show for Carter's was to appear on twenty 50,000-watt stations three mornings a week for a year and was the most extensively broadcast show Wilma Lee and Stoney have ever had. Stoney takes pride in recalling that Mr. Carter himself was an old-time fiddle fan and entertained sophisticated friends with his personal recordings of the Coopers.

The first two Rich-R-Tone releases appeared by early in 1948. Their third release was to include "Tramp on the Street." Unfortunately for them, Molly O'Day's Columbia recording of the same song came out before theirs, which was then hastily released in an effort not to lose too many sales. After the Rich-R-Tone discs had been on the market for a brief period, with good response in sales over the air and at personal appearances, complaints of bad packaging and breakage on mail orders (which were being shipped from outside Wheeling) grew more frequent. Finally, while response was still eight to nine hundred orders a day, the record offer was taken off the air.

With records, then, Wilma Lee and Stoney found they had even more to learn about the ins and outs of show business. One big lesson had to do with the way they got new songs and the complications which arose in recording new material. Thus far in their career, they attained songs in a traditional manner. Wilma Lee's ability with shorthand was a real benefit, and it "hardly ever cost more than a dime" to get the words to a song off a jukebox. Bill Carver recalls the source of most of the Coopers' songs at that time:

> I know that Wilma Lee and Stoney, from doing radio shows, when they came to Blytheville they had a satchel, maybe two, of songs that was old as the hills. And their material was all this old material that they'd gathered over a period of years. Back, I guess, when her mother and father sang—the Leary Family sang together. Probably a lot of the sacred, country-gospel songs came out of that. There at that time, wasn't a thing of doing each other's songs, couldn't have been. Each one had to reach back and grab an old type song. Unless, of course, at that time people like Mel Foree were traveling up and down the land representing Acuff and Rose songs, and sometimes he would come by and bring a song that somebody had done. And he'd want different groups to do it, you know, to get it hotter in the country. But it took awhile for that to work, and it was a slow process compared to what we've got now.

With their recording of Bill Monroe's "Wicked Path of Sin," the Coopers encountered some problems which they had not anticipated:

> SC: Yeh, that brings us back again, you know, Wilma could take off things in shorthand. She hasn't practiced in a long time, but she used to could get it right, well, she got it at least the second time that Bill done it. Then was when Bill would write his songs and go ahead and do it, but what we didn't know was that there was an ethic here in Nashville that they didn't do each other's songs and things like that.
>
> RC: Well, you heard it on a live performance, then?
>
> SC: Yeah, we heard him on the Grand Ole Opry on Saturday night sing it.
>
> WLC: Well, when we'd hear something we'd like, we'd stop the car if we were traveling. I'd just write the words down, and he'd get the tune. So that's how we got that. He did it one Saturday night we were traveling, and we stopped the car and got the words off. And we liked the song, so we started doing it. When we recorded, we just recorded that one, so. . . .
>
> SC: We love Bill Monroe, you know.
>
> WLC: So we found out later that he went up through—I don't know if he had it in the can, you know, had it recorded but not released, or not—but anyway, he went up through Virginia and there was the "Wicked Path of Sin" all over the jukeboxes—ours. His song he had written and . . .

RC: And he didn't even have it out?

WLC: And he didn't even have it out yet.

SC: We thought he had.

WLC: We didn't really know he'd written the song. Because, you know, they'd sing songs they didn't write. Just something we'd get out.

SC: At any rate, we were ignorant of the whole thing. And then I found out he did write it, and I thought Bill would be happy, you know, about it. And I was there at the Opry one Saturday night, and I said, "Bill, sure do like that "Wicked Path of Sin." I said, "You know, we recorded it." "Yeah, I know," he said, "Don't it seem to you a little when you sing other people's songs, after awhile you sort of get yourself patterned like them?" That really hurt me, you know. Of course we're the dearest of friends now. But it really hurt me because I held him so high.

RC: He didn't get that first crack at it.

SC: That was it. And I guess he thought it was unethical—and perhaps so. But of course. . . .

WLC: Back then it was the radio.

RC: You had a different way of getting songs back then, didn't you?

WLC: That's right, and it was a song we liked. And when we recorded, it was a song we liked, that one, so we recorded it.[6]

Despite various complications, the Rich-R-Tone releases proved the salability of the Coopers' music. Jim Stanton remembers their "Tramp on the Street" and the Stanley Brothers' "Little Glass of Wine" as the biggest sellers in the Rich-R-Tone 400 series. He also recalled an incident which affected the present name of Wilma Lee and Stoney's band. The first Rich-R-Tone releases identified their group as "Stoney Cooper and the Clinch Mountain Boys." This band name, of course, was also used by the Stanley Brothers, and at Carter Stanley's insistence, Stanton convinced Stoney to alter the name of their group. "The Clinch Mountain Clan" provided a suitable change.

Fred Rose of Acuff-Rose had noted the success of Wilma Lee and Stoney's recordings. On a trip to Nashville with Gene Johnson, their manager at WWVA, Stoney was approached by Rose about signing with Columbia. By the time Stoney had returned to Wheeling, Rose had consulted with Art Satherley, and a contract was formally offered to them. The major label was attractive, of course, and they accepted. At the time of the agreement, however, the musician's union had suspended all recording in an effort to combat the replacement of live radio entertainment with recorded music, a last effort in the musicians' effort to secure a separation between the two media. The Coopers could do no recording in the meantime. The union's position finally weakened, and their first

Columbia session was scheduled for April 8, 1949, to be held in the Tulane Hotel in Nashville.

While Wilma Lee and Stoney were in Wheeling there were several changes among their band members. Bill Carver remembers coming to Wheeling with the Coopers and being the first dobro player on the WWVA Jamboree. He remained with them until 1951, then worked as a stage musician at WWVA for two years before moving to Indianapolis, where he later returned to music with a gospel group and eventually rejoined the Clinch Mountain Clan on the Grand Ole Opry. Replacing Carver in 1951 was Buck Graves, who formerly played with Esco Hankins and others. Graves later accompanied the Coopers in their move to Nashville and established himself in Flatt and Scruggs' band. In the very early fifties the Coopers hired their first banjo player, a North Carolina musician named Chuck Henderson, who had been in Wheeling previously. In 1953 or 1954 John Clark began to play banjo with them. In their first few years at Wheeling, a young fiddler named Tex Logan, taking leave from his studies at M.I.T., joined the Clinch Mountain Clan for a period of roughly a year, after which he returned to his education at Stoney's encouragement. The bass player-comedian role within the group changed hands several times. After Ab Cole was Smiley Sutter ("Crazy Elmer"), "Dapper Dan," and Woody Woodham, who made the move to Nashville. After the Coopers had been in Wheeling for a time, Jimmy Crawford began to play steel guitar with them and also accompanied them to the Opry. This roster is certainly not complete, for other musicians were used at various times, both session musicians and sidemen on the WWVA Jamboree.

Wilma Lee and Stoney firmly established themselves at WWVA, and it was from this stage that they were introduced to most of their present-day audience.[7] The WWVA listening area was immense, extending well into Canada, and frequent personal appearances gave them the kind of audience rapport that they maintain today. They taped a fifteen-minute program, aired daily on WWVA at 11:15 P.M., and appeared weekly on the Jamboree. Much of the other time was spent traveling to and from dates. The artists at WWVA paid the station five percent of all personal appearance profits, and for the ten years the Coopers were there, they were the top name on the station's "artist service" list. A genuine interest in meeting and pleasing their audience made Wilma Lee and Stoney's performances fast-moving and balanced, with "something for everybody." Comedy sketches, sometimes extended, were a part of the show, and Bill Carver remembers a skit entitled "The Ghost Walks at Midnight," which they performed in earlier years to the delight of children at schoolhouse dates, using portable blue lights to create an eerie effect. In addition to a rigorous public appearance schedule, the Coopers owned their own record shop in Wheeling.

Following their last contract period with Columbia, the Coopers were interested in becoming associated with a new label. Columbia was not an exclusively country label, and the Columbia country artists receiving the most promotion at the time had been signed since the Coopers (under Don Law, who succeeded Art Satherley). Wesley Rose took an interest in Wilma Lee and Stoney because they had been among his father's "talent," and in 1955 he offered them a contract with Hickory. It was a new, minor label at the time, but they were assured of a better exposure to the country market and felt it was a step in the direction towards Nashville. With the first Hickory session they began to use electric guitar in the group, played by Chet Atkins, who also supervised the early Hickory sessions.

After ten years at WWVA, Wilma Lee and Stoney moved to Nashville and joined the WSM Grand Ole Opry on February 1, 1957. In terms of record sales, their most successful years came shortly thereafter. In 1959 two of their releases, "Big Midnight Special" and "Come Walk with Me," were among the top ten country western hits. In 1960 they had one song in this category, "There's a Big Wheel." Wilma Lee and Stoney's years with Hickory were their most prolific for recording, with a heavier emphasis upon gospel material than before. On October 28, 1965, they signed with Decca, and although under contract with Decca for four years, Wilma Lee and Stoney had only five recording sessions during this period.

Among the musicians making up the Clinch Mountain Clan at live appearances during the sixties were Joe Edwards (electric guitar), L. E. White (guitar and third vocal part), Victor Jordan (banjo), and Lou Stringer (bass). In 1967 Bill Carver returned to Nashville with the Swanee River Boys gospel quartet, and within three years he was again appearing with Wilma Lee and Stoney. With Carver the dobro sound, which had been absent during most of the Hickory and Decca periods, returned to the band. More recently, banjo player Mike Lattimore has joined the group. Appearing frequently with her parents since they joined the Opry and adding a strong vocal part was Carol Lee Cooper, who for a time was married to Rev. Jimmie Rodgers Snow, evangelist-son of Opry star Hank Snow. She managed her own vocal backup group, the Carol Lee Singers, doing session work in Nashville. Except for periods of Stoney's ill-health during the sixties, Wilma Lee and Stoney maintained their rigorous live appearance schedule since coming to Nashville, traveling up to 100,000 miles a year.

On the Opry the Coopers made their "mountain" sound a fixture among the long-established performers, those who preserve the sense of country music tradition from that stage. They have been closely associated with the Acuff "school" for a number of reasons—because of specific borrowings from the Acuff style and repertory, and, more importantly, from the performance milieu in which all entertainers of this period got their start. Wilma Lee's vocal style, which has been the real backbone of their sound, is an excellent case in point. Her singing is characterized by a driving, open-mouthed delivery, phrasing which emphasizes clear pronunciation, and a tendency to sustain notes rather than embellish them. Much of this straightforward style is shared not only with Roy Acuff, but also with "old country church singing." As Wilma Lee evaluates the style herself, it is related to both the type of song which she sings and the performance situation:

> I like story songs. And I'm just a plain ole country singer. I just sing like I learned, and I never had no voice training or nothing like that. I just do what I can do. And I always thought that it was important to say your words where people could understand. Especially if you're singing a story song—you're going with the story of that song. That's what people's gotta hear to like it. And if they don't understand the words, then they don't get the story. So I always tried to speak my words plainly, that they would know what I was singing.

Wilma Lee's philosophy is a practical one for an entertainer of her era performing live on radio or at personal appearances. Her exceptional ability to project in singing fulfills a concern for full communication with her audience. As Bill Carver implies in describing Wilma Lee's success at this attempt, a singer in a live situation cannot afford to depend solely upon a strong microphone to convey her song:

> When you've got the right P.A. set, and it can be understood and heard clear, I've never seen her fail to encore continuously on the songs that she does—no matter how long she does them or how often she does them.

Wilma Lee's inclination toward a story song can be seen in both her gospel and secular material; and because her repertory emphasizes both kinds of songs, her image has not been suited to singing much of the material which has characterized more recent female vocalists. Despite the pressure of the trend toward "cheating" songs and a few recordings which were somewhat out of her image, Wilma Lee, as Bill Carver explains, has relied on the traditional story song topics and point of view:

> When you think of Kitty Wells and people on down after this, they did a different kind of song. It had some similarity, a country sound, but they sang about love affairs and slipping around on a back street. Now Wilma Lee has stayed with the story type song and has never sung it personal, where it personally involved her, that she could possibly be one of the ones that was slipping around on a "Back Street Affair"—I think that was one of Kitty's big numbers. . . . So she's stayed with the story type song, and therefore possibly it has hindered her from being as popular as some of the girl singers that have had big hit records. Because naturally we know that anything that exploits a divorce, or this, that, and the other naturally sells, you know; where the other type song, there's a different class of people that listens to that mainly. Although others do buy it. She sells, Stoney and her sell, I think, to a more settled type of people, whether it be middle-aged, whether it be younger type people or the older.

Besides vocal parts and instrumental breaks, Stoney's most important role within the band has been as front man and decision maker, and as such he is constantly sensitive to the audience while on stage:

> RC: Do you have any kind of format or order that you present the songs in? How has that changed over time, or has it?
>
> SC: Well, yes, it's changed over time, because you learn a little more as you go along. And your audience teaches you the best, if you'll just watch 'em. We like to start fast. We're that type of act, you know. There's some that could start with a ballad. We're not the type singers that have, you know, just a beautiful listening voice to listen to. We've got to excite the audience. And this is the way, I think. You have to go with your strongest points. We open with the "Midnight Special." It's rolling, you see. Well, then, the next, we may drop to a slower song for the next one; but then we're right back up again with the next one, which is normally my fiddle tune.

Although there is a standard program in mind, Stoney may alter it according to the audience response. Here Bill Carver describes his ability to keep control of the show and the audience's interest:

> Stoney is good at gauging an audience—by that I mean feeling an audience out. Starting out with a certain type of a song that they don't seem to be responding to, and he'll stay with it; whether it be instrumental, or

whether it be the fast intro song or the slow song. So he can just kind of gauge that. If the audience doesn't begin to respond immediately, then he'll change the routine. If it seems good to begin with, then we do have a routine that we go through with.

RC: Do you think that many of the modern country acts are able to do that?

BC: No, I don't, because they've never learned it. And in the second place, 'course I'm not calling any names so it doesn't matter, but a great majority of them don't even know that. They don't know to feel of an audience and they really couldn't care less. Because they've had a couple of hit records and since they're new in the business, they walk out and do a couple of hit records and think that's all that's necessary. Years ago when we went out, you had to give the people a show. You'd have to go out, one act, and do an hour and a half. And you had to entertain people; if you didn't, they'd get up and walk out. So we would do songs, we'd do trios, we'd do solos, we'd do duets, we'd have comedy, we had instrumentals; we loved to touch everybody and do the type songs that would probably hit everybody, from a lively song to a good ballad, a good hymn, a good solid trio number, you know, to try to reach everybody.

Success at personal appearances is insured by being flexible enough to appear continually to the audience. Radio involves a remote audience with less direct feedback, but because a product is being represented, the concern for a broad audience appeal is still basic. Bill Carver characterizes Stoney as "one of the best pitchmen in the business," a quality perhaps more desired of a musical entertainer in the earlier days of radio, when the performance pattern was different in a number of ways:

RC: Do you think pitching was more important when they were starting out playing on the radio?

BC: I think so, 'cause they had a closer relationship with the people. For instance, you were able to speak more direct to the people who you're working to; where now you've got somebody between you and the people—usually the announcer or front man who's usually in front of the audience. It makes quite a bit of difference to know that you're second or third down the line. But then, in those days you were talking more directly to the people. You were working to them in the show dates, and then you went out and either you'd speak to them direct or over the radio. And what they sold, they pretty much were sold on themselves before they would pass it on to the people. They would do that, they had confidence in it.

The emphasis on record sales in the present-day music industry has influenced many entertainers in their approach to live performances, but as Stoney explains, he and Wilma Lee have resolved to concentrate on giving a good performance each time they appear rather than continuously promoting a "latest release":

> RC: It seems like you all are so much more effective on the Opry than some of the newer people, because you come across and put the audience at ease. It's a little bit more of a salesmanship thing than, you know, "knock 'em out with a hit record."
>
> SC: Well, I'm glad you detected that, and I'll tell you why. Because you're a musician yourself, first of all; and you have detected that we're not going out there to knock 'em in the aisles. And the minute we get over that and just go out there and get an encore, that's when you do good work. And we stopped doing that because after "The Big Wheel" we tried desperately, floundering around to please this A & R man and this one—"get that big, big one." Look, that big one is what the people make big for you. And unless you can do it in its natural way and you have found that song that fits your image and what you handle best, forget it. So now we take an ordinary, basically good song and go out and say, "Let's sing to the air audience, and maybe the people in here will like it, too." And they do.

Many times in live performances Wilma Lee and Stoney will do traditional or well-known numbers which they have never recorded. While under contract to record companies the Coopers have had problems with material—much of their repertory is not what the companies have considered "hit material" at the time, and many of the new songs and follow-ups on earlier hit material did not really fit their style. Because relations with a hit-oriented company have been constraining, Wilma Lee and Stoney now contract their own recordings individually, and, as Stoney explains, they have decided to select their own material and fully determine their own image:

> Now we know. We listened to a few too many people, you see. This is what can happen to an act. Now, that's what I meant, I don't think we'll go with that studio, that company that wants to rule you, and "We're gonna look for a song." *We,* you know. "*We're* gonna look for a song for you." I don't think we'll ever want with that company again. I think we'll lease all of ours.
>
> RC: Want to have your own head about it?
>
> SC: Yes sir, we will do whatever we feel that we're capable of doing, and no more. And if they want them, fine; if they don't, then we'll put them out ourselves. I think we'll be ahead, don't you?

In this decision the Coopers are overcoming a conflict which has slowly been developing between their own pattern of performance and that of performers who place a higher stock in record sales. The fact that they themselves can best manage their own recording affairs attests to a live-performance orientation and an established audience. As Wilma Lee describes, their success began before recordings became the dominant media:

> Really, we're a standard. We made our name in the days of radio, see, like Acuff. And you don't really have to have hit records. . . . Records really ruined the business for lots of entertainers, see, 'cause everybody can't be on the Grand Ole Opry, or everybody can't be on the Wheeling Jamboree. And there's not that many places for the entertainers to go now. So, really, the record business ruined the live entertainment part of radio stations for young talent getting started.
>
> SC: 'Cause I could pinpoint the map and show you the stations that had live talent, and I don't mean just one or two bands; I mean seven or eight, at thousand-watt stations.
>
> WLC: Just all over; just everywhere.
>
> SC: All live talent.

In both their use of traditional material and the move to small-label recording, Wilma Lee and Stoney have much in common with many bluegrass groups who presently find their audience somewhat out of the mainstream industry market. Although not regarded as strictly a bluegrass group, they have, in the course of their career, maintained many overlaps with the bluegrass style and repertory.[8] Within the past several years Wilma Lee and Stoney have been frequently booked at bluegrass festivals, and here a new audience has been opened to them, one which again requires the ability to cope with live-performance dynamics. Their success with festival crowds reflects both that ability and the basic appeal of their music to any country audience whose tastes are traditional or retrospective.

For the most part, however, Wilma Lee and Stoney Cooper still depend primarily on an air audience, one which responds to their personal appearances and to their sponsor's product. Record sales, in one way or another, are mainly promoted from a live-performance situation, either on radio or at personal appearances. Their territory has greatly expanded, but the essential relationship to the audience is the same as when Wilma Lee and Stoney began on radio. They know that their best fans are those who have listened to them the longest, and they feel a responsibility to this audience for their popularity. Elkins, West Virginia, the town which was their original home base and where Wilma Lee attended Davis and

Elkins College, honored them on 16 November 1973 with Wilma Lee and Stoney Cooper Day. A dedicated turnout characterized this event, as has been the case at most of their personal appearances through the years. Wilma Lee and Stoney remember it as the most satisfying moment in their career and a true indication that their mode of music and entertainment, although a little out of phase with the hit-minded industry, is still enjoyed by an audience consisting of people rather than record sales statistics.

NOTES

1. Research for this project was originally submitted as a part of coursework under Dr. Henry Glassie at the Indiana University Folklore Institute. Quotations within the text are taken from the following interviews: with Wilma Lee and Stoney Cooper (Nashville, Tennessee; January 3, 1974); with Jim Stanton (Johnson City, Tennessee; January 5, 1974); with Bill Carver (Nashville, Tennessee; August 13, 1974). The present article only scratches the surface of a rich vein of oral history open to those interested in country music. The Coopers are excellent interview participants, and I have been pleased to learn that Fred Williams of Kelley, Iowa, has begun a long-term, in-depth series of interviews with them.

2. See Neil V. Rosenberg, *Bill Monroe and His Blue Grass Boys: An Illustrated Discography* (Nashville, 1974), 21–24.

3. *Checklist of Recorded Songs in the English Language in the Archive of American Folk Song to July 1940,* issued by the Library of Congress, lists the following entries "by Mr & Mrs Jake Leary, Ted Henderson, Wilma, Geraline, and Cathaline Leary—Tygart Valley homesteads, Elkins, West Virginia, (collected by) Gordon Barnes, 1939":

Crawdad Song 3574 BI
The Jericho Road 3574 B2
Old Black Mountain Trail 3576 Al (Wilma Lee, Geraline & Cathaline).

There is no mention of the material collected from the Learys in Washington in 1938.

4. A 1966 publicity release by Bill Williams of WSM Public Relations reports that, while in Blytheville, Stoney won a national contest sponsored by *Southern Farmer Magazine* by selling 10,000 books over the air in three weeks.

5. There was some disagreement among my oral sources about the Rich-R-Tone sessions.

6. Neil Rosenberg reports that the Stanley Brothers (on Rich-R-Tone during the same period) also released their version of a song learned from Monroe, "Molly and Tenbrooks," before Monroe's recorded version was issued. See "From Sound to Style: The Emergence of Bluegrass," *Journal of American Folklore* 80 (1967), 143–144. Jim Stanton comments that in both cases he was

unaware of any irregularity until the matter was later brought to his attention and the discs had already been out for some time.

7. Attesting to the rapid growth of their popularity in the WWVA listening area, the Harvard University Library of Music named Wilma Lee and Stoney as "the most authentic mountain singing group in America" in 1950. See Linnell Gentry, ed., *A History of Country Western and Gospel Music* (Nashville, 1961), 208.

8. The Coopers' relatively early use of the five-string banjo-dobro combination and borrowings from early Monroe gospel material are perhaps their strongest connections with bluegrass. Their secular repertory has also been influential to bluegrass; Wilma Lee and Stoney's versions of two older songs in particular, "Ruby (Are You Mad at Your Man)," which was taken from Cousin Emmy's version and recorded by Wilma Lee as "Stoney (Are You Mad at Your Gal)," and "Sunny Side of the Mountain," taken from the original by Big Slim, the Lonesome Cowboy, both were popularized by the Coopers' recordings and later became standards in the bluegrass repertory. For further mention of Wilma Lee and Stoney's exposure to bluegrass audiences and the musicians associated with bluegrass who have played in their band see Douglas B. Green, "Wilma Lee and Stoney Cooper," *Bluegrass Unlimited* 8:9 (March 1974), 25–27.

Bernard C. Hagerty

WNAX: Country Music on a Rural Radio Station, 1927–1955

At the time of publication, the author of the following article was a political organizer on the staff of U.S. Senator James Abourezk of South Dakota. He wrote and was responsible for persuading Senator Abourezk to introduce the American Folklife Preservation Act in the Senate. Much of the information was gathered in interviews he conducted, in person and by telephone, with former musicians and employees of radio station WNAX; this material is now in the Oral History archives of the University of South Dakota at Vermillion.

Yankton, South Dakota, is a small town of about 12,000 souls, nestled on the banks of the Missouri River, across from Nebraska. The economy of the area, as of most of the Upper Midwest, is based on farming and stock raising. Aside from some historical interest as a capitol of the Dakota Territories, and some damn fine catfish from the Missouri, there is little to distinguish Yankton from any of a hundred other similar towns in the region. Yet Yankton boasted, and still has, one of the most successful and influential radio stations in that part of the country. This article is about that station, and about the years, from 1927 to 1955, when radio station WNAX featured live country music.

It is, I am sure, known to the readers of *JEMFQ* that many of the early radio stations were founded for reasons that had little to do with a pure and unsullied love for radio broadcasting as an art form. Usually, stations were started to boost the sale of a particular company's product. In this part of the United States, seed companies were particularly fond of starting radio stations to encourage their sales. At one time this led to the amusing situation of Shenandoah, Iowa, supporting two stations, each with twenty or thirty performers, boosting rival seed companies, with KFNF owned by the Earl Mays Company, and KMA by the Henry Fields Seed Company. If one added up the total number of people who worked for these two stations at one time or another, it would probably exceed the population of the town.

It is easy to understand, in a general way, how it was useful to a firm to own a radio station, and how country music could have been a very helpful promotional tool. What is not so well understood, however, is the depth and breadth of such rural stations' integration into the social and economic fabric of the communities they served. Stations such as WNAX had quite an impressive economic base, founded not only on their provision of services, such as market reports and weather, but also on their social function as a center of community activities and as provider of the specific, listener-oriented, participatory brand of entertainment exemplified by country and hillbilly music. Thus, in focusing on the mechanics of a single radio station in a part of the country which is still, so far as I know, rather underexplored by folklorists, I hope to give a few small insights into the history of country music, and at the same time, to give a little recognition to one of the more colorful and significant radio stations of the live broadcasting era.

Radio station WNAX was the brainchild of Chandler "Chan" Gurney, son of D. B. Gurney of Yankton, owner of the Gurney Seed and Feed Company. Chan is still [1975] one of Yankton's leading citizens, and served as a United States senator. It seems that, sometime in 1921 or '22, Chan got the idea that the family seed business wasn't doing as well as it might. Being a progressive-minded young man, he therefore approached his father with the suggestion that it might be a good idea to found a radio station as a promotional gimmick, as some others had done. D. B. agreed that this might be a good thing, and sent his son down to Shenandoah, Iowa, with instructions to take his time, at least two weeks, in looking over KMA, also owned by a seed company, to learn what he could about radio.

Chan, though, after seeing an operating station, couldn't wait that long. In fact, he was back in Dakota the next day, fired with enthusiasm. He and E. C. "Al" Madsen immediately set about constructing a transmitter, reputedly working from plans in a *Popular Mechanics* magazine. (This story may be apocryphal, since I could find no plans for a transmitter in *Popular*

Mechanics at the time this was all happening. It's the way Chan Gurney tells it, though.) The intrepid inventors pieced out their good old Yankee avarice with good old Yankee ingenuity. When a rather large vacuum tube ran too hot, they obtained a metal milk crock, filled it with a coolant oil, and immersed the tube. The antenna was a wire strung between two windmills on neighboring farms. On November 9, 1922, the Department of Commerce granted a broadcasting license to Dakota Radio Apparatus Company, E. C. Madsen, founder, and the station went on the air.

It proved to be an abortive beginning, however. The owners quickly discovered that there weren't enough radio receivers around to make the venture profitable. After a short period, they went off the air. While they were on the air, they did broadcast live music, by locals rather than professionals, but no record remains of this period. Nevertheless, the license was retained, and in 1926 the Gurney Seed and Feed Company, judging that times were more propitious, took over direct control of the company. They began broadcasting again in 1927.

To celebrate their return to the airwaves, the Gurneys conceived a gala event; a live, on-the-air fiddle contest, to be judged by the listeners. A Western Union station was set up in the living room of the D. B. Gurney home, where the contest was to be held. The musicians played, and the announcer asked the people to vote. And vote they did, 8,700 telegrams poured in from all 48 states. When the flurry of paper cleared, the winner was an amiable, big-gutted Irishman named Happy Jack O'Malley. He was the first entertainer hired, and was soon joined by an entire orchestra. Lewis Johnson, a fine old-time fiddler still residing [1975] near Winifred, South Dakota (and still placing high in the annual Yankton Old-Time Fiddlers Contest), recalls a contest about that time with Happy Jack; "When the contest was over, Happy Jack and me were even. So we played, and then played again to break the tie. Happy Jack won, and went on to be a star on WNAX. Me, hell, I went back to the farm."

At the same time, a number of other musicians, a complete studio orchestra, was hired. Within a very few years, the station was dominant in its own region and heard literally throughout the country. One small example may be adduced to demonstrate the coverage WNAX achieved. During World War II, sailors on a certain ship, stationed at San Diego when not at sea, made it a custom to call in every week, and request certain numbers to be played at a certain time. They would then hook the radio up to a microphone, invite the local ladies on board, and hold a dance on the fantail, or whatever the correct nautical term is.

WNAX's great range was due to a number of fortuitous coincidences. Although it was not a powerful station, its spot on the dial, 570 kc clear channel, was quite good. In addition, the land contours were favorable (don't ask me how, I'm not an engineer), and the ground conductivity was excellent. At the present time, the signal is "shaped" toward the north, carrying very well to Minnesota and Canada, in order to protect a station in the South. Until after World War II, however, the coverage was well-nigh universal. Although by no means unique, this range was one of the factors which allowed WNAX to be a successful station.

The Yankton radio station also quickly developed a reputation, among musicians working the radio circuit, as a good berth. The competition for jobs was quite intense, and it is a great pity that the many hundreds of audition discs made are now lost.

There were, really, two categories of musicians appearing on the station. The first were the touring groups, from Chicago or St. Louis or even further. These were generally ambitious types, lured by WNAX's large audience, hoping to make a name for themselves, or to sell records. Such groups and singers would usually stay for short periods, two weeks at most, and then move on. The second category included the station's own live talent staff, on a regular salary and obliged to appear on the station's showcase programs, the Sunday Get-Together and the Missouri Valley Barn Dance. It should be noted that all of the station's talent staff were professional musicians. Although a number of them lived in Yankton, none could honestly be described as "local talent."

The salary of a country musician on WNAX, while never opulent, and probably not comparable with the salaries paid by some of the bigger stations to their stars, seems to have been adequate. Moreover, even during the Depression, it was steady. Rex Hays, one of my informants and formerly musical director at the station, describes a typical incident at another station which, he says, paid less well than WNAX. The musicians, he claims, had been making $14.00 a week, and were thus overjoyed when the station manager announced that they were all getting a raise, to $17.50 per week. Two weeks later, the station went broke, and they were all fired. This sort of thing seems to have been rare at WNAX, though a number of musicians recall salary cuts during the Depression.

The station as a whole prospered during the thirties. In 1933 their broadcast power was increased to 2,500 watts, and in 1935 to 5,000. (I must digress for a moment to discuss the historic dates and figures in this article. They are often in conflict with other published dates for the events mentioned, and figures are also often changed. For example, even the FCC is unsure what the original wattage of the station was. Most of the figures I give are from an internal portfolio prepared in 1954 by the Katz Agency of Sioux City, the station's PR firm. Their information is often incorrect, however, and wherever possible I have checked it with government or other official records. This is probably the most accurate material published, but I am sure there are a number of factual errors. The station's own records are lost, thrown out by succeeding changes of ownership.)

In 1938 the Gurney Company sold out to Cowles Broadcasting, which also operated newspapers in Minneapolis and Des Moines. This sale was the result of an unfortunate case of tunnel vision on the part of Chan Gurney, who by then owned the station as a result of his father's death. Chan Gurney is a member of one of Yankton's leading families, popular enough to have been elected to the U.S. Senate, and smart enough to have, by most accounts, done a good job there. He is a forthright, proud, talented man, not given to making mistakes. Yet, in this case, he totally failed to see the potentialities of a radio station as an independent operation. He didn't think the seed business needed that kind of a boost any more, so he sold the station, for a rather small fraction of its present estimated $3 million value. He later saw his error, and this sale is still a sore point with the former senator.

The Cowles ownership continued former musical policies, and went one better by inaugurating the Missouri Valley Barn Dance, copied from WLS and other national trend-setters. While the Cowles ownership was eventful in music and personalities, there is little station history that need detain us in a discussion of country music. Around 1954, the station was sold again, and the new owners, faced with television and a whole new entertainment and music complex, ended live broadcasting.

In discussing country music on WNAX, it would be impossible to mention all the singers, musicians and groups who played on the station, or even any good fraction of them. Textual analysis of the music, of course, is beyond the scope of this article, which is too long anyway. I think, however, that, by drawing on the memories of some of the musicians who played on the station, such as cowboy singer Eddy Dean, who came on the station in 1929; John Matuszka, a classically trained violinist; and others, we can show the routine of the station, and evoke a little bit of its atmosphere.

It must be emphasized, first, that while country music was king on WNAX, it was by no means sole monarch. In addition to those who could be put under the aegis of "country" which ranged from old-time fiddlers and traditional balladeers to cowboy singers, there were numerous others, popular musicians, ethnic musicians, and even big-band swing musicians. The only universally known musician to come out of the station, in fact, is Lawrence Welk, whom nobody, ever, has accused of being country. The musicians, too, had quite a free-and-easy attitude toward their own styles of music. On their own shows, of course, they played what they were best known for. But a single musician might play as many as seventeen programs in a single day, especially if he was a member of the orchestra. Rex Hays has drolly described for me the frantic routine of grabbing new sheet music, and even new instruments, a dozen times a day during thirty-second commercial breaks.

Thus, versatility and an easy unorthodoxy were the order of the day. A cowboy singer like Tex Randall would think nothing of asking a big-band clarinetist like Rex Hayes or a classical musician like John Matuszka to back him up on a lonesome ballad. Another cowboy singer, Billy Dean of Sulphur Springs, Texas, even filled in for a while in the Bohemian band, plunking away happily to Czech folk tunes on his five-string banjo. Tex Randall (from Kokomo, Indiana) did the same on guitar. Bert Dunham and Zeke Martin, two of the more facile guitar players on the station, backed up everybody. Even Happy Jack, the undisputed dean of the staff, regularly backed up other musicians on his fiddle.

There was at least one exception to this live-and-let-live philosophy, and that was George B. German. His reluctance to back up others, or to have them back him up, had nothing to do with arrogance, for a more amiable, unassuming man could hardly be found. Rather, it is a tribute to the purity of his music, and the stark simplicity of the cowboy idiom. As a teenager, George B., as he is universally known, went to Arizona for his health and became a protégé of the great Romaine Loudermilk. George consciously styles his singing after Loudermilk, and one of the prize exhibits in the Yankton Territorial Museum, of which he is curator, is a cowboy hat willed to him by Loudermilk. It is, appropriately, placed on a cowboy, sitting in front of a campfire braiding a rope. George B. knows only very basic chords, and uses a simple thumb strum—no fancy displays of virtuosity, thirty-seven bar runs, or the like. His singing style is similarly simple. Yet his version of "The Strawberry Roan" is as good as any I've ever heard. He used it to introduce his program each day.

There are two points to this. The first is that technical virtuosity is not the essence of musical performance. It is possible, or at least it used to be, to be a great performer without possessing flashy instrumental or vocal technique. The second is that, as my informants agree, the instrumental accompaniments were usually rather simple. Great virtuosity, while sometimes present, was usually subordinated to the demands of the music.

There were, of course, exceptions to this, as to every rule. The aforementioned Zeke Martin and Bert Dunham would still qualify as hot guitar pickers. Jessie Mae Norman, of the husband and wife team of Ben and Jessie Mae, apparently played excellent lead lines on her metal, resonator-equipped National mandolin. (Ben, by the way, while running a business full time, is the only person I found who still plays regularly on the radio, on a small station in Winner, South Dakota.) And, of course, if you've got a good fiddler, you let him play.

Which brings us to the subject of Happy Jack O'Malley. He has been mentioned before, but he still deserves a few more words. Happy Jack was by far the best-known musician on the station to people in the Yankton area. He has, in fact, assumed the proportions of a legend. His own proportions weren't exactly small, either. He was, by common consensus, a very good fiddler, if probably not a great one. He had a wide repertoire of old-time, hillbilly, and Scotch-Irish fiddle tunes, and sang a little bit too. His greatest asset, and one of the station's biggest selling points, was his Uncle Dave Maconesque character. His family still runs Happy Jack's two restaurants in Yankton, and I would recommend them to anyone going through that part of the country.

The number of musicians who played on WNAX is quite staggering, and, as I have said, runs the gamut of country and hillbilly music. Let me just mention a few of the names: Eddy and Jimmy Dean, and later their nephew Billy Dean, all from around Sulphur Springs, Texas; Utah Slim and Sweetheart Mary; comedians Helen and Toby, and Quarantine Brown; blind pianist and singer Homer Arp; the Nelson Family; the Kactus Kids, from Blue Island, Illinois; the Novelty Boys and Cora Dean (Willie Pierson, Cora Dean's brother, played guitar and helped in the vocals, being particularly well known for his version of Tex Owens' "Cattle Call." He tells me the group started singing in 1938 in Boston, Massachusetts. The story was too long to get over the phone, but someday I'd like to hear how three country musicians from Hiawatha, Kansas, and Utica, South Dakota, started to sing in Boston); Marge and Betty, the Carson Sisters, who featured an Ozark hillbilly style, complete with yodeling; Al's Rhythm Rangers; and Delores Hill.

One of the more successful programs in the 1940–1955 period was the Missouri Valley Barn Dance. The format was simple: the largest hall or stage available in Hitchcock, South Dakota, or Sioux City, Iowa, or wherever, was rented and on Saturday afternoon, everybody, and I do mean everybody, was piled into a bus and taken to the chosen spot, where they first broadcast live for an hour, then stayed to play for the dance afterward. In the recollections of the local people who grew up listening to WNAX, this program almost invariably is the one that stands out.

At the beginning of this article I promised to discuss the economic base which enabled rural radio stations such as WNAX to employ country musicians. To appreciate this, one must realize how important a radio station was, and still is, in rural areas. In many ways, it affects the rural residents' very livelihood. In the Yankton area, farmers decide when to market their cattle, or corn, or hogs, on the basis of the daily market reports from Sioux City on WNAX. It is nice if they know how the markets are doing in Chicago, but they absolutely have to know how they're doing in Sioux City. Similarly, the weather is of great importance to them. In the city, the weather report isn't so crucial; the urban dweller likes to know whether he should take a raincoat, and if next week is going to be good for a picnic, but it doesn't really affect him deeply. But to a farmer, the forecast, long range and short range, is crucial. If it rains too much, he can't plow. If it doesn't rain at all, the corn burns up. He needs to know if he can space his work in the fields out over several days, or whether he should work by moonlight, and plan on going to town tomorrow, when the weather will turn bad. And finally, the rural radio station is the only media outlet which spends any time on the problems and concerns of the farmer. George B. German, for example, made a transition from cowboy singer to farm reporter, running around the country getting interviews and opinions on his "RFD with George B." program.

In other words, the rural radio station has a ready-made audience. Rural people have to listen to a radio station, they have no choice. In such a situation, before the advent of television, it was logical for a radio station, which was an important facet of its listeners' economic life, to attempt to maximize profits by becoming also a part of its social life. The provision of entertainment was a logical means of both fighting off competing radio stations providing the same economic services, and of painlessly extracting the largest possible amount of loot from the farmer, through advertising.

But the entertainment function of a rural radio station in the days of live broadcasting cannot be exactly equated with that of the present-day television station. Television is a passive entertainment form; one sits in front of it and is entertained. Radio, on the other hand, at least until the early fifties, was a far more participatory medium. True, people sat around it, but that is not all they did. Let me give a few examples of the participatory vigor of WNAX's listeners:

- In 1945, the station held a celebration in Yankton, complete with a Typical Mr. and Mrs. Midwest Farmer Contest. It drew 70,000 people.

- In 1952, when the station was well past its prime, a single show, "Your Neighbor Lady," drew more than 102,000 pieces of mail.
- A single daily advertising spot in 9 weeks brought 2,521 orders for, of all things, bronzed baby shoes.

Of course, musicians were the biggest draw. The Bohemian Band, with John Matuszka leading and reading song requests in Czech, caused sales of Grain Belt Beer to jump like the proverbial goosed bullfrog. A cracker company sponsored another show, the Stump-Us Gang, and their Tune Crackers. Readers would send in the name of a tune, and a boxtop from the sponsor's product, in an attempt to stump the musicians. Entries were drawn by lot each day. The musicians I was able to reach who played in this group are unanimous in claiming 500 or more boxtops per day. Even allowing for exaggeration, that's one hell of a lot of crackers.

And, of course, the biggest attractions of all were the individual stars. The Bohemian Band was nice, but it was much easier for a teenage girl to get a crush on Billy Dean than on a whole band full of people who talked funny. One of the more amusing sidelights I ran into in gathering material for this article was the conviction, held in all honesty and humility by each and every musician I interviewed, that the amount of mail they got was a phenomenon peculiar to themselves. They didn't realize that the other entertainers got that much, too! One former employee of the station recalls that favored entertainers were often presented with cakes, and similar signs of esteem, through the mail. The number of such culinary tidbits received every week by the station was apparently in the hundreds. And as for letters, Billy Dean recalls receiving as many as 1,600 per week. The average for Billy and other entertainers was undoubtedly much less, but it still adds up to an impressive volume of mail.

In summary, country and hillbilly music on rural radio stations during the era of live broadcasting should not be seen as a primitive phenomenon caused by a lack of technological capacity for recorded broadcasting; nor should it be considered, as it so often is, only in relation to the rest of the entertainment industry, although it is true that changes in that industry were chiefly responsible for the decline of live broadcasting. Rather, it should be viewed as an integral part of the economic, social, and sometimes political complex of services which radio stations profited by providing to rural populations. In the process, radio stations such as WNAX, along with the record companies, benefited folklorists, and all who are interested in America's musical history, by bringing to the surface a large part of our rich folk music tradition.

Simon J. Bronner

Woodhull's Old Tyme Masters: A Hillbilly Band in the Northern Tradition

In his "Introduction to the Study of Hillbilly Music," D. K. Wilgus states "that hillbilly music is a phenomenon solely of the South in general and of the Southern Appalachians in particular is a myth in the best sense of the word."[1] Despite this statement, the myth of southern origin is a persistent and recurring theme in the literature of country music study repeated by various historians of the music including Bill Malone, Fred Hoeptner, Robert Shelton, and others.[2] The main historical bias is a case of conclusions based on incomplete evidence. The research in the field has been based on available commercially recorded phonograph records and limited fieldwork. These materials have been traditionally southern in nature and leave out a whole segment in the development of country music.

Unrecognized sources of country music need more documentation and analysis to determine the effect of southern exposure on existing old-time music traditions. Other evidence is needed to test various theoretical bases underlying the diffusion and adaptation of the country music tradition. Is it true, for example, that "[country music's] manifestation was of the South; its essence was of rural America"?[3] These questions are being considered as collections continue to increase at centers like the Archive of New York State Folklife in Cooperstown, New York.

In the process of this continuing research and fieldwork with Central New York musicians, references were constantly being made to a source of influence of local origin. "Woodhull's Old Tyme Masters," originating from Elmira, New York, is this band whose radio and live appearances reflected and continued a northern old-time music tradition.

The band is unique and significant for several reasons. It reflects many of the musical traditions of the Central New York area predating the major influences of recording and radio. Second, it was one of the very few hillbilly bands from the Northeast to commercially record. Third, it is part of the family tradition which includes the phenomenon of family bands.

Today, Floyd Woodhull, one of the original members of the band, still remembers the history and music of that era. The information he provided along with research from other sources produced the following history.[4]

In 1895, Elizabeth Blanche Schmidt came to Elmira, New York, from an isolated village named Snowshoe, Pennsylvania, to find work. As an avocation, she played guitar and knew some traditional square dance calls, such as the "College Lancers," "McCloud's Reel," "Irish Washerwoman," and "Soldier's Joy." Her repertoire also included hymns usually reserved for church or home singing, including "The Old Rugged Cross" and "In the Garden."

Fred Woodhull had arrived in Elmira from PenYann, New York, shortly before Elizabeth. He worked as a construction worker for a dollar a day, twelve hours a day, but managed to keep up his fiddling in his few spare moments. He met Elizabeth Schmidt shortly after she arrived in Elmira, and they started playing house dances together, usually receiving three dollars apiece, which seemed a great improvement over their current occupations.

These house dances and kitchen hops were a unique social creation allowing farmers in rural settings to find release from the rigors of their work and reinforce community and kinship ties. It also served as a center for the transmission of oral traditions emphasizing repetition and participation in musical and social traditions.[5] These dances are described by Floyd Woodhull in the following exchange:

> Q: How did the house dances take place?
> A: They were all farmers and they would be in the winter because farmers after they get their field worked, all they have is barn chores. They'd have them any night—they wouldn't have to be a weekend night. They'd have them on a Monday night or a Wednesday night or a Tuesday and they'd start eight o'clock and take about an hour out for supper. Set all the furniture out in the yard, it didn't make any difference if it was snowing or not and dance in two or three rooms. The music would get in one corner out of the way and it was pretty near all square dance. Once in a while you'd play a waltz or something but not very often.[6]

Other descriptions of house dances in nearby counties agree with this account with the addition of food as an intrinsic ingredient of the affair. The context of the early music from these accounts is dance, and this becomes evident by the large number of dance tunes and calls in the repertoires of local musicians. House dances experienced their greatest popularity during Prohibition when neighbors would bring hard cider and home-brewed whiskey to the affairs. They faded after Prohibition as radio and large dance halls became popular. Different accounts place their demise at the late twenties or early thirties.

Besides dances, other vocal traditions included religious hymns, "coon" songs, and broadside verses. These broadsides were single printed sheets available for five cents from general stores, peddlers, music shops, and neighbors. Songs on these sheets included popular songs such as "In the Good Ol' Summertime," and "Golden Slippers." Songs already in the oral tradition were also circulated, including "The Ship that Never Returned," "I Had But Fifty Cents," and "Darling Nellie Gray." Topical songs of local interest also found their way on these sheets, including "Murder in Cohoes" and "The Johnstown Flood."[7]

Square dance calls and vocals were diffused through an aural process. Floyd Woodhull, for example, stated that:

> I always use the "Arkansas Traveller" for a certain dance, "Down the Center, Cut-off Six," it's not a singing call, it's a shouting call but I have other callers who use a different melody for it. This happens all the time. Callers would come to where you're playing and if you had a new call, you'd see them with a pencil and paper. Nobody complained that they couldn't use it . . . everyone used what they wanted and everyone was delighted because I could call it and another caller would call one—I had used pretty near the same thing but he had a style.[8]

Through the factors of repetition and participation, the repertoires of local musicians and callers not only were transmitted but underwent stylistic changes occurring up till the present day.

Other contexts for the music were family reunions, which were large affairs reinforcing kinship ties and intrafamily traditions. Another source was community focal points. This was often the general store, still a common sight in Upstate New York. As an example, one former general store in Oaksville, New York, always had two fiddles present, encouraging musical and narrative exchanges.[9]

After Fred Woodhull married Elizabeth Schmidt, they continued to play house dances and other small functions until 1916. In the winter of 1916, Elizabeth contracted asthma, curtailing the effectiveness of her calling and seriously impairing her health. Their thirteen-year-old son, Floyd, had been learning the piano and joined his parents that winter playing house dances. During this time, Floyd's mother taught him what calls she knew to accompany the tunes he had previously learned from his father.

Between 1916 and 1928, Floyd played small dances with his father. Floyd played piano until his eyesight seemed to get worse, at which time he switched to accordion. They were often joined by Floyd's brother, Herb, who played harmonica, and "Uncle" Billy Held, who played Hawaiian style steel guitar. Billy Held was no relation to the Woodhulls but assumed the "Uncle" title to reinforce the popular family image. His presence is significant in placing its early role in country music in perspective. His Hawaiian stylings adapted to square dance tunes was influenced by touring Hawaiian bands like the Irene West Royal Hawaiians and others appearing in theaters and chautauquas in the area.[10] This account again places the appearance of adaptations of Hawaiian stylings to country music at about the time of World War I, paralleling experiences of early Southern hillbilly recording artists such as Darby and Tarlton.[11]

The third Woodhull brother, John, was playing violin at this time. When he expressed interest in joining the family at the dances, he was encouraged to play guitar. While John was learning guitar, Herb picked up the tenor banjo. The plectrum banjo was present in square dance music bands in Central New York at least to the turn of the century, if not before.[12] However, the appearances of Eddie Peabody and Harry Reser gave forceful impetus to the instrument's rising popularity. This points out the constant interchange between popular and folk traditions.[13] The performance of vaudeville shows on a New York circuit including Albany, Binghamton, Elmira, and Buffalo both utilized folk materials and introduced new ideas to the existing tradition.

During these formative years of the Woodhull performances, they often assumed a "hillbilly image," dressing up in old farmers' clothes, large glasses, fake beards, and floppy hats. Asked about this aspect of their performance, Floyd Woodhull made the following comments:

Q: What was your father's name?
A: Fred. We all had trade names in the band: his name was Pop, mine was Ezra, and my brother Herbert was Zeke, and my brother John was Josh.
Q: Were those again for the hillbilly image?
A: Yes.
Q: When was that popular?

A: I can't really tell you how far back but from the farm dances in the houses, it just leaned naturally toward a farmer or hillbilly image.

Q: Was it a southern hillbilly?

A: Oh no, no. Of course I have the utmost respect for the South, don't get me wrong but I think it was a hillbilly, the hills of this area and *that* [emphasis is Floyd's] was the image. A farmer's image or a hillbilly image but not a hillbilly like you connect with moonshiners like you say Tennessee or something like that. It's not that type.

Q: They would know it was a sort of dressing up, but they still enjoyed it?

A: Oh yeah, that was half the deal!

Q. Why do you think that was?

A: I think it was a matter of fun. Of course you didn't have television then and any personal appearance with a disguise or costume was a big thing.[14]

It is unclear whether these statements parallel or dispute the notion of the "southern hillbilly image."[15] Certainly, there is the indication that the combination of "hillbilly" and "music" was not just a southern phenomenon.

In 1928, John "Tiny" Taggart, who played bass, was added to the Woodhull band, now featuring Floyd Woodhull on accordion and degan bells, Herb Woodhull on plectrum banjo, John Woodhull on rhythm guitar, and Fred Woodhull on fiddle. In October of that same year, they officially assumed the name of "Woodhull's Old Tyme Masters." They became one of the very few "professional" country bands, usually playing six nights a week in a hundred-mile radius of Elmira, New York. They performed at dances in barns, rural school districts, grange halls, and dance halls. The only exception to this routine was a special concert such as the one [in which] they appeared with Art Mooney at the Strand Theater in Elmira. The significant fact is that they stayed within the original traditions, applying them to different contexts within the same geographic and cultural sphere.

They broadcast over the radio, buying time from the stations once a week to play their music and advertise their dances for the coming week. Other bands employing this same technique at the time included The Rusty Rubens, The Lone Pine Ramblers, The Sherman Family, The Trailblazers, The Tune Twisters, The Harper Family, and The Bennett Family. They would broadcast over WESG-Elmira, WELM-Elmira, WCHU-Ithaca, WGY-Albany, and WKRT-Cortland to the Central New York area.

The "Old Tyme Masters" retained the same personnel for almost twelve years. In 1940, however, Fred Woodhull decided to retire. Ramson

Woodhull's Old Tyme Masters, 1939. Left to right, Herb Woodhull, John Taggart, John Woodhull, Fred Woodhull, and Floyd Woodhull

Terwilliger from Binghamton, New York, replaced him on the fiddle. By this time, the band had gained a popular reputation through their broadcasts and appearances in the Central New York area. Increasing numbers of requests from their audiences for recordings prompted Floyd Woodhull to attempt to record commercially in 1941. He describes the events in the following dialogue:

> Q: How did you make the records? How did that come about?
> A: You won't believe this, Simon—because I sent a sample disc that we made at the radio station on a soft wax disc: two sides—two square dances—first-class mail. I got the address from Victor in New York and the next week I got a letter back with a contract. Now the reason for that was this: at the time they had been searching for a recording band for square dances because they hadn't found anything they liked.[16]

It is curious that almost no recorded legacy exists for the pre-World War II era of country music in New York, considering the increasing evidence of a large amount of country music activity in New York.[17]

The years after World War II were difficult ones for the band. The increasing popularity of radio and other types of entertainment cut into the Woodhull's audience. They sold the "Old Barn" in Elmira Heights which they had used every Saturday night for dances. John Woodhull left the band to pursue a business venture. Eventually, only Herb and Floyd Woodhull remained from the original band. Finally in July of 1953, after twenty-five years as an entity, Woodhull's Old Tyme Masters broke up. None of the band members resumed their music, except for Floyd, who formed "Sammy and Woody" as a part-time venture, usually playing in taverns and inns. He still found an audience for his music despite the pressures of rock and roll and modern country music on the area's musical tastes. He had a personal influence, however, beyond just his musical influence. By remaining in a small area all his life, he often played to audiences of almost all friends, acquaintances, and family. Musically, his band is still often mentioned as an influence. Many of their calls can still be found at performances and dances throughout the Central New York area.

The Woodhulls operated under an already active country music and dance tradition adapting and selecting aspects of other traditions including popular, regional, and folk. The amalgamation of these streams of culture interacted and complemented the contexts of family, dance, and community. These elements in the northern country music field are part of a continuing tradition on which subsequent study will shed more light.

NOTES

1. D. K. Wilgus, "Introduction to the Study of Hillbilly Music," *Journal of American Folklore* 78:309 (July–September 1965): 206.

2. See Bill Malone, *Country Music U. S. A.* (Austin: University of Texas Press, 1968); Fred Hoeptner, "Folk and Hillbilly Music: The Background of their Relation," *Caravan* 16 (April–May 1959): 16; Robert Shelton, *The Country Music Story* (New York: Bobbs Merrill Company, 1966).

3. Wilgus, 196.

4. Interviews with Floyd Woodhull, 24 April and 5 May 1976. Correspondence with Floyd Woodhull, 22 April 1976, 3 May 1976, 12 May 1976, 19 May 1976. Interview with Harvey Harper, May 5, 1976. Interview with Jim Wright, Jerry Lang, and Charley Hughes, April 10, 1976. My thanks to the Chemung Historical Society, Country Music Foundation, Bob Pinson, Radio Corporation of America, Morris Distributing Company, and the New York State Historical Association for their help.

5. Discussion of these house dances appears in Robert D. Bethke, "Old Time Fiddling and Social Dance in Central St. Laurence County," *New York Folklore Quarterly* 30:3 (September 1974): 163–184. See also Simon J. Bronner, "Ken

Kane and the Adaptation of Tradition," *Archive of New York State Folklife* (May 1976).

6. Interview, May 5, 1976, with Floyd Woodhull, Elmira, New York.

7. Interview, May 3, 1976, with Ken Kane, Toddsville, New York, and manuscripts loaned from his personal collection. Interview, May 5, 1976, with Floyd Woodhull, Elmira, New York.

8. Interview, May 5, 1976, with Floyd Woodhull, Elmira, New York.

9. Interview, April 13, 1976, with Ken Kane, Toddsville, New York.

10. Interview, May 5, 1976, with Floyd Woodhull, Elmira, New York. In an interview with Roy Smeck, April 15, 1976, he also mentioned the Irene West Royal Hawaiians as the first slide guitar he heard. Roy lived in Binghamton, New York, at that time and was born in 1901. Stephen Calt cites Sol Hoopi as appearing in Binghamton, New York, at that time also in his liner notes to Yazoo 1052.

11. Malone, 119.

12. Interview, January 9, 1976, with Nick Conti, Binghamton, New York. Interview, May 5, 1976, with Floyd Woodhull, Elmira, New York. Stephen Calt, liner notes to Yazoo 1052.

13. This point is further noted in Wilgus's "Introduction to the Study of Hillbilly Music," 195, and in Ray Browne, ed., *Folksongs and Their Makers* (Bowling Green, Ohio: Bowling Green Popular Press, 1971). Reser and Peabody were specifically mentioned by Floyd Woodhull as influences.

14. Interview, May 5, 1976, with Floyd Woodhull, Elmira, New York. See also unpublished manuscript, "An Interview with Tessie Sherman," by Michael O'Lear, Archive of New York State Folklife (1973).

15. Malone, 43. Archie Green, "Hillbilly Music: Source and Symbol," *Journal of American Folklore* 78:309 (July–September 1965): 204–228.

16. Interview, May 5, 1976, with Floyd Woodhull, Elmira, New York.

17. Correspondence with Roy Horton of Peer International, May 4, 1976.

Summer 1976

Robert Coltman

Roots of the Country Yodel: Notes toward a Life History

Yodeling is farthest famed as an exacting Swiss vocal expression, but the alternation of full and falsetto voice of which it is composed is found in many places. In America it has become a cowboy sound, due largely to the striking influence of Jimmie Rodgers and the many singers, good and bad, who took their cue from him. The closer one's acquaintance with the evolution of yodeling in country music, the more vital Rodgers' contribution shows itself to be. That it could cross two decades to survive, little changed, in Hank Williams' yodeling, while rapid musical change was going on all around, testifies to Rodgers' impact. Yet country yodeling is more than a matter of one Mississippian working in isolation. Rodgers fused several traditions: popular yodeling together with a number of less formal options for use of the falsetto. The following is far from definitive, but it is a start on a little-discussed subject.

The Alpine Style. While research in America on the yodel has so far been slight, the outlines of the matter are clear enough. The yodel seems to have begun not as entertainment but as simple communication. By producing a piercing tone and greater volume than a shout, it enabled mountain-dwellers to catch each other's attention at some distance. In time, so the story runs, yodelers developed a repertoire of sounds which were understood as simple signals, a good deal more melodious than arm-waving.

The technique is simple enough, though its effective use as music requires considerable control. The human voice has more than a single range; there is a one-to-two-octave upper range overlapping some six tones or so with the highest notes reachable by the lower; in tone and pitch they stand in a contrast not unlike that of the ukulele and the guitar. Explanations of how this occurs vary in usefulness; a practical one comes from a longtime friend of the author's, himself an enthusiastic and accomplished yodeler. Bill Briggs suggests the upper range as a harmonic of the lower: the vibration of half, rather than the full length, of the vocal cord.[1] He theorizes that the yodeler trains himself to emphasize the distinction between the two voices, making it sharp and producing the celebrated "break," while other singers intent on developing range and consistent voice quality may make the transition as imperceptibly as they can—hence the inability of some singers to find the yodel break. "Sopranos," he explains, "may sing in the harmonic all the time," instancing a woman trained as a soprano who could use her full lower voice only after she had been taught to yodel.

It is in making the yodel behave, in the characteristic oscillation between the two voices, that the art arises. In the simplest yodels, such as Jimmie Rodgers used, the high and low notes are made to form harmonically pleasing intervals, usually 6ths. As the *Harvard Dictionary of Music* notes, the low tones commonly use "low vowels" a and o, the high tones, e and sometimes i; u is also encountered among the high notes. Alpine yodelers have evolved this simple principle into something ornate and often beautiful: an echoing, kaleidoscopic stream of alternating tones, golden or raucous, which during the latter part of the 19th century became a bravura art. Composers like J. K. Emmett created pieces like the widely performed "Cuckoo Song," one of several distinct pieces by that name, and some quite beautiful renditions reached records in the first two decades of the 20th century. Briggs speaks highly of the British recordings of Mirma Reverelli: "She expressed an ease and joy in just doing (no strain), obviously tripping out with her own sounds." The yodel by now had become a theatrical standby, passing into the repertoires of touring vocalists in America. Few firm data are available on the inclusion of yodeling acts in the numerous traveling shows of the 1880–1920 period, particularly in the hinterlands of the South, but we can be sure that yodeling was available to American record buyers as early as 1905 or so. And the records sold widely, reaching many more people, especially in rural areas, than would ever hear a yodeler on stage.

Concert performers like Frank Kamplain (Gennett) and George P. Watson (Victor) presented their "Alpine specialties" to full orchestra accompaniment in the European manner, but the yodel quickly fitted into more mundane arrangements. Ward Barton was making guitar-accompanied yodel recordings for Victor by about 1917, for example, using a vaudeville style not very different from Wendell Hall's: a piercing conservatory tenor and a plucky-strummy sort of playing. In his stagy phrasing, smart diction and elegant melodic embellishments he is thoroughly urban, but his treatments trot out many of the elements Rodgers would soon be using. And, of course, the vaudeville inspiration for aspects of Rodgers' style need scarcely be pointed out.

Barton recorded, about nine years before Rodgers, a yodeling version (with revised text) of "Sleep Baby Sleep"—hardly the "mountain" standard it has been claimed to be, but rather a descendant of a towny-sounding 1869 hit by S. A. Emery, certainly a key to the genesis of Rodgers' singing and yodeling, as it had become a yodel standard by about 1920 and possibly much earlier.[2] It helps us conclude that when Jimmie Rodgers decided to use the yodel he was departing in no way from entertainment tradition; "Sleep Baby Sleep" was a cover of an established hit. So was "Rock All Our Babies to Sleep," which had been yodeled in 1924 on a Columbia record by Riley Puckett. Puckett, indeed, was the principal early country musician to demonstrate fascination with Swiss yodeling's sound and use of image. He, too, is in the line of descent of the popular "Sleep Baby Sleep" yodel and all, and in other songs like "Strawberries" he evinced enthusiasm, though no great yodeling ability—suggesting that for a young blind Georgian committed to a career in music in 1924 (as for, say, a Nova Scotian like Wilf Carter trying to make a dent in U.S. country music in the 1930s) the yodel was a technique rare enough to make a singer stand out from the mob, yet popular enough to make him attractive.[3] It was, in any case, not a bad risk. Puckett would soon go on to conventional vocalizing at which he was infinitely better, but his recordings may have been the final link in the chain of events that turned Jimmie Rodgers' mind toward use of the yodel.

Black Yodelers. But in one respect Rodgers was innovative beyond all argument: he was the first singer clearly to establish the yodel as an echo and comment on the blues. This was not simply more of the same thing Ward Barton had been doing, and few other white singers were capable of working as near to the bone of black tradition as Rodgers. In later life, when he signed to play in black as well as white shows, or traveled to Jackson, Mississippi, not far west of his hometown of Meridian, to jam with the local cadre of well-known black bluesmen, who welcomed him as readily as any black visiting musician,[4] he was continuing a familiarity with blacks and their music which began in his boyhood water-carrying days on the railroad, and which few other whites would have found easy to sustain. His blue yodeling expresses that ease as matter-of-factly as it does the brisk and breezy personality he derived from vaudeville performance.

It is easy to intuit, though difficult to prove, the black roots of Rodgers' yodeling. Russell notes that many blacks use a falsetto device, an octave leap at the ends of words: "the effect was rather of a whoop or howl than the seesawing about the voice's breaking point which makes a yodel."[5] He also notes minstrel use of yodeling as far back as 1847, and minstrel men did try to ground their technique on generally recognizable black models. In addition, we find ample use of the falsetto and some true yodeling in African tradition,[6] and in Rodgers' home state the falsetto is one of the distinguishing features of the Delta blues. Rev. Ishmon Bracey claimed that children would yodel when he was a boy, "but it wasn't like [Rodgers'] yodel. . . . At first we'd hear us' voice echo down in the woods, and we'd echo back, and then we started from there."[7] It looks as if we could establish a fairly close correspondence between Rodgers' yodeling and that of Delta musicians like Tommy Johnson.

"That was the beginning of that voice changing, I'd call it, or yelling," Johnson's contemporary, Rev. Rubin Lacy, says of the Crystal Spring singer's eerie register shifts in "Cool Drink of Water Blues" and other songs.[8] We must remember that though Johnson first recorded about six months after Rodgers, his is no copy, but a distinct style. There is no "yodel-ay-ee" in the white manner; the break is there but the effect is wholly different. Where the typical cowboy yodel is brassy and outspoken, where Rodgers' yodel is cheery and upbeat, Johnson's is secretive, brooding, harrowing. As practiced by a few Delta musicians up to the present (one being the late Howlin' Wolf), it has no emotional identity with the Rodgers yodel at all.

If we try to look behind Johnson for the roots of black yodeling, we find the trail even more badly obliterated than that of the Alpine art. Listening to the mass of blues recordings made between 1920 and 1940, there is not enough yodeling to establish a line of inquiry. Mississippi is at the heart of it, and urban blues singers used it not at all. Vocal cries like Blind Lemon Jefferson's are common enough. Field hollers, wordless moans or wails sung almost absently while following a mule or chopping weeds did sometimes use the falsetto, but in no very organized way, and the field holler has been heavily overworked as a source without enough concrete evidence. Nevertheless, the weight of blues impressions is convincing, and we must assume that a vital root of Rodgers' yodeling, if we could follow it, would take us to a black yodeling source, possibly offhand use of falsetto by the black railroad workers Rodgers knew as a child.[9]

The Blue Yodeler. Once Rodgers had recorded his first Blue Yodels, everything changed. His suave, rueful vernacular songs made him the first real people's popular singer, stylistically ten years ahead of his time, breaking the long dominance of golden voice and stage manner. All this was not to be digested at once, and imitators often sounded inane; indeed, the typical Rodgers hit was fragmentary, insubstantial, held together by his wry, remarkable personality and the signature of his yodel. Hearing it, one catches one's breath as his voice slips mischievously over the break. Doubtless he was well aware of the yodel's value to his career; virtually all his songs had it worked in somewhere, and he wore each yodel like an old shirt, supremely at ease. In his throat it shed its Swiss starch and its black introversion, the voice blurring upward as easily as water over a mossy stone, making other popular singers of the time sound as if they were standing at attention wearing tight-fitting tuxedos. Rodgers' yodeling is perhaps the simplest type of all, scorned by many yodel devotees. But what he did with it was magnetic, inimitable, and not at all easy.

Few working in country music, indeed in blues, could remain unaware of Rodgers. Some, like Bulow Smith of the Perry County Music Makers, found it both prudent and enjoyable to learn and perform each new Rodgers song as soon as the record came out. The yodel was something singer after singer had to try, whether it worked or not; an instance is Sara Carter's strange falsettoless false yodel in the Carter Family's "Lonesome Pine Special." A fairly long list of blacks, as well as whites, recycled some element of Rodgers' music or lyrics, and even his personalized yodel, though less assimilable, passed into black hands, particularly among the black variety singers like the Mississippi Shieks, but also among straight blues singers like Skip James. The black Mississippian "Big Road" Webster Taylor (whose nickname derives from one of Charley Patton's main songs) evidenced direct Rodgers influence by making a brave stab at the white-style yodel, "yodel-ay-ee" syllables and all. All of which suggests that some blacks perceived something satisfactory about Rodgers' blues derivations, whitened though they might be.

Cowboy Yodeling. A third bona fide root of country yodeling appears to be the cowboy yodel, though association with the movie cowboy image since the 1930s has muddied that trail (and, incidentally, reintroduced many Swiss elements). When we try to pin down, not merely vague generalizations, but firm statements about the nature of early cowboy yodeling, we find little that is reliable. There are vague traditions—

nothing substantiated—about use of quasi-musical, soothing sort of crooning to herds at night; Thorp denies even this, saying he heard only a "low hum or whistle," and says nothing about yodeling.[10] Rodgers' wife, Carrie, felt the blue yodel had a plains origin, but she may merely have been romanticizing.[11] In the he-man atmosphere of the range, it might be that the falsetto was regarded as feminine, and avoided accordingly. But certainly cowboys used falsetto yells, and their ee-yow and ki-yippyyay crept into some song choruses. Why not yodels as well?

We can answer only that the evidence, one would think, should be stronger than it is. One problem is that cowboy singing, almost more than any other kind, is largely documented in print rather than recordings, so that a seemingly trivial matter like use of the falsetto break easily escapes notice. The memories of the few survivors of the pre-Rodgers era are highly colored by the subsequent popularity of the cowboy yodel, and even the existing field recordings, most of them done through the field research of the Library of Congress, were mainly made during a period postdating Rodgers' recording career and are thus at least theoretically subject to the researcher's old bane, contamination of data. It is tempting, and probably defensible, to theorize that the traditional cowboy yodel, if such a thing ever reached the status of music, was a falsetto melodic device like what Eddie Armold used in "Cattle Call," rather than a conventional yodel. Curiously, when Ken Maynard recorded his "Lone Star Trail" in 1930, that native Texan and veteran of Wild West shows, presumably familiar with the Jimmie Rodgers recordings which had been blanketing the south for three years, chose to use not a true yodel, but a falsetto holler which (subjectively) sounds rather convincing. We are left to wonder whether the late cowboy star was doing something he'd heard cowboys do in the early decades of this century.

By the middle 1930s a number of singers had developed the cowboy yodeling style into something far removed from Rodgers' modest beginnings, and during the next 20 years much would be borrowed from the Alpine yodelers—not just yodeling techniques, but images of Swiss chalets and Alpine moonlit nights and romances with little Swiss girls which sorted oddly with hoots and saddles but testified to the elasticity of the western myth. The Nova Scotian with the supple, sandy voice, Montana Slim (Wilf Carter), was an early user of the new cowboy image and the new yodeling. Fine singers such as the Girls of the Golden West, Caroline and Mary Jane Dezurik, and Patsy Montana, especially the last, developed it into a high-powered popular vocal technique while Gene Autry was welding cowboy and yodel indissolubly together in the minds of movie fans. Doubtless the most fervent injector of Swissness into modern yodeling, and one of the best of the athletic school of cowboy yodelers, has been Yodelin' Slim Clarke, whose brazen machinegun yodeling in classics like "I Miss My Swiss (And My Swiss Miss Misses Me)" fascinated the author at a tender age, and no consideration of cowboy yodeling can exclude Elton Britt, whose powerful "Chime Bells" and fine minor-flavored "Cowpoke" are yodeling classics.

But such proliferation of popular yodeling styles (often, as Briggs points out, sacrificing the range, tone and resonance of the best yodeling for rapidity, vowel changes and use of the tongue to achieve extra consonant sounds) is useful here principally as an illustration of the degree to which the early history of yodeling has become obscured by later developments. As with black yodeling, we find slim evidence for many of the assumptions that have been made about early cowboy yodeling, yet the assumptions sound reasonable. We are left to wish for aural evidence, and constrained to realize that the hour is very late for anything of the kind to turn up.

Multiple Sources. We have come this far only to repeat that we cannot, as yet, trace the yodel as satisfactorily as we would like. One doubts that the Alpine, black and cowboy roots are sufficient by themselves to tell the story, for the falsetto, though rare, is alive in many places. Consider that southern white singers often use brief falsetto breaks at the ends of words (a practice cultivated, incidentally, by the contemporary country singer Tanya Tucker)—hardly more than a vocal crack, but quite intentional and distinctive. Some of the use of falsetto by early country singers like Riley Puckett and Al Hopkins is plainly inspired by Swiss-derived vaudeville in the Ward Barton strain, but others are more puzzling. There is Georgian Earl Johnson's use of a falsetto harmony on his refrains, probably a leftover from minstrel shows. There is Kentuckian Dad Crockett's use of a short vocal refrain, all in falsetto, on his banjo piece "Sugar Hill"; Uncle Dave Macon does similar things now and then. Jimmie Tarlton's odd yowling yodels do not sound as if they derived from Rodgers. There are more. A little farther afield, we find the shrieks and calls of Cajun music, extended into Mississippi in the vocal accompaniments to the fiddle music of Hoyt Ming. The white south would appear to have something to do with the falsetto, if not the yodel.

It may be that falsetto has long been an option for rural cultures both in the United States and elsewhere, and that the yodel proper has been one of several ways in which it could be applied. Certainly anyone who has let out a good scream knows where the falsetto is and how to use it. On the other hand falsetto never quite achieved legitimacy until Rodgers triumphed with it; it may have been felt to be an informal novelty, a gimmick like playing rubber balloons or musical saws, fit for hollering out in the field but not for singing in the house.

If this is so, then we are prepared to see the yodel in a crossways perspective: a rarified musical delight for the European connoisseur, but to the rural American southerner a musical oddity accidentally elevated to legitimacy by a unique performer. This may explain the yodel's decline since 1950, an odd contrast to its three decades of popularity. It is as if the yodel cannot survive as a mainstream technique on its own merits, but depends on the occasional popularizer with the magic touch—like Rodgers—to capture the imagination of the public. Under Rodgers' head of steam it became a potent device, poignant and startling, a sudden shift in aural perspective nothing else matches. It may awaken from its present eclipse only at the touch of an artist of equal power and originality. Yet as Briggs remarks, "the full range of what is available in this art form has barely been explored," which makes one eager to see what the yodel's next growth stage will be.

NOTES

1. This and subsequent observations by Bill Briggs are taken from his letter to the author, March 18, 1976.

2. "Sleep Baby Sleep" was also recorded, interestingly enough, by the black vaudeville singer Charles Anderson, as Tony Russell points out in his *Blacks, Whites and Blues* (New York: Stein Day, 1970), 66.

3. Paul Oliver, *The Story of the Blues* (Philadelphia: Chilton, 1969), 57.

4. The resident musicians of Jackson were no third-raters, including at various times Ishmon Bracey, Charlie McCoy, Tommy Johnson, Rubin Lacy, Johnnie Temple, and the Chatman brothers of Mississippi Sheiks fame. See David Evans, *Tommy Johnson* (London: Studio Vista, 1971), 40–43.

5. Russell, 67.

6. Paul Oliver, *Savannah Syncopators: African Retentions in the Blues* (New York: Stein & Day, 1970), 63.

7. Quoted in David Evans, "Black Musicians Remember Jimmie Rodgers," *Old Time Music* 7 (Winter 1972/3): 13.

8. Quoted in Evans, 40.

9. Charles Wolfe, "The Perry County Music Makers," *Devil's Box* 26 (September 1974): 38.

10. Austin E. and Alta S. Fife, eds., *Songs of the Cowboys,* by N. Howard "Jack" Thorp (New York: Bramhall House, 1964), 18.

11. Quoted in Bill C. Malone, *Country Music: U.S.A.* (Austin: University of Texas Press, 1968), 96.

Winter 1976

Norm Cohen

Riley Puckett: "King of the Hillbillies"

The realm of country music is saturated with royalty. There are doubtless more kings and queens than footmen and chambermaids. My subtitle is an epithet that was frequently applied to Puckett in advertisements and news articles from the 1920s and 1930s, but I have no intention of justifying the title as belonging to him alone. Nevertheless, Puckett's influence and popularity were so widespread during the halcyon years of his career that superlatives in his case are not wholly without justification. Hardly a professional country musician who grew up in the Southeast in the period between the two World Wars did not listen to Puckett's music and feel his influence—at least, this is the impression I have formed from numerous interviews, my own and those of others, in the past dozen years or so.

Puckett was not one of the legion of recording artists who enjoyed a spurt of popularity and faded during the Depression, never to regain the limelight. He was but fifty-two years old when he died, and still quite active in the world of country music. But he died before interest in country music took a serious turn, and I have found no interviews of him—either by journalists or academics.

John Edwards was the first country music historian to try to piece together the story of Riley Puckett's career. His brief biography, published in *Disc Collecter* in 1959, drew principally on an account in a song folio, *Bert Layne and His Mountaineer Fiddlers with Riley Puckett and Richard Cox;* on brief Columbia catalog blurbs; and on a few tidbits from

143

Edwards' American correspondents: Clayton McMichen, Gid Tanner, Bill Bolick, Bob Hyland, Wilbur Leverette, and others.[1]

My own early interest in Riley Puckett was a consequence of an enthusiastic response to hearing recordings by the Skillet Lickers nearly fifteen years ago. I leaped into print in 1965 with a study of the Skillet Lickers because D. K. Wilgus, editing the special "Hillbilly Issue" of the *Journal of American Folklore,* lacked one article to round out the issue.[2] My account, resting more on enthusiasm than knowledge, was published several years before it should have been, and for years after I intended to put together a proper study of this band, one of the most important in the early years of hillbilly music on record. So much has been written about the members of this assemblage in recent years that I do not feel pressed anymore to set the record straight; other writers have done much of that for me. And after country music historian Donald Lee Nelson visited Riley Puckett's widow, Blanche H. Bailey, two years ago, I felt that I could confidently leave the task of revising the Puckett biography to his hands. Unfortunately, ill health has prevented Don Nelson from continuing the fine series of studies that he had been writing for *JEMFQ;* therefore, I have decided to use some of Nelson's findings to amplify and correct the account that I wrote in 1965. I am grateful to him for the material he has made available to me, and regret that he has not been able to sketch out the Puckett story himself.[3]

George Riley Puckett was born on May 7, 1894, near Alpharetta, a small town about fifteen miles northeast of Atlanta, Georgia. His father, James Puckett, died when Riley was young. He and his one brother, James Jr., were reared by his mother, Octavia, who was not particularly musical. When Riley was still an infant, a doctor treated an eye ailment with sugar of lead solution, which caused near-total blindness. He could, according to his widow, distinguish light from dark, though some accounts denied even this. In about 1901, his mother placed him in the Georgia Academy for the Blind in Macon; there he was given some lessons on the piano. Blues writer Simon Napier had once speculated that Puckett and Blind Willie McTell had crossed paths, as McTell had also attended the Macon Academy for the Blind; in fact, he even suggested that McTell was the "old darkey" Puckett mentioned in his spoken introduction to his bottle-neck style guitar solo of "John Henry." However, as McTell did not attend the Macon Academy until the 1920s, there is little basis for that speculation—apart from the more general fact that both musicians frequented the Atlanta area.[4]

Puckett's doings between his leaving the Macon Academy and 1922, when WSB began broadcasting, are very hazy; his musical associates have no recollection of him during those years, and his wife did not meet him until 1925. The sketch in the Bert Layne folio states he learned to play banjo when he was about twelve years old, and then learned to play guitar. His wife claimed that he could play piano, mandolin, and violin as well, but on record he played only guitar and banjo—and the latter only on some of his early recordings.

Riley always made his living as a musician, playing on street corners, in concerts, and at parties. He did a little carpenter work; he could read Braille, and also knew telegraphy. He built himself a crystal radio set and used to listen to popular songs of the day. His widow recalled that he would whistle fragments of fifty or sixty different songs during a day. He could identify friends and acquaintances by the sound of their footsteps.

In March 1922 the *Atlanta Journal* opened station WSB, the first commercial broadcasting unit in the South.[5] On September 9, Fiddlin' John Carson became the first (to our knowledge) traditional rural musician to broadcast over the airwaves. Two weeks later, the Hometown Boys, a band including Clayton McMichen, Miles and Charles Whitten, and (perhaps later) Ted Hawkins and Boss Hawkins, made their first appearance, much to the delight of the listening audience. On September 28, Riley Puckett joined the band on radio, and the *Journal* noted the following day,

> On the Home-Town boys' fine program were the "Old Cabin" song, a wonderful yodeling solo, by Riley Puckett; "Ring Waltz," "Sweet Bunch of Daisies," "St. Louis Blues," "Wabash Blues," and other hits. Already favorites at WSB, the Home-Town outfit scored a knockout by introducing Mr. Puckett as one of their stars Thursday night.

How he first got involved with the band I have not been able to determine. Blanche Bailey felt that he had teamed up with Ted Hawkins sometime after leaving the Macon Academy. Lowe Stokes also recalled that Puckett and Hawkins and some fiddler played together around Atlanta at bars, picnics, and on the streets.[6] Although the picture is hazy, it does seem clear that the musicians such as the Home-Town band were trying to make a reputation in the idiom of contemporary music of the day as much as with older traditional material. On the other hand, such already well-established musical fixtures in Atlanta as Gid Tanner and Fiddlin' John Carson were definitely of an older musical generation—a distinction that Clayton McMichen was to draw many times and with much feeling in his later years.[7] How, then, Tanner and Puckett happened to go together to New York City to record for the Columbia Phonograph Company in

March of 1924, I do not know. Late in February they made test recordings in Atlanta, and were invited to New York the following month. In two days (March 7–9) Tanner and Puckett recorded seventeen numbers: two by Tanner alone, six by Puckett alone, and the balance by the two together. All but one of Puckett's solos were pop songs from the 1890–1920 period. Tanner's selections, and the duets, were of a much older vintage. The first release (Columbia 107-D) from this session, Puckett's vocal and guitar on "Little Old Log Cabin in the Lane" and "Rock All Our Babies to Sleep" (with Tanner's fiddle added on the former title), was issued in the regular pop music series on May 20, 1924—Columbia's first venture into the hillbilly music field. Altogether, fourteen of the seventeen numbers were released between May 1924 and June 1925. The initial response must have been quite favorable, as in September 1924 the pair was invited back to New York for a three-day recording session (September 10–12) at which thirty-seven numbers were recorded, twenty-six of which were soon released. Puckett dominated this session: ten of the numbers were by him alone, and another ten featured him with unaccredited fiddle accompaniment by Tanner. Only four were solos by Tanner. This trip was also significant in that Puckett brought banjo as well as guitar with him; these were his only recordings on any instrument other than guitar.

Very early the following year, Riley was in a serious automobile accident with Ted Hawkins (and possibly others). Hawkins required hospitalization for some six months; Puckett needed special care while he convalesced at home in Thomaston, Georgia. His nurse was to become his wife, though both of them were engaged to others at the time they met. They were married on May 18, 1925. The newlyweds were given a honeymoon trip to New York by Columbia that June, and on the 15th through 17th Riley recorded twenty selections, only seven of which were issued.

In the following years, Blanche drove him countless miles by car to numerous engagements throughout the Southeast. They would, for example, leave Macon at midnight and drive straight through to Nashville, some 350 miles distant. On November 25, 1930, a daughter was born; she was named Blanche, after her mother. Clayton McMichen asserted that Riley and his wife quarreled frequently and that eventually she left him; but Blanche assures me that this was not at all true. In general, in his later years McMichen bore Puckett much ill will, and criticized his musical skills and his character on several occasions.

Puckett's guitar playing was unique, both in sound and in style. In fact, on the basis of sound alone I feel certain that he is the unaccredited guitarist, on Columbia recordings, for comic singer Oscar Ford, for the string-band identified on record as McCartt Bros. and Patterson, and for blues singer Virginia Childs. His principal musical hallmark was his use of bass runs, often long, often double-or-quadruple-time; seldom chromatic. How he played the guitar seems to have been a matter of considerable interest—and also disagreement. In his 1959 article, John Edwards wrote that Puckett probably played left-handed. The evidence for this may have been—at least in part—a Columbia catalog photo inadvertently printed in reverse. Also, Bill Bolick may have written Edwards to that effect; when I spoke with him in 1965 about Puckett he told me that Puckett played left-handed, but with the guitar strung normally. The bass runs, he said, were played by his index and middle finger, picking upwards. Doc Hopkins told me at the same time also that Puckett made his bass runs with two fingers.[8] Mac Compton, a Dallas fiddler, told folklore student Lewis Wills (in the summer of 1968) that he had traveled on tour with Tanner and Puckett in the late 1920s and early '30s, and that Puckett played without his thumb, using his index finger for the bass runs, picking upwards like flamenco guitarists. Fred Stanley, another musician of that period who occasionally played with the Skillet Lickers, wrote me that "I never saw anyone pick guitar like Riley Puckett. He used a steel pick on his fore finger of the right hand and he got the bass runs with his middle finger." Clayton McMichen told me that Puckett played with a finger pick on one finger and picked upwards. Bert Layne agreed that he used a steel pick on his forefinger. On the other hand, Lowe Stokes told me that Puckett used finger and thumb picks. Dwight Butcher told Gene Earle that Riley used a thumb pick to make his bass runs, and Charlie and Obed Pickard Jr. stated that, according to their father, Dad Pickard, Riley used only a thumb pick, and picked both upwards and downwards with it. J. Laurel Johnson, another Dallas fiddler, told Lewis Wills that Puckett picked downward with the thumb and then brushed downward with his fingers. Asa Martin told me that Puckett played with a thumb pick, and only occasionally in concert used finger picks.[9] It strikes me as remarkable that so many musicians, several of whom I have other reasons to believe generally reliable in such matters, could have such different views on how Puckett played. One might conclude that he played in several styles, but the sound of his playing is so consistent on record that such a possibility seems untenable. Can we conclude no more than that he made his bass runs with either his thumb or with one or two fingers, picking either upwards or downwards? So it seems, for the present.

The question of Riley's guitar playing inevitably leads to his status as a back-up guitarist for fiddlers. The two fiddlers who probably played more with Puckett than anyone else did—Clayton McMichen and Lowe Stokes—spoke (to me and others) slightingly of Puckett's back-up work; that his timing was bad, that he would often throw the fiddler off; that it was difficult to play with him. Bert Layne, McMichen's brother-in-law and another fiddler who played frequently with Puckett, had no such recollections. And other musicians who either played with Riley or at least heard him offered no complaints. Doc Roberts, another outstanding old-time fiddler, reminiscing about Puckett, noted tersely, "And don't you think he couldn't follow a fiddle."[10] Perhaps all parties are correct. I have witnessed many disagreements in recent years, when bluegrass guitarists first began adopting the lead-guitar work of Doc Watson, Clarence White, and a few others, about the propriety of such a style for back-up. Surely when the rhythm is held by a solid bass fiddle, the guitarist can indulge in a little fancier picking than he should dare if he were providing the only rhythm foundation. Was the Skillet Licker's banjo, played by Tanner or Fate Norris—which everyone agrees was deliberately placed far from the microphone because it would otherwise drown everyone else out—providing a rhythm foundation? However one is inclined to respond to this disagreement, I think that the ultimate test of the effectiveness of Puckett's guitar back-up should be the recordings that he made. And the evidence, Stokes' and McMichen's complaints notwithstanding, is that both of them were able to produce some outstanding fiddling even with Puckett's unorthodox backup.

I have alluded to McMichen's comments on Puckett's character. He recalled that Riley was unreliable; that when they went out on recording or concert dates, he would always be off chasing some woman. Lowe Stokes recalled that Riley was "the crabbiest guy you ever saw." Asa Martin had quite a different opinion. He first met Riley while he was working on WHAS and Riley and Clayton were on WCKY, in Covington (probably in about 1934). They all had rooms in the same rooming house. Once in a while on a night when they weren't working Mac and the other boys would go out for a night on the town. But Riley, Asa recalled, was a good family man, and never went out. One morning, after Asa had heard Riley play "Alabama Girls" he said to him that he liked the runs Riley had put in it. After a moment's silence, Riley asked gruffly, "Well, what of it?" and was silent again for a while. Then he asked Asa what were the chords that Asa had used in "Tiptoe through the Tulips." They exchanged musical ideas; after that, Asa recalls, they were very good friends.

Whatever the inner tensions that beset the Skillet Lickers—and I have only touched on some of the problems here—to the fans, such difficulties must not have been apparent. The Skillet Lickers were one of the most popular of the bands of the late 1920s, and even McMichen acknowledged that Puckett was largely responsible for their popularity. Of course most fans were not enthused primarily by his guitar playing; it was his singing that won so many admirers. Puckett had a strong, clear, pleasant voice; he enunciated clearly and was easily understood. His range was about an octave and a half: from B below low C to G above middle C, though in falsetto (as in his yodeling) he could easily reach high C. He did not have a highly decorated style, as did his fellow North Georgians, John Carson or, to a lesser degree, Gid Tanner. Nor did he have the almost conversational presentation that Clarence Ashley or Dock Walsh could slip into. He did not sing nasally, nor did he have a pronounced accent. His voice was, though less mellow and more piercing, practically that of a pop singer of the day. And in that regard, it fit his repertoire. Of the slightly over 100 recordings he made by himself for Columbia, over half were pop songs from 1880 to 1920. Many of those were quite contemporary. The distribution of his nearly 100 recordings for RCA Bluebird in 1934–1941 is similar. On the other hand, there were some surprises in his repertoire. His version of "Casey Jones" was quite unusual, and not at all like the standard vaudeville version. But when I asked his widow what his favorite songs were, she mentioned "Let Me Call You Sweetheart," "Red Sails in the Sunset," and "If I Could Hear My Mother Pray Again," the first two pop hits of 1910 and 1935, respectively; the third, a not very old gospel song.

In the five years following his marriage to Blanche, Riley recorded extensively for Columbia. In September 1925, at Columbia's first out-of-town recording session, held in Atlanta, he recorded fourteen guitar/vocal solos. In April 1926, he and Tanner were joined by Clayton McMichen and Fate Norris and made their first recordings as the Skillet Lickers— eight selections were made and issued. At the same spring session, Puckett recorded eight solo numbers and four duets with McMichen, who was credited only on one of the labels, and that under the pseudonym of Bob Nichols. Two times each year thereafter, through 1931, Columbia sent a recording unit down to Atlanta and other southern cities to wax their ever-growing roster of blues, hillbilly, and jazz artists. In November 1926 the foursome, now well-known on disc as Gid Tanner and His Skillet Lickers, with Riley Puckett and Clayton McMichen, recorded ten more tunes. (McMichen's name was added after these November sessions as a consequence of his complaining that he was not getting deserved credit.) In addition, a new group consisting of McMichen, Puckett, and clarinetist

K. D. Malone recorded four songs as McMichen's Melody Men; Puckett recorded four solos, and Puckett and McMichen recorded four duets. Blues singer Virginia Childs was backed up for four tracks by Puckett (and possibly McMichen) at this session.

In March–April 1927, the Skillet Lickers recorded ten numbers; McMichen (as Bob Nichols) and Puckett recorded fourteen (joined by Bert Layne, fiddle, on a few); and Puckett recorded two guitar instrumental solos. Also at this time the whole gang—Tanner, McMichen, Puckett, Norris, and Layne—recorded the first of many extremely popular skits, "A Fiddlers' Convention in Georgia," issued in two parts. In October–November 1927, Puckett made six solo recordings, three duets with Bob Nichols (McMichen), eight tunes with the Skillet Lickers, eight with McMichen's Melody Men, and two duets with singer/guitarist Hugh Cross. The first two sides of the Corn Licker Still series were recorded on this trip. Issued in December 1927 (Columbia 15201-D), this disc sold just over a quarter-million copies—probably the best-selling item in the entire Columbia hillbilly 15000-D series.

In April of 1928, the Skillet Lickers recorded eight tunes, and in addition Puckett recorded six solos, five duets with McMichen/Nichols, four duets with Hugh Cross, two titles with McMichen's Melody Men, and six skits. In October were six more by the Skillet Lickers, four duets with Cross, five solos, four skits, four duets with McMichen, and eight numbers with a new recording group called The McMichen-Layne String Orchestra, probably consisting of Puckett, guitar; McMichen, Layne, and Stokes, fiddles (or viola); clarinet by either K. D. Malone or Bobby James; and an unidentified string bass. In addition, Puckett backed up the McCartt Brothers and Patterson for two selections (probably made in Johnson City, Tennessee, just before the trip to Atlanta). McMichen's Melody Men also recorded in these sessions, but Puckett was probably not with them at the time.

In April 1929, the Skillet Lickers recorded eight tunes and two skits, in addition to which Puckett made six solos, two duets with Hugh Cross, two numbers with Fate Norris and the Tanner Boys (Gid and Arthur), and two duets with Arthur Tanner, and backed up Oscar Ford. In the fall sessions for that year were the usual eight pieces by the Skillet Lickers and eight skits, five solos, a duet with fiddler Bill Helms, two duets with McMichen, and a duet with Colon "Red" Jones. Jones, who also recorded with Puckett in the 1930s on Decca, was a car driver for the Pucketts for several years. The son of a Baptist preacher, he came from Hazelhurst, and practically lived with the Pucketts from 1928 to about 1936.

McMichen's Melody Men recorded four pieces at this time, on which Riley may have been the guitarist.

In April 1930, the Skillet Lickers waxed another eight tunes and eight skits. Puckett also made six solos, two duets with McMichen, and two with Lowe Stokes. In December came another eight by the Skillet Lickers and six more skits, six solos, two duets with Stokes, a duet with McMichen. The final Columbia session was held in October 1931 and included six numbers by the Skillet Lickers, six duets with McMichen, two duets with Gid Tanner, four solos, and four songs with The Hometown Boys (Bill Helms, Puckett, and Gid Tanner).

Not long after the latter sessions, the Skillet Lickers broke up. There had been friction among the members almost from the beginning. McMichen always felt that while he did all the work (in particular, the lead fiddling), Tanner got all the credit. Furthermore, Mac was interested in playing more modern music than the old-time hoedown music of the Skillet Lickers, and regarded Tanner and Norris as a generation behind him; I have discussed these facets of McMichen's attitudes in an earlier *JEMFQ* article (see Ref. 7). Judging from clippings in McMichen's scrapbook in the 1931–1933 period, the name "Skillet Lickers" was used by various groups. In 1931 at WLW, a photo showing McMichen, Slim Bryant, Pat Perryman, and Johnny Barfield was labeled the Skillet Lickers. In October 1932 at WCKY the band seemed to consist of McMichen, Layne, Bryant, and Jack Donegan. But in December of that year, at the national old-time fiddling contest, a Skillet Lickers photo showed Layne, McMichen, Bryant, and Puckett. Meanwhile, McMichen began to use with increasing frequency the band name "The Georgia Wildcats"—a band of changing personnel that never, to my knowledge, included Riley Puckett.

Gid Tanner and Riley Puckett did not record again until March 1934; then a new "Gid Tanner and His Skillet Lickers," consisting of Gid and his young son, Gordon, on fiddles, Puckett on guitar, and Ted Hawkins on mandolin, recorded an extraordinarily long two-day session for RCA Victor in San Antonio, Texas. The foursome recorded, in various combinations, forty-eight sides, all of which were issued on the then-new Bluebird label. At this time were recorded what must surely have been the Skillet Lickers' best-selling titles: "Down Yonder," "Back Up and Push," "Soldier's Joy," and "Flop-Eared Mule." Gid Tanner never recorded again commercially, and the name the Skillet Lickers was retired with him.[11] Riley continued to record for RCA: six numbers in Atlanta in July 1934; ten in Atlanta in August 1934; ten in Charlotte, North Carolina, in

February 1936; twelve in Rockhill, South Carolina, in February 1939; twelve in Atlanta in August 1939; eight and six in February and October 1940, respectively, in Atlanta; and six in October 1941 in Atlanta. In addition, in about September of 1937, Puckett and Red Jones recorded a dozen pieces for Decca in New York City. The 1941 recordings in Atlanta were Puckett's last.

In addition to this heavy recording schedule, Puckett performed throughout the Southeast during the Depression years. Between 1934 and 1937, he played on radio stations in Covington, Kentucky, Huntington, West Virginia, Gary, Indiana, and Chicago, Illinois. He then returned to the Atlanta area. He was playing on a radio station with a group called The Stone Mountain Boys in Cedar, Georgia, in 1945 and 1946, when he took sick. A boil on his neck developed into a serious infection, but he refused to become concerned about it until it was too late. He developed blood poisoning and died at Gray Hospital, on July 13, 1946. He was buried on the 17th at the Enon Baptist Church in College Park, survived by his wife, daughter, and brother. Among the pall bearers were Gid and Gordon Tanner.

In 1958, Bob Hyland recalled, in a letter to John Edwards, his impressions on seeing Puckett and others in the early 1930s:

It was on a cold Sunday in Columbus, Ohio, back in the mid '30s at a huge auditorium. It was a big show with many fine groups and singers such as Arthur Smith, Paul Warmack and His Gully Jumpers, Uncle Dave Macon, Riley Puckett, Clayton McMichen's Georgia Wildcats. Mac and his Wildcats were at that time on the Grand Ole Opry from WSM in Nashville. Much to the surprise of many he introduced Riley and said that he was the man who on Columbia records for many years had brought into our homes via the phonograph many of the old tunes and ballads. He went on to say that when not playing as a lone troubadour he played with the Skillet Lickers, which "should have been Riley Puckett and His Skillet Lickers, but due to a hitch in the contract, Gid got the credit." He mentioned making many records with Riley and asked how many still had a record of them doing "Little Log Cabin in the Lane." A surprising number of hands went up from the audience and of course I held mine up high. He then announced that "they would do it together exactly as they did for Columbia records several years back." I can almost hear the cheers that went up from the packed house. When I returned home, I put the disc on to hear again, and even the tempo did not seem to vary in the least, from the performance that day. To have seen this blind singer seated there on his chair singing with Mac playing that wonderful fiddle accompaniment was something never to be forgotten and the disc will always serve to bring that performance to life once more, in sound at least. Riley also sang "Trouble in Mind" that day, a song which at that time was sweeping the country in folk music circles. Of course it was superb also.[12]

After his death, as in his life, Puckett remained an influential figure in the world of hillbilly music. His songs and style made an impact first among his fellow southern musicians, and in later decades among young northern revivalists who were just discovering the world of old-time hillbilly music. One can scarcely meet a southern musician who was alive during the 1930s who does not remember seeing Puckett or playing with him. Without a doubt, the image he presented to his fans was a one-sided one; yet those who knew him intimately were probably too entangled in his career to report objectively on his other facets. The music without the persona is an incomplete legacy; yet there are limits to how deeply the music historian can probe without violating his subject's rights of privacy.[13]

NOTES

1. The letters on file in the archives of the JEMF. Other sources in this paragraph are: John Edwards, "A Tribute to Riley Puckett," *Disc Collector,* no. 12 (ca. 1959): 8–9; and *Bert Layne and His Mountaineer Fiddlers with Riley Puckett and Richard Cox* (n.p., 1936?).

2. Norman Cohen, "The Skillet Lickers: A Study of a Hillbilly String Band and Its Repertoire," *Journal of American Folklore* 78 (July–September 1965): 229–244 (JEMF Reprint No. 5; also reprinted in Linnell Gentry, *A History and Encyclopedia of Country, Western, and Gospel Music,* 2nd ed. (Nashville, Tenn.: Claremont Corp., 1969), 234–254.

3. Information from Mrs. Blanche [Puckett] Bailey is taken from a personal interview by Donald Lee Nelson during the summer of 1974; my own telephone interview with her (August 3, 1974); and a letter from her to me dated July 16, 1974.

4. Puckett's years at the Macon Academy are not completely certain. Lee Jones, the school's superintendent, wrote me (January 25, 1965) that Puckett was mentioned in school reports as a student in 1901–1902, but the report did not state what class he was in. Since he was only seven then, it seems unlikely that he could have been enrolled more than a year or so before that. Blues historian Pete Lowry wrote me that when he inquired at the same school for information about McTell and Puckett six years later, he was told by the same Lee Jones (September 14, 1971) that they were unable to find any record of either of the two men in their files. McTell had told Alan Lomax that he had attended the school some time in the 1920s. See Lowry's article, "Blind Willie McTell," in *Blues Unlimited,* no. 89 (February–March 1972): 11–12.

5. Archie Green discusses in more detail the role of WSB in early country music history in his "Hillbilly Music: Source and Symbol," *Journal of American Folklore* 78 (July–September 1965): 204–228 (JEMF Reprint No. 4).

6. All references to comments by Lowe Stokes were taken from my interview with him at his home in Chouteau, Okla., on April 30, 1972.

7. More details are given in my article, "Clayton McMichen: His Life and Music," *JEMF Quarterly*, no. 39 (Autumn 1975): 117–124.

8. Interviews with Bill Bolick and Doc Hopkins were conducted at UCLA on March 16, 1965.

9. Sources for information in this paragraph: Frank Stanley to me, April 13, 1971, and July 26, 1971; interview in McMichen's home at Battletown, Ky., May 25, 1969; Bert Lane, telephone interview, October 27, 1974; Charlie and Obed Pickard Jr. interviewed by Anne Cohen at JEMF, UCLA, October 27, 1968; Asa Martin, interview at his home in Irvine, Ky., June 18, 1976.

10. Interview in his home in Richmond, Ky., May 26, 1969.

11. This may not be quite correct; an unidentified fiddler accompanied Puckett at his 1936 session in Charlotte, N.C., though I doubt that it was Tanner.

12. Letter to John Edwards, June 19, 1958.

13. Further information on Puckett and his musical companions can be found in the following sources—in addition to articles already cited above: "Clayton McMichen Talking," a transcription of an interview with Fred Hoeptner and Bob Pinson, in *Old Time Music,* nos. 1–4 (Summer 1971–Spring 1972); Stephen F. Davis, "Uncle Bert Layne," in *Devil's Box Newsletter,* no. 26 (September 1974): 19–27; "A Skillet Licker's Memoirs," by Bert Layne, as told to Margaret Riddle, *Old Time Music,* no. 14 (Autumn 1974): 5–9, and no. 14 (Winter 1974/75): 22–24. Six LP reissues devoted to the Skillet Lickers provide extensive annotations: County 506: *The Skillet Lickers;* County 526: *The Skillet Lickers,* vol. 2; Rounder 1005: *Gid Tanner and His Skillet Lickers;* GHP LP 902: *Riley Puckett;* Voyager VRLP 303: *A Corn Licker Still in Georgia;* Folk Song Society of Minnesota, FSSM LP l5OOl-D: *Gid Tanner and the Skillet Lickers.* (The last two are now out-of-print.) An abbreviated Riley Puckett discography on Columbia appeared with the article, "Riley Puckett—1894–1946: Country Music Pioneer," in *CMF Newsletter* (September 1970): 3–4. A complete discography of all sides recorded as by Gid Tanner and His Skillet Lickers was compiled by John Edwards and issued posthumously in *Quarter Notes: A Record Collector's Guide and Market Place,* 1:2 (Autumn 1962): 3–9.

Vocalion Records

Old Time Tunes

ELECTRICALLY RECORDED

Play on all Phonographs

THE BRUNSWICK-BALKE-COLLENDER CO.
Manufacturers—Established 1845
CHICAGO

·5199 - LAY MY HEAD BENEATH A ROSE
    SWEET ALLALEE
      Vocal - McFarland and Gardner

·5208 - I AM A MAN OF CONSTANT SORROW
    DOWN IN TENNESSEE VALLEY
      Vocal - Emry Arthur

·5222 - GWINE TO RAISE A RUCAS TONIGHT
    CHICKEN REEL
      Warren Caplinger's Entertainers

·5235 - LES BACKER'S YODELING BLUES
    DOWNHEARTED YODEL BLUES
      Vocal - Les Backer

·5231 - LITTLE BESSIE
    MY MOTHER
      Vocal - Buell Kazee

·5245 - NO NOT ONE
    WHY NOT TONIGHT
      Arthur's Sacred Singers

·5028 - HAND ME DOWN
    MY WALKING
    CANE
  I WAS BORN FOUR
    THOUSAND
    YEARS AGO
    McFarland and
    Gardner

·5124 - I WILL SING OF MY
    REDEEMER
  WHEN OUR LORD
    SHALL COME
    AGAIN
    McFarland and
    Gardner

·5125 - MIDNIGHT ON THE
    STORMY DEEP
  CARELESS LOVE
    McFarland and
    Gardner

·5120 - MY CAROLINA
    HOME
  OLD BLACK SHEEP
    McFarland and
    Gardner

Vocalion Records
Old Southern Tunes

ELECTRICALLY RECORDED
PLAY ON ALL PHONOGRAPHS

Anne Cohen and Norm Cohen

Folk and Hillbilly Music: Further Thoughts on Their Relations

Anyone who concerns himself seriously with the folk music of a society eventually comes to the questions of origins and dissemination. What is the source of the musical style? What factors loom large in the transmission of the music from one generation to the next? How do these questions relate to other parameters of the culture? The most successful attempts at dealing with such questions have been those framed in terms of an ideal "folk society" in the sense of one that is homogeneous, relatively isolated from outside influences, and stable. Although such descriptives may have been true of Appalachia a century or two ago, they have not been applicable since Reconstruction days. And the extent of inhomogeneity, instability, and cultural cross-influence has been increasingly marked since the early decades of this century. In the past few decades, students of Appalachian music have grappled with the problems of musical style and change in a context that admitted the borrowings from several other musical genres. In the attempt to evolve some meaningful statements it was found necessary to expand the older terminology that divided music into "folk," "popular," and "art." The term "hillbilly" music came into use in a well-defined academic context in the 1950s, although it had been used in an imprecise (though effective) manner in the popular press for some decades earlier.

Another term, "citybilly," first appeared in print in 1948 in Charles Seeger's first record review column in the *Journal of American Folklore*.[1]

Although no definition was given, the context of Seeger's discussion implied that he used the term to apply to folk music as performed by non-folk performers in nontraditional styles approaching those of the concert stage. Seeger's brief remarks indicated that he was groping for a convenient terminology to use in categorizing recordings for the benefit of his readers. His term is, in retrospect, a useful one, but it can be understood only in the light of a more precise definition of "hillbilly" music.

The "folk music revival" of the 1950s saw the birth of many short-lived periodicals dealing with various aspects of folk music; the most influential, and the only one to last into the present, was *Sing Out*. In early years, *Sing Out*'s editorial orientation was toward that music that was relevant to the urban experience. The music of rural America, while not ignored completely, was apparently of secondary interest. In this framework, "hillbilly" music was not necessarily seen as folk music—or even relevant to folk music. A short-lived periodical whose last editor tried to provide a different balance was *Caravan*. Begun in August 1957 by Lee Shaw, *Caravan* was a free mimeographed publication whose editor noted, in the inaugural issue, "material content will depend on the readers." In August 1958, as the format changed to a smaller size and offset printing, the magazine included an article by Roger Lass on bluegrass music, one of the first in a magazine directed toward the urban folk music audience. The February–March 1959 issue announced that Billy Faier had become editor; he held that position until the magazine's demise in July 1960, with the 20th issue. Under Faier's editorship, several articles focusing on hillbilly music were published: by Archie Green on "Will the Weaver" and on recorded hillbilly analogs of G. Malcolm Laws' syllabus on American balladry from British broadsides; by John Edwards on Buell Kazee and on the humorous skits such as the Cornlicker Still series recorded on the Columbia label during the 1930s; and by Joe Nicholas on Uncle Dave Macon.[2]

An expert banjo player with an ear for the traditional southern banjo styles, Faier was obviously aware of the differences between the various traditional styles, folk and hillbilly, as distinguished from the citybilly music that was then in such vogue. During a trip to Los Angeles in the spring of 1959, Faier met Fred Hoeptner, a devotee of many years of hillbilly, western, cowboy, jazz, and folk music. Both of them were performing on the Sunset Strip—Faier at a folk music club, The Unicorn, and Hoeptner down the street in a jazz band. Having learned something of Hoeptner's interests and views from Archie Green, Faier solicited from him an article for *Caravan* on the subject of folk and hillbilly music.

That article was soon submitted, and published in the 16th and 17th issues of *Caravan* titled "Folk and Hillbilly Music: The Background of Their Relation."[3] Our own choice of title is meant to indicate the importance we attach, eighteen years later, to his article.

In his article, Hoeptner sharply reprimanded both the revivalists and the folklorists for their inattention to hillbilly music, and for their failure to appreciate its impact on, and relation to, folk music. Noting that there was no convenient definition of "hillbilly music" in print, Hoeptner proposed his own: that style of music native to the culture of the common folk class of white people in the southeastern United States, played by stringed instruments, and relatively little influenced by musical developments occurring after 1941.[4] Hoeptner saw hillbilly music as one branch of "country" music—a field he divided into (a) hillbilly (including such artists as Flatt and Scruggs, Bill Monroe, Jimmie Osborne, and Roy Acuff); (b) western (Bob Wills, Tex Ritter, and Sons of the Pioneers) (c) modern country music; and (d) rockabilly (Elvis Presley, Carl Perkins). Contrasting hillbilly music with what was at the time being marketed as folk music (Charles Seeger's term "citybilly" applies to what Hoeptner was then describing as folk music), he noted, " 'hillbilly' records were performed by people in whose culture the material (i.e. songs) existed; whereas most 'folk' records are performed by urban folk singers who imitate folk style."[5]

Later, he stressed both the traditional folksinger's and the urban folksinger's dependence on hillbilly music by observing that "the urban folksinger is obtaining his style and material increasingly from hillbilly styles and developing on them, especially the instrumental style. Even the more authentic folk artist that is discovered in the field and recorded on a folk specialty label can hardly not have been influenced, at least some, by hillbilly music."[6]

Here we are not concerned with the issue of the influence of hillbilly styles on citybilly styles, though it is an important development that deserves attention. (The obvious influence of the Carter Family on citybilly singers and guitarists is perhaps but the tip of an immense iceberg that floats uncharted on a sea of cross-cultural influences.) But we do wish to probe further the relationship between hillbilly music and the noncommercial folk music whence it sprang.

Some of the questions we are concerned with are: (a) Is it most useful to regard hillbilly music as belonging to a specific time period, as Hoeptner did, or will our discussion be more instructive within another framework? (b) If we choose another framework, then within its terms, what are the differences between hillbilly and folk music? Are they parallel developments, or sequential—or is one a subclass of the other? What are the factors responsible for the differences between them?

Shortly after Hoeptner's provocative article appeared, D. K. Wilgus's doctoral dissertation was published: *Anglo-American Folksong Scholarship Since 1898.*[7] Perhaps not many who read Hoeptner's article were also moved to read Wilgus's masterful treatise on a half-century of American scholarship in the field of folk music. (The title notwithstanding, Wilgus's survey was not confined to Anglo-American material, nor to "songs" to the exclusion of other types of folk music.) In scattered passages, Wilgus touched upon hillbilly music and its relationship to traditional folksongs and to the collection of the academic fieldworkers.[8] Wilgus offered a definition of "hillbilly" that put the relationship between hillbilly and folk music in clearer perspective than did Hoeptner's:

> hillbilly. 1. Of or pertaining to commercialized folk or folkish songs (or the performers thereof) largely derived from or aimed at white folk culture of the southern United States, beginning in 1923. 2. Of or pertaining to that style—a blend of Anglo-Irish-Negro folksong and American popular song—on which the commercial tradition was based and developed.[9]

With the benefit of nearly two decades of scholarship on hillbilly music's backgrounds and development behind us, we can see the advantages of Wilgus's definition over Hoeptner's. From Hoeptner's approach we see clearly that he has a particular musical style in mind—as shown by his cut-off date just prior to the social and economic upheavals initiated by the Depression and amplified by the Second World War.[10]

Wilgus avoids any specific stylistic characterization, suggesting that hillbilly music can, and does, continue to undergo change under the impact of a variety of musical influences. In his first definition he provides a beginning date which implies that records played a dominant role in this new development. His second definition, however, can be applied to the pre-1923 commercial media that held a similar relationship to the folk culture as did recordings—that is, fiddlers' contests and conventions, tent and medicine shows, radio, and other forms of live entertainment.[11] We consider that the medium of phonograph recordings was both qualitatively and quantitatively different from these earlier manifestations—a point we shall elaborate later—and affected both repertoire and performance in a manner that the previous commercial media did not. Thus we prefer to reserve the term "hillbilly" for the postphonograph period, and regard hillbilly music as having started in 1922–1923 with the first commercial recordings of traditional southern performers.

If we can agree, then, that hillbilly music is accurately characterized (whether de jure or de facto) by commercial recordings following 1923, let us consider for a moment the noncommercial folk music that we recognize as the principal well-spring for hillbilly music. Early folksong collectors began to canvass the rural South around the turn of the century looking for what they regarded as the dying remnants of the old Anglo-American culture. They found it in abundance. And, as with the moribund heroines of opera, the dying notes have lingered on far beyond anyone's expectations. The great English folk music collector, Cecil Sharp, advised by an American correspondent of the musical fruits that were ripe for picking, spent forty-six weeks in the mountains between 1916 and 1918 and noted down over 1,600 different versions of some 500 songs. Sharp found very little instrumental music—a few jigs played on fiddle—and only one instance of singing with instrumental accompaniment.[12] And yet, a scant decade later (and only five years after the first commercial recordings of traditional southern folksingers and musicians), there was a thriving commerce in "hillbilly" music. By then, 1927, close to two thousand 78-rpm records were available in stores throughout the South featuring hundreds of guitarists, fiddlers, banjo players, and stringbands. Where were the headwaters of this gushing torrent, if early explorers like Sharp had found such a desert landscape, instrumentally speaking?

While a few folksong collectors in the 1920s had been aware of these commercial recordings and even cited and transcribed them on occasion, the scholarly community for the most part regarded commercial products as antithetical to its notions of folk culture. Hoeptner, Wilgus, Archie Green, and a few other writers, had posted their indictments, which need no reiteration here. And following their lead, in the early 1960s a growing recognition of the importance and significance of hillbilly music could be detected in both the fan-oriented journals and the academic publications. Soon it had come to be the accepted position that the early hillbilly recording artists were folksingers and folk musicians pure and simple, and that the talent scouts of the record companies who found and recorded them were next of kin to the academic folksong collectors who had scoured the same hills before them.

Yet, while we are basically in accord with this more modern view of the role of hillbilly music, it is somewhat misleading. If the mere fact of commercialism is of such an incidental nature, how can one account for the rapid changes in commercially recorded "hillbilly" music between the 1920s and the 1970s, while collectors can still go into the hills of North Carolina, West Virginia, and elsewhere, and record instrumental styles and songs scarcely different from those of a half century ago? And, even more pointed a question: why is it that the academic collections of the 1920s reveal so different a repertoire from that recorded by the A&R men of the same period?

There are several answers to this latter question, one of which parallels the answer to the query why Sharp found no instrumental music. In the first place, it is often the case that performers respond to what is requested of them. Folksong collectors, basically antique hunters, have their antennae tuned for the old and arcane. Sharp was not interested in instrumental music; he did not search for it; and it was not offered to him.

But, in a sense, this can be only part of the truth. For example, collectors (or A&R men) don't necessarily request individual ballads or songs; more likely they request, or hint at, broad areas of material. Here, then, may lay the key. Perhaps the reason Sharp collected no instrumental music was that he was not present at, or was not interested in, those occasions on which instrumental music is played: at dances, parties, and public assemblies of various sorts. He visited individuals in their homes and got the kind of music that was usually performed by individuals in their homes: ballads, lullabies, children's songs, etc.—that body of music D. K. Wilgus has labeled the "domestic tradition."

We would like to suggest the term "assembly tradition" for that realm of music, generally different in style and repertoire from the domestic tradition, and usually having an instrumental component, which was performed at public gatherings.[13] The assembly tradition is the music that functions in the context of a much expanded audience: local dances, parties, cornhuskings, land sales, weddings, medicine shows, fiddle conventions and contests, political rallies, street singing, church music, and even professional concerts, such as those presented by groups like the Carter Family or the North Carolina Ramblers long before they began making records. In a sense, this public component was the "hillbilly" tradition long before the advent of hillbilly phonograph records.

When a folksong collector such as Sharp visited the mountain folk, he made it clear that he was interested in the material of the domestic tradition, and this is what he got. When the early contacts were established between singers and musicians and the representatives of the commercial phonograph industry, there could have been little if any doubt in the minds of the performers that this was public entertainment, and that the assembly tradition was what was expected and what was appropriate under the circumstances.

Assembly music was much more responsive to contemporary popular musical developments than was the domestic tradition. The domestic was largely the older component, the material learned orally in the folksinger's youth without thought of commercial value or current vogue. It was so much a part of the individual's private cultural heritage that it was probably inconceivable to many would-be entertainers that it had commercial value—any more than a contemporary urban singer would offer up a lullaby or jump-rope rhyme or ditty such as "Happy Birthday." By contrast, the assembly music was greatly affected by then-current musical idioms that were enjoying national prominence, such as jazz, pop, blues, and ragtime.

When the more ambitious musicians began to make commercial records in the 1920s, they found themselves confronted by a new circumstance. A customer could purchase a single disc and hear its contents again and again. If another record was to be sold, a new song would have to be recorded. Thus the mere fact of recordings forced the previously slow rate of musical change to accelerate markedly. The record company scouts and executives, operating under the ethic of a northern industrial culture, encouraged novelty and change (though not so much as to threaten the survival of the entire musical idiom).

This character of phonograph records is the justification for our earlier categorization of recordings as qualitatively different from the commercial media that preceded 1923. A singer or band could sing the same dozen songs on a tour of personal appearances that led to a different town in the Southeast each weekend of the year; but as soon as a performer decided to become a recording artist, he had to expand his repertoire. The difference may also be quantitative, because recordings, sold by mail order through Sears, Wards, and other catalog houses, could blanket the South more effectively than any network of personal appearances could have done.

But old music survived even as the new was created. Those men and women who chose to make their livings by their music were required to create and/or learn new material. But their roots in traditional culture were deep enough to ensure that the new hillbilly songs were still folk-like in quality. Gradually, the new music drew less and less on the folk tradition, although it fashioned new pieces in the contours of the old. These new pieces were often learned by noncommercial, nonprofessional singers and musicians, and accepted into their repertoires. So where we had folksongs that became hillbilly songs, now we had hillbilly songs that became folksongs. Now a different problem poses itself. If we have acknowledged the qualitative change in hillbilly recordings between 1923 and a decade or two later, and if we agree that hillbilly music had a measurable impact on the folk culture, then how do we account for the fact that the published field collections show such slight historical trends as far as changing styles and contents go?

The answer must lie, again, in the interests of the collectors—the predilection for older material already noted above and discussed at length elsewhere.[14] We have argued, then, that the academic collectors and the A&R men of the early hillbilly recording industry were collecting at opposite ends of the total spectrum of southern mountain folk music. Is there some collection that is a representative sampling of the assembly tradition at some given point in history? We think that hillbilly recordings made by the earlier recording artists in the first year or so of the industry, before their repertoires were likely to be affected by the industry itself, would be a good indicator of the assembly tradition at that time. This approach in turn raises the question whether the early A&R men were selective in the material they recorded. Since most accounts would lead us to believe that initially the artists could record whatever they wished, we think we can neglect this possible source of bias, particularly if we include in our survey songs recorded but not released.

Accordingly, we have tallied about 280 selections made in the first years of hillbilly recordings—1922 through the end of 1924. Eighteen artists are involved: Samantha Bumgarner and Eva Davis; Fiddlin' John Carson, A. A. Gray, Bascom Lamar Lunsford, Uncle Dave Macon, David Miller, Charles Nabell, Land Norris, Fiddlin' Powers and Family, Riley Puckett, George Reneau, Eck Robertson, Connie Sides, Roba Stanley, Ernest V. Stoneman, Gid Tanner, Ernest Thompson, and Henry Whitter.[15] Of these 280 pieces, the origins of about 30 are indeterminate to us at present. The remainder can be classified as follows:

British origin (pre-1800)	2%
Native American origin	
Tin Pan Alley origin, 1860–1900	26%
Tin Pan Alley origin, after 1900	6%
Folk (or early minstrel) origin pre-1900	59%
Folk origin, after 1900	7%

One hesitates to place too much confidence on statistics based on such a small sampling, but it is nevertheless startling to find that a scant 2 percent of the items are of British origin, and that practically one-third are of Tin Pan Alley origin. Most academic field collections yield practically the reverse distribution.[16]

If one were to analyze the contents of hillbilly recordings after 1924, one would find an even smaller fraction of pieces that are of British origin, and probably slowly diminishing figures in the other categories, as the fraction of new hillbilly songs, composed by the artists or by other contemporary songwriters such as Bob Miller, Carson Robison, and Andrew Jenkins, rose in proportion.

One possible objection to using this group of 1922–1924 recordings as a basis for drawing conclusions about the assembly tradition before ca. 1920 is that many of these artists were already professional before they started making records. Perhaps their repertoires were not representative of nonprofessional singers and instrumentalists? Wouldn't it be better to look at the recordings of those artists who, to the best of our knowledge, were never professional, but simply made a few recordings for the novelty of it and then disappeared from the scene? Unfortunately, while there were many such persons during the 1920s and 1930s, they did not abound in the first few years that are under discussion. The industry turned to names that were well known locally for their first recording artists. But we still think we can make do with what we have. We doubt that there is a great difference between the repertoires of the professional and the nonprofessional performers of the period. People who are interested in songs—whether for commercial reasons or not—will learn a lot of them, both old and new. Hillbilly artists with large recorded repertoires—such as Riley Puckett, Uncle Dave Macon, Charlie Poole, Asa Martin, and Ernest V. Stoneman—did not sing new songs to the exclusion of the old by any means.

As the hillbilly phonograph industry took shape and grew, it quickly expanded beyond the confines of a public folk tradition and took on the character of a commercial folk-derived tradition. Rapid growth necessitated an expanding repertoire, which led to the composition of new pieces. Many of these new pieces later entered folk tradition (principally the assembly, but occasionally the domestic tradition as well), but not to the extent that older songs and styles were driven out. The relatively slight impact on the domestic tradition meant that most folksong collectors did not find great changes in the repertoires that they sampled. But the assembly tradition changed considerably, though by no means as much or as fast as hillbilly music itself did. In the years after the First World War, elements outside the southeastern Anglo-American folk tradition played an increasing role in hillbilly music, to the point where many Southeasterners became quite conscious of the gap between contemporary country-western music and the then-current assembly tradition — which now was often called hillbilly music; hence the chronological cut-off in Hoeptner's definition.

We have contrasted the content of the field recordings of Cecil Sharp in 1916–1918 with the early commercial hillbilly recordings of 1923–1925, Of course, there were more inclusive field collections, at least by the 1920s. Early folklorists who were more catholic in their collecting habits were Robert W. Gordon, Frank C. Brown, and John Lomax (later joined by his son, Alan). All of these men were already making cylinder recordings in the field prior to 1920. [Editor's note: while John Lomax made cylinder records prior to 1920, it is doubtful that they were made in the field.] It strikes us as no coincidence that the collectors who had the best luck at sampling the assembly tradition were those who used recording equipment; the likelihood of a collector hand-transcribing the singing and playing of a stringband, for example, seems small. Whether it was the availability of recording equipment that incited these collectors to sample the assembly tradition, or, conversely, the prior recognition of the existence and importance of such a tradition that made them realize the necessity of field recordings, we do not know. But we feel there is a correlation. It further strikes us as interesting that Gordon and Brown did not publish much of their own collections (Brown's collection was edited for publication after his death). Can it be that these scholars felt the inadequacy of the printed page in capturing the essence of folk music? In this connection it should also be noted that Alan Lomax has been a pioneer in the publication of recordings, as opposed to printings, of folk music.

Our main conclusions then are: that it is useful to regard Anglo-American folk music before the advent of the phonograph record as having had two components — a private ("domestic") tradition and a public ("assembly") tradition. The latter layer spanned a continuum that ranged from public but noncommercial (and nonprofessional) to commercial/professional.[17] Folksong collectors sought in particular the domestic tradition, but often got some of the other as well. In truth, the two traditions no doubt shaded into one another. Commercial A&R men unwittingly drew upon the assembly tradition almost exclusively. Thus we can say that the early phonograph industry did indeed document folk music traditions of the southern mountains in the early 1920s, even though the styles and repertoires so recorded vary considerably from the academic collections of the same period. Taken together, the academic and commercial collections provide us with perhaps our closest approximation to the total range of southeastern folk music of the 1920s.

NOTES

1. Charles Seeger, "Reviews," *Journal of American Folklore* 61 (1948): 215.

2. See the following articles in *Caravan:* "A Discographical Appraisal," 15 (February–March 1959): 7–13; "Buell Kazee: A Biographical Note," 17 (June–July 1959): 42–43; "Buell Kazee: A Discography of his Early Recorded Work," 17 (June–July 1959): 44–45; "The Grand-Daddy of American Country Music," 18 (August–September 1959): 36; "Macon Discography," 18, 38–43; "Will the Weaver's Hillbilly Kinfolk," 18 (August–September 1959): 11, 14–23; "A Discography of Columbia Rural Drama Records," 19 (January 1960): 36–37, 41.

3. The article appeared in two parts: In *Caravan* 16 (April–May 1959): 8, 16, 17, 42; and 17 (June–July 1959): 20–23, 26–28. The two parts were reprinted together in *Pictorial History of Country Music,* vol. 2, edited by Thurston Moore (Denver, Colo.: Heather Enterprises, 1969): 18–23. This volume also was published as a section of the 1966 edition of *Country Music Who's Who.* Successive footnotes refer to the pagination of the original *Caravan* articles.

4. Part I, p. 16. In a footnote, Hoeptner noted that the harmonica and kazoo were the only nonstringed instruments in stringbands.

5. Part I, p. 17.

6. Part II, p. 28.

7. D. K. Wilgus, *Anglo-American Folksong Scholarship Since 1898* (New Brunswick, N.J.: Rutgers University Press, 1959).

8. Probably not many readers of *Anglo-American Folksong Scholarship Since 1898* knew that its erudite author was also "the perfesser" who reviewed hillbilly recordings in *Disc Collector.*

9. Wilgus, 433.

10. In retrospect, however, one might argue that his inclusion of Bill Monroe and Flatt and Scruggs in the hillbilly category signaled his intention to include early bluegrass music in general; however, the style generally recognized as "bluegrass" did not emerge until the 1940s.

11. That is, the performers were professionals and semiprofessionals whose music was derived from, and was addressed to, that culture.

12. Cecil J. Sharp, *English Folk Songs from the Southern Appalachians,* edited by Maude Karpeles (London: Oxford University Press, 1932, 1960), p. xxvii.

13. In his record reviews for *Journal of American Folklore,* D. K. Wilgus used the terms "domestic" and "frolic" traditions to designate these two components of American folk music. Recently, Richard K. Spottswood, in an album he edited for the Library of Congress (Folk Music in America, vol. 14: *Solo and Display*

Music, announced but not available as of this writing) used the title "display music" in approximately the same sense that we use "assembly tradition."

14. This issue was discussed in some detail in Norm Cohen's "Tin Pan Alley's Contribution to Folk Music," *Western Folklore* 29 (1970): 9–20.

15. A few other artists from this early period are, for one reason or another, omitted from this tally. Their omission does not change the numbers significantly. Of the artists included in this survey, three are of particular interest because their own recorded repertoires (up through 1924) were much more heavily weighted in favor of Tin Pan Alley songs than the average figures given in the text. They are Riley Puckett (50 percent), Ernest Thompson (55 percent), and Connie Sides (100 percent).

16. Two large collections that indicate rather catholic interests on the parts of the collectors are Vance Randolph's *Ozark Folksongs* (Columbia, Mo.: 1946–1950) and the *Frank C. Brown Collection of North Carolina Folklore* (Durham, N.C.: 1952). These are, respectively, 18 and 15 percent of British origin, and, respectively, 3–4 percent and 4–9 percent of 19th-century Tin Pan Alley origin (the spread in figures represents the uncertain origins of some pieces). The Western Kentucky Folklore Archive, an unpublished collection that seems to be very unselective, is about 9 percent of British origin and about 11–17 percent of Tin Pan Alley origin. Most published collections contain far fewer Tin Pan Alley songs and far more British titles than this archive does.

17. By "commercial" music is meant music performed in the context of a paying audience; by "professional" musician is meant one who receives payment for his services. These two need not necessarily go hand in hand; for example, a folk musicologist could obtain field recordings from a folksinger without compensating him, and then release the recordings commercially. "Semiprofessional" is a useful term to apply to performers who play for pay, but make their livings principally by other means.

Archie Green

Commercial Music Graphics #44: John Held Jr.: Jazz Age and Gilded Age

"Jazz Age," the term, implies a given musical form but essentially it marks a particular time period: 1918–1929. We Americans have frequently segmented our history by special nomenclature—Jacksonian Era, New Deal, Age of Reform, Gilded Age, Gay Nineties, Mauve Decade. When we date the Jazz Age to the time between the close of World War I and the catastrophic October crash which opened the Great Depression, we suggest not only the passage of years, but also an exotic flavor, a syncopated beat in these brief years. The parallel term "Roaring Twenties" has been used to designate our gaudy national spree and its large quest for open excitement. Jazz-fresh, buoyant, daring—became the perfect aural marker for this public high.

Jazz of the 1920s, of course, still echoes on numerous reissued LPs edited from 78-rpm discs of the period. However, the Jazz Age as a state-of-mind can best be recalled by naming a set of nonmusical personalities—F. Scott Fitzgerald, Clara Bow, Rudolph Valentino, Al Capone, Babe Ruth, Lucky Lindy, Will Rogers—all representative of some highly visible aspect of American life. This decade also was fixed in imagination by fiction, sports, drama, film, and graphic art, which projected into popular consciousness a set of stock figures, among them the flapper, the collegiate sheik, the gangster, the worldly newspaperman, and the joiner (Babbitt). An important documentarian in art of some of these figures was John Held Jr. Not only did he bring sheiks and shebas into sharp focus, but in cartoons for *Life, Judge, College Humor,* and other magazines, he gave youngsters new codes to emulate.

Recent critics have noted correctly Held's prime role as Jazz Age delineator. Richard Merkin, of the Rhode Island School of Design, likens him to artist Charles Dana Gibson (1867–1944), who created the Gibson Girl in the 1890s. Held, in observing the flapper and teaching her tricks, "set the style for the era: clothing, coiffure, manners, figures of speech, and most important of all, a youthful, exuberant, and all-encompassing impudence." Held's razor-thin girls, in bobbed hair and scanty dresses, determined beauty pageant standards not abandoned until the 1930s. Similarly, his saxophone-tooting, gin-guzzling college boys were found on campus until youth's values were altered in the New Deal period.

My initial attention in this series was directed to commercial art used by the sound recording industry when announcing its discovery of old-time and mountain music. As the series grew, I broadened it to include related musical expression, as well as many artists not connected in any way with phonograph records. My main area for exploration presently is the interaction of art (formal, academic, popular, commercial, untutored, idiosyncratic) with folk and folk-like music. I am especially concerned with those artists who have pioneered in the depiction of folk music or have added fresh vision to our understanding of its social role.

Some students of American music link jazz, blues, and folk forms into an integrated and continuous whole, while others place jazz and folk in discrete bins. We know that jazz developed, in this century, from a traditional base to a contemporary experimental configuration, and moved from being an exclusive Afro-American folk creation to a worldwide music. Desirous of charting artistic response to these changes, I devoted a recent feature to Miguel Covarrubias, selecting for explication some of his Harlem drawings of Negro performers and audiences from the mid-twenties. This close look led me to John Held Jr., for his very name has always been tied to jazz. Although Held and Covarrubias worked for many of the same magazines in Manhattan and often heard the same musicians, they were artistic ages apart in what each offered.

To my surprise, in a search of Held's art I found no Negro musicians in any of the lowlife settings where jazz was born. Instead, his musicians were all white, young, collegiate, and often engaged in activity to which music seemed auxiliary. Two of these Jazz Age drawings are reproduced here from *Held's Angels* (1952) in which Held and Frank B. Gilbreth Jr. looked back at collegiate life of the 1920s. For this book, Held selected more than 150 illustrations, ranging from single-figure line drawings to two-page spreads teeming with football fans or party goers. Although these are printed in black and white, some were originally rendered in pastels or watercolors, and published as *Life* covers. (This reference is to the humor magazine, 1883–1936, which preceded the photojournal.)

All the art in *Held's Angels* depicts the Roaring Twenties, but no drawing is dated individually, either by actual time of composition or by previous publication. A few of the cartoons retain their original captions or other internal signs, such as "The Spirit of St. Louis" on a flivver. These captions and signs together, however, help stamp the Jazz Age upon *Held's Angels* technically removed in publication by decades from the 1920s.

Held's cartoons of fraternity and sorority revelers are much more important today as period pieces, and as wry anatomical studies than as exact musical portraiture. Richard Merkin has identified "The Dance-Mad Younger Set" (p. 172), first published in 1927 as a *Life* cover, as the quintessential Jazz Age drawing. Yet, within it no one dances to music, and a four-man band (sax, ukulele, drums, piano), relegated to the room's margins, is curiously passive. If this is a milestone of the Roaring Twenties, it suggests that the "roar" was nonmusical, and that collegiate combos played more pallid sideline music than hot jazz. Central in Held's drawing, however, is a guiding notion of sin, of unashamed necking on the stairway. In a metaphoric sense, the term "Jazz Age" as applied to Held's art slips away from rhythmic or improvised musical expression to hedonistic conduct, to the breaking of puritanical codes, and to the public display of sensuality.

No museum catalog or art book is known to me which brings together the full range of American jazz depiction—performers, whether downhome creators or Gershwin-like interpreters; setting, as far apart as juke joint, speakeasy, concert hall, or festival circuit. When such a compilation is gathered, without question, John Held Jr. will hold a significant and honored position, not because he translated pulsating sound into visual art, but because his cool pen helped extend the word "jazz" to cover a turbulent decade in national life.

In this connection, we note the phrase "danced the jazz" spoken on an Uncle Josh recording in 1909, and "jazz," the word for an energetic music, first printed in the *San Francisco Bulletin* in 1913. Scott Fitzgerald's *This Side of Paradise* (1920) told postwar collegians that they belonged to a special generation, soon named "lost" by Gertrude Stein. Fitzgerald himself labeled youth, mood, and era in *Tales of the Jazz Age* (1922). Obviously, a musical form—long in birth in Afro-American folk

society—was not named on one baptismal day, by one song, or by one set of doting parents.

Corey Ford, editor of Columbia University's *Jester* in 1921 and a humor writer of considerable talent for the full decade, has paid warm personal tribute to Held as a shaper of mores for Ford's generation:

> Fitzgerald christened . . . the Jazz Age, but John Held Jr. set its style and manners. His angular and scantily clad flapper was accepted by scandalized elders as the prototype of modern youth, the symbol of our moral revolution. Frankly I had never seen anything remotely resembling that fan-

tastic female until Held's derisive pen portrayed her. My guess is that she sprang full-blown from his imagination: flat-chested, long spidery legs ending in stubby feet like hooves, her brief skirt riding high to reveal the rolled top of a stocking and a glimpse of flesh, cloche hat on close-bobbed hair, a precise dot of rouge below each cheekbone and a matching crimson mouth. *Betty Co-Ed has lips of red for Hah-vud.*

We took his exaggerated cartoon types to heart and patterned ourselves on them. Each new Held drawing was pored over like a Paris fashion plate, girls cropped their hair and rouged their cheeks and shortened their skirts to be in style, galoshes and raccoon coats were indispensable to every male undergraduate wardrobe. So sedulously did we ape his caricatures that they lost their satiric point and came to be a documentary record of our times.

Nearly all present-day commentators relate Held only to the Jazz Age, but his reflections upon music were sharply divided into two distinct time periods, each demanding a different style within his art. The flaming youth of the 1920s called mainly for pen and ink line drawings. By contrast, the heroes and heroines in Held's Gilded Age art, as well as in the folksong books he illustrated, called for linoleum blockprints or pen

drawings on scratchboard resembling "early" woodcuts. This use of an antique or pseudo-woodcut style was deliberately pegged to subject matter, but also was functional in New York's competitive art world of the 1920s. Held's style for flappers had been fixed in the public eye by his magazine work early in the decade. When his friend Harold Ross asked him to contribute to the "infant" *New Yorker* during 1925, Held turned to a sharply different melodramatic style combining satire and nostalgia. Frequently in this "old" work he identified himself, tongue-in-cheek, as "A sentimental Engraver" or "Engraved by John Held Jr. adelving into yesteryear."

Two "yesteryear" items are reproduced here which comment on music and drama. The contrast between these and the jazz items listed is strong. If Held reduced his flappers to silhouetted abstractions, he drew their grandmothers as buxom, bustled, and waspwaisted heroines. This contrast literally was one of garb—brief underwear versus heavy corset, but, of course, Held was concerned with sensibilities far beyond dress. In the 1920s, he was an active shaper of then-current strands of humor, but when he looked back to the close of the nineteenth century, he was not a direct participant. In his retrospective vision, Held sought absurd and pathetic situations, and presented them as a parodist. We can assert that Held was a superb caricaturist in all that he undertook, but that he cloaked himself in separate mantles as he shuttled between two eras. Our appre-

"There ARE SONGS THAT MAKE YOU HAPPY

There ARE SONGS THAT MAKE YOU SAD"

ciation of his skill is enhanced when we know that he was a prodigious worker, who completed illustrations simultaneously in both styles to meet the demands of rival editors.

A word on the usage, "Gilded Age," is necessary at this juncture because it has not been applied previously to Held's "woodcuts." Mark Twain's first novel, *The Gilded Age* (1873), was a portrait of bloated and vulgar life after the Civil War in Washington. Twain lampooned opulent tycoons and free-spending politicians alike; his title entered common speech to describe the last three decades of the nineteenth century. If we date the Gilded Age to the years 1876–1900, we suggest that it opened with the Philadelphia's Centennial Exposition's stress on technological progress. Also, these years included two specialized segments, the Mauve Decade and the Gay Nineties. We know that life was then infrequently cheerful for blacks and immigrants new to urban, industrial life; yet for many Americans this quarter century was truly abundant and expansive. New national magazines as diverse as *Popular Science* (1872), *Scribner's* (1887), and *Vogue* (1892), in colorful pictures and prose, proclaimed that convenience and elegance were at hand. President Cleveland, at the White House in 1893, by electric wire turned on all the white lights at Chicago's Columbian Exposition—some to light halls of glistening machinery, and some to light Little Egypt's belly-dancing "tent."

Although Held's burlesques in woodcut style are black and white, I believe that they reflect the gilt seen by Mark Twain as well as the lights turned on by Grover Cleveland. For those of Held's contemporaries to whom the decade of the 1920s was too disruptive (modern, fast, immoral), the near past in the Gilded Age seemed properly bright. There is no evidence that John Held Jr. was ever mired in personal nostalgia for the close of the last century, nor that he rejected that special period with radical social criticism. His engravings were formal, structured, explicable, and obviously comic, yet they were not acid in the tradition of Daumier, Hogarth, or Posada. Instead, Held's depiction of sin, drink, and poverty dissolved tragedy into bathos. Essentially, he mocked the festive Gilded Age and its Victorian morality to which many Americans attempted to "return" after World War I, when they could not accept the turbulence of the 1920s.

Because Held is valued today largely for his Jazz Age signposts, we know more about the evolution of his pen and ink style for vamps and parlor snakes than about the origin of the woodcut style for his early belles and beaux. I have been especially curious about Held's gilded people, for within the span of attention to their lives, he illustrated a series of folksong books. To place these contrastive styles and themes into a time frame, I note a few facts about the artist's life.

Born in Salt Lake City on January 10, 1889, Held received some formal art training from sculptor Mahonri Young, but also trained himself pragmatically as a sports cartoonist on the *Salt Lake City Tribune.* Still in his teens, Held sold his first work to *Life* (1904), and, like countless other creative youngsters, he journeyed to New York (1910) for both freelance and ad-agency work. His flappers emerged gradually in the pages of *Vanity Fair,* and sister journals, after he was home from war service (1918). Held is often credited with "creating" the flapper, but he did not invent the word; it had been used in Northumbrian colloquial speech during the 1880s to describe young women who were unsteady, lacking in decorum, or indulging in vice. Carried to America, this pejorative term was made to order for the new Everywoman.

While Anita Loos asserted in the novel of that title that *Gentlemen Prefer Blondes,* and red-head Clara Bow flounced on screen, Held also pictured his liberated flappers in provocative or foolish circumstances. Blonde, or otherwise, in her revealing skirts and swinging beads, she was compellingly vital in all her actions. Frequently, Held's cartoons used caption puns—word inversions which caught both the naivete and sophistication of his lads and lasses. Typical is his *Life* cover in watercolor, "The Faded Blonde" (August 11, 1927), in which a winning flapper on her knees is rolling dice. The word-play caption, of course, comments on girl and game alike.

In summary, when Held is tied to the Jazz Age, we imply neither delineation of black musicians, downhome or uptown, nor even music in the hands of a Paul Whiteman or Bix Beiderbecke. Rather, we mean jazzy youth in caricatures which evolved early in the 1920s. The chronology for Held's Gilded Age art (also labeled "yesteryear," "pseudo-woodcut," "Gay Nineties") extends over a much longer time span than a decade. Richard Merkin has suggested that Held, early in 1925, had "concocted a melodramatic woodcut style" for Harold Ross at the *New Yorker's* inception, because the editor was apprehensive about repeating the already well-known flapper profile from established magazines. I believe this explanation is too compressed to be entirely accurate.

Ross and Held had been friends since school days in Salt Lake City, where both were cubs on the high school paper. While on *Stars and Stripes* in Paris, Ross began to dream of an innovative magazine, at once irreverent, elegant, and critical. Before he could actually launch the *New Yorker,* he edited in the early 1920s the prosaic *American Legion Weekly,* for which occasionally, to entertain the veterans, he purchased a Held cover drawing of flappers. Ross was eager to use Held in his new magazine (first issue: February 21, 1925), but in no position to generate immediately within his friend's mind a wholly new style nor an inclusive grasp of the ethos of a bygone era.

In its natal year of 52 issues, the *New Yorker* featured 24 of Held's contributions, the first of which was "The Rumrunner's Sister-In-Law" on April 11. However, the earliest dated example of this type, known to me, is "The Shot-Gun Wedding," which appeared on May 30 with the date of composition, 1923, blocked out. Subsequently, in *The Works of John Held Jr.* this cartoon was republished with its original internal date retained. A close examination of Held's two dozen cuts for the *New Yorker*'s first year indicates that he had thought about his Gilded Age subjects and had completed several prints long before Harold Ross gave him an open platform.

My assumption of the gradual development of Held's "yesterycar" style is confirmed by Carl J. Weinhardt Jr., of the Indianapolis Museum of Art, in *The Most of John Held Jr.* (1972). Weinhardt carefully traced Held's Gay Nineties art to the influence of his father, a skilled printing tradesman and copperplate engraver as well as a cornetist and leader of a brass band. Hence, musical performance and woodcut technique were part of John's childhood learning experience. During his apprenticeship on the *Salt Lake City Tribune* young Held experimented with satiric linoleum blockprint cartoons of lowlife in the city. His uncle Pierre, also a skilled mechanic and pioneer electrician, specialized in "doctoring" slot machines in the crib houses and gambling dens to which Utah's hard-rock miners flocked. From time to time, John accompanied his uncle on work rounds, absorbing lore, in his own words, from "the whores, the pimps, the gamblers, the hop-heads and the lenient police," who had known "The Mormon Kid" during his "wild free existence" in Utah.

In his early years in New York (1910–1914), Held again took up linocut style and subjects, and executed a marvelous Frankie and Johnny series, described below. Also, Held used this same antique format to prepare work neither nostalgic nor satiric in tone. The earliest dated example, known to me, of such a representative print without a hint of parody is "Ship Bonita Salem," made in 1918 for an unpublished book. Weinhardt sums up Held's *New Yorker* debut in precise terms: Ross urged Held to return to the early blockprints of their youth. Already bored by stereotyped flappers, he turned to this "new" genre with alacrity and brilliance, making his Gilded Age figures as memorable as those of the Jazz Age.

In the early *New Yorker* Held was in magnificent artistic company: Rea Irvin, Helen Hokinson, Peter Arno, Ralph Barton, Miguel Covarrubias, and Reginald Marsh. Each had chosen a section of Manhattan life for special attention in a contemporaneous style, but only Held looked back consistently to a past of ear-piercing, buggy stripping, bustle soldering, and corset lacing. In prints titled "Horse Whipping the Masher" and "The Soubrette Sings a Racy Song to the Man in the Box," he not only poked fun at vanished times but also established a scale against which to judge the "mashers" and "soubrettes" of the Jazz Age. Held's work in the *New Yorker* never seemed to be related to the magazine's reportage or reviews, but in time his own "thesis Americana" threaded individual engravings into categories—for example, Wages of Sin, Theatre Fraught with Romance, Songs Without Music, Moments in the Faint Rosy Past, Morals for Young and Old.

While caught up by these sentiments, Held collaborated with Frank Shay for three song collections published by the Macaulay Company: *My Pious Friends and Drunken Companions* (1927), *More Pious Friends and Drunken Companions* (1928), and *Drawn from the Wood* (1929). Frank Shay, a Greenwich Village bookseller and Cape Cod resident, was one of the informal band of scholars, writers, concert performers, and record company scouts who popularized folksong in the 1920s. Hence, Shay shared many roles with Robert Winslow Gordon, James Weldon Johnson, Carl Sandburg, John Lomax, and Ralph Peer. In his three anthologies, Shay freely mixed traditional ballads, sentimental ditties, and hoary chestnuts—at times offering valuable folksong variants from his own wanderings (the Canadian Rockies, a Standard Oil tanker, army camps in France). For these books, Held brought together cuts from the *New Yorker* and other sources. I do not know how long Held continued as "an engraver of yesteryear," but some of the best work in this vein was newly prepared for James Geller's *Grandfather's Follies* (1934), an easygoing commentary on nineteenth-century melodrama.

I have not encountered any correspondence by either Shay or Held about their songbooks, or business records of the Macaulay firm on these three anthologies, and would welcome reference to such material. At one level, to the consternation of scholars, Shay cheerfully jumbled folk and Tin Pan Alley material; at another level, he helped widen the audience for American folksong. Held was also free in his labels, indiscriminately using phrases such as "American folksong," "old song," "old ballad," or "a song from the dear dim past."

Frank Shay was not unlearned in matters of categorization, for in the preface to *My Pious Friends* he anticipated that symphony music lovers would dismiss his songs and ballads of conviviality. Further, he wrote, "The folklorist will dismiss them with the phrases profane and vulgar. To him they are but the product of low resorts, gutter songs, the communal musical expression of an artistically destitute society." It seems unnecessary today to be reminded that the lore of "destitute society" is often both rich and telling. Dialogue between Frank Shay and his academic peers about song can be documented, but because commentary on artistic depiction of folksong is virtually nonexistent, I doubt that any folklorist ever discussed Held's when they were current.

One of Held's picture books, *The Saga of Frankie and Johnny,* deserves fresh scholarly attentions. It was issued in December 1930 by Walter V. McKee of New York in a limited edition of 2,500 copies, 50 of which were bound with extra illustrations. Carl Weinhardt has dated the execution of these linocuts to about 1914 in New York. I would be pleased to learn whether or not Held tried to publish his folksong book before 1930, and the circumstances of eventual acceptance of the manuscript.

Held needed no collaborator for this traditional narrative stemming from a murder in a St. Louis bordello on October 15, 1899. In a short preface he confessed that he had learned "Frankie and Johnny" in Utah from "a colored piano player, who was called 'Professor' in a parlor house" belonging to Madam Helen Blazes. As a boy John had delivered, to various parlors of joy, business cards engraved in his father's shop. For each of the ballad's stanzas he prepared a full-page "woodcut," twenty-three in all, embellishing other pages with some two dozen small prints. During February 1954, in its third issue, *Playboy* magazine reproduced twelve of Held's Frankie and Johnny cuts, placing the ballad's characters in fully appropriate company. Fortunately, the whole book was reproduced in 1972 by offset lithography, and it is currently [1978] available from publisher Clarkson Potter of New York.

Very few American folksongs have inspired whole sequences or cycles of visual art. Thomas Hart Benton, beginning about 1927, made a handful of oil paintings and lithographs based on specific traditional ballads and fiddle tunes; Miguel Covarrubias illustrated "Frankie and Johnny" in the form of a printed play by John Huston (1930); Palmer Hayden placed the John Henry narrative in twelve strong paintings between 1944–1954. However, John Held Jr. anticipated all of these efforts. Can we identify other American folksongs in graphic art before Held turned to Frankie and Johnny about 1914?

A few technical points may help readers and viewers who come to Held anew. The word "woodcut" is used ambiguously in commentary on his work. Held clearly learned engraving and woodcutting from his father, and, as a boy, worked in this medium "for the Politz Candy Kitchen on Main Street" (Salt Lake City in about 1900–1904). In 1905 on the *Tribune* he started cartooning with linoleum blockprints on linocuts, a method to which he later turned for "Frankie and Johnny." His early *New Yorker* work was also in the form of linocuts, but some of the later cartoons for this magazine were rendered in pen on scratchboard — a technique faster than linoleum engraving. Although Held rigorously kept his "past" and "present" work apart, in 1931 he offered a series of unusual single-page pairings to *Liberty* magazine, placing an "old" scratchboard piece and a "new" pen and ink piece together to demonstrate thematic and stylistic contrast.

A word on size: Held's reproductions in books and magazines were generally reduced in size, for example, "Jesse James," a small linocut in the *New Yorker* (September 29, 1928), was 14 × 11¾ in original measurement. During the 1960s a number of "large" prints were hand pulled from original linoleum blocks and sold in New York galleries at hand-some prices. Finally, a comment on "woodcut" sources: Held was largely self-taught, but his Gilded Age art was centered in the genre of early English chapbooks, cheap broadside ballads, sensational almanac illustrations, and lurid theater posters. We need considerable analysis of Held's place in the tradition of ephemeral broadside art.

In selecting but a few examples of Held's musical graphics, I have neglected the sweep and depth of his life. In the 1930s, with the Jazz Age behind him, he turned to writing, to animal painting and sculpture, to work in wrought iron, and to farming. No comprehensive biography of him is yet available.

Margaret Held, his widow, in a 1964 sketch touched on several details concerning Held's early interest in music and drama. Young John's mother, Annie Evans Held, had been an actress in the Salt Lake Theater where her father was the stage carpenter. Thus, John actually saw some of the melodrama he later recalled in scratchboard drawings for *Grandfather's Follies*. John Shuttleworth, an editor of *Judge* in the 1920s, recalls his friend Held as a banjo picker, mandolinist, and folksinger. This latter attribute was also reported in a *Vanity Fair* note on Held's novel, *Grim Youth* (1930). Not only was the versatile artist commended as a gentleman farmer, but he was praised, as well, as an "unrivaled tap dancer" and "singer of cowboy laments." To close, we need only add that this Utah-born singer of cowboy laments died at Schuyler Farm near Belmar, New Jersey, on May 2, 1958.

In demarcating Held's art by era, I have not suggested that one period was superior to the other. His stamp upon the Jazz Age is indelible. While his evocation of gilt and gaslight makes a fine comment on American life, it is not essential for comprehending the Gilded Age. As a folklorist I am pulled to both ages depicted by Held. We no longer know whether jazz is folk or chamber music, and we have surprisingly little folkloric study of the journey made by jazz away from its home bases. Held did not focus closely on this journey or on the nuances of jazz performance in the 1920s, but his art, now, does help all of us see music as a key symbol for a past decade.

Conversely, Held's "woodcuts" helped bring to life the stories within particular folksongs, but he did not create special symbols to mark Gilded Age music. Through Held's lens, today, we see these songs as appealing but distant, suggestive but safe. Even when he illustrated some of Frank Shay's risqué songs, Held bathed them in a wholesome light. The analogy which comes to mind is Carl Sandburg, on stage when the Shay-Held anthologies appeared. There was no way that Sandburg could dress a song up or down to cheapen it or to destroy its core emotion. Likewise, the ruffles and flourishes which Held placed in engravings did not detract from the basic content and message of his songs.

I am keenly aware as a ballad scholar in the 1970s of difficulties in looking back at folksong art of the 1920s. We assert today that folksong is best presented on concert stage or festival circuit with respect for its native esthetic. (With others I had advanced this "straight code" during the 1960s, for presentations from Carnegie Hall to Berkeley's Greek Theater.) Nevertheless, present-day questions which trouble me are: Must an artist be as realistic and factual in his visual depictions as an outsider should be in concert presentation? How can we shape an appropriate norm for evaluating any artistic depiction of folksong? One such standard was established as early as 1889 by Thomas Eakins in his quiet and realistic portraits of cowboy musicians. Another was set in the mid-1920s by Miguel Covarrubias' broad caricatures of blues singers in Harlem. Still another is found in the pastel shades and bogus sentimentality of Alice and Martin Provensen's work for the *Fireside Book of Folk Song* (1947). A fourth norm appears in Ben Shahn's near-mystical ballad booklets such as *The Cherry Tree Legend* (1953).

Ultimately, we respond to any artist's work in terms of competence and craftsmanship, as well as of our own sense of meaning within subject matter and style. Looking at Held's "woodcuts" today, I feel close to his musical companions: Frankie and Johnny, Jesse James, Casey Jones' wife, sailors returned from the sea, coffin-carrying gamblers, grog-house and pawn-shop sots. I like his soulful zither players and his romantic guitarists, as well as his smug listeners to "newfangled" cylinder records. I am not aware of any personal nostalgia for the world of Diamond Jim Brady and Lillian Russell, or Admiral Dewey and Anna Held, but I am conscious of continuity and constancy in Held's ballad heroes and heroines.

John Held Jr. did not view his parents' years (nor his childhood) in mordant terms, nor did he reduce Gilded Age culture to treacle. He helped Americans during the Jazz Age to define their particular time and to appreciate their near past. But his sheiks and shebas, so modern in the 1920s, are now as distant from us as the Gay Nineties were to Held's collegiate fans. Today, all of his figures—thin and full, new and old—are part of a shared national past. Held's caricatures of flappers and their escorts as well as of belles and their beaux continue to function for us as we look ahead to the twenty-first century, still encumbered by the nineteenth.

Loyal Jones

Buell Kazee

One folksong scholar called Buell Kazee "the greatest white male folk singer in the United States." He was one of the several musicians who made records when the recording industry was in early bloom, who took up another profession, and who was rediscovered as a musician much later. Those who collected 78-rpm records, several scholars, a good many lovers of genuine traditional music, and his neighbors in eastern Kentucky swore by him as one of the great singers and one of the very best banjo players in the mountain frailing style. With the folk revival in the '60s and '70s, he was sought after, and he gave concerts or appeared in festivals at Newport, the Smithsonian, the Universities of Chicago, Illinois, California at Los Angeles, Temple and Simon Fraser (Vancouver), Berea College and Fresno State, the Seattle Folk Song Society, Mariposa and the Mountain Heritage Festival. Folkways issued an LP, and he was visited by many admirers, delighted to discover that the man who had recorded for Brunswick the last three years of the '20s was still alive.

Buell Hilton Kazee was born August 29, 1900, at the head of Burton Fork in Magoffin County in the mountains of eastern Kentucky. His parents were Abbie Jane and John Franklin Kazee, both singers. His mother sang the old ballads and his father was noted for his hymn singing. His sisters sang the "tender love songs" such as "Come All Ye Fair and Tender Ladies."

> Musicians came to our house, because of the girls [his sisters] more than anything else, I guess. They were very pretty girls, and popular, and they

183

attracted young men. Then my father was a strange person. He never went to school more than the second grade, but he was one of the greatest readers I've ever known. He would sit by the fireplace at night and read books to us. People liked to come by and talk with him. He was affable and had a great following. Mother was a staunch mountain woman in character and life. There were four boys and two girls living together in that big log house—a double-room log house, with chimney between, of hewn logs.

We just sang by nature. Everybody sang and nobody thought there was anything unusual about it. And a good many people around us did. Down the road almost in sight was Preacher Caudill's family. They were all singers. They had a banjo, the first one I ever saw. They called it a "peanut" banjo. It was a little fellow. They played that and they played the fiddle down there.

Banjo players especially were numerous:

Everybody played the banjo—not good but whacking at it, and you could find homemade banjos around. I'd hear others play; they'd come there and pick the banjo and play the fiddle—sit up half the night with that kind of music. I'd listen to them. . . . Bate LeMaster was the leading banjo-picker in the community and Clint Bailey was the leading fiddler.

I started picking the banjo when I was five years old—a tack-head banjo. I went to Aunt Sade's [Bailey, his mother's sister] one night. They had one over there that they'd worn out, they thought. There was a hole in the head where your fingers rest. It was homemade with a walnut neck. The Bailey boys were all good carpenters, and they had made the banjo. I cried for that one, and they gave it to me and I carried it home under Dad's coat, trying to keep it out of the rain. Sherd [Sherman] Conley was always catching animals and tanning their hides, and he caught a cat, skinned and tanned that hide and put it on the banjo. . . . I began to pick with thumb and forefinger. I picked most of the melody with my thumb. I'd hit the thumb string and then hit the melody string. Then I began to frail—no melody at all. I learned to pick out the tune with my forefinger, picking down with the back of the nail. "Lord Thomas and Fair Ellender" was the first tune I ever learned. Mother had sung that ever since I could remember.

Buell played that homemade banjo until he was ten or eleven years old. Then he bought another one from a neighbor named Ben McCormick which had a "brought-on" (manufactured) head with brackets and a homemade neck. It cost him $3.00, and he played it for many years. Ben McCormick was one of the persons who taught him special techniques in playing.

The Kazees had migrated from Virginia to Floyd and Johnson Counties of Kentucky in the last century, taking up land there under land grants. Buell thought that the family name had originally been Case, pronounced with two syllables. Some of the descendents of these early settlers spell it Keesee, others Kozee. Buell's mother was a Conley, a common name in the Burton and Mash Fork area of Magoffin County, and he was related to numerous Baileys on his father's side. His mothe, Abigail, was a "serious religious person"; everyone respected her. She felt it was all right to clap her hands and praise the Lord but she was opposed to dancing and had reservations about the music associated with dancing. John Franklin Kazee took an occasional nip of whiskey and was more frolicsome. Yet he was "a great singer of religious songs," as Buell recalled. "Father had a great voice, though he never knew it. . . . He knew how to interpret songs." He was "churched," expelled, from the church for his drinking, but he went to church anyway and helped lead the singing, not abashed by the broken relationship. Eventually, no doubt under Abigail's influence, he forsook his wayward flings and became a serious church member.

The conflict between religious and secular music, as well as related traditions, was mainly unspoken, but it was a profound problem which was with Buell throughout his life:

> Our house became a social center. The girls [he had two sisters and three brothers] would get out and pick beans all day, and they might say, "Let's have a bean stringing." The boys'd say, "Let's have a dance." Well, Mother couldn't take that, and for a long time she fought it off. But a few times they over-powered her and they had some dances. I remember Clint Bailey playing the fiddle and Bate LeMaster the banjo. . . . Mother got talked about for letting us dance, so she put her foot down. . . . We look back with condescension now, but there was a great deal of evil connected with these occasions. There was a lot of blackguard talk when they got drunk. People didn't want their girls to go to places like this.

Evil and its opposite, righteousness, were of great concern to the people of his community. There were two churches on Mash Fork, into which flowed Burton Fork. Both were Baptist, but one was a Missionary Baptist Church (Southern Baptist) and the other a United Baptist Church, which leaned back toward a more rigorous Calvinism. They were effective in setting the moral and religious tone of the community in which Buell grew up, and they personally affected him. He learned the two kinds of music, the unaccompanied "lined-out" singing of the United Baptists, and the more revivalistic music of the Missionary church. He professed a religious commitment in a revival at the Mash Fork Baptist (Missionary) Church, and by the time he was seventeen, he was preaching.

> Along about 1912 or 1914, I was picking the banjo, picking all of the tunes, hoedowns and ballads, like I do now. But I joined the church and I was told, not formally, that the banjo did not go with religion. I could understand why. It had a pretty bad reputation. It had been a lot of places where a lot of things were going on that shouldn't. It was the frolicking atmosphere that had surrounded the banjo, and the people looked upon the fiddle or banjo as the sort of thing that went with that crowd, you know. So I had to kind of mute the banjo. I played it at home, but I never got out with it much, though. I realized that if I became a preacher, I wouldn't be allowed to pick the banjo. The sentiment would be against it.
>
> So, I knew the conflict was there, but it began to decrease by the time I was growing up. While nobody thought of bringing a banjo to a churchhouse, it wasn't terrible to play by the time I became a young man.

Instinctively, he did not mix his preaching and revival singing with his banjo picking and entertainment. This was the beginning of two distinctly separate careers—so separate that years later fellow preachers were surprised to hear that he was a well-known folk artist and folk enthusiasts were unaware that he was a preacher.

He liked to entertain. He spoke of teaming up with his high school principal, Ollie Patrick, and entertaining around the county:

> Ollie played a mandolin and fiddle. He could violin or fiddle it. I played the guitar, mandolin and banjo. We got together and became well known as entertainers. Sometimes in the summertime on the dirt streets around the courthouse, we'd get the instruments out and sit there and play in the moonlight, and people would sing. We'd have a great time. We were entertainers.

He spoke eloquently about the get-togethers in his or other musicians' homes, when a special magic would prevail:

> Picking the banjo by the fireside at night, you know, it would lead up to a mood. It'd get so everything you'd touch would be good. You wouldn't miss a note. Everything you played had a soulful quality about it—an emotional quality. That was the thing that made it good. Now it just couldn't come up like we're doing now. You can't sit down here and say we're going to demonstrate this and demonstrate that and do it that way. It doesn't

work that way at all. The fiddler and the banjo picker—that was, I think, the famous combination of the mountains and the best—would start on a tune and it would get so that the fiddle bow would just dance on the strings. It'd just tip the strings, and by that time the whole thing was just running by itself. The banjo picker and the fiddler were simply in an emotional automation. They sat with their knees interlocked. Your right knee would be between my knees, you see, and your left knee on the other side—be so close together it would just weave itself together till there was just one beat all the way through.

He had the ministry in mind when he entered Magoffin Baptist Institute, a high school. Yet music was a strong interest, and it was there that he was exposed to other traditions.

When I got to high school, I was hearing all of the modern things. I got my classical education right across the lane from the high school dorm where I lived from Mrs. Polly Hazelrig, a widow, a good singer, maybe not as trained as some, but she had a wonderful voice. She sang in the church choir at Saylersville and all around. Her sons gave her a Chippendale model of the Edison phonograph and she had two drawers of records, nearly all classical. I would go over there and sit and play those records. You can't imagine how much I learned to appreciate good voices.

His appetite for classical learning was fed at Georgetown College, where he enrolled after high school and a year of preaching and missionary work. In fact, at Georgetown, a central Kentucky college supported by the Kentucky Baptist Association, there was little attention given to traditional folk arts. Buell left his banjo at home, thinking it would be inappropriate there. However, he noticed that the ballads he was studying in his English course were some of the same ones still being sung in his native county. He began to realize also that the culture he came from—the tales, the words and expressions—were related to the life and language he was studying in literature classes. He commented that he decided his mother was an Elizabethan type of woman. So he brought his banjo to school and began to give programs. In fact he brought two banjos, the one he bought from Ben McCormick and the one given to him by his Aunt Sade, along with a dulcimer he had obtained from a neighbor family. He donated the older banjo and dulcimer to the college to start a museum. He was saddened to learn later that a group of students had broken and ruined the instruments in foolishness attending initiation rites for freshmen. This was perhaps another indication of how little his contemporaries thought of folk culture.

He majored in English and Greek and Latin in college and studied voice, aiming at improving his knowledge and skills for the Christian ministry. His voice teacher was a Mr. Bonawitz whom he described as "an unusual man . . . from the German court opera and from England, well known, with a wonderful voice." He attempted piano lessons, but he could not learn to play the instrument by note after his many years of playing by ear. He finally gave it up, although he continued to play the piano by ear and often accompanied himself in singing religious songs and love songs in what he called his "good voice," meaning his trained voice. He did, of course, learn to sight-read music for singing, as a part of his voice training.

He listened to classical composers and had the opportunity of hearing such accomplished singers as John McCormack and Lawrence Tibbett. He learned to appreciate opera, and later sang operatic airs for his own enjoyment. He organized a glee club. He considered pursuing a career in music, as a concert singer. He was also interested in composing. Even before college, he had tried his hand at composing songs similar to the parlor songs of the day. Yet he never wavered in his determination to become a preacher, and he took Bible courses. Most of his musical studies was aimed toward his chosen career. He had done revivalistic singing along with his preaching even before he entered college.

During the summer of 1925, after graduation from Georgetown, Buell gave his first real folk concert, in the gymnasium at the University of Kentucky.

W. S. Taylor was the dean over there then. He'd heard me entertain the Kiwanis Club at Russellville one time . . . and he invited me to come there. I did it in tie and tails. Anybody that appeared in anything like that did it formally. I had a dress suit and I picked the banjo in that. It was a good concert though. I had a lot of folks down from the mountains who came to hear it.

I got the idea that I could make something out of it. I played the banjo and lectured. I gave the mountain tunes. I gave hoedowns and ballads mostly. One of my music teachers played piano accompaniment to some of my ballads. Then I had another feature—Negro spirituals, and I dressed like a finely-dressed Negro performer, in blackface and wore a long coat and a big hat. I came out in concert style . . . and sang Negro spirituals. They were good too. I mean I did well with it. I never made any money at it, then.

His first job after college was as director of religious education and music at the First Baptist Church of Chickasha, Oklahoma, but, as he put it, "they had some problems that I didn't want to get into . . . and I came back home."

> I was out of a job and my teacher, Mr. Bonawitz, had heard from a woman in Ashland who had a music school, and she wanted a man to help her—to take over business management. So I went up there and we made a deal. I lived there for a year or more. I soon saw that her school wasn't as substantial as it looked to be in the beginning, so I dropped out of that and took my own private studio-taught voice. I studied with a tenor from St. John the Divine in New York. He came to Ashland for the summers, and I studied with him there. . . . When I began teaching, of course, I learned more than I did studying. I stayed in Ashland another year and got a call to go to Cumberland College, Williamsburg, Kentucky, and teach voice and Bible which was just my dish.

While Buell was in Ashland, he was "discovered":

> I was down in this music shop there listening to records, and he [the man who owned the store] was making money hand over fist, because Armco Steel Corporation had attracted a large group of people who were in that level. The man was a very sharp business man. He said, "Do you know any of this music?" I said, "I know all of it." He asked if I played anything. I said, "I play the banjo." "Where's your banjo?" "It's in my studio." He went up there with me, and I played a tune or two and sang a ballad or two, and he said, "Boy, they'll throw their arms around you in New York." I didn't know what he meant. He was a scout for Brunswick. So in three weeks we were in New York, recording. . . .
>
> We went up on the train, and we had a big time. This man [W. S. Carter] went with me. He had plenty of money. He thought the Brunswick Company would take care of all expenses. I only got $40 a record the first time . . . and the fare had to come out of my earnings. I think I made nine records—$360, and when we took the train fare out, there wasn't much left. I believe he also took something out for the hotel.

His first recording was "John Hardy" with "Roll On, John" on the reverse side. Vernon Dalhart and Carson Robison came to hear him record. They were very popular at the time through their recordings. Buell remembered Dalhart as "a big handsome fellow . . . as nice as he could be." He commented to Buell, "Boy, you've got something there." Buell had the same problem that Dalhart, a light opera singer, had—somehow to forget all of his voice training and sound "country" or folk. He felt that Dalhart over-nasalized in order to sound like a traditional singer. The key, rather, was to sing with a tight voice, to sing high in the throat, instead of from the diaphragm as a trained singer is encouraged to do.

> I had to make a record seven or eight times to get it bad enough to sell.
> They'd say, "Buell, that's fine but it won't ring on a cash register." I'd ask,
> "Well, what do you want?" "Well, that vibrato and resonance, if you can
> cut that out." If you want to sound country, you sing with a light throat.
> But I can hear the trained voice all the way through my recordings.

The fact that recording companies were never interested in his "good" voice was a disappointment to Buell. He took his music seriously, both the folk and the trained-voice material. No one in commercial music appeared interested in the latter. He recorded a great deal of material in his trained voice—religious songs, love songs, popular numbers and a few show tunes, but all were done on poor equipment and are not adequate for a record. On the relation between his two singing styles, he said:

> I have always tried to keep in the trained voice—I don't know what you
> call it—some of that plaintive sound, the heart of singing, not let it become
> purely mechanical. I think that is a good thing to retain. Now if I'm inter-
> preting folksongs, I sing as they [the folk] did. I appreciate all kinds of
> music.

He mentioned that the main reason he began recording for Brunswick was that he had a $1,250 debt from college for $3.00-per-hour voice lessons that he was anxious to pay off. As it turned out, this was not a very good way to make money, since on most he received only a flat payment and no royalty.

> You see, what they did was to release records every month. If you released
> ten records on a fellow, people would buy two or three of them, that's all,
> but if you put them out one a month, they'd buy all of them, if they liked
> you. I'd make lots of records at one recording and they'd release them one
> each month.
>   I was about to go with Victor when they raised the price they paid on
> my records. That's why I got $75. My contract had run out. They were very
> much surprised that I would do a thing like that. I said, "Well, I haven't
> heard anything about a renewal." So they upped the price to $75. Then we
> thought that was very good.

He remembers being in Salyersville and hearing someone say, "There's Buell Kazee. He'll never have to work another lick—making all that money on records." He cut a total of fifty-eight sides (of which fifty-two were released) between 1927 and 1929.

> They said it took 5,000 records of each to supply the trade, with samples and all . . . I don't believe I was ever a big seller. The second time I went to record, they told me my best seller was 15,000 records. I guess that was pretty good then. That was "The Roving Cowboy" and "Pretty Mohee." I sold a lot in Texas.

He would have sold more records, no doubt, if he had been interested in promoting them, but this notion did not appeal to him:

> They wanted me to go to Texas and places like that and play the county and state fairs, and they also wanted me to go up the hollows to every picture show and popularize them [the records]. I didn't have time for that. I never went into it with that idea . . . I got a letter from Jimmie O'Keefe in New York wanting me to go to Chicago and be on the staff of, I guess it was WLS. That must have been 1929. . . . Well, I couldn't go that way. My life was cast in a different direction, you see, and there wasn't any reason to consider it. He said he'd recommend me, that I had a good chance; they were asking about me. But I never gave it a second thought. I was going to preach all of my life.

In 1928, Buell married Lucille Jones of Corbin, Kentucky. To them were born two sons, Allan in 1930 and Philip in 1933. He must have been happy in the marriage, for when his wife left him in 1940, he called it "one of life's great tragedies" which brought him "great anguish and embarrassment." Buell spoke very little about the break-up of his marriage except for his great sorrow and feeling of anguish and embarrassment. He had seen the break coming for a year or more, and he prayed that it would not come. When his wife went away, leaving the boys with him, he went through a dark period, both personally and spiritually. He wrote in his book, *Faith is the Victory,* "I . . . had prepared to fold up my ministry and retire to seclusion," but his faith held strong and he realized that he was not alone in trouble. "My experiences are not singular," he wrote. "Many a life has been shattered by sorrow. I was preaching a life of faith; now I was to see if it worked." His faith did work for him, and out of his travail came the above-quoted book. This experience had a profound effect on him. It made him a more humble man, one who was tolerant and sympathetic toward others. It heightened his sense of tragedy. He said once that the tragic ballads were especially meaningful to persons who themselves had experienced deep trouble. They had a cathartic effect and thus were important psychologically, he thought.

He ran the household and reared his two sons, with help from a niece, Luva Preston, who lived with them while attending high school and who assisted with household chores. Both Allan and Philip became Baptist ministers, with pastorates in Tennessee. Phil is a banjo picker and singer in the style of his father, performing most of Buell's favorites.

Buell married Jennie Turnmeyer, a teacher, in 1950. Her mother and maternal grandparents were natives of Magoffin County. She supported Buell in his ministry and musical career. She accompanied him on many of his trips to festivals, such as to the Mariposa Festival in Canada and the UCLA festival. After he retired from the active ministry, they moved to Winchester, Kentucky, where they lived until he died on August 31, 1976.

Although Buell aimed to preach all of his life, he did consider secular pursuits and, in addition to teaching in a voice studio, he taught for a year—Bible and voice—at Cumberland College, then a junior college in southeastern Kentucky, supported by Kentucky Baptists. He left then to explore the possibility of getting on the Chautauqua lecture circuit with his musical program, but before this opportunity materialized, his father had a stroke and he remained in Kentucky. He taught private voice students in Corbin and Williamsburg for a year and then went into business with his brother-in-law to run music and appliance stores in Corbin and Harlan. At first business was good, but since many of the sales were on time payments, the stores went bankrupt in 1930, when miners were laid off in the Depression.

The Brunswick Company also went broke in 1930, and that was the end of Buell's recording career—at least for thirty years. He turned to preaching full-time and singing at revivals and other religious functions. He served a church in Morehead for twenty-two years, taught for seven years at the Lexington Baptist Bible College and then became pastor of a new church, Devondale Baptist, in Lexington which he served for twelve years, until he retired from the active ministry at the age of sixty-nine.

Buell's ministerial career was not unrelated to his other career in traditional music, although he tried to keep the two separate. He was a traditional person, and he cared little for innovations in either music or theology. He thought the Nashville Sound was a long way from country and the folk. Likewise, he thought modern church practices and much that modern ministers were preaching and doing were a long way from scriptural teachings as he understood them. He never took the easy way of conformity, and thus his ministry was at times a rocky road. He scolded church members, theologians and administrators from his denomination alike. He deplored all of the emphasis on "programs" in the Southern Baptist Convention and other denominations, in place, he thought, of spiritual commitment. He preached a simple gospel of reconciliation to God, and faith, and he believed that "works" would follow. He believed that Christians should be alert to the temptations to get involved in good programs as a substitute for this relationship with God. He held to the belief that the church is not of this world and should keep "unspotted from the world." He spoke out against and wrote to Billy Graham about his emphasis on worldly success, for example, having persons on his show that are successful in sports or show business. His scorn was total for the evangelist who had the yo-yo champion of the world on his television show. Buell's comment was that "my witness, alongside his, would not be worth a nickel, even with my fifty-seven years of preaching." He did not understand how Johnny Cash could appear in Billy Graham's crusades and play Las Vegas too. "I just don't see how he could mix it that way," he said. This observation explains why Buell never wanted to mix his banjo playing and ballad singing with his preaching. It did not seem appropriate to use one to promote the other.

His stands on religion put him at odds with many of his fellow Southern Baptists, and he believed that gradually he came to be ignored at associational and state meetings when nominations were open. But he stuck to his beliefs which had been forged through private study, thought and prayer. He had his associates and followers, however, who liked what he preached. He published two books on religion, *Faith is the Victory* in 1951 (Crescendo Book Publications) and *The Church and its Ordinances* in 1965 (The Challenge Press). *Mused Uncle Mose* (privately printed) was a collection of sayings attributed to the janitor of his church in Morehead. He had a third theological book almost ready for publication at the time of his death.

He had also written an autobiography, which is unpublished, and had begun a book on his banjo techniques. He tried his hand at composing songs, first with popular parlor-type songs when he was in high school. He sent these early compositions off to what he called "the Sucker Center" and paid them to "publish" them, getting several printed copies in return. "I had to learn my lesson like everybody else," he said. His best-known composition is "Steel A-Going Down," that resulted from his working on the railroad with black steeldrivers when he was a youth. He was very much interested in using traditional materials in compositions for choral groups. This idea had been in his head from college days when he was impressed with the fact that Percy Grainger, the English composer, had based many of his compositions on folk tunes. One of his favorite religious songs was "The White Pilgrim" (sometimes "The Lone Pilgrim") composed by B. F. White and appearing first in *The Sacred Harp.* Buell and Lewis Henry Horton (who taught music at Morehead, Transylvania, and the University of Kentucky) published a cantata based on this song which is still available from the Belwin Mills Co. in New York. The foreword was written by George Pullen Jackson. He also composed an operetta entitled *The Wagoner Lad,* from one of his favorite folksongs. This composition contained some of Buell's favorite folksongs, and he envisioned it in a festival-like setting. Of the songs he recorded, he composed "The Cowboy's Trail" and "The Dying Cowboy" and wrote the music for "The Hobo's Last Ride."

> I wrote the words and music to "The Cowboy's Trail," and I tried to put into that one everything about the West you could get in—the pony, the Indian, ranch lights—more of a novelty than anything. It is pretty—turned out well. Indian stories are popular with us people, and the Indian coupled with the West, with the cowboy, I guess, has been a popular thing for a long time—even behind my memory.

While he was recording for Brunswick, he was asked to write some skits that might be recorded, since those done by the "Skillet Lickers" band had proved popular. He composed and recorded two, "A Mountain Boy Makes His First Record" and "Election Day in Kentucky." These are humorous pieces, but Buell did not look on them as major accomplishments.

During the years when he was preaching full-time, he also continued to give programs of folk music. Through his friendship with Lewis Henry Horton of the Morehead State College music department, he performed for students at least once a year, and most of his folk concerts were local. He had no trouble with his parishioners about his secular music because, as he said, "they like it too." And he added, "I never mixed it with the church." He did evangelistic singing "all over the country, with great preachers in time gone by." He was also in demand as a revival preacher, although he commented that he was "more a man to strengthen the spiritual life of the church" than he was a straight evangelist.

The recordings Buell made between 1927 and 1929 were soon unavailable in this country after the collapse of Brunswick, but they were reissued in the British Isles and Australia and were available longer there, although Buell did not receive royalty payments for these repressings. It was not until 1958 that a new record on Buell Kazee was issued. Gene Bluestein, teaching at the University of Michigan and traveling in eastern Kentucky in 1956, was directed to Buell by Leonard Roberts, a folklorist. Bluestein was well acquainted with Kazee's recordings but was surprised that he was still living and performing. He spent two days interviewing Buell and recording him in his living room. Buell maintained that he had no idea that any of the material would be used, other than in Bluestein's doctoral studies. Yet Bluestein sold the material to Folkways, and a record, *Buell Kazee Sings and Plays* (FS3810), was issued. Buell was unhappy with the results and commented as follows:

> He spent a couple of days with me recording, just like we're doing now. It was not professionally done. I mean by that I did not play well. I was doing just like I would pick up a banjo here and pick something for you. It's not good. The conversation's not good. I remember using the word "quirlicue" [curlicue] twice. I know there's no such word. That embarrasses me. I made some remarks that he ought not to have put on there. I said Vernon Dalhart copyrighted "The Prisoner's Song" and made $60,000 out of it. That was an awful statement to publish, you know. It's on that record. I wouldn't have said that for anything in the world.

He also regretted that he had sung only fragments or incomplete versions of some of the songs that appeared on the record. He felt that it was not a good representation of his repertory. And he reported difficulties with the business side of the record. He acknowledged that he had been notified that a record was to be made, but added:

> I kept waiting for a contract and couldn't get any. Finally I wrote to the man [Moses Asch, President of Folkways] and told him not to issue it unless he was going to give me a royalty on it. He wasn't going to give me anything. . . . I finally had to sell it to him. I beat him around until I got one royalty check—a hundred and some dollars. It was about two years before I got that. Then I got one a year or two later, after browbeating him, and finally I told him to make me an offer and I'd sell it to him.

Although Buell did not like the Folkways recording and though it does have shortcomings, it is nevertheless an important record, in sound and word, of Buell Kazee, his life and music. It is a great pity that it was not done under more ideal circumstances, with Buell prepared to present material worthy of his sensitivity and talent.

Perhaps the problem with Bluestein and Folkways kept him from making another album in the latter part of his life. He was taped with good equipment by John Cohen, a filmmaker and record producer, around 1965 and by Mark Wilson, who then worked for Rounder Records, in 1972. Both Wilson and Cohen were much interested in his banjo tunes, but Buell was reluctant to be presented as just another mountain banjo picker. Wilson reports that, even though the recordings were done for a record, "We both decided not to pursue the project further, largely because of differences in what we wanted out of the record. I wanted more banjo solos—he wanted 'Steel A-Going Down,' et al." Buell himself made a professional recording in Newark, Ohio, arranged by his nephew Lewis Franklin Kazee, who played guitar accompaniment. This recording was not as good in quality as the ones made by Wilson and Cohen. This writer talked with Buell about the possibility of making a record a year or so before he died. He was willing but wanted to be in control of the material so that it reflected his tastes and best skills. Unfortunately, money was not available to do the album at the time, and no recordings for that purpose were done. However, June Appal Records of Whitesburg, Kentucky, will shortly release a record based on the Mark Wilson tapes mentioned above.

Rediscovery in his older years was not a totally happy experience for Buell. He enjoyed the notice he received, enjoyed talking to interested persons and performing before appreciative audiences. Yet he had a strong reserve that kept him from being influenced too much by fame. Also, he was not altogether charmed by some of the young folk revivalists who appeared at his door or whom he met or observed at festivals.

> Of course I'm pretty conservative, when there's a Biblical reason for it. I believe that many of the things we are smiling at as if they were products of ignorance, we haven't investigated the Bible thoroughly on. I don't like to scissor the Bible. There is some reason.

He was concerned with modern morality, and yet he had a tolerant view of human nature, from his basically Calvinist theological position. But he was not just traditional in religious matters. He had an old-fashioned patriotism, and he was constantly being offended during the 1960s with the anti-Vietnam protests and related social turmoil. He played the Newport Folk Festival in 1968, along with Pete Seeger and Joan Baez. He had been invited to play before but declined because he thought it might be rowdy. He said it was actually a calm affair. But he was cornered by reporters who nudged him into saying things about his fellow performers and their "protest" music that he later regretted. He sang at a festival at the University of Chicago organized by a group of students and spent the night on a knotty couch in a dormitory. But he had many good experiences at festivals and concerts elsewhere—at the Universities of Illinois and Indiana, UCLA, Morehead and Fresno State, Campbellsville and Berea Colleges, in Seattle, at Mariposa and elsewhere.

He usually didn't like just to appear on a program. He wanted enough time to tell the story of his music, to create a spell, in much the same way that Jean Ritchie does in concert. He did not like to rush through a ballad and cut out verses. He was witty and entertaining in his comments. He was the master of his material and instrument. He put on a good show, but there was more to him than that. He had an integrity and sincerity about him that impressed those who heard him. Many might not agree with his ideas or his interpretation of his culture, but he was respected.

A few words on his singing and playing style are in order. As has been said before, he had two styles of singing—in his folk voice and in his trained voice. His voice tone (especially in the high ranges), articulation, and timing were certainly improved by his voice studies. Yet, he tried to sing in the authentic way he had learned as a boy, when he sang folksongs. "I can almost go back to my original voice," he said, and yet he also said that he could hear his trained voice coming through even as he strove for authenticity.

His banjo style was what some have called "frailing" and others "clawhammer," known throughout the Appalachians and elsewhere. He said, "I play like the fellows around Mash Fork played. That's the only way I know." He did have one distinctive variation in his thumb movement. Most frailers let the thumb drop from the fifth string to the second or third strings occasionally to get extra notes. This is usually called "drop-thumb" picking or "double-thumbing." Buell achieved the same result with an occasional backward stroke of the thumb—that is, he brought his thumb up across the desired string, instead of picking the string with the usual downward motion. He had another somewhat unusual technique of alternating between the lower two strings and the upper two with the downward beat of his index finger, particularly when he was keeping rhythm as he sang the melody. This produced a rocking sound of high-low, high-low notes. He preferred to call his style "picking" rather than frailing because he carefully articulated the tune with a downward stroke of the nail of his index finger. His accompaniment is distinctive, especially on the ballads. It is a rapid welter of sound but with the tune creeping along at his singing tempo, discernible from the other sound. He also did an up-picking style that is common, but he rarely used it. On some slow-tempo songs he strummed as if he were playing a tenor banjo. He played in some eleven tunings of which he said, "I learned most of them from somebody else." The banjo he played for almost fifty years was a Gibson ("The Gibson"). He bought it at Scott's Music Store in Ashland after his first recording session in 1927 (he borrowed a banjo for the first session).

The Appalachian Mountains have bred many fine musicians, and Buell Kazee was among the best. He was an extraordinary ballad singer, with a versatile voice and a profound sense of the place of the ballad in musical literature. As a Baptist minister, he had a deep sense of tradition, in both theology and music. Because of his ministerial duties, he had relatively little time for folk music, but what he did, he did with integrity and arresting style. He knew many rare ballads and songs, and he was knowledgeable in music and folklore, so that he preserved with discerning ear and voice the modes and style from another age. Bess Lomax Hawes introduced him at the Newport Folk Festival as the man from whom so many modern folksingers had gotten songs. He was an important link with traditions that are becoming less distinct as styles and customs change.

NOTES

Most of the information for this story of Buell Kazee's life came from interviews by the author on July 10, 1974, March 20, 1975, and May 13, 1975; from tapes made by John Cohen and Mark Wilson and from the following sources: "Discography of Recordings by Buell Kazee," *JEMF Quarterly* 6 (Spring 1970): 19–22; "Buell Kazee Talking to Joe Bussard, Wilson Reeves, and Leon Kagrise," *Old Time Music* 6 (Autumn 1972): 6–10; brochure notes to Folkways FS 3310, *Buell Kazee Sings and Plays* (1958).

Charles Wolfe

Columbia Records and Old-Time Music

To what extent did the commercial record companies of the 1920s accurately document the traditional music of the rural South? And what effect did this documentation process have on the music and the musicians? These are the classic questions confronted by anyone seriously pondering the relationship between traditional music and commercial country music. One approach to the problem has been to compare the songs found on commercial recordings with those found in the standard folk song collections of the same general era.[1] Another might be to compare the list of songs recorded by Library of Congress researchers in the 1930s with a master list of those songs recorded by commercial companies.[2] But perhaps the most basic approach is to look more closely than we have before at the exact content of the commercial companies' recordings, at the kinds of material they released, and how well various types of material sold. This kind of overview of the commercial series would look not so much at the individual songs, or the individual artists—both of which have been the standard approaches in the past—but rather would look at a record series in a broader, more general vein: at the release patterns of song genres, at sales patterns of song genres, at distribution methods and promotional devices, at the image the commercial companies themselves had of the music. What is needed at this stage is hard statistics instead of romantic pictures of far-sighted recording pioneers wandering into the mountains with a carload of wax discs and a love of the common people. The early recording business, after all, was a business; one cannot assess the effect of commercial recordings without understanding something about how the business worked.

Yet that is easier said than done. While key pioneer recording executives like Ralph Peer (Victor), Frank Walker (Columbia), Art Satherley (American Record Company), and A. C. Laibly (Paramount) have been interviewed about their careers, none of them was able to offer specific statistics about sales and marketing, perhaps because they were all more involved in finding and documenting talent rather than actually selling it. Company files, in many cases, no longer exist, or have become hopelessly lost as the independent record companies of the 1920s were sold, merged, and dissolved repeatedly throughout the years. Yet one can, by using just the phonograph records themselves, generate a surprising amount of usable statistical data: one can, for instance, generate profiles of what kinds of records were released, in what years, and by what kinds of artists. Surviving catalogs and advertisements can give us some idea of distribution and marketing strategies, and occasionally older performers come up with royalty statements, correspondence, and contracts. And in a few cases, we have even more data: such a case is Columbia Records, and such is the justification for this pilot (and highly preliminary) study.

Few readers of *JEMFQ* need an elaborate introduction to Columbia records, or to its famed 1920s series, the 15000-D series, "Familiar Tunes—Old and New." Most of the old-time records of the 1920s were released in various special numerical series designed to appeal to southern audiences and designed for marketing in the South.[3] Columbia's 15000-D series was one of the most successful of these series. During its eight years of existence (1925–1932), it brought to the American people the music of the Skillet Lickers, Charlie Poole, Riley Puckett, Vernon Dalhart, and many other important early country performers. A fuller history of Columbia's corporate genealogy and its early entry into the country music field can be found in standard references by Goodrich and Dixon[4] and Green.[5] For the purposes here, suffice it to say that Columbia was one of the first companies to record and market old-time music— it began in early 1924, barely months after John Carson's famous first recording for OKeh—and it was the very first company to initiate a separate series for white southern music.

From its inception in early 1925 until its demise in November 1932, the Columbia 15000-D series produced 782 records; one release number was apparently never issued, thus making the actual total of records in the series 781. The first title in the series was Ernest Thompson's "Alexander's Ragtime Band"/"The Mississippi Dip," and the last record

in the series was Bob Miller's "The Crash of the Akron" backed with the Columbia Band's rendition of "Anchors Aweigh" (15782-D). The Columbia 15000-D series contained more releases than any of the other major "old-time" numerical series of the 1920s (OKeh, Paramount, Brunswick, Vocalion, Victor, and Gennett). Columbia's series accounted for about 20 percent of all the old-time material issued prior to 1932. In addition, Columbia's technology was as good as or better than that of its competitors; the sound of its records was loud and clean, and the discs themselves were remarkably durable, able to survive numerous playings on the old lathe-like Victrolas and still sound decent. Unlike many other records produced in the 1920s, the Columbia records were laminated, using a sort of sandwich construction which helped hold the discs together even when they suffered substantial cracks. Finally, Columbia's distribution seems to have been wider than that of companies like OKeh, Vocalion, and Brunswick; Columbia 15000-D series records have been routinely found by record collectors not only over the South, but even into the Midwest and Far West. Columbia had pressing plants at Bridgeport, Connecticut, and Oakland, California, and both plants produced old-time material in the 15000-D series. Columbia and Victor were the only two companies to achieve anything resembling national distribution with the "old-time" series—though it has to be noted that by far the largest percentage of the sales was in the South. All of these facts help justify using Columbia as a starting point for the study of how old-time music was produced and marketed.

In making this preliminary analysis of the Columbia 15000-D series I have drawn upon the music contained on the records themselves, the research done by numerous people who have interviewed former Columbia artists, and my own extensive interviewing of old-time artists associated with Columbia. But two important sets of data have really formed the basis for the study: the coupling notices of the releases from the Columbia files and the sales figures for the individual records in the series. A note is in order about the provenance of each.

The coupling notices were company file references which gave basic information about the origin of the record: they contained the exact title as it would appear on the record label, the artist reference as it appeared on the label, the name of the song's composer (if any) and a reference to the publishing company owning the song, the number of records initially pressed, and additional number of labels printed for possible future pressings, the date the record was released (not the date of recording), the date the record was first listed in the monthly catalog supplements, and the master numbers of the songs. As far as I can determine, these data were first gathered and codified by singer-disc jockey-scholar-teacher Bill Randle and were presented as an appendix to his dissertation, "History of Radio Broadcasting and Its Social and Economic Effect on the Entertainment Industry 1920–1930" (Case Western Reserve University, 1966). Since then they have been widely circulated among collectors and students of the music. Randle has recently published a similar set of coupling notices for the Columbia 1-D popular series, with a fuller explanation of the notices and their significance.[6]

The sales figures for the issues in the Columbia 15000-D series were obtained by David Freeman, one of the country's leading authorities on, and collectors of, old-time music. These figures had been filed on a series of note cards in the New York offices of CBS, and in their original form represented month-by-month orders on each record in the series. Freeman reports that these figures appear to have been kept rather carefully from 1925 to about 1930; when the Depression knocked the bottom out of record sales, the cards were updated more carelessly, and in fact sales figures for many of the 1932 sides were apparently not even entered. Thus there is some doubt that the figures give a completely accurate picture of retail sales. To complicate matters more, Columbia apparently for a time had a no-returns policy on selling records to its wholesalers, which means that sales reflected in these figures could refer to wholesale sales that were not necessarily passed on to consumers. Nonetheless, these sales data are the only remotely reliable indicators of actual record popularity in the 1920s, and are vital to establishing an honest profile of the records' impact on southern society. We are very grateful to Dave Freeman for making these sales figures available for this study.

These two sets of data, used in conjunction with the records themselves, allow us to study the Columbia series from two perspectives. First, we can see it as a collection of songs, preserving a variety of vocal and instrumental styles, of song texts and instrumental tunes. To a rather limited extent, the collection can be seen as an analogue to the written collections of folklorists like Brown, Cox, and Randolph. It can be seen, to an extent, as a passive reflector of southern culture. After all, most of the records in the series were made "in the field" somewhere in the South. Until recently, it was assumed that most old-time records were done in New York, with "field trips" being the exception rather than the rule. In 1925, the first year of the 15000-D series, this was certainly true. But all Columbia records after May 1925 were electrically recorded, and this new process made field recording much more feasible. In the fall of 1925

Columbia began to make regular lengthy trips to Atlanta and customarily recorded there twice a year through 1931. Other, though less important, trips were made to Johnson City, Tennessee; New Orleans, Dallas, and Memphis. After 1925 as many as 75 percent of the titles released in the 15000-D series were recorded in the South. Well over half the releases in the series were recorded in Atlanta (cf. below).

Unlike the folklorists' field recordings and collections of written texts, commercial phonograph records did not simply reflect passively their culture. These records almost all reentered the culture that produced them, sometimes in the tens of thousands, and almost certainly influenced the culture they were documenting. They were an active influence as well as passive reflector. Columbia's series pumped into the southern musical culture 11 million records between 1925 and 1932; that is over 22 million song or tune performances, and in most cases each record was listened to by several people. If the other old-time series did only half as well in sales in the South, probably as many as 65 million old-time song or tune performances flooded into the southern culture over this same seven-year period. This is especially impressive when one realizes that the population of the South during this time was barely 30 million.

THE MEN BEHIND THE SERIES

Before evaluating the 15000-D series as a collection of "texts," it is important to know something about the collectors and something of the principles under which the collecting was done. The 15000-D series was the brainchild of A&R pioneer Frank Walker. Along with Ralph Peer and Polk Brockrnan, Walker was largely responsible for developing the commercial country music industry. Walker was interviewed in 1962, a few years before he died, by Mike Seeger, and the interview reveals a good deal about the man and his values.[7] Walker came from a rural background in upstate New York and joined Columbia in 1921. He was apparently responsible for bringing Gid Tanner and Riley Puckett north to record in 1924, and by 1925, with the new electrical technology produced by Western Electric, he was one of the first to go into the field. Walker was genuinely sympathetic to the music he recorded and referred to the typical southern performer as a "poet"; he seemed to have a good grasp of what constituted traditional material, though he recognized the tendency for singers to change and adapt texts. Still, he recorded mainly what he thought would sell, and never really thought of himself as preserving culture. He had nascent standards of professionalism; he complained that many acts he recorded had limited repertoires of "eight or ten things," and recalled that when one found an artist who had an expandable repertoire, who could learn new material readily, "you hung onto him."

Walker worked closely with developing the 15000-D series during its first three years of existence and personally supervised most of the field-work himself. But gradually, as the system settled down, he delegated responsibility to various assistants. One of the most important of these was Wilbur C. "Bill" Brown. Not much is known about Brown's background; he was apparently a native of Atlanta. He worked closely with Walker from his earliest field trips; he helped locate talent, he worked with the artists, helped choose repertoire, and helped loosen them up if necessary. A member of Jess Young's band told me: "Old Bill Brown, he was always there with that bottle, wanting you to take a little drink to relax you." Brown worked so closely with the Skillet Lickers that he was roped in on several of their skits and made at least a couple of tours with them. By 1930 Brown had left Columbia and was serving in a similar capacity for the Brunswick-Balke-Collender Company. His whereabouts today are unfortunately unknown, though as late as 1951 he was still working in Atlanta.

Two younger men became increasingly active in the series during the late 1920s: Dan Hornsby and Bob Miller. By 1929 this team had pretty much replaced Walker and Brown, with Miller taking Walker's supervisory role and Hornsby working closely with the artists. Miller, born in Memphis, eventually gained fame as a prolific songwriter, music publisher, and promoter; his songs included "Eleven Cent Cotton" and "Twenty-One Years." Under a variety of noms de plume he recorded many sides for the 15000-D series and later for other labels. Hornsby, for his part, was an Atlanta native who had solid training in pop music and sang in a rich baritone voice. He recorded numerous times with pop artists like Perry Bechtel, and occasionally sang on records by the Skillet Lickers and Jess Young's band. After Columbia closed its Atlanta office, Hornsby continued to work in Atlanta radio, doing commercials and mainstream music, and was later associated with politician Gene Talmadge.

Although both Miller and Hornsby were from the South, both were interested in more commercial, pop-oriented music; they saw little of the charm of the old music that attracted Walker, and they generally pushed the recording sessions they were in charge of more in a pop direction—or as far in a pop direction as they could. By the time the Delmore Brothers made their recording debut in Atlanta in 1931, Miller and Hornsby were insisting that their artists have "original material."[8]

METHODOLOGY

How did Walker and his crew go about finding and locating talent to record for his series? This is a complex problem, and one which I plan to explore at length in future studies; for now, however, a few cogent points may be in order. In a few cases, Walker and his counterpart at Victor, Ralph Peer, actually placed notices in local papers advertising their field trips.[9] But as the field techniques became perfected, most field trips were set up far in advance, and the people who appeared had in many cases been auditioned earlier by one of Walker's men, or recommended by Columbia dealers. By 1929 Hornsby was even touring radio stations in the South looking for likely talent.

Atlanta became a sort of field headquarters for the company. Victor and Columbia had studios for a time in the same building on Peachtree Street, and the offices were across the hall from each other. One old musician told me: "There were two doors down there when you got up there; on one side was what they called The Riley Puckett door; on the other side was what they called The Jimmie Rodgers door." Hornsby kept a well-stocked library of old sheet music in a room next to the studio, and on occasion would duck into this room to verify some lyrics that a musician had forgotten. Columbia customarily paid expenses for musicians to come to Atlanta to record, and Columbia's fondness for using the Atlanta studio grew as time wore on. After 1925, as much as 66 percent of the 15000-D series releases were recorded in Atlanta. The only other field site to yield much material for the 15000-D series was Johnson City, Tennessee; trips to New Orleans, Dallas, and Memphis yielded some fine blues but relatively little old-time material.

This reliance on Atlanta as a field base, to the exclusion of other sites, naturally affected the geographical range of the performers represented in the series. North Georgia performers absolutely dominated the 15000-D series; performers from "outlying" areas were either not represented well, or were represented by other companies whose recording centers were more accessible to them.

Over 300 different recording groups show up in the 15000-D series. Some groups, however, had interchangeable members, and some groups were musicians who had recorded before under different names. Well over half these groups recorded only one record. At the same time, six groups accounted for over 50 percent of all the releases in the series. These groups were:

(1) The Skillet Lickers constellation, with its off-shoot bands headed by Riley Puckett, Clayton McMichen, Lowe Stokes, Fate Norris, and others;

(2) The Smith Sacred Singers-M. L. Thrasher groups from north Georgia (though Thrasher and Smith split from each other, the groups shared several key members);

(3) Darby and Tarlton, recording always under their own names only;

(4) Vernon Dalhart, with occasional pseudonyms;

(5) Charlie Poole and the North Carolina Ramblers; and

(6) The Leake County Revellers, from Mississippi.

Dalhart alone accounted for one-third of all sales prior to 1929.

Walker and his co-workers did not hesitate to influence the nature and direction of the music when it suited their purpose. For example, Walker seemed possessed with the idea of finding a singing group to compete with Victor's highly successful Carter Family; he apparently groomed the Blue Ridge Mountain singers for this, and members of the Chumbler Family recall being asked specifically to try to sound like the Carters. In doing things like this, Walker might well have distorted traditional singing styles or repertoire. But in other cases he went out of his way to preserve more archaic music forms when the artists wanted to go modern. Walker apparently insisted that Charlie Poole retain his trio format when Poole wanted to expand to a larger band. Walker held the Skillet Lickers together when they wanted to break up and forced Clayton McMichen to play older fiddle tunes when Mac really wanted to experiment with jazz or western swing or popular pieces. Often Hornsby and Miller corresponded with performers for months before a session, discussing tune selections. Certainly during the last three years of the series, Columbia chose very selectively from the repertoire of its artists, and often these selections were dictated by originality, prior copyrights, and other recordings of a number.

TYPE OF SONGS IN THE SERIES

How much traditional music was represented in the 15000-D series? This is a debatable point, considering the current unsettled definition of traditional music. But a place to start is the copyright references that show up in the coupling notices. Generally speaking, about 25 percent of the songs in the series have such copyright notices. However, the notices do not include older copyrights, and they do include a few blatant attempts to copyright traditional material. (In 1927, for instance, Carson Robison copyrighted a version of "Barbara Allen.") But many of the copyrights listed in coupling notices are accurate. The percentage of copyrights increased as the series moved into the early 1930s and as Hornsby and Miller took over. In 1927–1930, with Walker still a force in the series, the copyrighted songs hovered between 15 percent and 20 percent. In 1931 the figure rose to 30 percent and by 1932 to 76 percent.

The percentage of copyrights, though, only tells us that, even by the vague business standards of the 1920s, Columbia recognized much of its old-time product as Tin Pan Alley in origin. Indeed, one has to remember that the series was called "Familiar Tunes—*Old and New* (emphasis added). Copyrights do not tell us much about the type of music in the series, or even the type under copyright. To learn that, we have to delve into the songs themselves. Walker told Seeger that he had four main categories for the series' material: (1) jigs and reels; (2) event songs; (3) heart songs; and (4) gospel songs. It is noteworthy that this division reflects only distinctions of song type rather than provenance; there is no distinction of traditional from nontraditional material.

With this in mind, I have somewhat expanded Walker's categories to allow for such distinctions and to account for other occasional types that show up in the series and have devised the following list of categories:

A. Traditional instrumental tunes, played primarily on the fiddle or occasionally on the banjo, guitar, harmonica, or mandolin.

B. Traditional songs: songs widely recognized as traditional in a conservative sense, or found in standard collections.

C. Prewar pop songs, which includes popular Tin Pan Alley songs published prior to 1916.

D. Postwar pop songs: popular Tin Pan Alley songs published during or after 1916, but not country songs composed by the artists themselves at or near the time of recording.

E. Event songs: songs composed and recorded in direct response to a national tragedy, scandal, or issue.

F. Comedy recordings include humorous songs as well as skits like "A Corn Licker Still in Georgia."

G. Gospel songs include sacred harp material, quartet material, convention songs, and solos or duets of sacred material.

H. Original country vocals: new material written by old-time singers and directed toward an old-time audience, such as McMichen and Layne's "My Carolina Home."

I. Original instrumentals: instrumental tunes originating with their performer(s).

N. Cajun music: the small number of field recordings made of Cajun performers in 1928.

This classification scheme has a number of admitted flaws. I am aware that many songs in category C (prewar pop) might well have been learned from tradition or by some of the performers. I have, for instance, included "The Little Old Log Cabin in the Lane'' in the prewar category. Though it has been widely reported in tradition, it does have a definite Tin Pan Alley history. The gospel songs category includes both prewar and postwar material and some genuinely traditional material. It now seems clear that many of the gospel artists in the series (certainly including Smith and Thrasher) sang from the paperbacked "convention'' books, and these routinely included songs of all three types. On many of the comedy records (especially the skits), there are traditional music and a few traditional jokes, even though the bulk of the skits themselves were written by individuals like Hugh Cross, Walker, and Hornsby. The distinction between postwar pop and original country vocal categories becomes at times tenuous, especially when dealing with some of Bob Miller's products. Finally, the setting of 1916 as the dividing line between "old" and "new" pop songs may seem somewhat arbitrary. But my feeling is that 1916, the year before America entered World War I, was a cultural watershed of sorts, and that once America emerged from the war it moved quickly into the age of mass media and "modern times."

A final problem in dealing with this system—or with any such system—is the simple mechanics of applying it. For this study, I have tried to listen to as many of the records in the 15000-D series as possible and to assign each song to one of these categories. I have personally listened to about 70 percent of the selections; some records have not turned up in accessible collections. In some cases, category assignments have been made on the basis of title and/or coupling notice information, with the uncertainty that such a process entails. Some songs have not been traceable to any one certain category, and some have been tentatively assigned to categories which may, with later research, prove erroneous. For these reasons, the following statistics must be seen as tentative and preliminary.

I have also limited the study to the years 1925 through 1931; 1932 was not included because hardly any of the sales data were available for that year. Thus, the study reflects the 15000-D series from Columbia 15000-D through Columbia 15726-D. Since one release number was not issued, the scope of the study includes 726 records, or 1,452 tunes. Some 1,427 tunes are reflected in these statistics; the balance could not be identified well enough to place in any category.

With these qualifications, we can then turn to the Columbia collection as a whole and explore the relative percentages of song types contained in it. Overall, the average percentages of song types throughout the period from 1925 through 1931 are as follows:

A. Traditional instrumental—10.5 percent
B. Traditional vocal—22. 9 percent
C. Prewar pop songs—16.2 percent
D. Postwar pop songs—12. 5 percent
E. Event songs—3.4 percent
F. Comedy—5.5 percent
G. Gospel—19.4 percent
H. Original country vocal—6.5 percent
I.   Original instrumental—2.6 percent
J.   Cajun—0.5 percent

A breakdown of categories by year reveals that:

1) In every year but one the series released more traditional than popular material. In most years, though, the percentage difference between the two categories wasn't very significant. Generally speaking, about one-third of the records released were some sort of traditional music.

2) There were more old (pre-1916) pop sides issued than new (post-1916) sides. Of course, most of the mainstream pop sides were issued in the Columbia 1-D series, and some of the 1-D series releases were very popular in the South (e.g., the series by Moran and Mack, the Two Black Crows; individual sides by Vernon Dalhart, Ukulele Ike [Cliff Edwards], and Ford and Glenn).

3) Instrumental sides were always outnumbered by vocal sides. Walker recalled in his interview that instrumentalists were far more common than singers, but most of the sides in the 15000-D series had some singing on them. The gap between instrumental sides and vocal sides grew larger as the series developed.

4) There was a slow, steady rise in the number of original country vocals, reflecting the increasing commercialization of the music.

5) The percentage of gospel releases was steady throughout the seven years of the study, usually hovering between 18 and 20 percent of the

releases. In fact, the relative percentage of gospel releases was the steadiest of any of the categories.

6) If one would combine categories A, B, and C to get a composite category that might be generally labeled "old secular songs and tunes," this category would account for almost half of the releases. This suggests that the key element in the series was nostalgia rather than genuine traditionalism. This composite percentage, though, gradually decreases through the years, until it reaches 42 percent by 1931.

7) It is instructive to compare the figures in categories A–J with a similar set of figures for Columbia's parallel 14000-D blues series. This series was also developed by Walker, and he supervised many of the recordings in it at the same field sessions that yielded the 15000-D selections. In Dan Mahony's excellent study of this series,[10] he devised a classification system different slightly from that presented here and computed the following percentages of releases:

vocal blues — 25.3 percent
vaudeville vocals — 33.7 percent
pop/standard vocals — 7.0 percent
religious songs — 12.8 percent
sermons — 5.4 percent
West Indian songs — 0.4 percent
instrumental blues — 3.9 percent
instrumental fox trot — 11.5 percent

In a very rough sense one could compare the 15000-D series' "traditional" category with the "vocal blues" category, in which case the percentages (25.3 percent vs. 23.4 percent) are quite close. Gospel-religious music in both series runs about the same. It should be noted, too, that Mahony is quite cautious about his categories and principles in assigning tunes to those categories, and generally distinguishes vaudeville vocals as mainly vocals by female singers, regardless of the nature of the song.

SALES OF DIFFERENT CATEGORIES

The type of music released in the 15000-D series really tells us more about Columbia's expectations than anything else; it shows us the kinds of music they thought they would sell. To test the accuracy of these expectations, we must turn to the sales figures themselves. It is these sales figures which reflect the 15000-D series as an active influence on southern culture, and it is these figures that really show how successfully Walker and his associates designed their product.

The 726 records released in the 15000-D series through 1931 sold a total of 11,316,000 records: an average sale of about 15,600 per record. The best-selling record sold slightly over 300,000 copies; the poorest-selling, barely 500. Some records were kept in the catalog longer than others and thus had a longer selling life. Some records originally released in 1926, for example, were still selling in 1930. Some early records in the series established themselves as "standards," while later records by the same artists were deleted from the catalog when the stock on hand was exhausted; in other cases, records were repressed. It is important to remember that the sales figures used in this study are cumulative sales totals of all sales for a record throughout all the years that record was available. Without further data, it is impossible to break the sales down to a year-by-year basis, to determine if buying patterns shifted within the seven-year span covered by the study.

Later studies will chronicle the specific "greatest hits" of the 15000-D series. My concern here is with presenting an overview of the sales picture. This overview, however, must take into account the role of the best-seller, because Columbia sales were a significant function of big-selling records. For instance, fifteen records in the series sold in excess of 100,000; their combined sales accounted for as much as 23 percent of the total sales in the series. In other words, 2 percent of the releases brought in 23 percent of the sales. When these records and their sales are subtracted from the general sales, the average sale in the series drops from 15,600 to 12,300 copies.

In many cases, a record would have different song types on each side. To reflect this possible division, the following data have been reduced to "sides" rather than "records." In computing the total sales, for instance, if a record had two sides, both of which were the same song type, then the data would reflect twice the actual sales figure. The total record sales of 11,316,000 represent 22,632,000 sides. In most cases it is impossible to tell what side of a record was a hit side; for purposes of distribution and influence, both sides of the record were equally available to the audience.

The biggest average record sale was generated by event songs, 42,690. Most of the successful event songs were issued in the first two years of the series. After event songs, comedy sides had the biggest average sale, then traditional instrumentals and songs. The smallest average sale was for gospel songs.

Some types of song were more likely to produce smash hits than others. Event songs, of course, was the category most likely to produce more hits per release: almost 8 percent of event song releases sold over 100,000 copies. Other categories generating a number of big hits included traditional instrumentals and postwar pop.

The total of both "traditional" categories, A and B, produced 37.1 percent of all the sales; the total of both "popular" categories, C and D, produced only 26.5 percent of the sales. This should make folklorists happy, for it suggests that the collection, to an extent, functioned more as a folk influence on the culture than a pop influence. Fifteen of the big smash hits were traditional; only six were popular. Comparing the cumulative sales of these two combined categories with their cumulative releases, we can see that traditional material sold slightly better than expected (37 percent sales for 33 percent releases), while pop as a whole (C and D) sold worse than expected (26.5 percent sales from 28.7 percent of the releases). If we add the comedy totals to the traditional totals (for, in fact, many of the skits contained traditional music), the total sales account for 43 percent of the overall sales. About four out of every ten recorded songs in the 15000-D series sold by Columbia from 1925 to 1931 were traditional songs of some type.

How much was the popularity of the individual artist a factor in these sales? If people bought, say, Riley Puckett records because they were by Riley Puckett, then the above figures have to be evaluated in a slightly different light. This is a highly complex question which I plan to reserve for a future separate study; my feeling now is that many record buyers bought the song rather than the singer. However, it is a fact that, of the fifteen highest selling Columbia 15000-D titles, two artists (Vernon Dalhart and the Skillet Lickers) had eleven. Of course, this could be a result of the fact that Dalhart and the Skillet Linkers recorded more than others; and of course, they could have been recorded more because they sold well. Without some rather complicated statistics, this issue will be hard to resolve.

DISTRIBUTION PATTERNS

According to the coupling notices, new Columbia records in the 15000–D series were released every ten days. In the early years of the series, two records were released every ten days; in later years, as the number of releases was stepped up, as many as five records were released every ten days, or as many as fifteen per month (in 1928). Monthly catalog supplements were issued for the Columbia 15000-D series, often with photos and write-ups about artists. Columbia dealers were sent advance listings of the new records and allowed to pre-order titles they thought would sell; this "preview" technique probably dictated the initial pressing orders for the releases. Though there is little evidence that Columbia forced its new releases on its dealers, the dealers were apparently not allowed to return unsold records.

Newspapers of the late 1920s are full of advertisements for Columbia records, usually sponsored by local Columbia dealers. Many of the advertisements have mail order coupons in them, suggesting that some Columbia sales were made by mail. In 1928 and 1929 Columbia records were also advertised and sold by Montgomery Ward, one of the country's major mail order houses; Ward's 1928 catalog listed ten Columbia 15000-D series records, and the 1929 catalog listed 52 records. (Of the ten records listed in the 1928 catalog, three were among the top seven sellers, and two others sold well above average; was Ward's selling proven hits, or generating hits?) Ward's distribution certainly expanded the Columbia sales pattern beyond the South, and helped popularize the series.

It is almost impossible to say how much money Columbia made from their old-time records. They apparently sold records to their dealers at between 35¢ and 40¢ per disc; with the average record selling 15,600, the company would have taken in between $5,000 and $6,000 per disc. This would not have been all profit, of course; out of this would have come production costs (about which we know nothing), overhead, and fees (usually a flat $50 per side). Doubtless, artists were exploited under this system; even those who received royalties usually got only a fraction of the profits generated by their hits. It is not surprising that virtually none of the artists saw record-making as a serious way to make money.

CONCLUSIONS

We must be extremely cautious about applying the results of this highly preliminary study to the early country music industry as a whole. Columbia was only one of seven major companies operating and at best represents only a fraction of the industry as a whole. A number of factors, not the least of which was Frank Walker, might well have operated to make Columbia untypical. Columbia's sales figures, to be sure, seem roughly compatible with those we have seen from Victor and Gennett. However, the song type content of the other companies remains to be explored, as do their marketing methods and philosophy.

There is also the problem of seeing the sales figures in perspective. I have argued elsewhere, as has Norm Cohen, that there were very few, if any "million-sellers" in the country music world of the 1920s. The Columbia figures seem to bear this out. Yet even today the typical Nashville country album sells only between 20,000 and 30,000 copies, and it has only been in the last three years that a country LP has "gone platinum"—actually sold a million copies. (This was Willie Nelson and Waylon Jennings' *Outlaws* on Victor.) In this light, a sale of 20,000 copies to the much more limited country audience of the 1920s is indeed impressive. In fact, the average sale of records in the 15000-D series is somewhat higher than has been previously estimated. Doubtless the Depression seriously affected record sales; the average sale of records released in 1930, for instance, was 2,480; by 1931, this figure had fallen to 886. Of course, older records still in the catalog were continuing to sell during these years, though certainly in smaller numbers.[11]

Finally, the study reveals that the Columbia series contained a substantial amount of traditional material and that this material sold very well. By no means can we see the series, in the older simplistic mode, as a collection of folk songs; it contains as much pop culture as folklore. This analysis of the Columbia series suggests that old-time music (or what some scholars still call hillbilly music), as a genre, was an amalgam of traditional songs, older popular songs, religious songs, and new material which had a rural flavor: an amalgam which had as its common denominator a sense of nostalgia. But given the commercial goals of those who produced the series, the wonder is that the traditional content is as high as it is. Part of this can be ascribed to the audience that supported the series; perhaps the impulse that made people across the South buy traditional tunes on record was the same impulse that caused them to preserve the old tunes in the first place. Whatever the case, it seems clear by now that this first generation of country records can no longer be ignored by anyone attempting to deal with the traditional music or culture of the rural South.

ACKNOWLEDGMENT

Special thanks to David Freeman, not only for providing the valuable sales figures for the 15000 series, but for advice and suggestions for the entire study and its conclusions. Thanks also to Stephen F. Davis, Mary Dean Wolfe, and my research assistant, Betty Dalton, for helping with the statistics.

NOTES

1. See, for instance, Norm and Dave Cohen's review of John Cohen and Mike Seeger, eds., *The New Lost City Ramblers Song Book* in *The American Folk Music Occasional,* edited by Chris Strachwitz and Pete Welding (New York: Oak Publications, 1970), 78–80.

2. No one to my knowledge has done this, but a start in this direction would be the *Check List of Recorded Songs in the English Language in the Archives of American Folk Song to July, 1940* (Washington: Library of Congress, 1942). This list gives, in alphabetical order, all the titles of the numbers recorded by the field workers of the 1930s—though often the LC title for a tune is different from the commercial record's title of the same tune.

3. Many of these have been published in the *JEMFQ*'s continuing series entitled "Commercial Music Documents."

4. John Godrich and Robert M. W. Dixon, *Blues and Gospel Records 1902–1942* (London: Storyville Publications, 1969), 15–19. Also see the late Walter C. Allen's fine "Introduction" to Dan Mahony, *The Columbia 13/14000-D Series* (Stanhope, N.J.: Walter C. Allen, 1961).

5. Archie Green, "Hillbilly Music: Source and Symbol," *Journal of American Folklore* 78 (July–September 1965): 204–218. Also available as a JEMF reprint.

6. Bill Randle, *The Columbia 1-D Series* (Bowling Green, Ohio: Bowling Green State University Press, 1975).

7. My thanks to Mike Seeger for making available a tape copy of his complete interview with Walker. Part of this interview, somewhat imperfectly transcribed, also appears in Josh Dunon and Ethel Raim, *Anthology of American Folk Music* (New York: Oak Publications, 1973).

8. A detailed account of this 1931 session appears in Alton Delmore, *Truth is Stranger Than Publicity,* ed. Charles Wolfe (Nashville: Country Music Foundation Press, 1978), 31–40.

9. See Charles Wolfe, "Ralph Peer at Work: The Victor 1927 Bristol Session," *Old Time Music,* no. 5 (Summer 1972): 15; also see Charles Wolfe's note on Walker's Johnson City session (with advertisement reproduced) in *Journal of Country Music,* no. 3 (Fall/Winter 1973).

10. Mahony, *The Columbia 13/14000-D Series,* 12.

11. The question of just how typical the Columbia sales were in respect to those of similar old-time issues is difficult to answer with our current limited data. Some sense of perspective is possible, though. In the JEMF files are almost com-

plete sales data for the Asa Martin-Doc Roberts releases on the Gennett and various affiliated labels. These figures reveal that best-selling records by this group on Champion sold just over 20,000, and that the average sales for releases on Supertone (the Sears label) were 4,100; on Champion, 5,340; and on the original Gennett label, only 335. These figures suggest that Gennett sales were nowhere near those of Columbia. On the other hand, some limited sales data from the Georgia Yellow Hammers' sides on Victor suggest sales approximating those of Columbia; the Yellow Hammers' biggest hit, Victor 20943 ("Picture on the Wall"/"Carolina Girl") topped 100,000, while other nonhit sales hovered around the 10,000 mark. Norm Cohen's remarks in Johnny Bond's recent annotated discography of Jimmie Rodgers (JEMF, 1978) reveal that even Jimmie Rodgers may well have produced only four records that sold over 250,000, and that many of his later releases sold fewer than 50,000 copies.

Gene Wiggins

Popular Music and the Fiddler

While working on a perhaps inexcusably complete study of the record-ings of Fiddlin' John Carson, I browsed through many of the lists of dealers in old sheet music. I collected a good many specimens of "pop" material which turned "hillbilly," even when they had nothing to do with John. A somewhat descriptive treatment of items which became fiddle tunes and of what the fiddlers have done with them may provide some things worth thinking about. Even some consideration of the verbal con-tent may be worthwhile. It is true that in some cases fiddlers today are unaware that words once existed for their tunes. Gordon Tanner was sur-prised when I told him his "Whistling Rufus" once had words, and Jack Weeks was surprised to be told the same of his "Twinkle, Little Star." Undoubtedly the tune always has been the major consideration, but ver-bal content may have had a little influence in causing fiddlers to adopt the tune, even when the words later passed out of memory. I would not press the idea far on the basis of so few examples; but it appears that in the songs adopted as fiddle tunes, the "coon song," the "Indian song," and the "Southland song" loom even larger than they ever loomed in popular music in general.

Without claiming to be complete, I hope to note a large fraction of the items which fit well the description "piece of popular music which became a fiddle tune under the same or a similar title." I shall not deal with such things as "Turkey in the Straw," "Arkansas Traveller," "Golden Slippers," "Old Dan Tucker," and "Listen to the Mocking Bird."

Beyond the fact that the established or disputed origins of these items are relatively well known, they do not seem to fit the description well. We would have to admit that by reasonable definition they were "popular" music at one time, but if we go back to the eighteenth century, the same is true of such things as "Soldier's Joy."

Items fit the description "fiddle tune" well if they have been played, and sometimes as strictly instrumental numbers, by a considerable number of fiddlers. I believe they also have a fair claim if they have been recorded without words, or played as contest pieces, by fiddlers who were generally traditional in repertoire. This at least suggests that they may have had a wider usage than we happen to know about, that they may have made a real crossover and should not necessarily be regarded merely as popular tunes some fiddler happened to play.

Alphabetical order seems as good as any:

"Alabama Jubilee" was a 1915 song with words by Jack Yellen and music by George L. Cobb. There are 64 measures of the song. I have never heard old-time fiddlers or other "folk" types use more than the last 32, but there is repetition in the first 32 so that we do get more than half. The words used by any hillbillies I ever heard did not clearly show this to be a "coon song," but they did present a Deacon Jones rattling bones and a Parson Brown dancing around like a clown. One familiar with the cliché contrasts and parallels of religious and secular activities in "coon songs" could recognize even abridged versions as being in this genre. In the full original version we are invited to hear "darkies" play a "ragtime treat." The invitation to hurry somewhere and hear black music was another song cliché.

This tune used to be a great favorite with fiddlers in Tennessee and Georgia, I know, and I would guess it to have been even bigger in Alabama. It was a favorite guitar piece of Georgia's Hoke Rice. In the 1930s its words were parodied into the theme song of a program which emanated, very early in the morning, from WDOD in Chattanooga. Its real name was "The Bust o' Dawn Show," but either mistakenly or facetiously it usually was called "The Busted-on Show." They would sing,

Hail, hail, the gang's all here
For the Busted-on Jubilee.

It may be worth noting that the same pair of men who wrote this piece also wrote a song which has had considerable country usage—"Are You From Dixie?" At any rate, I shall note, further on, other "popular" composers who contributed songs as well as fiddle tunes to country music. There must have been something "country" about them.

Bill Bailey, Won't You Please Come Home was a 1902 song by coon shouter-composer Hugh Cannon. It is supposed to have been written about an actual Bill Bailey who lived until 1966, denying that he was turned out by his wife, as the song related.

Cannon was a song-and-dance man as well as a composer, and one of the songs he performed—"I Got Mine," by John Queen and Charles Cartwell—had some hillbilly popularity. It was recorded by John Carson, Riley Puckett, Ernest Thompson, Chitwood and Landress, George Holden [John McGee] and Peg Moreland. This was one of the few latter-day "coon songs" of a derisively humorous nature in which whites pretended to be blacks rather than just talking about blacks.

I know the "Bill Bailey" tune to have been more popular with fiddlers, at least in areas where I have lived, than its limited recording history would suggest. In my experience, fiddlers usually have called it simply "Bill Bailey." They usually have sung no more than the chorus, and often have played no more. I have never heard a clear use of the original Negro dialect, and suspect that few fiddlers have even known the song originally was in such dialect.

Black Hawk Waltz originally flourished as a piano composition by Mary E. Walsh. There was a piano arrangement which was more impressive than it was difficult, and I believe a piano version was offered by the Sears Roebuck catalog in a limited offering of sheet music in the 1930s or 1940s. Naturally, some fiddlers adopted the tune, and it is frequently heard at contests.

Chief Black Hawk made war against the United States twice—in the War of 1812 and again in 1832. While in captivity he dictated an autobiography which helped to make him, in time, a romantic and admired figure. The world of popular music was very Indian-conscious in the late nineteenth century and early twentieth. A real male Indian was needed to balance all those fictitious female Indians, two of whom gave their names to fiddle tunes, to be noted below.

The Bully of the Town is the usual folk title of a tune and song which is known to have existed as a folk song before a version appeared in the Broadway play *The Widow Jones* in 1895 and was published in 1896. Printed versions have been titled "The Bully Song," "May Irwin's Bully Song," "The New Bully," etc. Fiddlers' versions are more like each other than they are like the printed versions, but I remember encountering, during World War II, an old fellow who remembered *The Widow Jones*.

There seemed to be no distinction in his mind between the folk version and the version employed in the play. That fiddlers are melodically more like each other than like printed versions does not mean that there has been no influence at all on them of the melody as printed.

In printed versions the singer labels himself (or herself—I suppose May Irwin was pretending to be a man, but I am not sure) "a Tennessee darkey."[1] I do not believe this was done when hillbillies sang the song. My impression is that, as with "Bill Bailey," whites lost the idea of a black persona. White origin is barely possible, even though Charles Trevathan, who caused the printed version to be a printed version, said he heard the basic song sung by Mama Lou at Babe Connor's place in St. Louis. A valid general rule, even though it reflects a strange way of thinking and even though there are exceptions, is that when hillbillies pretended to be black they did so in pretty, romantic songs such as "Kitty Wells," "No More the Moon Shines on Lorena," "My Pretty Quadroon," "The Yellow Rose of Texas," and some of Stephen Foster. In the case of "The Yellow Rose of Texas," they even had a statelier and more solemn melody than the original. When something like the original was revived on the Hit Parade, the "rose of color" becoming a "little rosebud" and her "darkey" a "feller," some of the hillbillies called their melody the "old" melody. This tendency may be behind the whitening of "Bill Bailey," "Bully of the Town," and other songs which once contained first-person blackness.

"The Cat Came Back" is an 1893 song by Harry Miller. The melody was elaborated into a fiddle tune which once had some usage. R. P. Christeson presents it with the comment that it was played in Missouri in the 1930s but is not any more.[2] A version perhaps more clearly based on the song's melody was fiddled by Doc Roberts on Gennett 101. The 1893 song version is close to that sung by John Carson in 1924 on Okeh 40119, except that it is longer and is in Negro dialect.[3] There seems to be no reason for the dialect except that dialect was popular in 1893. It is a folksy type song. Lots of folk and folksy songs are about invincible animals— bears and foxes that can't be caught, goats that regurgitate red shirts to flag trains, horses that can't be ridden, an intractable bell cow, an indestructible grey goose. Here a cat comes back from each of a series of attempts to get rid of it. Most of the attempts, a priori, would be thought to involve extreme overkill. Yet all choruses except the last begin, "But the cat came back." In the last his ghost comes back. Like "Our Goodman," which often has been made to include automobiles, "The Cat Came Back" has been adjustable to modern technology and to a much altered cosmic view. In the original,

One time did gib de cat away to man in a balloon
An' tole him for to gib it to de man in de moon.

In Cisco Houston's version the cat is taken to Cape Canaveral and fired into space.[4] Even then he comes back.

Chicken Reel was published as a piano composition by Joseph M. Daly in 1910. He seems to have been both composer and publisher. The sheet music is by "Daly Music Publisher, Boston, Mass." and also carries the notation "Entered according to act of Parliament of Canada in the year 1910 by Jos. M. Daly at the Department of Agriculture." Other pieces of sheet music indicate a registration with the Canadian Department of Agriculture, but it seems especially appropriate that an imitation of a chicken should be registered there. Daly's notation, however, does not stress the chickenesque quality. The opening slide which is the most characteristic part of fiddle versions is not even represented by a slur mark.

One can write the essential "Chicken Reel" as eight measures of sixteenth notes. Using the same time system, the 1910 piano version has 112 measures, but it is mostly repetition. The melody does shift from C to F and bring in a strain that is no longer heard to my knowledge, but there is not much that a fiddler would yearn to add to the tune as usually heard today.

There is the alternate title "Performer's Buck" and the direction "not too fast." Thus it may be that the North Georgia title "Slow Buck," used by the Skillet Lickers on the label of Columbia 15267, and used verbally by other fiddlers in the area, is not as new or local as it may seem. There was a 1911 Victor recording of "Chicken Reel" by Arthur Collins. Since he was a singer, I assume there have been words; but the only ones I ever heard could not have been on a 1911 record.

Dill Pickles or *Dill Pickles Rag* was written by Charles L. Johnson in 1906. Fiddlers usually call it "Dill Pickle Rag," and it has been a great favorite.

Down Yonder remains the buck dancing and clog dancing favorite in Georgia. Once I fiddled some other tune for a bunch of cloggers, with less than perfect results. A guitarist explained to me, "It doesn't make any difference what you're playing; they'll always be dancing 'Down Yonder.'" In north Georgia, the tune is generally credited to Gid Tanner, though Gid's son Gordon, who fiddled it on Bluebird B-5562, tells me that Gid did not even learn to play it on the fiddle until it was evident that the record was selling well. I have heard two separate apocryphal stories as to how the Skillet Lickers came to think of such a title.

Actually the song came out in 1921 and was recorded the same year by the Peerless Quartette. It was by L. Wolfe Gilbert, who in 1912 had written the words for "Waiting for the Robert E. Lee" (Lewis Muir wrote the music). At about the peak of the popularity of "Hawaiian" fad, in 1916, Gilbert also wrote the words to "My Own Iona" which was Hawaiian to the extent that it was first popularized in Honolulu, though it was written probably in New York and finally got to Georgia on Okeh 45142, by the Scottdale String Band. The music (by Anatol Friedland and Carey Morgan) is strongly suggestive of the "Indian" song "Snow Deer," reminding us that we were not safely out of one fad before we got into another.

Gilbert, in "Down Yonder," consciously was trying to write a song like "Waiting for the Robert E. Lee." He confessed this after a 1952 piano recording by Del Wood was released, made under the impression that "Down Yonder" was a public domain fiddle tune.

Fifty Years Ago is a tune which has just come to my attention. Quite recently Charles Wolfe sent me a tape of this tune by Wyzee Hamilton (Herwin 75542), and more recently Marcus Bailey sent one of a much later rendition by Herman Johnson. After a search that turned up a 1952 song of identical title, three "twenty years ago" songs, and two "hundred years ago" songs, I still cannot give author or date of the song behind this fiddle waltz. However, there is one, and it is on an Edison cylinder by Ada Jones and Len Spencer. The title of the cylinder is "The Golden Wedding."[5] It presents a dialogue of a couple on their golden wedding anniversary. Appropriate songs are interpolated. "Silver Threads among the Gold" of course is one, and another is the song that became the fiddle tune. It may not have been called "Fifty Years Ago," though this is the tag line of one section and the likely title.

Georgia Camp Meeting is the usual title for what is properly "At a Georgia Camp Meeting." Kerry Mills wrote it in 1897, and it is supposed to have started the cakewalk. It describes one. There is a "coon camp meeting" at which the older folks become full of religious zeal. Untouched by such zeal, the young folks hire a brass band and the festivities are climaxed by walking for a cake. The old folks disapprove at first but finally join in. This idea of religious arousal opposing a secular frolicsomeness basically very like it and the religious finally surrendering to the secular became standard in coon songs. It is possible that there was some carryover from the way whites belonging to more sedate denominations once ridiculed whites of more Pentecostal habits.

The lyrics, except for the phrase "way down in Georgia," seem not to have appealed to hillbillies, but the tune did. Oscar Ford used a tune based on it, and stole that phrase from it in his song "Georgia's My Home" (Columbia 15634). Earl Johnson recorded a "Way down in Georgia" on Okeh 45559, which leaves the impression he got the title phrase from the Mills song.

"Georgia Camp Meeting" was recorded in purely instrumental form by the Leake County Revelers on Columbia 15409-D, and the instrumental "Peaches Down in Georgia" by the Georgia Yellow Hammers on Bluebird B-5126 owes much more to "Georgia Camp Meeting" than to "Everything is Peaches Down in Georgia."

Hesitation Blues or *Hesitating Blues,* or the same essential tune under still other titles, has usually been done with words but was done in purely instrumental fashion by Reaves White County Ramblers on Vocalion 5217. There are several things to indicate that the essential tune had a folk existence prior to W. C. Handy's 1915 "Hesitating Blues." One is that there was another printed version, "Hesitation Blues," about the same time.[6] Another is that folk versions, though recognizably the same basic tune, are not very much like Handy's music. Another is that few hillbillies have used any of Handy's words. Uncle Dave Macon used four of Handy's lines in his version, which was titled "Hill Billie Blues" (Vocalion 5041), along with some lines from the other printed version and some lines from God knows where. Handy did not even have the meaning of hesitating implied in many folk versions, which seem to allude to the technique of "hesitation" in dancing, which peaked in popularity about 1913. Handy advises against procrastination in general and expresses special displeasure at a telephone operator's slowness in giving him a girl's number.

A simple version of the tune was a favorite of Fiddlin' John Carson. He is known to have used it to promote Senator Tom Watson, Governor Cliff Walker, Governor Gene Talmadge, and (my order is chronological rather than climactic) True Blue beer.[7]

I'll Be All Smiles Tonight certainly has been more of a song than a fiddle tune, and I would not have included it had it not been played by Harold Zimmerman in the finals of the 1978 Tennessee Valley Old-Time Fiddlers Contest. He showed that it makes a fine fiddle tune. He also provided a reminder that the act of making a popular song into a fiddle tune can come long after the song has left the "popular" category. In this case we can see that perhaps only part of the song ever was in the "popular" category, strictly speaking, and that perhaps none of it was. We find the words to this song (by M. J. Ludlow) essentially as done by the Carter Family in an 1891 collection of songs that are more "art" than "popular." But the melody given there (by George Powis) is not the same melody at all. We may have the lyrics to an art song, later done to a folk or popular melody which finally became a fiddle tune.

I'll Meet Her When the Sun Goes Down was an 1882 song by William Walsh. I am still without a copy of the original music, though I have one of the cover and of the song "Standing by the Gate" which was printed under the same cover. However, when we put together the music as given in a Scottish tune book, the lyrics as quoted by Douglas Gilbert,[8] and the recordings of John Carson, we see that we have a popular song which in considerably altered form became a fiddle tune.

Drastic differences between Carson's versions of things and the original versions do not necessarily represent the results of a long historical process. He probably played hob with the 1914 "I'm Glad My Wife's in Europe" and the 1917 "Dixie Division" almost as soon as those songs appeared, though what he did with them could not be heard on records until a few years later. However, in this case I suspect that Walsh's song was modified by people other than John. A verse apparently based on it appears in a collection of Negro folk rhymes.[9]

John did the tune with lyrics as "Meet Her When the Sun Goes Down" on Okeh 45353 and in strictly instrumental form on the skit record "The Old Gray Horse Ain't What He Used to Be," Okeh 45471. The tune may never have been fiddled by many people, but it deserved to be, and I suspect it was. I have tried it on younger fiddlers, and they had never heard it before; but the response of Uncle Jim Cofer, who is past ninety, was "Lord, yes."

"My Little Girl" was a 1915 song, music by Albert Von Tilzer, words by Sam Lewis and Will Dillon. It does not lend itself to the virtuosity fiddlers like to display today, but in the 1930s, when string bands were less ostentatious, it was popular—as a plain instrumental, with the original lyrics, and as a parody. In the parody, the girl was not—as in the original—many miles away. She threatened to be many miles *around*. If I remember correctly the parody began:

> My little girl, she is a whopper,
> She weighs fully three hundred pound;
> And if she keeps on gaining,
> She'll be many miles around.

It ended:

> I see the lane down in the wildwood,
> Where you promised to be true.
> My little girl, if you keep on gaining,
> 'Twill be hard for you to get through.

I believe Arthur Smith and his Dixie Liners were, on radio, frequent perpetrators of this.

My Nellie's Blue Eyes has a chorus which has belonged to four different types of music. It was an Italian folk song which eventually was popularized by Caruso. William J. Scanlan in 1883 added two other parts to this chorus and produced "My Nellie's Blue Eyes," which finally became a hillbilly song. Scanlan also wrote the Uncle Dave Macon favorite "Peek-a-Boo" and a "Molly O!" which is strongly suggestive of what Ahaz Gray and the Leake County Revelers called "Merry Widow Waltz" (quite unlike the Lehar waltz usually called that). There undoubtedly was an inexplicable touch of hillbilly in Scanlan. I do not know that "My Nellie's Blue Eyes" has been recorded by an old-time fiddler since it was done by Arthur Smith on Bluebird B-7325, but I remember it as once rather popular.

"Pray for the Lights to Go Out" was a 1916 song with words by Renton Tunnah and music by Will Skidmore. It is classified on the cover as "A Negro Shouting Song" and as "That New 'Ballin' the Jack' Song." It goes further than "Georgia Camp Meeting" by presenting a situation in which the line between religious ecstasy and concupiscence (not just frivolity) is thin. It is not in dialect but attempts to seem colloquial by putting in apostrophes where they make no sense as well as where they do. "Lovin' " and "slippin' " are all right, but there is no sense in "turn'd" and "throw'd." While the narrator sets the action in a church where his father was a deacon and includes "Father" in the action, there is not much of a first-person feeling. The song really belongs with those songs that talk about blacks, and there is nothing in the text itself as I have it to indicate that the people are blacks. I cannot say about the "set of extra comedy choruses" which one could get for twelve cents more. These well may have included the words which, according to Tony Russell, are the title of a version by black singer Hambone Willie Newbern—"Nobody Knows What the Good Deacon Does."[10]

For present purposes, the notable rendition is the one which caused Russell to make this observation—the "Wait for the Lights to Go Out" of Walburn and Hethcox (plus an uncredited second fiddle) on Okeh 45305. I don't think their wait had much standing; I always heard *pray*. It used to be done by Uncle Dave on the Grand Ole Opry.

"Red Wing" is a 1907 song, words by Thurland Chattaway and music by Kerry Mills. We saw Mills as composer of "Georgia Camp Meeting" and shall see him again as composer of the "coon song" "Whistling Rufus." He emerges as the favorite "pop" composer of the fiddlers, and, as a violinist, might be pleased could he know this. When we consider that the "coon songs" were likely to be snappy, danceable things (in vaudeville often accompanied by a dance) and that two of them adopted by the fiddlers were by Mills, we doubt that we should accuse the fiddlers of much fondness for the verbal content. We now have the question of whether or not there were melodic traits likely to be found in the "Indian"

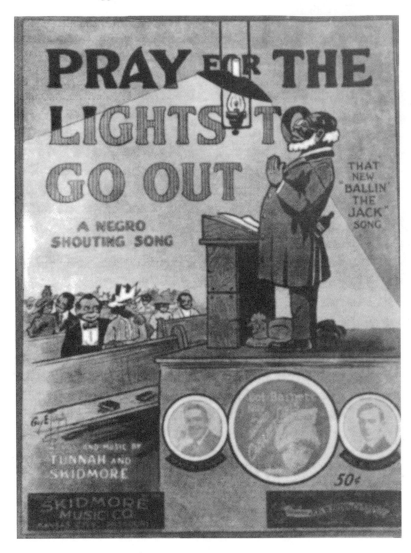

songs such as "Red Wing." I think there were. It would have been because their composers were imitating each other rather than because of any basis in real Indian music. More frequently than songs in general they seem to have melodic phrases calling for feminine rhymes in the lyrics and to have a lot of short phrases contrasted with longer ones. This can happen in other music, and the truth is that "Red Wing" is pretty close to the Schumann composition popularly called "The Happy Farmer"; but the "Indian" songwriters seem to be especially addicted to contrast in phrase length. For instance,

> She sang a lay,
> A love song gay,
> As on the plains she whiled
> away the day.

St. Louis Blues was a 1914 song by W. C. Handy, composer or re-composer of "Hesitation Blues." I remember it as done in at least one contest by Arthur Smith. It also was a favorite of Sawmill Smith, who was an outstanding fiddler, even though he was not recorded. He is mentioned by Charles Wolfe in a book on Tennessee music.[11]

Silver Bell was a 1910 song with music by Percy Wenrich and words by Edward Madden. It has been even more popular with country players of fretted instruments than with fiddlers, but popular with fiddlers too. "Indian" songs were shamelessly imitative of each other. Ada Jones played the squaw on at least three Edison cylinders that are the same in cast (a brave and a squaw) and plot (brave woos squaw and takes off somewhere with her). Vocabularies are similar and of course don't include the ugly word "squaw." Tunes are no more different than would be expected when one was called "Silver Bell" and the other "Silver Star" (the other was "Rainbow"). What I mean about short phrases in "Indian" songs will be clearer after a transcription of the way the "Silver Bell" of Ada and Billy Murray sounds. There are detached syllables which are equivalent to phrases.

> Ada: Be-
>   Neath
>   The
>   Light
>   Of a bright,
>   Starry night
>   Sang a lonely little Indian maid, "No lover's sweet serenade
>   Has ever wooed me!"
>
> Billy: As
>   In
>   A
>   Dream

It would seem
Down the stream
Gaily paddling his tiny canoe
A chieftain longing to woo
Sang her this song:

(The dominant voice of the chieftain is that of Ada, who sounds too female and too British for a chieftain, but she could sing like blazes.)

Your voice is ringing,
My Silver Bell.
Under its spell,
I've come to tell you of the love
I am bringing
O'er hill and dell.
Happy we'll dwell, my Silver Bell.

As "Snow Deer," Ada was involved with a cowboy, but all else was much the same.

Sweet Bunch of Daisies is an 1896 song by Anita Owen, who was very justly called "The Daisy Girl." She seems to have spent most of her time sitting around writing waltz songs about daisies in the key of A-flat. It has been a great favorite with fiddlers. It was the express favorite of Jess Young, and when he died it was fiddled on the stage of the Radio Playhouse in Chattanooga, as a memorial, by his friends Bob Douglas and Roy Cross. I have heard it done other than as a waltz only once, but it was done very effectively in 4/4 time at the 1978 Yellow Daisy Festival at Stone Mountain, Georgia.

Twelfth Street Rag was written as a piano piece in 1914 by Euday L. Bowman. Lyrics were written by James Sumner in 1919 and by Andy Razaf in 1942. The Razaf lyrics, which (like many lyrics written for already existing melodies) tout the melody, say it was written in Kansas City. If this is true, the street of the title may be a street there.

This tune was popular congruently with jazz players and fiddlers. I believe this number is the only one on which we can hear Pink Lindsey and His Bluebirds. The other side of Bluebird B-6221 is a song by Marion ("Peanut," "Curly") Brown, who played on John Carson's last session as well as with Bill Gatin's Jug Band and with the Bluebirds. Pink Lindsey, who also was a voice on some of the skit records, was the Bluebird fiddler. His son Ray was the tenor banjoist.

Twinkle, Twinkle, Little Stars was an 1876 song by Fred MacEvoy. I suppose the history of the fiddle tune's title, which seems invariably to address only one star, begins with the rhyme "Twinkle, twinkle, little star/How I wonder what you are," and the little Mozart melody that goes with it. We should note also an 1855 song by John P. Ordway called "Twinkling Stars Are Laughing, Love." Undisguised appropriation of bits of earlier works seems not to have been considered stealing in the old days, so MacEvoy had an unworded instrumental introduction to his song which clearly is indebted to Ordway. He then began the lyrics with a close approximation to Ordway's title—"The pretty little stars are laughing, love." Earl Johnson's fiddle version on Okeh 45156 is the only one I have heard which suggests the Ordway-based, wordless part of MacEvoy's song. Other fiddlers have been fairly close to the worded part.

Fiddlers seem always to address only one star, but the MacEvoy title was "Twinkle, Twinkle Little Stars," rhyming with the alternate title "Meet Me at the Bars." One is gratified to learn that these are the bars of a fence down by "grandpa's meadow." The picture shows a trustworthy looking boy and girl standing on opposite sides of those bars.

Under the Double Eagle was written by J. F. Wagner, an Austrian composer who died in 1908. Like "Over the Waves," it is more "art" than popular in origin, but I am going to include it anyway. The title may have puzzled others as it once puzzled me. As a child I knew that a double-eagle was a twenty-dollar gold piece and wondered why anybody would get excited about what was under one of those. My sheet music cover shows an eagle with two heads, and I assume that such was a symbol of the Austro-Hungarian Empire, for which this is said to have been the "semi-official march."[12]

Waiting for the Robert E. Lee has already been mentioned as the work, in lyrics, of "Down Yonder" composer L. Wolfe Gilbert. It appeared in 1912, music by Lewis F. Muir. According to one source it "was inspired by a scene on a levee in Baton Rouge, Louisiana, witnessed by the lyricist: the sight of Negroes unloading the freight from a Mississippi River boat, the Robert E. Lee."[13] If this is accurate, we must assume Gilbert was joking when he wrote Harry Golden, "Harry, now that you're down South, would you please let me know what is a levee?"[14] It would be a likely assumption, anyway.

In the song, we are not in Louisiana but in "Alabammy." Alabama has been the favorite locale of "coon songs" and "Southland" songs for the simple reason that "Alabammy" can be rhymed with "Mammy," as it is in this song. The statement is that the boat has come to carry the cotton away, though it is a fair guess that something was unloaded first. Our characters, however, don't seem to be either loading or unloading but just having a good time. A cylinder record by Arthur Collins and Byron Harlan presents the song as a stichomythic dialogue between the two and brings in a little of the idea of the religious yielding to the earthly which seems to have been almost required in "coon songs" in which there was a group, rather than just mooning lovers or warring spouses.

Even the preacher,
He am the banjo teacher!

The tune is not done much by fiddlers today, but it was popular on the Grand Ole Opry in the 1930s.

The Waltz You Saved for Me is a 1930 composition, music by Wayne King and Emil Flindt, lyrics by Gus Kahn. Of several fairly recent waltzes that have been played in fiddlers' contests, it is the one that has been played by so many fiddlers that its inclusion here seems proper. Present-day fiddlers are an eclectic lot—there always were some who were that way—and only when several adopt a newish number do we feel that something of general significance may have happened.

Washington and Lee Swing is a 1910 piece, music by Thornton Allen and M. W. Sheafe. The initially published words were by Thornton Allen and C. A. Robbins. Many schools have had *their* words. It was more popular with fiddlers in the 1930s than recording history would show.

Whistling Rufus is another Kerry Mills piece. The melody dates to 1899. The words, credited to W. Murdock Lind in some copies, may not be as old as the tune. According to sheet music dealer Larry Floyd, apparently old and wordless copies exist which give no date or publisher. The story back of the words (which concern a black guitar player who was called a one-man band) may have existed before the words were written. Charles Wolfe has a wordless copy with the following statement:

> No cake walk in the Black Belt District in Alabama was considered worthwhile unless "Whistling Rufus" was engaged to furnish the music. Unlike other musicians Rufus always performed alone, playing an accompaniment to his whistling on an old guitar, and it was with great pride that he called himself "The One Man Band."

Most fiddlers today, I believe, know no words to this tune. The bulk of the recordings appear to have been wordless, but according to Charles Wolfe, there have been several with words, including those of Welling and McGhee, McLaughlan's Old Time Melody Makers, the Short Brothers, and the McGee Brothers. The title character has the surname Blossom (some singers on record seem to say Johnson), and the McGees called the song "Rufus Blossom." More about their version will be found in Charles Wolfe's *Three Tennessee Folksingers*.

This song manages to speak of Alabama without rhyming it with mammy. It rhymes Alabammer with hammer (Rufus had a head like one). The tune has been very popular with fiddlers and still is. Some used to achieve a whistling effect by bowing partly behind the bridge, but this was more appropriate and more impressive than it was agreeable and I think it isn't done any more.

Probably all readers who follow the fiddlers will feel that I have omitted at least a couple of tunes which should have been included, and they no doubt are right. Charles Wolfe, who read this piece in draft, felt something should be said about how these pieces got to the fiddlers—what he calls the "conduit." The trouble here is that I do not have the discographical and other resources. It is through his help that I am able to say something along these lines. Many of these pieces, he notes, were recorded by jazz bands prior to any country recordings, and some appeared on piano rolls. This involved not only pieces which might seem to be likely jazz

Pieces—"Georgia Camp Meeting," "Bill Bailey," "Whistling Rufus," "St. Louis Blues," "Hesitating Blues," "Washington and Lee Swing," "Dill Pickles," etc., but some that may not seem so likely, such as "Sweet Bunch of Daisies" and "Over the Waves." Other types of recordings, such as quartette recordings, doubtless were involved too.

Fiddlers with one foot in the "pop" camp, such as Clayton McMichen and Jess Young at an earlier date and Bob Wills at a later one, must have been especially important in causing certain tunes to make a crossover. Radio no doubt had its importance, and some fiddlers who did not record at all may have had their importance; but it seems likely that fiddlers, in earlier days just as now, were more likely to learn from recordings. Obviously a recording can be played as much as is necessary while radio is less at the learner's command. It seems probable also that fiddlers have always tended to turn to recordings of something like "hit" status. I daresay that no fiddler of the past suffered as many requests for anything as the modern fiddler does for "Orange Blossom Special," but it is safe to say that popularity made a difference. Some very popular recordings of tunes mentioned above would include the Blue Ridge Highballers' "Under the Double Eagle" (as well as the later Bill Boyd version), the Scottdale String Band's "My Little Girl," the 1926 McMichen "Sweet Bunch of Daisies," the Blue Ridge Ramblers' "Washington and Lee Swing," and the Curly Fox "Fifty Years Ago." A tune might owe its survival for a number of years to rather obscure recordings but owe its present-day popularity and many of the details of any present-day performance to Bob Wills.

We should remember that a printed source is not necessarily the ultimate source. Perhaps most of all in the case of "Chicken Reel," but in the case of other pieces dealt with here too, it is reasonable to suspect an existence prior to the printed version. Had such songs as "Battle of New Orleans," "Bonaparte's Retreat," and "Hop-Scotch Polka" been written before any of the related fiddle tunes were printed or recorded, one could find himself writing about how the fiddlers had appropriated these. There has been no intent in this article to question the inventiveness of the fiddlers. Art and popular music owe more to folk music, though the debt is harder to document, than has been given back.

NOTES

1. James Jacob Geller, in his *Famous Songs and Their Stories* (New York: Macaulay, 1931): 97, states that Trevathan learned the tune from blacks in Ten-

nessee. His book includes this song as well as "Bill Bailey" and two songs to be noted later in this article—"At a Georgia Camp Meeting" and "Waiting for the Robert E. Lee." The "Bully" and "Bailey" songs also can be found in *Songs of the Gay Nineties* (New York: Amsco, 1943). Ann Charters, ed., *The Ragtime Songbook* (New York: Oak, 1965), includes all the songs mentioned in this note except "Waiting for the Robert E. Lee," but this book, while informative, is performer-slanted and alters texts to avoid references to race.

2. R. P. Christeson, *The Old-Time Fiddler's Repertory* (Columbia: University of Missouri Press, 1973), 8.

3. Lester S. Levy, *Flashes of Merriment: A Century of Humorous Songs in America, 1605–1905* (Norman: University of Oklahoma Press, 1971): 238–240. More of the original sheet music is reproduced in Robert A. Fremont, ed., *Favorite Songs of the Nineties* (New York: Dover, 1973): 52–54, but a page of "additional stanzas" is not included.

4. Vanguard R L 7624–8 *Folksong and Minstrelsy*.

5. I have the collection of cylinder recordings made up by the late Fred Harrington. He did not provide recording numbers. This collection, items from it, and additional material were available at the time of publication from Merrit Sound Recording, 223 Grimsby Road, Buffalo, New York, 14223.

6. See Abbe Niles, "Notes to the Collection," in W. C. Handy, ed., *A Treasury of the Blues* (New York: Charles Boni, 1949): 243–244.

7. *Folio of Standard Songs,* rev. ed. (Boston, New York, and Chicago: White Smith Music, 1891): 27–32.

8. *Kerr's Collection of Merry Melodies Arranged for the Pianoforte* (Glasgow: J. S. Kerr, n.d.): 16; Douglas Gilbert, *Lost Chords: The Diverting Story of American Popular Songs* (New York: Doubleday, Doran and Co., 1942): 145.

9. Thomas Talley, *Negro Folk Rhymes* (New York: Macmillan, 1922): 332.

10. Tony Russell, "Back Track: Walburn & Hethcox," *Old Time Music* 29 (Summer 1978): 16.

11. Charles K. Wolfe, *Tennessee Strings: The Story of Country Music in Tennessee* (Knoxville: University of Tennessee Press, 1977): 50.

12. *Baker's Biographical Dictionary of Musicians,* revised by Nicolas Slonimsky, 5th ed. (New York: C. Schirmer, 1971): 1732.

13. David Ewan, *American Popular Songs from the Revolutionary War to the Present* (New York: Random House, 1966): 420–421.

14. Harry Golden, *So What Else Is New?* (New York: G. P. Putnam's Sons, 1964): 21–22.

Fabrizio Salmoni

Country Music in Italy: A Matter of Controversy

American country music in Italy has not had the exposure and popularity which it has enjoyed in other countries such as England, Holland, and Japan. Difficult though it is to find all of the reasons for this lack of success, nonetheless we can point out three main factors which approach the problem. First, Italians are aware of the enormous cultural distance separating them from the American South and its customs, morals, values, symbols, and lifestyles. Secondly, most Italians show a certain distrust towards country music because to them it apparently does not possess aesthetic traits sophisticated enough to compete with other musical genres, such as rock or opera. Last but not least, country music cannot easily reach the taste of an audience which, for ideological reasons, often resists the infiltration of the pop scene by "overly American" cultural models. In fact, the presence in Italy of a strong and influential political left constitutes a relevant cultural factor.

Generally, foreign observers blame the vivacity of social relationships as the cause for the never-ending instability within Italy. Actually, some commentators suggest a positive interpretation of the situation: turmoil, ferment, and constant dialectical controversy make Italy a country politically problematical but culturally rich. Therefore, the cultural debate cannot overlook the ideological disputes and the extent of social change. This is a peculiarity which ultimately has the utmost importance for the investigation of any Italian phenomenon.

Before getting into substantive discussion, I feel it necessary to clarify the exact translation of *popolare*. It is not possible to translate this word with the American adjective *popular,* even though we will meet the Italian word connected with categories such as *music* or *culture*. In Italy, an advanced industrial society dominated by the media, the adjective *popolare* tends to be associated with ideas such as "free from current conditioning," "regional," or even "belonging to a pre-commodity model of society." In all these examples of usage, *popolare* maintains a good degree of flexibility, although it usually relates to an idea of spontaneity of the lower class and working people. *Popolare* offers a version of the behavior or point of view of ordinary people, when these do not reflect, or only superficially mirror, the values and patterns of the dominant culture. In this paper, I will translate this key Italian term with the circumlocution, "of the people."

Here I seek to establish to what degree the Italian public has recognized and accepted country music as a definite genre. A good starting point is to focus on the channels through which some knowledge of the music has reached the public. Record companies in Italy form one such channel. One might try to gather information from them, using their sales indexes, but even these data cannot provide a clear view of the situation, mainly because the country music market is based almost exclusively on imports. Only a long and careful survey through the major import sales dealers can perhaps shed a little light on the matter. Nevertheless, one can attempt some observations.

Some early official attempts to introduce country-western music in Italy have been those by the Italian CBS with the publication of a few Johnny Cash albums, and by EMI with a sampler entitled simply *Country Music*. The latter LP presented miscellaneous pieces performed by major Nashville stars. Very little indeed has been done by RAI (the state-owned radio network in Italy) or national television. These sources have always been so culturally backward and conformist that one cannot expect the bureaucrats, who manage them under governmental mandates, to take bold steps forward to unexplored and untested ground. From the mid-1960s to the early 1970s, RAI broadcast a weekly thirty-minute program entitled "Songs of the West" (*Le canzoni del West*) which did no more than announce the pieces. The fare was taken from the sound tracks of western movies (Italian as well as American), or from LPs of artists such as Woody Guthrie and Pete Seeger (from a series of six albums published by Albatross, the French-Italian equivalent of Folkways).

A mysterious vocal and instrumental group of doubtful American origin, Rocky Mountain Ol' Time Stompers, rounded out the RAI selection with classics like "Home on the Range," "Swannee River," and even "Yankee Doodle." One of the Stompers was probably a singer who had been popular in Italy in the early 1960s, and who had used an imitative American pop style. This program subsequently changed its name to "Country & Western," and adopted a repertory of country rock origin but also introduced pieces by the New Lost City Ramblers, Johnny Cash, Merle Haggard, Sonny James, and Buck Owens. Some of their songs were taken from the EMI sampler mentioned above; Guthrie and Seeger also remained on the list. Every now and then some instrumentals taken from a pair of albums published by Joker, a small Italian label, would be inserted. These Joker LPs, entitled *Greats of the Banjo,* offered reissues of period material by musicians who had been associated in one way or another with the folk revival: David Lindley, Roger McGuinn, Eric Weisberg, and others. Joker had already published, among other things, a double album by Jack Elliott and Derrol Adams, which formed a rather hodge-podge collection of selections originally belonging to a variety of musical styles (from "John Henry" to "Worried Man Blues" to "Going down the Road Feeling Bad").

Another point must be mentioned about the situation in the 1960s before rock made its conquest of the Italian teenage market. In general, American folk music was misconceived as being entirely cowboy music. In actual fact, numerous original versions of Nashville hits circulated (for example, Jim Ed Brown's "The Church"), but these were indiscriminately submerged in the tide of imported American pop music. Unknown to most listeners, there were even Italian covers of country hits such as "Busted" (Harlan Howard), "Honey" (Bobby Goldsboro, Roger Miller), and "Ringo" (Sons of the Pioneers).

American ethnic and folklore studies developed in Italy in the early 1950s, nurtured by a small group of pioneering enthusiasts. These studies, in contrast to those of other European countries, never developed sufficiently to attain real prominence, nor even to insure the addition of new scholars to the field. Research in and classification of regional Italian folklore had been undertaken under the auspices of the Instituto Ernesto De Martino, which occasionally turned its attention to international folklore. Alan Lomax, during his travels in Europe in the mid-1950s, had stayed in Italy, and in the course of his activities, had collaborated on research in Piedmont and in the South. It is possible, in my opinion, that an initial interest in American folk music evolved from connections maintained by Lomax and the New York group "People's Songs" with a few Italian folklorists. The fact is that it was precisely in those years that a bond—even an ideological one—developed between Italian folklorists and singers who were soon to be protagonists of the folk revival in the United States.

Some of the Italian folklorists followed Gramscian methods, an analytic/interpretive approach developed by Antonio Gramsci, a leading Marxist intellectual imprisoned by Mussolini. Over the years, the progressive political revision by the Italian Communist Party (PCI) helped transform most of Gramsci's cultural suggestions into sterile ideological conformities. This transformation undermined considerably the serious development of American folklore studies in Italy. A conspicuous tendency among the left wing was one of often arbitrarily interpreting the cultural expressions of the people as indirect political messages. Basically, starting with the principle that the proletariat is potentially a revolutionary class, its cultural expressions, or at least those of some of its sectors, must then, in a fundamental way, reveal a revolutionary spontaneity.

The Italian left has often made this hypothesis an article of creed, and has taken refuge in it during those moments when the left most sharply felt the symptoms of a cultural identity crisis. The musical heritage of the leftist militants, historically, is made up usually of anthems, political songs, and traditional songs (often in dialect) with no explicit political content. Thus, a striking contradiction occurred between this heritage and the musical tastes of thousands of pop-rock-influenced young militants. Most of them resolved this contradiction by keeping their political activity separate from their musical entertainment. Hence, performance of national and international folksongs at times filled the generation gap and masked the problems with expressions of international solidarity.

Furthermore, then as well as today, and for reasons which need investigation in detail, a conformist tendency transcended political positions, causing the consumer public to adopt a subservient attitude toward a mistaken concept of "learned" culture. This tendency denigrated a cultural product which did not display "artistic features." The interpretation of the concept "artistic features" varied, of course, according to one's point of view. The left usually attributed artistry of the people to national or local cultural expression uncontaminated by the media or popular forms. As a consequence, the left has shown a predilection for folklore, especially from third world countries, better yet if Latin (Cuba or Chile). As for the conservatives' point of view, "artistic features" remained a property of the traditional forms of "high culture" (classical music, opera, theater).

When applied to the United States, this widespread attitude has, understandably, often caused an important revolutionary role to be attributed to the proletarian and subproletarian black, especially after the urban ghetto revolts in the late 1960s, and the formation of militant organizations such as the Black Panthers. Indirectly, a genuine but indiscriminate sentiment of solidarity against the racism of the American system motivated this characterization of the American black. Italian leftists preferred black music over country music. The former, from blues to jazz, represented an expression of oppositional culture; the latter represented the notoriously conservative, if not reactionary, values of southern white society.

Many Italians still find it problematic to come to terms with country music, a genre cherished by an American audience composed mostly of factory workers and lower-middle-class people—that is, the social strata traditionally interested in supporting the political left in Europe. How could this class, or at least substantial parts of it, back the policy of aggression in Vietnam? How was one to accept a genre which was nothing but a transposition into music of a movie like *The Green Berets*? There simply could not be much room in Italy for country music during the Vietnam years. The anti-American feelings among the militants of the PCI, who in the 1950s had carried on a struggle against the NATO military bases in Italy, had temporarily merged by the late 1960s with the hostility towards the United States on the part of the "Vietnam generation." This new protagonist on the political arena sustained the major burden of the antiwar protests and then, in large measure, differentiated itself from the PCI by giving rise to organized movements to the left of the PCI beginning in 1969.

In that year, the Laterza Publishing Company printed a selection of texts bearing the significant title *Lead Poison on the Wall, Songs of the Black Power*.[1] This collection followed in the wake of a series of similar enterprises involving American scholarship. The prevailing attitude was the one described above: attention focused primarily on the radical aspects with which the American left was also concerned. Certain arguments raging among American folklorists (for instance, the role of the rural folksong transferred to an urban context by musicians unfamiliar with its original surroundings) were observed with great interest. The Istituto Ernesto De Martino published in its internal bulletin some letters by Alan Lomax, John Cohen, B. A. Botkin, and others, debating these subjects.[2]

As early as 1954 a small anthology of protest songs of the American people had been compiled and published under the title *Listen, Mr. Bilbo* (*Ascolta, Mr. Bilbo*). It presented, among other things, a few texts by Woody Guthrie, a brief biography of him, and a discussion of the relationship between the song "Tom Joad" and John Ford's movie *The Grapes of Wrath*.[3] In 1958 a small book appeared dedicated to American songs celebrating heroes and outlaws.[4] Another collection followed simply entitled *Folksongs*.[5] Next, Richard Dorson's *American Folklore* (*Il folklore negli Stati Uniti*) appeared in translation. Finally, Francesco LaPolla's analytical article "The American Folksong in the Nineteenth Century" (*"La folksong americana nell'Ottocento"*) became available.[6]

The years 1968 to 1972 marked a significant interruption in such publications. In that period a widespread organized movement to the left of the Communist Party sparked controversy, discussions, and theoretical debate. The PCI, also frightened by the Chilean coup in 1973, since that moment hastened the revision of many of its positions and assumed a subordinate role in relation to the Italian majority party. This political fear gradually determined behavior in cultural matters for the ensuing years. The veerings in party line which characterize its recent history have had strong repercussions on the PCI's cultural policy. Having considerably revised its former analysis of the question, the PCI today is the most active organizer of rock concerts in Italy, aimed towards gaining prestige with the young.

Rock concerts by foreign musicians in Italy had been canceled for several years because of frequent riots. The high cost of tickets sparked these riots. Many young people accused concert promoters of speculating on music which "belonged" to youth. Several groups of youngsters crashed these concerts, clashing with the police. Some of these instances turned into riots in Milan and other large cities in the early and mid-1970s, at the appearances of bands such as Grand Funk Railroad, Led Zeppelin, and Santana. In all those cases police used tear gas to subdue rioters.

After a few years of silence, the Communist Party involved itself in concert promotion by guaranteeing profits to promoters and providing order. Its purpose was to gain popularity among the young, hungry for good music, and at the same time to gain prestige as a law-and-order party among the middle class.

In 1972, some members of the same group of people who had been responsible for the publication of earlier American folk material offered a retrospective analysis of the folk revival.[7] It is interesting to note, by looking at publication credits, that so far no new interpreters of American folk music had surfaced in Italy at a scholarly level. One can only guess at the many reasons for this lack of fresh recruits: (A) the fact that the published material circulated only in the limited circles of specialists and enthusiasts; (B) people were concerned with being considered excessively pro-American; (C) an inability to get beyond the narrow limits of the field of folksongs to address a wider field of inquiry; (D) the difficulty in disentangling oneself from problems caused by the convergence of folk forms with others of pop origin.

A major study appeared in 1975 on Woody Guthrie's life and work. The author, Alessandro Portelli, is an instructor in Anglo-American literature at the University of Siena as well as a folklorist (he had previously edited the collections *Folksongs* and *Songs of Black Power*). Portelli's work is possibly the most serious and accurate on the subject. However, although he includes an introduction to and a short discussion of country music, the old methods of approach prevail. Portelli chose to emphasize a few examples of songs concerned with social themes, or songs picked from the repertoires of early hillbilly musicians. Examples were: Uncle Dave Macon's "Down the Old Plank Road," "Roll down the Line," "Governor Al Smith," "All I Got Is Gone," or the Dixon Brothers' "Weave Room Blues." He then concluded that in spite of these and a few other rare cases, today's country music "is the vehicle for the most reactionary material the United States media industry can produce in a cultural field."[8]

Portelli portrayed country music as a substantially negative phenomenon, the result of an irreparable devolution of a misled evolution—a cultural expression once treasured by a subordinate class, formerly able to express its values at the folk level. Essentially, he felt that businessmen appropriated the music of the people for profit and transformed it to the point that it lost connection with its original roots and became something totally shaped and controlled by a commercial elite.

Nevertheless, Portelli made a valuable contribution by discussing the question of validity in the relationship between folk music and political song. He interpreted Woody Guthrie's character in the light of the singer's artistic journey, and of his progressive awareness culminating in militant engagement. The result is a very positive assesment of Guthrie as "the greatest revolutionary American poet." To Portelli, Guthrie offers an exemplary demonstration of how an artistic form such as music can be restored to its original social milieu in a way that makes it possible for the people to reappropriate and use it constructively.

What of the large Italian audience which takes no part in the ideological disputes, and which has, after all, its own indirect autonomous power of judgment despite its subjection to market regulation and a powerful promotional apparatus? For the majority of this audience, especially the younger set (prime consumers of recorded music), the very name *country* is vague and lends itself to generalizations and misconceptions. The idea of *country* is commonly associated with those forms of country rock of California origin represented by groups like the Byrds; Crosby, Stills, Nash & Young; Pact; and some of the early Eagles' output. To many, the spectrum of country rock artists runs more widely from Jackson Browne and Emmy Lou Harris through Linda Ronstandt and Michael Nesmith, to the Nitty Gritty Dirt Band, Charlie Daniels, and the Marshall Tucker Band.

This whole set of musicians by now has its stable Italian following which is formed in part by the rock audience. A limited number of broadcasts by RAI (in special programs for the young) and frequent programs on the independent radio stations (usually in the evening hours given over to "rubriche," that is, broadcasts on a predetermined theme), reach these listeners. This music is looked upon as one island in the jagged archipelago of rock, as consumable music, without a history, music that does not warrant deep investigation.

Specialized magazines deal with such material to a limited extent— some to speak well of it, some to speak badly, or even to neglect it. For example, the magazine *2001*, dependent on music publishers, is well disposed towards it. *Gong* and *Muzak,* which belong to a certain youthful "intelligentsia" of the new left, are substantially disdainful of it. The name *new left* is commonly given to nonhomogeneous political forces, which have placed themselves to the left of the PCI, beginning in 1969. Hence, the new left includes a wide range of positions which have in common different levels of criticism towards the so-called ideological revisionism of the PCI. *Muzak,* before its close in 1976, included some notable exceptions with articles by Portelli, who concentrated his attentions on the folk, ethnic, and precommercial aspect of American music.

A minor branch, commonly labeled *progressive country* in Italy, departs from so-called country rock. The former, considered to be closer to folk origins of American music, is reworked in a modern key, and stripped of the "backwoods" aspects which characterize it as ethnic music. Progressive sound comes out clean and perfect, and its outlines leave plenty of room to virtuosity. Exponents are young instrumentalists who rework traditional pieces and bluegrass. These performers are usually promoted by minor labels such as Flying Fish and County. Some enjoy a certain fame (perhaps greater in Italy than the United States). This is the case, for instance, with stars like David Bromberg, Norman Blake, and Stefan Grossman.

The progressive country audience is often made up of hi-fi lovers who have a keen appreciation for excellent recording quality. These listeners also enjoy the quality of sound reproduction of such music on stereo sets, a sound quality which is based on the technique of the heightened tonal contrasts obtainable from acoustic instruments. This somewhat snobbish audience, satisfied with special choices and unwilling to subject itself to the coarseness of the "real thing," has its own publication, the title of which is borrowed from a product of American cinema, *The Wild Bunch* (*il Mucchio Selvaggio*). The magazine dedicates space to "real country" music, its origins, and pioneer musicians from the precommercial era. Its editors, who had earlier also been the first to deal with the subject of country music in a column in a hi-fi monthly, undoubtedly can be credited with having promoted awareness of the matter in Italy, but they have usually been made the butt of bitter criticisms by part of their audience.

One such criticism touches the method with which country music is presented. The magazine presentations simply follow an outline based on each artist's discography; the reference to the discography is the guiding theme of every article, while analysis of the phenomenon is superficial, though rich in detail. The remaining impression indicates that the author is well supplied with a collector's mass of information, and that he dribbles it out pedantically, sometimes with a certain exhibitionism, taking good care not to divulge the sources of his knowledge (the articles include no footnotes). However, the major criticism that can be made of *Mucchio Selvaggio* is that even though it also celebrates the annals of old-time music, it is always the Brombergs, Blakes, and Grossmans who are the real protagonists. These revivalists and others are touted as the most significant exponents of progressive country, which the staff of *Mucchio* still considers the most worthy of note in the realm of country music.

Nevertheless, the magazine did succeed in bringing out of hiding and into contact with each other people who soon turned out to form a set interested in country music at various levels. *Il Mucchio* even revealed the existence of local groups who play bluegrass, old-time music, and country rock. Such performers, for the most part, do not define themselves politically, nor claim an ideological justification for their choice of music. By contrast, various semiprofessional or nonprofessional rock groups do claim a radical stand. Those who say the American myth is dead, notwithstanding groups with names such as New Hillbilly String Band, Old Banjo Brothers, Kentucky Fried Chicken Boys, have given concerts almost anywhere: private clubs, public meetings, schools, etc.

In the spring of 1979 one such group from Milan, the Southern Comfort String Band (seven members aged about twenty), toured the province with a show bearing the fascinating title "Old time & bluegrass, the evolution of the music of the American people from its old forms to commercial." According to the review in *Mucchio* "the show lasts two hours and is mainly suited to a young audience; with appropriate modifications it could be presented to even younger listeners (elementary and junior high) that is, by including pieces which would encourage active participation on the part of the children."[9] The Southern Comfort String Band also had previously accredited itself through a concept show entitled "The Labor and Union movement in the United States from 1870 to 1940 as seen through the music of the people."

Many of these youthful performing groups are influenced by country rock, progressive country, and bluegrass. They are also inspired, in some cases, by single tracks which have been popularized from the sound track of successful movies. Examples are: "Foggy Mountain Breakdown" from Arthur Penn's *Bonnie & Clyde;* "Dueling Banjo" from *Deliverance.* In all this confusion, one can even come upon oddities such as an Italian version of "Six Days on the Road," recorded live at a free festival, and transformed into a song in support of the squatters in Milan in 1975. This song's Italian title is *"Questa casa non la mollero"* ("I'm not going to let go of this house"); it addresses the line of policeman sneering at the squatters with expressions such as "assembly of cowboys" to indicate their arrogant pose and predisposition towards violence.

Old-time music does have a limited circulation in Italy, tied to specialized labels such as Rounder, Old Timey, and County. Made-in-Nashville country music means everything that runs from Kenny Rogers to Dolly Parton to Merle Haggard. Straight Nashville music does not enjoy much popularity in Italy, and the private radio stations tend to throw it into the category of "easy listening." Undoubtledly the Italian audience perceives a cultural distance even more than a quality-determined one, whether it be toward old-time music or toward the Nashville sound. Lack of knowledge sustains this distance. Badly expressed prejudices (country music equals reactionary music), confused ideas, and the ambiguous relationship between Nashville country and pop also contribute to barriers. The understanding of texts could further add to the distancing process. In Italy both the patriotic and the sentimental rhetoric of many country songs, not to mention the frequent excessive celebration of macho attitudes or behaviors on the part of good old boys, and also a certain oppresive exhibition of religiosity, might not be acceptable.

From the point of view of the Italian market, bluegrass, because of its originality and gaiety, could no doubt acquire a real audience if adequately promoted. The complexity of instrumental and vocal techniques could engage the interest of those attracted by virtuosity. Bluegrass flirts with urban and progressive audiences, thus providing itself with good references in the eyes of that part of the Italian public which needs to be assured of the acceptability of the genre.

In 1978, Albatross issued the first bluegrass record released in an Italian edition which included introductory notes on the back cover. This LP featured the Bray Brothers & Red Cravens and was the Italian reprint of *Prairie Bluegrass* (Rounder 0053). Although the record is an excellent one, the introductory notes could not be worse. They describe bluegrass in awkward terms and are quite inaccurate. These notes reveal how much still has to be done in the field.

Italian audiences remain unaware of the folk origins of country music and, hence, cannot approach it critically. Further, most Italians remain unaware that country music expresses aspects of national tradition which have managed to remain alive and widespread among people despite commercial distortion. This kind of phenomenon has not occurred in Italy, nor perhaps in all of western Europe. The local and regional traditions have never melted into distinct national cultures; therefore, a process of commercialization has never begun. The failure of the Italian folksong revival relates to the Italian misunderstanding of American country music. Italian folklorists should be first to face these problems from fresh perspectives, but to do so must imply a willingness to part with sterile sectarianism. If and when Italian scholars face country music openly and with determination, they shall open up new directions for understanding the American experience.

NOTES

1. A. Portelli, *Veleno di piombo sul muro, Le canzoni del Black Power*. Laterza, Bari, 1969.

2. Istituto E. De Martino, "Discussioni in USA sulla nuova canzone," *Strumenti de lavoro* 3, July 1966.

3. R. Leydi, T. Kezich eds., *Ascolta Mr. Bilbo: Canti di protesta del popolo Americano*. Avanti, Milano-Roma, 1954.

4. R. Leydi, ed., *Eroi e fuorilegge nella ballata popolare Americana*. G. Ricordi, Milano, 1958.

5. A. Portelli ed., *Folksongs*. Guanda, Parma, 1966.

6. F. La Polla, *La Folksong Americana nell'Ottocento. Studi Americani* 16.

7. R. Leydi, ed., *Il folk music revival*. Flaccovio, Palermo, 1972.

8. A. Portelli, *La canzone popolare in America: La rivoluzione musicale di Woody Guthrie*. DeDonato, Bari, 1975, 48.

9. *Il Mucchio Selvaggio*, 16 (February 1979): 19.

Linda L. Painter

The Rise and Decline of the Standard Transcription Company

During the 1930s and up to the early 1950s music broadcast over radio was primarily from electrical transcriptions. The 16″ ETs were a development of the earlier 16″ vitaphone discs which had been used for sound for motion pictures; vitaphones were sent to movie theaters to be played in synchronization with the film print. The same presses and playback equipment for vitaphones could be used for transcriptions. In fact, RCA entered the transcription business when vitaphones became obsolete after the perfection of the sound-on-film process. Art Rush (who later became business manager for the Sons of the Pioneers) was working part time at RCA when he discovered that their vitaphone presses were being cut into scrap iron to sell to Japan. Horrified at the waste of these machines (worth $16,000 each) Rush convinced the RCA executives to start a transcription company and halt the destruction of the presses. RCA agreed and in 1934 appointed Rush as its West Coast manager for their new Electrical Transcription Department.

Shortly after RCA's Transcription Department was created, two other Los Angeles-based transcription companies were formed—C. P. Mac-Gregor and Standard Radio. Los Angeles during this time was a thriving center for country and western music, and RCA and Standard Radio recorded many artists in that field (MacGregor specialized in dramatic shows), thereby contributing greatly to their later success. In spite of the important role played by the transcription companies for all types of musical performers, nothing has ever been written on them—how they were formed, and how they operated. The company which was particularly important to country and western as well as popular artists was Standard Radio, based in Hollywood, California. Standard was formed in 1934 by Jerry King, who was then general manager of KFWB radio station (owned by Warner Brothers). While he was working at KFWB, King, unbeknownst to Jack Warner, began recording some of the Warner Brothers artists on transcription discs—an orchestra led by Kay Kayser with Ginny Sims as vocalist, and Paul Whiteman's quartet, the King's Men. King sent samples of these recordings to firms representing radio stations, and at the Ed Petry Company a man named Ed Voynow contacted a friend of his, Milton Blink (who at the time was selling recordings of the events of the World's Fair), to sell King's new line of transcription programs. Blink was impressed with the artists as well as the quality of the recordings and sold the shows to the Seminole Paper Company for approximately twenty cities. King was so pleased with Blink's salesmanship that he flew to Chicago to meet him personally.

By this time, Jerry King had made a series of recordings by the Sons of the Pioneers (102 selections). Blink admits to having tried to discourage King from recording this group:

> "But," said Jerry, aghast at my lack of talent taste, "they yodel in harmony." And indeed they did, most effectively in their famous theme, "Tumbling Tumbleweeds." Well, it takes a big man to admit he's wrong, doesn't it? So I went out and sold the Sons of [the] Pioneers to a few national mail order sponsors like Sterling Insurance and Willard's Message for Stomach Sufferers [for WBBM radio station in Chicago].[1]

Blink convinced King to produce a general music library to be leased to radio stations. King took Blink's advice and got the backing of Seth Ely. According to Blink, "Jerry figured that by using mostly studio talent from his station, we could produce 200 selections as a starting library and add 20 a month, and we could get off the ground if we secured one-year contracts from at least forty stations."[2] Blink signed with Standard Radio for the Chicago contract, at $250 per month, so he could continue supplying discs to WBBM. He went on the road for three weeks to sell the library, covering one and two cities a day "from the Twin Cities down to Louisville and from Pittsburgh to Denver." He signed fifty stations in those three weeks, and Standard Radio was now officially in business, starting its service in May of 1935. Later in 1935, Blink bought out Seth Ely's share in the business and became vice president of Standard

Radio, operating out of Chicago, in charge of six salesmen (each covering a region of the United States) as well as representatives in Canada and Europe; advertising; publicity; promotion; and producing recording sessions that were made in the Midwest and on the East Coast. Now that Standard Radio was under way, King left KFWB and assumed his role as president of the organization. He was in charge of artists and repertory, and the administration of the Hollywood office which handled recording, scriptwriting of shows, continuity writing to accompany each selection, payments of recording fees to music publishers, contractual agreements with artists and with the radio stations.

Standard Radio built up a top-quality general music library and helped many types of performers in their careers. Some of the artists who recorded for Standard before recording for commercial conpanies were Nat King Cole, Spike Jones, Les Paul, Kay Starr, Art Tatum, Frankie Laine, Mike Douglas, Lawrence Welk, the Sons of the Pioneers, and Jimmy Wakely and his Rough Riders (Johnny Bond and Dick Rinehart). The members of the latter two groups each recognized the important part that Standard Radio played in broadening their exposure and increasing their popularity. According to Blink, the Sons of the Pioneers's transcriptions were "highly successful and were really the forerunner of our general music library. . . . [Their selections] ran for years and years on radio stations. The stations had no trouble in getting local sponsorship."[3] King recorded the Pioneers in two further sessions in 1935, making a total library of 271 selections. The Sons of the Pioneers' library was retained, by Standard, as separate from their general music library and was sold, rather than leased, to stations.

Jimmy Wakely stated that he, Johnny Bond, and Dick Rinehart definitely owed much of their success to Standard Radio.[4] They had come to Los Angeles from Oklahoma in 1939, and were recorded that same year by Standard. Their popularity soared with the exposure they were given and led to their signing recording contracts with major companies (Wakely, Decca; Bond and Rinehart, Columbia). In 1939, they recorded for Standard as Jimmy Wakely and his Rough Riders; in 1941, as Johnny Bond and his Red River Valley Boys. (They also went on to record for other transcription companies—World, as the Rodeo Boys; NBC, as the Jimmy Wakely Trio.)

Recording of Artists. Until 1948–49, when tape was developed, all recordings were made directly onto the master disc. In 1934–35, the master consisted of wax; after 1935, acetate. To record directly onto the master, some problems arise—the group recording must do it perfectly the first try or a new master has to be brought out and the whole session begins again. A typical recording session, before the advent of tape recordings, might run as follows:

A studio is rented and the artists meet there with the studio's engineer; Standard's chief engineer, and musical director; and a Musician's Union representative who makes sure they do not run into overtime, or if they do that the group is paid for it. The length of time of the session depends on how many tunes are to be recorded and if the group needs to rehearse before actual recording begins. Artists such as the Sons of the Pioneers, for example, would need very little, if any, rehearsal time, because they were used to performing together; whereas vocalists who bring in studio musicians would need a longer time since they have not previously worked together. Some rehearsal is needed, however, for the engineer so that he can take readings and mix the sound properly. When Ernest Baumeister was chief engineer for Standard, he would turn over the final decision of sound to the leader of country and western groups, because he recognized that they knew best how their music was to sound (Spade Cooley, for example, liked a lot of bass on his recordings).

Next, a master would be put on the transcription recording machine. When wax masters were in use, they were delivered to the studios approximately 3″ to 4″ thick, then pared down on a cutting machine to make the top level, resulting in a 2″ to 3″ thick blank. They were then stored in a cabinet which was maintained at 72°. For 16″ discs, a 17 1/4″ diameter wax or acetate blank was used; for 12″ (such as the Pioneers library), the blank was 13 1/4″ diameter. The transcription recorders, prior to 1938, operated from the center of the disc to the outside; the opposite of how discs today are made. This direction was preferred because as the stylus was cutting into the disc to form the grooves, chips would fly out and towards the inside. If the disc was being cut from the outside to the center, then the chips would be in the path of the stylus. In 1938 a suction tube was developed that could be attached to the arm to pick up the chips. With the suction tube and the development of a hot stylus, recordings could be made to start on the outside of the disc, thereby making better use of the disc, as the outside is of higher quality. (The label on the disc indicated whether it should be played from the outside or inside.)

Now the session is ready to begin. The artists are cued either by a system of yellow, green and red lights in the studio—the yellow light signaling the group to prepare to start; the green, to begin; and the red, to stop—or by a simple hand cue given by the engineer. A verbal cue could not be used because the disc would pick up the sound and there was no way to eliminate it afterwards. After the first number, the group would stop and await the signal to begin their next tune. The engineer, meanwhile, is turning the disc two revolutions so that one song does not run into the next. Before tape recordings, the number of revolutions between songs could vary by as much as 1/4 to 1/2 a turn. This would occur because the group did not start exactly on cue. After tape was in use, Standard Radio standardized their revolutions to two, so the announcer at the station would know exactly where a selection began on the disc. (An arrow was cut into the master pointing to the starting place of the revolutions.)

The 33 1/3-rpm, 12″ discs which the Sons of the Pioneers made consisted of three songs to a side. If a mistake was made, the wax master would be taken off the recorder (to be reburnished later, for further use) and a new one put on, and the session would begin all over again. For 16″ discs such as those of Jimmy Wakely, five selections were on each side, and if a mistake was made on the last tune—and if it was small enough—they would let it pass, rather than start from the beginning. This was particularly true when recording large orchestras.

Finally, the session would be over, after lasting from two to six hours; the masters were then ready to send to the pressing plant; the final product being a 12″ or 16″ shellac disc (after 1945, vinylite). Standard used various pressing plants over the years, but primarily Allied, RCA, and Columbia.

The contracts for recording were made per session, with a one-time fee paid, and no royalties of sales, rentals, or airplay. Standard Radio's library consisted of various types of music, including popular, cowboy-hillbilly, novelty, classical, jazz, big bands, pipe organ, hymns, military bands, ethnic music, and others. The library also included jingles for all types of merchandise from dry cleaning to ladies wear to appliances; weather reports; and the most comprehensive sound effects library of any of the transcription or film companies (compiled by Rusty King, Jerry King's brother). Each type of music was designated by a letter, i.e., Q = instrumental novelty; R = vocal novelty; P = dance and popular music; V = hillbilly or cowboy (later changed to "folk"); U = hymns; T = concert music.

The studio that Standard rented for a recording session would depend on the type of music being recorded. The size of the group was, of course, a factor, but also to be taken into consideration was the sound quality to be achieved. Harry Bryant, former engineer at NBC and Radio Recorders of Hollywood (the latter was where Standard did most of their recording) stated that each studio was a little different; e.g., the best drama programs were recorded in Studio A; a moderate size orchestra sounded best in Studio B. He said, however, that he believed the engineers "had better control over sound if a studio is fairly dead; for a more lively sound, Radio Recorders built an echo chamber from which echo could be put on any microphone, then the sound would be mixed and the echo added in."[5] Also, with a fairly dead studio there were ways to brighten it up: using more wood and less celotex; portable splays could be placed around the musicians. When recording directly onto disc, less distortion was picked up, giving greater freedom than when recording onto tape. According to engineer Bob Nicholas, in the early years of recording it was believed that the studios should be dead, and felt curtains would be hung around the walls. He stated that when you now hear old discs being played, you can hear the difference between a dead studio and a studio in which they tried to brighten the sound.[6]

Continuity and Script Material. As soon as the musical selections to be recorded were chosen, a staff of men and women would begin writing the continuity for each piece. The continuity consisted of a short paragraph about each selection for station announcers to read when they played it. Below are a few examples of continuity for some Sons of the Pioneers selections:

"Auld Lang Syne" — This fine old Scottish air, one of the best loved folk songs of all time, played and sung as it would be by a group of cowhands gathered around the campfire after the day's work is done.

"Casey Jones" — What can be said about this best known of all old-timers. The Pioneers have varied the lyrics somewhat; they say these are the words handed down to them by their grandpappies.

"Echoes from the Hills" — This is a typical tune by the well-known writer of such melodies, Bob Nolan. It is a song of home-sickness, of a wandering boy, who no matter where he is, hears echoes from the hills.

"Song of the Pioneers" — A musical cowboy type of song, something new in hillbilly and western music. Verne Spencer wrote this number as a new theme for the group.

"Texas Crapshooter" — Hugh Farr's fiddle solo of the most prized accomplishment of the barn-dance fiddler.

The continuity would be typed on 8 1/2″ × 11″ sheets and sent to the radio stations weekly. Each paragraph was identified by the library number of the disc, and the number of the band (or, in the case of 12″ discs, whether the song was inside, center, or outside). For many artists, in addition to continuity, voice tracks would be recorded on discs to accompany the transcription. Voice tracks of an artist introducing his own band would give the appearance of a live, rather than recorded, show. In fact, an artist could be featured in a 15- or 30-minute show, and to the radio audience it sounded as though the musicians were appearing live at their local station. So that listeners could not be misled, however, the FCC created a ruling that every half-hour an announcement would have to be made that the program was recorded.

In addition to providing continuity so announcers could create their own shows, Standard also employed scriptwriters to put together weekly programs: "Broadway on Parade," "Eventide Echoes," "For Mother and Dad," "Modern Concert Hall," "Hollywood Brevities," to name a few. When Chuck Benedict was head of scriptwriting, he selected a staff that specialized in various types of music, so programs could be created featuring certain types of music: Hawaiian, Latin American Chamber Music, Country and Western, etc. He also wrote some of the shows, as did Lewis Teegarden, who was general manager and general counsel of the Hollywood Office. (Teegarden wrote "Eventide Echoes" and "For Mother and Dad.")

To eliminate long pauses between selections, radio stations always had two or three playback machines. This system allowed the announcer, while a selection was playing on one turntable, to "cue up" the next one on the second turntable and have it lined up ready for instantaneous play. Three turntables were used when harp interludes or voice tracks were to be played between selections. A series of interludes on the harp were recorded, which started in one key and ended in another, to match the proper keys of the two selections, creating a more fluid transition from one musical number to the next. For voice tracks and interludes, while a piece was playing, the next voice track or interlude and musical selection were put on the other two turntables and cued up for play. (The playback machines were also equipped to play either lateral or vertical grooved discs—World, for example, was vertically cut; while Standard was lateral. The label of the disc indicated whether it was lateral or vertical.)

Leasing Arrangements with Radio Stations. In order to compete with other transcription libraries, Standard Radio developed a general music library with a wide variety of music as well as recording the top artists of their fields. The Cowboy and Hillbilly section included Spade Cooley, Eddie Dean, Johnny Bond and his Red River Valley Boys, Jimmy Wakely and his Rough Riders, and Gene Autry; other artists included

Lawrence Welk, Gene Austin, the King Cole Trio, Bob Crosby, Tommy Dorsey, James Dorsey, Doris Day, Art Tatum, Les Paul, Jack Teegarden, and Freddie Martin. Radio stations leasing from Standard knew they would be receiving popular performers which would please their audience, as well as the current hit tunes (in order to keep their library current, Standard regularly deleted dated material). Transcription companies could compete with commercial record companies because in the early years the quality of transcriptions was better than that of 78s; a wider variety of material could be offered by transcription services; they offered services not available elsewhere; and prior to 1942–43, 78s were sold to radio stations by the record companies. (According to Jimmy Wakely, Capitol Records in 1942 or 1943 was the first to give discs to stations free of charge.)

Standard Radio employed six regional salesmen, and it was their job to meet with program directors of radio stations to convince them to lease Standard's library. They took along brochures and catalogs as selling aids. For any given area, the policy was to give exclusivity to the station, so that other stations in the listening area were not airing the same programs. The rates for leasing were based on the wattage of the station and ranged from $125 to $300 per month. Each station had a choice of a one-, two-, or three-year contract. Signing a contract with Standard Radio entitled the station to the basic library (which started in 1935 with 200 selections and grew, at its peak, to 5,000 selections), approximately 80 new selections each month, weekly continuity service, large filing cabinets in which to store the 16″ discs, 3″ × 5″ card files in which to store continuity (ca. 1940, the 8 1/2 × 11 sheets were replaced with a card file system), and the opportunity to purchase the newest RCA playback equipment on a two-year financing plan (rather than having to pay in one lump sum to the dealers). For a few years, Standard offered three types of library services: a tax-free service, which consisted of public domain and BMI material (ASCAP was refusing to grant permission to radio stations to play their music, while trying to raise their rates. BMI was formed by the radio broadcasters to compete with ASCAP. The discs during this time had BMI printed in large letters on the label so announcers could easily identify material which was safe to play); two types of limited services—Plan B, which emphasized "string, concert, choral, and novelty music;" Plan C, emphasizing "standard and current popular dance and novelty selections, with limited coverage of concert and more serious types of music."[7] However, sometime after 1940 they converted to one system.

In addition to salesmen going out on the road, Standard Radio also manned a booth at the annual convention of the National Association of Broadcasters in order to promote their library service. The convention was held alternately in eastern or western sections of the United States, and radio personnel from all over the country attended. Jerry King, Milt Blink, the musical director, and the salesmen were required to attend, bringing new material to demonstrate and be available to answer all questions. As a promotional item, each year Standard prepared a "blue 10" recording to be given away.

By 1947 Standard Radio had grown so much they had to leave their offices at 6404 Hollywood Boulevard to move into larger quarters at 140 North La Brea. At this time the name of the organization was changed to Standard Radio Transcription Company. Their new location, however, did not contain studio facilities, and Standard continued renting space at Radio Recorders, Columbia and NBC.

Recording in Foreign Countries. One year in the mid-1940s, Standard Radio created quite a stir at one of the NAB conventions. Harry Bluestone, musical director at that time, had gone to Mexico to record. It was his belief that good talent could be found anywhere in the world, whereas the prevailing attitude was that it would be impossible to find good musicians in some of the foreign countries. In addition, most of the transcription companies did not have the technology available to record "on the road." During the Musician's Union strike from late 1947 to early 1949, while other companies were reissuing older material from their libraries, Standard and Capitol sent men to Europe to record talent. In two trips, 1948 and 1949, each lasting approximately three months, Bluestone recorded enough material for Standard to issue for the next few years. In 1948 tape was first beginning to be used and with the new portable equipment available it freed the engineer from depending on locating an actual recording studio, though one would be used if available. On the first trip, Bluestone and engineer Bob Callen took a Rangertone tape recorder and went to Paris seeking talent. A major problem developed, however, of which they were not aware until they returned to Hollywood. Bluestone had been sending the tapes back to the Hollywood office for editing and rerecording; but it turned out that the electrical current frequency in France fluctuated throughout the day and was not maintained at 50 cycles. Jack King, Jerry King's son, remembers receiving the Paris recordings and hearing the speed change as the frequency had changed. King located a musician with perfect pitch and by using him along with a variable-speed turntable, managed to rerecord the material onto master discs. During the 1949 trip, Bluestone and Standard's new chief engineer, Ernest Baumeister, used a Stancil tape recorder and had Stancil build a special power generator so that when converting the French 50 cycles into the U.S. 60 cycles, the frequency remained constant.

In addition to returning to Hollywood with a lot of fine music to add to Standard's library, Bluestone also brought a young singer he had found performing in a Paris dance hall—Robert Clary. He had been recorded during the first trip, and when Standard released his recordings, they were deluged with fan mail and decided to bring Clary to the United States. Shortly after arriving, though, Clary left his "mentors" to strike out on his own. He was successful, and millions of people all over the world now know him for his role in the television series *Hogan's Heroes*.

The Decline of Transcription Companies. In the 1930s there were approximately 750 radio stations in the United States and six transcription companies leasing libraries. Standard Radio at that time had approximately 350 stations under contract. As more and more radio stations were formed, the number of contracts increased, and, according to Milt Blink, at their peak Standard had "almost 1,000 stations, and our library had 5,000 selections; our monthly release was 100 selections, and we furnished forty hours of mimeo'd program continuity per week, along with jingles for local advertisers, theme songs and spoken intros by our top talent, four-way file cards, cabinets, the works."[8]

Standard Radio's peak, however, was not to last long, as the need for transcription companies diminished. With the advent of television, fewer and fewer people depended on the radio for their entertainment. Sponsors were now backing television shows, taking needed revenue away from the radio stations. Simultaneously, the quality of commercial recordings increased; the development of the LP process meant that many more selections could be put onto a smaller size disc; and record companies began giving away promotional copies of their discs to stations. Program directors all over the country began either canceling or not renewing their library services with the transcription companies. When the number of remaining stations still under contract with Standard Radio diminished to 300, King and Blink decided to liquidate their contracts by giving the stations the opportunity to buy the discs in their library for a one-time fee of $1,000. They successfully terminated each contract in this way, and in the spring of 1954 Standard Radio Transcription Company closed its doors.

NOTES

1. Milton Blink, *Beyond the Caul: A Reminiscence* (unpub. typescript, October 1978): 26

2. Blink, 27.

3. Interview with Milton Blink, March, 1982.

4. Interview with Jimmy Wakely, June, 1982.

5. Interview with Harry Bryant, April 9, 1982.

6. Interview with Bob Nicholas, March 3, 1982.

7. Standard Radio *Yardstick* (ca. 1940).

8. Blink, *Beyond the Caul,* 27.

Willie J. Smyth

Early Knoxville Radio (1921–1941): WNOX and the "Midday Merry Go-Round"

During the "golden years of radio," between the mid-1930s and the 1950s, Knoxville, Tennessee, radio stations provided channels for the development of the careers of a spectacular list of performers. WNOX, Tennessee's oldest station and number eight in age nationwide, came to be known as a "stepping stone to the Grand Ole Opry" because of the number of stars recruited for the Opry from WNOX stages. Many people claim that because of WNOX Knoxville could have become the country music capitol of the world.

Knoxville has long been recognized for its role in the development and dissemination of country music. Charles Wolfe, in particular, has drawn attention to the contributions of Knoxville's musicians to the early recording industry. In 1924, the Aeolian-Vocalian Company recruited singers Charlie Oaks and George Reneau from Knoxville to journey to New York and become (along with Am Stuart and Uncle Dave Macon) Tennessee's first country music stars. Vocalion continued to play an important role in encouraging early Tennessee musicians by maintaining talent scouts and distributing records through Knoxville's Sterchi Brothers' Furniture Company. Knoxville has received additional notoriety for being an early center for fiddle contests and "old-harp" singing schools.[1]

Unfortunately, little information has surfaced about the role of Knoxville radio in the history of country music. This neglect is at least partially because scholars of country music have had little tangible subject matter to examine. Unlike the processes involved in trying to understand a singer or a song through a study based on interviewing artists or listening to phonograph records, the method of discerning the nature and importance of early radio shows has been encumbered by the unavailability of the artistic product itself.[2] Only in the past few years have scholars realized the importance of documenting country music radio history and have begun searching for and examining radio transcription discs and other related data. This article assembles newspaper clippings, interviews, and a transcription disc to explore the first twenty years of Knoxville's WNOX—from its inception in 1921 until 1941.

WNOX had an inauspicious beginning as a primitive radio station built in 1921 by Stuart Adcock for the People's Telephone and Telegraph Company. The station operated under the call letters WNAV at all of fifty watts and was probably housed in the basement of the company's Vine Avenue and Market Street building.

Adcock operated WNAV for the next few years, eventually building larger studios for the station in the St. James Hotel. An official broadcasting license was granted to WNAV in April 1925. Shortly after this, Adcock purchased the station for $3,000 and applied to the Department of Commerce for a change of call letters. Thus, WNOX was born.

It was about this time that WNOX broadcast "Mac and Bob," probably the first of a long list of famous hillbilly performers to work for that station. Lester McFarland recalls how he and Bob Gardner came to WNOX:

> Radio was just a toy then [1925]. We heard a guy singing out of key and decided, if they would let him sing, they would let us. They didn't have auditions—we put on a half-hour program. The manager of the station said he couldn't pay us anything but if we would come back next week he would pay us ten bucks. We were back.[3]

In 1927, Adcock sold WNOX to the Sterchi Brothers Furniture Company for the same amount as his purchase price. Sterchi Brothers maintained two studios—one located in the store's basement, which was used primarily for playing records, making station breaks and some recordings; the other, housed on the mezzanine floor of the St. James hotel, which was used for live broadcasts and occasionally for recording. Joe E. Epperson, an engineer for WNOX from 1928 to 1943, describes the situation:

> When I joined the station in 1928, this [basement] studio was used for a
> 1½ hour program of recordings from noon to 1:30 daily. The St. James Stu-

dio was used for live originations and for recordings when desired. The schedule at that time included a two-hour program on Tuesdays, Thursdays and Saturday nights. I remember such programs as Roger and Baxter Williams with Ruth Ferrel at the piano, Harry Nides, violinist, and one program which ran for an extended period on Saturday evenings. The MC was known as "Pay Cash Taylor" and the program was sponsored by JFG Coffee Co., Lay Packing Co., and others. There were remote point program pickups of local orchestras like Maynard Baird and his Orchestra, Skeet Talent, etc. Roger Williams and a person named Bob Anderson were the main announcers in those early days.[4]

Epperson remembers there being a number of hillbilly performers and shows but could not give specific details. Some facts about country performers on WNOX can be reconstructed from other sources, however. An extract from the *Brunswick 'Dixie' Supplement 1928* reads:

> The Tennessee Ramblers challenge any four-string band to an open contest for World's Championship. We advise any band seriously considering taking up this challenge to first hear 'Brunswick' record no. 257, [or to] tune in on Radio Station WNOX, Knoxville, Tennessee, some night and hear this band which is a regular program feature on this station.

Dwight Butcher while fifteen to sixteen years old worked on WNOX. It was there that he met Hugh Cross, who had his own show from 1926 to 1929. This was just before Cross was "discovered" and left for New York to record, and for WLS Chicago to perform.

In 1929 Brunswick-Vocalion held a recording session in the St. James Hotel studios. It should be assumed that at least some of the local talent which was recorded also played on WNOX.[5] Sterchi Brothers, as well as owning the WNOX studios in which the Brunswick-Vocalion recording session took place, was also the largest East Tennessee distributor for Brunswick records, for phonographs, and for radio sets.

At this date phonograph records were still more influential with country music fans than radio shows, if one can judge by the size of the audience that each reached. Radio was still somewhat of a novelty in 1928–1929; few homes had them. The Federal Radio Commission estimates that in 1924 there were 4 million radio sets in homes—one for every ten houses; in 1927 there were 10 million sets—30 percent of homes had one; and in 1936 there were 23 million—two for every three households.[6]

Radio sets in 1928 were expensive and of inferior quality. Joe Epperson describes the 1928 Knoxville "state of the art" equipment:

Generator supplies were necessary for the transmitter vacuum tubes since the tubes required "d-c." All a-c transmitter operation hadn't reached a state of perfection at that time. In fact, the majority of radio receivers were battery-operated, as radios using alternating current were just beginning to appear. The ones in use at that time usually had a built in a-c hum. Majestic, Philco and others were just beginning to manufacture a-c radios.[7]

In 1930, while still under Sterchi Brothers ownership, WNOX moved their studios to the seventeenth floor of the Andrew Johnson Hotel. In May 1932, Sterchi Brothers sold WNOX to Liberty Life Insurance Co. of Greenville, South Carolina, for $50,000. On December 5, 1935, Liberty Life sold the station to Continental Radio Co. (the radio subsidiary of E. W. Scripps Co.) for $125,000. The large cash appreciation in such a short time is testimony to the rising popularity of radio.

The acquisition of WNOX by Continental or E. W. Scripps Co. (Scripps-Howard) was pivotal in Knoxville country music history. The fact that Scripps also owned Knoxville's largest newspaper, the *Knoxville News-Sentinel,* proved helpful to WNOX. A review of the newspaper from 1934 to 1938 shows a dramatic increase in coverage of the station's programs beginning directly after the Scripps's purchase. Fortunately, the *News-Sentinel* staff's interest in the success of WNOX has left a wealth of information (in the form of articles, pictures, radio logs, and advertisements) about the station's shows and performers.

By 1935 radio had proven itself to be a commercially viable enterprise. The accessibility of relatively inexpensive sets—now, almost all run by alternating current—and the attractive programming offered by stations helped radio to surpass the phonograph as the most popular audio home entertainment mechanism.

Live radio shows or block programming were also being discovered to be the most popular radio format. George Biggar, ex-director of the WLS "National Barn Dance," writes:

> People want to hear the same type of program for several hours without turning the dials. Very few folk [hillbilly] musical programs of 15 to 30 minutes duration—spotted between other types of radio shows—have ever been successful. A minimum of one hour seems essential for building sizeable [and profitable] audiences for this type of program.[8]

An example of the importance of radio to early country performers is the fact that in 1936 the Monroe Brothers turned down an offer to make phonograph records because their live shows and radio appearances were so successful. In February 1936, when they were doing daily radio shows in Greenville, South Carolina, and Charlotte, North Carolina, Eli Oberstein, Victor A&R man, sent the Monroe Brothers a telegram stating, "We must have the Monroe Brothers on records stop we won't take no for an answer." Because of the success of the Monroe Brothers' shows and radio appearances, the offer held little interest and was turned down. After some persistence by Oberstein they finally agreed to go to a 17 February 1936 recording session.[9]

New ownership of WNOX brought a new staff. Richard Westergaard became station manager. In a fall 1982 telephone interview, Westergaard told me that he immediately tried to establish shows that would capture a large rural audience. Toward this end he hired Lowell Blanchard, a young announcer just out of the University of Illinois, whom he had known previously when both worked for a radio station in Des Moines, Iowa.

Blanchard had studied dramatics and broadcasting during his university years. He was a self-trained emcee who prided himself in his acting ability—especially his character portrayal involving regional dialects. Invited to join this growing station, Blanchard left WXYZ in Detroit and headed for Knoxville—a move which was to influence the lives of hundreds of country music performers.

Blanchard began his twenty-eight-year stay at WNOX in late January 1936. Upon arriving, Westergaard told him, "You are to become a hillbilly. Bring us hillbilly performers. Entertain with them as one of them." At this date two live hillbilly shows were being aired daily: Archie Campbell, known as "Grandpappy," had a fifteen-minute late afternoon program; and "Roy Acuff and the Crazy Tennesseans" performed from 12:15 to 1:00 p.m. Blanchard's first permanent WNOX job was to emcee and build up the "Crazy Tennesseans" show.

Roy Acuff had been playing with his band(s) in the Knoxville area since 1933. Radio logs indicate that the "Crazy Tennesseans" show began as a daily feature around 15 January 1935, and thus had existed for a year before Lowell Blanchard arrived.

Blanchard wanted to implement his ideas about successful entertaining. His first move was to organize a show which could be seen as well as heard. In order to cater to a studio audience the noon show was expanded to one hour and fifteen minutes and moved to the Old Sentinel building, then again moved to the second floor of the old Market House where remote broadcasts began. Admission was five cents per person. Spurred by a flood of advertising in the *News-Sentinel* and a lot of talented performers, crowds quickly began to fill the hall. A March 9, 1936, *News-Sentinel* advertisement indicates that Blanchard's programming ideas were taking effect:

> The "Crazy Tennesseans" are dressing up this week, really changing things about. This week they offer new costumes, new acts, a better show and what have you. According to Lowell Blanchard, "Master of Ceremonies," these changes are being made in order to give the visible as well as the radio audience a more professional show. "Grandpappy" might even get something new in the act.

Blanchard had begun what he was to become most famous for doing: polishing up acts, creating new gimmicks and material, and developing professional entertainers. With the extended time, more performers were brought into the program. The "Crazy Tennesseans" soon became more than Roy Acuff and the original band. For reasons which may be difficult to ascertain, Acuff and his band left WNOX in March 1936 to play on WROL, Knoxville's only other station. Some speculate that a disagreement (over whether the new revenues being brought in by the popular noon show would be shared with the performers) between Acuff and Program Director John Mayo led to Roy's simultaneous resignation/dismissal.

Blanchard was left with a big gap to fill with the absence of this talented group (which moved from WROL to the Grand Ole Opry in 1938). The fact that WNOX's noon show continued to grow in popularity is a tribute to Blanchard's skill as an emcee, performer, and talent hunter. After Roy Acuff's departure, the name was immediately changed to the "Midday Merry Go-Round." Radio logs first list the show under this name on March 18, 1936.

An array of talented performers was recruited to replace Acuff's group. The "Tennessee Ramblers" became the show's main hillbilly band.[10] In a fall 1982 telephone interview, Mack Sievers (Dobro player for the Ramblers) spoke to me about the band's beginning on the "Midday Merry Go-Round":

> We had a regular show by ourselves which was sponsored by J.F.G. [Coffee Company]. Then John Mayo and Lowell brought us on to the "Midday Merry Go-Round" when Roy went to WROL. At that time the Ramblers consisted of myself on Dobro; my sister Willie on guitar; our Dad "Fiddlin' Bill" Sievers; the Rainey Brothers from Petros who played guitars and banjo; and "Kentucky Slim" [Charles Ezra]. Our family did mostly novelty and Hawaiian numbers, the Raineys added real nice harmonies, and "Kentucky Slim" was our comedian.

Newspaper listings indicate that other regulars on these early 1936 shows included: "The Buckeye Buckaroos" (personnel unknown), "Guy Campbell and his fiddle," "The Tropical Islanders with Ed, Reese, and Roy—all playing Hawaiian guitars," "Grandpappy," "Lost John Miller" (singer, guitar player, and fiddler), and Arthur Q. Smith (singer/ songwriter).

Dennis and Louise Shehan, who worked at WNOX during the early years of the "Merry Go-Round," recalled how the shows were organized:

> Lowell would write out a schedule which gave everyone about ten to fifteen minutes. They'd get in three or four songs, then there would be a commercial from Scalph's Indian River Tonic. Lowell would regulate the performers—get them on and off in time—and he would tell them what he thought would and wouldn't go over with the audience. He provided a lot of the comedy, too, but mostly he polished up musicians. He used to say, 'We educate 'em and Nashville gets 'em."[11]

March 21, 1936, brought another live hillbilly show to WNOX. Blanchard and the regulars of the "Merry Go-Round" presented an extended version of the noon show at the Market Hall on Saturday nights. Additional performers were added to the 8:30–10:00 p.m. show. Admission was twenty-five cents. This show, first called the WNOX "Carnival," was to become the "Tennessee Barn Dance" in 1942.

Both the "Midday Merry Go-Round" and "Carnival" continued to draw full houses at the Market Hall. On May 24, 1936, WNOX began broadcasting from new studios at 110 South Gay Street. Both shows moved from the Market Hall to a new 800-seat auditorium which was built to handle the growing audiences.

The May 30, 1936, newspaper listing of "Carnival" performers shows a new group called the "Stringdusters." This band included Kenneth (Dude or Jethro) Burns on mandolin, his brother Aytchie on guitar and bass, Henry (Junior or Homer) Haynes on guitar, and Charlie Hagaman on rhythm guitar. The "Burns Brothers" had their own show on WNOX for about six weeks before adding Haynes and Hagaman and joining the "Merry Go-Round." The "Stringdusters" stayed together as regulars on WNOX until 1939 when Burns and Haynes left for Renfro Valley, Kentucky, to become part of the "Renfro Valley Barn Dance."

"Homer" Haynes and "Jethro" Burns became, of course, the famous comedy duo "Homer and Jethro." Burns remembers how Lowell Blanchard influenced them:

We had just been given the names "Homer" and "Jethro" by Lowell Blanchard. This guy taught us so much about show business. I hung around him
and picked his brain, because I knew that he knew all the stuff I wanted to
know. Really, I give him credit for everything I've ever done, because without him, I wouldn't have done anything. He couldn't teach me how to play,
but he taught me how to talk, sing, and all the other stuff I had to know.[12]

Under Lowell Blanchard's coaching many performers found themselves becoming polished entertainers. Blanchard had a keen eye for
spotting and developing what the rural audience wanted. He could
instruct performers on the art of ad-libbing, doing gags, and weaving stories between songs. Archie Campbell of "Grand Ole Opry" and "Hee-
Haw" fame said that Blanchard was instrumental in the development of
Archie's character. "Lowell would help write scripts and gags for
'Grandpappy.' He would also have a store of jokes for us to use."[13]

The comedy, hillbilly, and variety (the "Stringdusters," for example,
often would play a progressive "country jazz") format of these shows
proved to be an immense success. Local businesses were clamoring to
buy advertising space. Nevertheless, the performers were not all growing
rich from the station's profits. For the most part they had to supplement
their salaries by performing at local schools, halls, or wherever. The radio
shows would be used to plug the outside appearances of the performers.
Blanchard would book both local and traveling performers into jobs in
Knoxville and surrounding areas, usually touring with them as emcee.

The promise of a job playing for WNOX began to bring musicians
from out of town during these post-Depression years. A list of performers on the "Merry Go-Round" the week of September 17–24, 1936,
shows the addition of several regulars from out of state. "Monk and Sam"
(Charlie Henson and Sam Johnson), a comedy group; "Pee Wee" King,
famous singer and cocomposer of "Tennessee Waltz"; and "Curly Miller
and his Ploughboys" all came to WNOX more or less directly from
WHAS in Louisville.

In January 1937, Lowell Blanchard hired a group called the "Dixieland
Swingsters." They were to remain the "Merry Go-Round" staff band for
the next twenty-five years. Dave Durham, the band's fiddler and trumpet
player, tells how the band got started:

I was at WHAS Louisville playing with Clayton McMichen, Slim Bryant,
and the Georgia Wildcats from 1930–35. In about 1935 we broke up. Slim
wanted to keep a country band and wanted me to go to Pittsburgh with

them (but I didn't). I had a chance to leave with Gene Autry, too, but was married and decided to stay in Louisville and play trumpet with Clayton's Dixieland band. That's when I started working [playing fiddle] with Pee Wee King. I traveled with him a bit, but all at once Pee Wee decided to move to Knoxville. I stayed up there [Louisville] playing on WHAS with a group of my own until that folded in the fall of 1936. At that point I said I better go to Knoxville, so I went to the "Merry Go-Round" to see Pee Wee and Lowell Blanchard. We had put a group together in Knoxville and had a nightclub job offer. Lowell said to hold off on any offers because he wanted us for staff band. Well, we got the job about the middle of January. Then [one of the band members] Cecil Bell, he was a clarinet player, decided he didn't like country music, so he left. Our band ended up being Jerry Collins, piano; Cliff Stier, bass; Buck Houchens, fiddle, sax, and clarinet; Larry Downing, guitar; and myself on trumpet and fiddle.[14]

Pee Wee King stayed at WNOX for only a few more months, and then moved to the Grand Ole Opry and WSM, Nashville. Curley Miller moved to WMNN, Fairmont, West Virginia, then to the WWVA "Jamboree" in Wheeling, West Virginia.

Dozens of talented performers were attracted to the WNOX stages and the "Midday Merry Go-Round" in the next few years. A complete list of regular and guest performers (from 1936 to 1941) would total in the hundreds. Capitulating to lack of space, I will mention only some of the performers who became regulars on WNOX.

Buck "Huckleberry" Fulton, a singer/guitar player noted for his "country rube" humor, appeared as a regular from 1937 until the early 1940s. He would either solo or play with groups such as "Huckleberry and His Rangers" or "Huckleberry and the Tennessee Mountaineers." The "Mountaineers" played throughout East Tennessee. This group included Guy Campbell, fiddle; Bob Bennett, guitar and vocals; Buddy Wilson, guitar; and Smoky Mountain Rose, steel guitar.

In mid-1938, just after he and Bill split up their famous brother duo, Charlie Monroe was hired by Lowell Blanchard. Charlie's band at first consisted of Bill Calhoun, guitar and vocals; and "Lefty" Frizzell, mandolin (not the more famous recording artist). Zeke Morris then replaced Frizzell on mandolin. From WNOX the group moved to WDBJ, Roanoke. Charlie returned to WNOX for occasional jobs in the late 1940s and became a regular again in 1951–1952.

In late 1938 the Vaughn Four, a gospel quartet who changed their name in 1940 to the Swannee River Boys, played regularly on WNOX and the "Merry Go-Round." This group consisted of baritone and guitarist Stacy

Abner, high tenor; Buford Abner, lead; Merle Abner, bass, and, for a while, piano player.[15]

In 1939 Archie Campbell's group, Grandpappy and His Gang, consisted of Archie, Doug Dalton on mandolin, Gene McGee on guitar, Charlie Pickle on bass, a young tap dancer named Pete Hines, and Roy Lanham on guitar.[16]

Around 1940 Johnnie Wright and his brother-in-law Jack Anglin came to WNOX and formed a group with Eddie Hill which was first advertised as "Eddie Hill and His Mountain Boys." Jack was soon drafted, but Eddie and Johnnie Wright managed to keep the band together during the war years. They played under the name the "Tennessee Mountain Boys"—mostly at WNOX.

Bill Carlisle also arrived at WNOX around 1939, joined, at first, by his brother Cliff, Cliff's son, Tommy, and banjo player Shannon Grayson. Bill then began playing with Archie Campbell, doing songs and a comedy act. Bill created a character named "Hot Shot Elmer" who was always in the midst of comic antics—such as engaging in organized "on-stage" wrestling matches with a midget named "Little Robert."

In 1941 a teenager from Luttrell, Tennessee, named Chet Atkins heard that Bill and Archie were looking for a fiddle player. Mel Foree and Tommy Covington, who were both working for WNOX at the time, heard Chet playing at a party one night. They were impressed and set up an audition for him. He got the job. Atkins recalled those early days:

> The three of us started playing show dates right away. We would play high schools and theatres and small places like that. They paid me $3 a night. . . . We would work together for about 20 or 30 minutes then Archie would leave stage to put on his "Grandpappy" costume, and leave Bill and me out there to entertain. Then Bill would leave me alone and I would have to play a couple of solos on guitar. That was kind of tough because I was just a beginner. I remember one day playing "Bye Bye Blues" backstage at WNOX and Cowboy Copas (who was a regular on "Midday Merry Go-Round" in 1940–41) said, "Chet, I believe you're playing the wrong chord there." He was right. Anyway, after my solos Bill and Archie would come out and do comedy, then we'd all three do a finale.
>
> One night I was playing guitar in the back of Lowell Blanchard's car as we returned from a personal appearance. Lowell asked me how I'd like to be a staff guitarist on the station. He said that starting Monday I'd be the staff guitarist. That was 1942.[17]

Another regular act that appeared on WNOX around 1941 was the Cope Brothers—Charles on mandolin and Lester on guitar—from Bean

Station. Two friends of the Copes and another important duo to appear on Knoxville radio were the "Bailey Brothers," Danny and Charlie. The Baileys, however, established themselves on WROL so will be only mentioned in passing in this short history of WNOX.

Two points about the "Midday Merry Go-Round" are worth reiterating. (1) The show had a variety show or experimental flavor; while catering to a "country" audience, the show would not contain exclusively hillbilly music—the "Stringdusters" and "Dixieland Swingsters," for example, playing a mixture of country, Dixieland, swing, and jazz. And (2) comedy and/or levity were kings. The shows were laced with jokes and gags, many, if not most, master-minded by Lowell Blanchard. The country-comedy format of the show helped to develop some of the most popular rural comedians of our time, and also to eventually bring "country" humor respect and recognition at a national level.

I have chosen 1942 as the cut-off date for this essay because of the effect the war had on the arrangement of personnel at the "Midday Merry Go-Round." It should be apparent that even in prewar times, many groups had ephemeral existences. Members would come and go. Even within each "Merry Go-Round" show, personnel would trade off members for purposes of "backing up," etc. World War II brought rearrangements of even the most established groups. Members would be drafted or join the armed forces. New groups would be formed.

The postwar years would see WNOX reach its peak of popularity. The "Tennessee Barn Dance" and "Midday Merry Go-Round" attracted a constant stream of first-rate performers. Many who left for the war would come back to WNOX—other new "stars" would be discovered there. A partial list of the new personnel between 1942 and 1955 (excluding performers already mentioned) includes Ray "Duck" Atkins, Claude Boone, Bonnie Lou and Buster, Brewster Brothers, the Carter Family (Anita, June, Helen, and Maybelle), Martha and James Carson, Colorado Mountain Boys, Leonard Dabney, Flatt and Scruggs, Wally Fowler and the Georgia Clodhoppers, Don Gibson and His King Cotton Kinfolk, Farley Holden, "Salty" Holmes, Cotton Galyon, Lonnie Glosson, Homer Harris, Jamup and Honey, Johnson Brothers (Willie and Charlie), "Speedy" Kreis, Molly O'Day, Old Joe Clark, Emory Martin, Lilly Brothers, Louvin Brothers, Benny Martin, James Martin, Jimmy Martin, "Uncle Tom" Moore, Jimmy Murphy, Red Rector, Jack Shelton, Fred Smith, Roy Snead, Carl Story, Kitty Wells, and Mac Wiseman.

My attempt to review the content and some of the personnel from these early years of WNOX's "Midday Merry Go-Round" is in no sense meant to be definitive or complete. If this brief history serves to give the reader some sense of the importance of WNOX in the development of American country music or if it acts as a catalyst to bring out more information about WNOX and/or its performers, it will have achieved rewarding results.

NOTES

1. Charles K. Wolfe, *Tennessee Strings* (Knoxville: University of Tennessee Press, 1977), 11–35, passim.

2. See Charles K. Wolfe, *The Grand Ole Opry* (London: Old Time Music, 1975), 32.

3. Lester McFarland interview by Doug Morris, appearing in *The Knoxville Journal,* December 10, 1974.

4. Letter from Joe E. Epperson to Kim Stover, 24 August 1981 (used with permission of the author).

5. For a full account of the 1929 session and the personnel involved see Charles K. Wolfe, "Early Country Music in Knoxville: The Brunswick Session and the End of an Era," *Old Time Music,* no. 12 (Spring 1974): 19–33.

6. George C. Biggar, "The WLS National Barn Dance Story: The Early Years," *JEMFQ,* no. 23 (Autumn 1971): 107.

7. Epperson, 1981.

8. Letter from George Biggar to Joe Koehler of *Sponsor Magazine,* April 15, 1948.

9. Ralph Rinzler, "Bill Monroe," in *Stars of Country Music,* ed. Bill Malone and Judith McCulloh (Urbana: University of Illinois, 1975), 210.

10. This group should not be confused with "Dick Hartman's Tennessee Ramblers," "Cecil Campbell's Tennessee Ramblers," or the Kessinger Brothers who also played under this name. See also Charles K. Wolfe, "The Tennessee Ramblers: Ramblin' On," *Old Time Music,* no. 13 (Summer 1974): 5–12.

11. Interview with Dennis and Louise Shehan in Knoxville, July 25, 1982.

12. David Grisman, "Jethro Bums: Jazz Mandolin Pioneer," *Frets* (October 1979): 39.

13. Interview with Archie Campbell in Knoxville, August 18, 1982. See also *Archie Campbell: An Autobiography* (Memphis, Tenn.: Memphis State University Press, 1982), 61.

14. Interview with Dave Durham in Knoxville, September 19, 1982.

15. Wayne W. Daniel, "We Had to Be Different to Survive: Billy Carrier Remembers the Swanee River Boys," *JEMFQ,* nos. 65/66 (Spring/Summer 1982): 59.

16. For an account of Lanham's days at WNOX, see "The Roy Lanham Story," by Ken Griffis, *JEMFQ,* no. 36 (Winter 1974).

17. Chet Atkins, "Chet Atkins' Own Story," *Guitar Player* 6, no. 1 (February 1972): 22–23.

Chet Atkins with Mother Maybelle and the Carter Sisters

James P. Leary

Ethnic Country Music on Superior's South Shore

American folklorists, and country music enthusiasts generally, have long been interested in the complex relationship between Southern and Western traditional rural music and its commercially recorded and broadcast offshoots: hillbilly, western swing, bluegrass, rockabilly, honky tonk, and country. Meanwhile, a small but significant body of writings has focused upon the rural traditions of Northern musicians in New York state and the Canadian maritimes.[1] Praiseworthy inasmuch as they document the unmistakable existence of "Northern country music," these studies are overwhelmingly limited to monolingual performers of Anglo-Celtic origin. Yet, as Robert Klymasz's pioneering article on Ukrainian country music demonstrates, the multilingual progeny of Eastern European immigrants to the Canadian prairies likewise strum guitars and don cowboy hats.[2] A similar phenomenon prevails along the South Shore of Lake Superior.

Today that region's most characteristic musical style is a pan-ethnic hybrid dubbed "old time" by locals.[3] And while a precise analysis of the old-time music "sound" lies beyond the scope of this paper, its major features can be readily identified. The accordion is the primary melodic instrument. Vocals tend to be relaxed, open-throated, and conversational. Performances are dominated by waltzes, polkas, and an occasional schottische; and these dance tunes are drawn largely from non-English-speaking ethnic sources. Even so, a significant number of "country" songs penetrates the contemporary old-time repertoire. As Tom Johanik of The Polkateers put it recently:

> Most of what I play is old time. Like that first band I was with—Frank [Farkas] and Tom [Marincel] and me—that was pretty much all old time. . . . [Now] we play mostly old time. We play lotta country though. . . .We could play country music all night if we had to; we know enough of it.[4]

The presence of country music as a subsidiary but essential element in old-time music can be explained by examining the region's historical and musicological evolution.

European Americans settled along the South Shore of Lake Superior in the post-Civil War era as Yankee entrepreneurs financed or promoted the establishment of rail and shipping lines, mines, logging camps, and, eventually, agricultural settlements on cutover acreage. Old and new immigrants alike provided cheap labor for the vast "pinery"; for Houghton/Hancock's "copper country"; for the iron-rich Gogebic range mines at Ironwood/Hurley; for the granite and brownstone quarries of Mellen and the Bayfield peninsula; for the sawmills and loading docks of Ashland on Lake Superior's Chequamegon Bay; and for the farmsteads in stump-laden hinterlands. There were Irish and assorted WASPs hailing from Canada's maritimes and America's Northeast; there were Norwegians, Swedes, Swede Finns, and Finns; there were Germans, Italians, Swiss, and numerous Slavs, Bohemians, Croatians, Hungarians, Lithuanians, Poles, Serbs, and Slovaks.

Arriving singly, in the company of relatives, or in the midst larger groups of fellow countrymen, immigrants tended to settle in enclaves. In the city of Ashland, for example, Swedes and Norwegians dominated the West Side, while Poles, Bohemians, a handful of Lithuanians, and Swede Finns occupied the East End. Swedes, Finns, Croatians, Hungarians, and Slovaks clustered similarly in outlying villages or rural communities like Mason, Marengo, Benoit, Washburn, and Moquah. The general inclination of newcomers to live amongst people with whom they shared an Old World experience did not, however, result in ethnic insularity. In predominantly Slovak Moquah, to cite a typical case, there were also families of Bohemians, Poles, Swedes, and Finns; a few English, Irish, and Germans dwelled on the hillsides ringing the Moquah valley. Culture contact between these diverse peoples, consequently, was present from the outset in at least four overlapping socioeconomic realms. People worked together as wage earners in the woods, the mills, and on the docks; as rural laborers bent upon clearing land and establishing homesteads, they exchanged machinery and labor; they spent their money and sold or traded their produce in the towns; and they sent their children to schools. As a result of these common activities, assorted ethnics became conversant, albeit to a limited extent, with one another's speech and customs. However, English—the language of the "host" country, and more importantly of the workplace, the towns, and the schools—soon prevailed as the chief medium of interethnic communication.

A parallel pattern characterized the region's music. Since many musicians were numbered among the early settlers along Lake Superior's South Shore, a wealth of "foreign" dance tunes and songs dominated gatherings at homes, on outdoor platforms, and in newly erected ethnic halls. Predictably, such events were not exclusive, as people from various backgrounds assembled to dance and play music. In this way a Polish button accordionist might learn a Norwegian waltz, while a Swedish fiddler could acquire a Hungarian *czardas* or a Finnish polka. At the same time—while keenly aware and proud of their Old World heritage, and generally tolerant of others' ethnicity—these people, especially the youthful immigrants and children of the second generation, soon played and sang many American numbers. Dubbed *English* for linguistic reasons, these songs and tunes were learned, like the English language, in the aforementioned contexts of the workplace, the urban or rural neighborhood, the town, and the school.

Besides requisite patriotic anthems and Tin Pan Alley pop, the English songs and tunes learned in the late nineteenth and early twentieth centuries were exactly of the sort that evolved into country music in its various manifestations: Anglo-Celtic ballads, fiddle tunes, minstrel pieces, and sentimental parlor songs. It is, unfortunately, impossible at this point to offer a very detailed reconstruction of just how these interrelated genres were acquired by the Northern ethnics of sixty to one hundred years ago. Nonetheless—after more than a year's fieldwork in the region, and the perusal of newspapers and reminiscences by old-timers—I have assembled enough information to provide a general account.

As numerous folklorists have demonstrated, the lumbercamp was an important locus for Anglo-Celtic song-and-dance tune performances.[5] And, indeed, Franz Rickaby's *Ballads and Songs of the Shanty-Boy*—based on a 1919 trek across the northern tier of Minnesota, Wisconsin, and Michigan—attests to the presence of these forms along the South Shore of Lake Superior.[6] Rickaby's volume understandably neglects "foreign" singers of "English" songs, but certainly there were some.

Uusia Victor
Suomalaisia Rekordeja
Helmikuu, 1924   (February, 1924)
(New Victor Finnish Records)

The lumber camps provided immigrants with winter employment and, if one didn't squander it in taverns and sporting houses, cash payment. Some camps were a season's home for woods-wise Scandinavians and Finns; but the late Carl Gunderson, a Rice Lake Swede and former lumbercamp cook, also worked with Irishmen on the Flambeau River north of Ladysmith. Beyond vivid memories of breaking a rival cook's arm with a rolling pin, Gunderson came away with "Paul Bunyan's Ox," a version of the hyperbolic "Derby Ran," from the singing of "an Irish Jack."

> As I went down to Bunyan's camp upon a snowy day,
> I saw the biggest ox, sir, that ever was fed on hay.
> This ox was fat behind, sir, this ox was fat all 'round.
> And every foot on that old ox would cover an acre of ground.
> Maybe you don't believe me, maybe you think I lie,
> But go you down to Bunyan's camp and see the same as I.
> The horns that grew on that ox, sir, reached up to the moon.
> A man went up there in January and never got back 'til June.
> The man that killed that ox, sir, was drowned in the blood.
> And 40,000 other poor souls was carried away in the flood.
> The hair that grew on that ox, sir, reached up to the sky.
> The eagles built their nest up there, I could hear their young ones cry.[7]

In 1914 on the Bad River, Ashland County, nineteen-year-old Bohemianborn Jerry Novak signed on with a crew of Slavs ramrodded by Yankees and Canadians. These latter fellows did plenty of bawdy singing, Jerry told me in 1979; but, perhaps because he had a houseful of sisters to greet him in the spring, Jerry retained only a rousing and "clean" version of "The Shantyboy's Alphabet."[8] Energetic Anglo-Celtic fiddling and vigorous dancing also prevailed in the camps. Mike McCann, a Washburn County pioneer, observed in a printed reminiscence:

> Gee, if the young folks now could see some of them old lumberjacks wearing a pair of shoe packs or lumberjack rubbers before they came to swing, back off, and dance a jig before swinging! Them were really the days![9]

McCann, a fiddler himself, was Irish; indeed, many of the lumberjack fiddlers revered by old-timers were Irish or French-Canadian—men who had learned rollicking jigs and reels as part of their cultural traditions. Until his death in the early 1930s, at roughly eighty, Irishman Ben Gilpin was the city of Washburn's most famous fiddler. According to Ed Nelson, a Scandinavian admirer, this silver-maned former timber cruiser would often fiddle from the steps of his house.[10] The Donnelly boys were highly regarded in Barron County's Oak Grove township, while the "Frenchman" Bat DeMare was famed in Washburn County.[11] Fellow Canadian Leizime Brusoe of Rhinelander eventually recorded tunes like "Devil's Dream," "Fisher's Hornpipe," and "Money Musk" for the Library of Congress.[12] The fiddle, however, was also a favored dance instrument among certain Czech, Finnish, German, Polish, and Scandinavian immigrants; and many soon expanded their repertoires to include lumberjack favorites. The versatile Otto Rindlishbacher of Rice Lake (about whom more will be said later) was a Swiss German who made both simple cigar box and concert-worthy fiddles while distinguishing himself as a musician and publishing what the *Rice Lake Chronotype* termed "a booklet of peppy musical selections entitled *Twenty Original Reels, Jigs, and Hornpipes.*"[13]

Apart from the lumber camps's male preserve, ballad singers and lumberjack fiddlers held forth at dances in the homes, the halls, and on the outdoor platforms of rural villages and nascent townships. Bill Hendrickson, a Finn, picked up the broadside ballad "Willie Taylor" from the singing of Irishman Dennis Daley.[14] This fellow, who lived out his life as a bachelor in Herbster, Wisconsin, was likewise a noted fiddler.

> Bill Hendrickson: Oh, he was good, I'll tell you that.
> Eino Okkonen: He played square dances . . . alone even. . . . And then he'd get started, and he'd raise up and pretty soon he'd be standing up on a stool.
> Bill Hendrickson: Yeah. The crowd got big, y'know, and so they'd hear it all around.[15]

Within these contexts, Anglo-Celtic fiddlers were heard by many a young musician, whatever his chosen instrument. Harmonica players and accordionists like Slovaks Phil Johanik and George Letko, Finns Einard Maki and Bill Hendrickson, and Polish-American Felix Milanowski all learned to blow or squeeze out a stepped-up version of "Red Wing," along with "Golden Slippers," "The Irish Washerwoman," and "Turkey in the Straw."

The acquisition of new dance tunes demanded the parallel learning of new dance steps. Edith Hukkala recalls her Finnish-American mother's zeal:

> Oh, my mother used to go squaredancing. She used to walk three or four miles when she was twelve or thirteen. She was already adult enough to go to dances. They'd walk three, four miles to Highbridge and there was a caller

there. And then they'd play the violin. . . . Well, anyway, mother said that one time she came home so late from the squaredance that—her stepfather was getting up—she put the coffee on. And then she went to work in Ashland after that. See, in Highbridge there was mostly non-Finns. And they had a guy that could play concertina and they had a squaredance caller.[16]

In the Barksdale area, near Washburn, Vivian Eckholm Brevak grew up, amidst Swedes, Finns, Hungarians, and English Canadians. Vivian's father, Carl, was a Swedish-born fiddler with his store of old country tunes, but many of her most vivid musical memories centered on gatherings of "all kinds of people" in the homes of the McCutcheons, the Days, or the Cooks. In keeping with the crowd's varied composition there were "lotta square dances. Schottisches though, too, and old time waltzes, and polkas. Not modern stuff, though." Her longtime neighbor and friend Nelly Day Harvey chimed in, "And two-steps too. What they call polkas now, we used to call two-steps. And the broom dance, and the circle two-step." Square dances, however, were the most popular.[17] According to Vivian, much of their attraction resided in their simplicity. She compared modern squaredancing with its old-time counterpart:

This newer stuff, you can change, the caller can change from time to time when you go—the caller can change to something else, a diffcrent square. Then you gotta learn that. But the old time had its own way. They probably had four or five different drills that you learned. You learned these, see, so that it was fun to do it when you came there, 'cause you knew what you were in for when you started out. Not today, I don't like that today.

In his 1973 reminiscence, octogenarian fiddler and caller Mike McCann also expressed his preference for old-time squaredancing:

The old-time dancing they are trying to bring back now has something missing. The meter is different. The music is played by note and it hasn't got that old zip.[18]

Besides square dances, their tunes, and an occasional ballad, the Upper Midwest's old-timers also acquired "English" songs in school. As a young girl in Toivola, Michigan, "Jingo" Viitala recalled how

After the bell rang and we sat down, the teacher read the roll call. Then we had fifteen or twenty minutes of singing. How we loved to sing! Picture fifty or more kids of every size, age, and shape singing Irish ballads and Scottish folk songs with a broad Finnish accent! All Finns love music, and

when they sing together, they really lose themselves. We kids simply tried
to drown each other out. I can imagine we were heard miles away with the
doors and windows open.[19]

Fond of singing, Jingo and her friends copied the words of favorite
songs, both Finnish and English, into notebooks to be shared at informal
singing sessions. This practice, paralleling the accumulation of printed
broadsides and the formation of "ballet books" by Southern traditional
singers, was widespread in the region.[20] Jerry Novak similarly learned
many such, in his parlance school songs including rural favorites like
"The Old Gray Mare" and "Put on Your Old Gray Bonnet" as well as
minstrel songs like Henry Clay Work's "In the Year of Jubilo."[21]

The latter ditty's presence in the region was not surprising, given the
number of minstrel shows touring the north woods in the late nineteenth
and early twentieth centuries. As an important mill town on the Red
Cedar River and a burgeoning agricultural trading center, Rice Lake,
Wisconsin, boasted an imposing opera house where, in the spring of
1896, the Plantation Minstrels and Slayton's Jubilee Singers performed
for enthusiastic crowds.[22] During that era Ashland, Wisconsin—a mill
town, port, and railroad hub—likewise hosted companies like The Great
Barlow's Minstrels and The Dixie Jubilee Singers.[23] That such professional presentations were not lost on audiences of varied ethnic stock is
evident in an account from the *Ashland Daily Press* of "Home Talent
Minstrel Night" in the hall of St. Agnes's Catholic Church. While
roughly one thousand gathered, "Hilda Bloomquist recited a Negro
piece," and others enacted a "tambo and bones blackface minstrel show"
complete with "coon songs, which were all hits."[24]

The evening also included an Italian and Bear act by Will Garnich and
John Allo, in which the "Dago maka de beara clima the pole to the tele-
graph." And indeed numerous ethnic acts, along with light opera, were
common to the music hall scene. Scandinavian vaudevillians like Knute
Erickson and Hjalmar Peterson, aka Olle i Skratthult, put on plays and
sang humorous songs in Ashland County.[25] Meanwhile, entertainers like
Bell's Hawaiians, Moser Brothers, Swiss Yodelers, and the yodeling
Jolly Riggi Boys toured Rice Lake.[26]

While apparently distinct from Anglo-Celtic rural traditions, these acts
nonetheless subtly influenced regional acceptance of what was evolving
into the country music of today. As a Bondkomiker, or peasant comedian,
Olle i Skratthult donned "squeaky boots, overcoat, long scarf, peasant
cap with a big flower, and a blacked out tooth under straw colored wig."[27]
In this hick get-up, spouting jokes and poems in a rural dialect, Olle made

a distinct impression on Swedes like Birch Lake's Fritz Swanson, and Mason's Carl Swanson, who took in the comedian's Ashland performance just after World War I. At subsequent dances, with Fritz on accordion and Carl on banjo, the latter would "clown around" and "pull all kinds of foolishness."[28] Such rustic antics could hardly have been unlike the hillbilly and rube routines of Anglo-Celtic country performers—as carried on later in the persons of Archie Campbell, Minnie Pearl, Junior Sample, and others.

Hawaiian troupes likewise spawned admirers and imitators. In 1925, according to the *Ashland Daily Press,* "Sixty-six girls and young women met last night at the Ashland National Bank community room to form the Ashland Girl's Hawaiian Guitar Club."[29] A few years later, the eclectic Otto Rindlishbacher of Rice Lake was heading up "The Rindlishbacher Hawaiian Guitar Quartet."[30] Since the Hawaiian guitar inspired the steel guitar so ubiquitous in post-World War II country music, it is not unlikely that touring Hawaiian bands laid the seeds for an appreciation of whining strings in the upper Midwest.

A similar argument might tentatively be raised with regard to yodeling. Beyond traveling acts like the Moser Brothers and the Riggi Boys, yodeling Swiss performers like Barron County farmer John Giezendanner were also known in the region.[31] And while I will not push the inference, it is possible that such Alpine artists sparked a predisposition in some for the yodeling style of Jimmie Rodgers. But whatever their specific effect, it is clear that touring ethnic vaudevillians in the upper Midwest were emissaries of the extra-regional world and harbingers of developments to come. Their collective careers, which persisted until the onset of the great Depression, likewise overlapped with the technological innovations of radio and the widespread sale of authentic rural Southern phonograph records to national audiences—both of which developments accelerated Northern ethnic acceptance of emergent country music.

The phonograph industry, in existence since the 1890s, had a slow but certain impact on ethnics in the upper Midwest. The old-timers with whom I have spoken universally agree that by about 1920 their families either owned phonographs or had access to a neighbor's machine. Meanwhile, the small yet probably representative collection of 78-rpm records housed in Northland College's McDowell Archives, and the several dozen private collections that I have examined, suggest that the region's listeners prized records by performers of their own ethnicity most highly, but these collections also registered Anglo-Celtic records as a significant second choice.

Early entries include dance pieces like "Miss McLeod's Reel" with "The Irish Washerwoman" by Prince's Orchestra (Columbia A-1474). While marked by full orchestral instrumentation and a high art or "professional" rendition, these discs nonetheless carried tunes which were recognizably those heard at local get-togethers. When bona fide rural performers of ballads, sentimental songs, minstrelsy, and dance tunes became available in the mid-1920s, the region's listeners snapped them up.

But radio's emergence in the 1920s was an even more significant force not only in bringing extra-regional country music to the upper Midwest, but also in presenting regionally familiar tunes to audiences—thereby offering a kind of national sanction to indigenous rural music. In 1924 WLS of Chicago began its live broadcast of the "National Barn Dance."[32] Jingo Viitala Vachon recalls how radio affected youngsters in the woods of Michigan's Upper Peninsula:

> By the time I was a teenager, mountain music had swept like wildfire through our rural community. Since we didn't have any money to go anywhere, especially during the Winter, we stayed up all hours of the night listening to radios that ran on car batteries. We got to know the Drifter from Del Rio, Texas, the Callahan Brothers from WWVA, Wheeling, West Virginia, Patsy Montana, Arkansas Woodchopper, Skyland Scotty and Lulu Belle, Linda Parker and all the rest from WLS Chicago, Louise Massey and the rest from Des Moines, and of course Uncle Dave Macon the Dixie Dew Drop from Grand Ole Opry! And we mustn't forget the Carter Family from WJJD Chicago. We knew them all.[33]

In addition to spreading their music through the airwaves, "Barn Dance" musicians made tours through the upper Midwest in the 1920s and 1930s. The April 8, 1936, edition of the *Rice Lake Chronotype,* for example, reports that "The WLS Merry Go Round crew, featuring the Arkansas Woodchopper, will be at the El Lago Theater next Monday."

More importantly, touring, broadcasting, and recording hillbilly performers gave impetus not only to the region's preexisting Anglo-Celtic musicians, but also to youthful, second-generation ethnic-Americans. Jingo Viitala Vachon, soon the possessor of a $4.50 Sears Roebuck guitar, began to strum out "On Top of Old Smokey" (along with "Voi Emma" and "Kotilan Kulaiset Tansi") and yodel a la Jimmie Rodgers amidst parties with her neighbors. Rice Lake, Wisconsin, meanwhile experienced a fiddling boom in 1926 and 1927. According to the *Chronotype,* on January 1, 1926, the Sampson-Stinn Motor Company hosted a dance wherein participants listened to Henry Ford's old-time fiddlers on radio, then danced while local fiddler Steve Hawkins played, backed by his daughter on piano. On the subsequent March 24th Otto Rindlishbacher, inspired by Henry Ford's efforts to revive old-time fiddlers contests, organized just such an event.

Many of the contestants were former lumberjacks of British, Irish, or French Canadian stock: Manor, Tallman, Hitter, Miller, Stafford, Reed; Collins, Haughian; Gabriel, Brunette, LaBrie, and Crotteau. And yet there were also Scandinavians (Moe, Severson), and Germans (Immerfall, Reckenthaler, Gaulke), and Bohemians (Bretl, Jelinek, Wilda) who participated. According to the paper's account:

> The music played ranged all the way from Sailor's Hornpipe, Rocky Road to Dublin, Over the Waves, and Turkey in the Straw to classical Spanish airs played by Columbo Morrison and a little bit of jazz. . . . Henry Dietz said he hadn't had so much fun since the hornpipe in '76. Dump Blyton and Anthony Pecore jigged.[34]

This event's considerable success spurred similar contests in March and November of the following years.[35] And, probably as a result of his Rice Lake championship in 1926, W. W. Waite—a formidable trick fiddler able to play with the instrument upside-down, behind his back, and while held between his knees—performed over Minneapolis's WCCO radio station in 1926.

As Bob Andresen's researches have pointed out, barn dances in Chicago, Des Moines, and cities further to the south and west provided a model for Northern companies to follow. Minneapolis-St. Paul stations like WCCO, KSTP, and WDGY featured programs combining "ethnic Old Time with Country Music" from the late 1920s through the 1950s.[36] Situated on the interstate Gogebic Iron Range, WJMS (for Johnson's Music Store) served Ironwood, Michigan, and Hurley, Wisconsin. Its programming was highlighted in the 1930s by the weekly live performance and broadcast of "Pappy Eatmore's Barn Dance Jubilee." Besides Finnish and Italian bumpkin comics, the show starred a Scandinavian girl billed as Peggy Arizona (after WLS's Patsy Montana), and Curley Bradley and his Hard Cider Boys—none other than a Slovak, two Italians, and three Finns in cowboy suits playing western and mountain music.[37]

Beginning in the community events of the late nineteenth and early twentieth centuries, boosted by the onslaught of commercial recordings and radio broadcasts in the 1920s and 1930s, country music furthered its influence on Northern ethnics in the 1940s and the decades to follow through increased marketing and mass media exposure. By the early 1980s the repertoires of the ethnic-American musicians whom I encountered during fieldwork included country songs from every stage of the music's existence. There were the nineteenth-century sentimental numbers, cowboy ditties, and railroad songs that characterized the early years of recorded country music: "Little Rosewood Casket," "The Letter Edged in Black," "I'll Be With You When the Roses Bloom Again," "Cowboy Jack," "The Little Sod Shanty on the Claim," "Chisholm Trail," "The Wabash Cannonball," and "Wreck of the Old 97." From the 1930s came yodels ("Muleskinner Blues," "Cattle Call"), rural tearjerkers ("Old Shep," "Beautiful Brown Eyes"), and western swing classics ("Under the Double Eagle," "El Rancho Grande," "Wahoo"). The 1940s provided war-tinged titles like "There's a Star Spangled Banner Waving Somewhere" and "The Soldier's Last Letter," as well as hits like "Tennessee Waltz," "Born to Lose," "Pistol Packin' Mama," "Blue Eyes Crying in the Rain," "You Are My Sunshine," and "Mockingbird Hill." Honky Tonk cheating songs dominated those retained from the 1950s ("Your Cheatin' Heart," "I Walk the Line," "Four Walls," "Pick Me Up on Your Way Down," "He'll Have to Go," "Heartaches by the Number," and "Married by the Bible/Divorced by the Law)"; but also popular were Lefty Frizzell's sentimental "Mom and Dad's Waltz," Bill Carlisle's comic "I'm Too Old to Cut the Mustard," Ferlin Husky's gospel piece "Wings of a Dove," and the nostalgically rural compositions of Stuart Hamblen ("This Ole House") and Boudleaux Bryant ("Out Behind the Barn"). Finally, the 1960s provided the region's musicians with songs of rural displacement like "Detroit City" and "Green, Green Grass of Home."

Made possible by culture contact and media accessibility, further aided by the immigrants' desires to become "American," the widespread and sustained acceptance of country music by non-Anglo-Celtic Northerners also occurred for reasons which, although elusive, are of perhaps greater significance. Many old-timers told me that they were fond of country music because of its definite melodies, its avoidance of ear-shattering volume, and its danceability—qualities which they valued in their own ethnic music. On occasion, the boundaries between Anglo-Celtic and ethnic genres were even unwittingly dissolved. Vivan Brevak's favorite dance tune, which she invariably played with nuance and feeling, was "Mom and Dad's Waltz." However, she called the tune "Dad's Waltz" and, oblivious of its composition by Texan Lefty Frizzell, placed it alongside other esoterically named Scandinavian items in her repertoire: "Leonard's Waltz," "Polka Dad Used to Play," and so on.[38]

The themes of country music also affected Northern ethnics. Boom times ceased early in this century along the South Shore of Lake Superior, and many locals moved to find work in the Pacific Northwest, or in Midwestern industrial centers like Detroit, Chicago, Milwaukee, and Minneapolis. Those who remained in what soon became an economically depressed, marginal, "backwoods" region grew accustomed to hard work, struggles with the elements, and tight-knit communities bound together by kinship, taverns, and churches. Consequently, country music's "hillbilly" preoccupations with mobility, home, rural life, labor, exuberant sociability, loneliness, and religion were shared by the upper Midwest's "jackpine savages."

Perhaps for these reasons, Northern ethnic performers often made country songs their own. Walt Johnson, a Finnish-American vocalist, produced "half-and-half" or macaronic versions of country songs in which the English words of country standards like "You Are My Sunshine" and "Green, Green Grass of Home" alternated with Finnish translations. Jingo Viitala Vachon, meanwhile, has rendered the lyrics of many country songs wholly into Finnish—a process which, for linguistic reasons, resulted in hybrid texts neither English nor Finnish:

> Y'know, it's so hard to translate it ["The Wabash Cannonball"] literally. It's like [she sings]: Here's to Daddy Claxton, his name forever stands/ He'll always be remembered in the forests throughout the land. Well, here I'm singing about "Laxton's papa" [there is no 'cl' sound in Finnish], how he'll always be remembered. And where the part is, y'know: "His earthly race is over, and the curtains 'round him fall. How you gonna translate that in Finnish? So I've got it: [She says the Finnish words, then translates back.] "A race of life is over for him, and shadows are falling over him." That's the way I had it in Finnish, you can't do it any other way.[39]

Besides half-and-half songs and translations, Northern ethnics have also delighted in creating regional parodies of country hits. A Norwegian-American guitarist (whose name will be omitted since he has abandoned comic Scandinavian ditties and honky tonk heart-tuggers for hymns) used to entertain house-party revelers with a "yah shure" version of Bradley Kincaid's "I Was Born about Four Thousand Years Ago," in which he named and satirized local characters. Calling himself Haiki Lunda (Hank Snow in Finnish), Dave Riilta of Hancock, Michigan, was noted for converting "Is Anybody Goin' to San Antone?" into a song about Toivola and Tapiola, Michigan. Art Moilanen, proprietor of Art's

Bar and the Adventure Motel in Mass City, Michigan, was especially noted for his repertoire of parodies or, as he called them, "ad libs."

Art's Barroom (after "Detroit City")
Last night I went to sleep in Art's Barroom,
And I dreamed about that pulpwood pile back home.
I dreamed about my chainsaw, dear old ma and grandma;
I dreamed about those payments that are overdue so long.
I wanna stay here, I wanna stay here,
Yo, but I wanna stay here.
And have another beer.[40]

Stressing that "lotta them old Finn tunes have a comic streak too," Art also worked over "Born to Lose," "Tennessee Waltz," and "Room Full of Roses."

Drawing upon his affection for country melodies and his local tradition of Finnish humor, Art also composed new songs in an ethnic country mode. "The Lumberjack Song," with a tune reminiscent of Johnny Horton's "Sink the Bismarck," came about some twenty years ago.

When I owned the Rousseau Bar, the first year, I was still logging. And I took my crew to Art's Bar there for a breakup party. This is the time of the year when there's road restrictions on. And the ground gets too soft in the woods to do anything really. So that's known as the breakup time. That's when I made up the words to the song about the lumberjack:

The lumberjack, he came to town on a warm springtime day.
A smile he had upon his face, in his pocket was his pay.
He'd had a long hard winter, a-working in the woods.
A packsack upon his back had all his worldly goods.
For he's a rough and ready guy,
A lumberjack is he.
A good old rough and ready guy,
That's the way he's got to be.

He strode on into Art's Bar with a twinkle in his eye.
Plunked his paycheck on the bar and ordered up a rye.
He looked around and said, "Oh well, I tell you what I think.
"If you will ring that little bell, I'll buy the house a drink."

Jingo Viitala Vachon likewise delighted in composing country style songs embellished by a broad "Finnglish" accent. One began,"I'm chust a Finn from Is'pemin'/ t'at s'ovels ta iron ore," while another ("Eino Maki's Pig") chronicled the demise of a giant porker named "Uncle Ned."

Distinctive, long-lived, still vibrant, ethnic country music along the South Shore of Lake Superior—and indeed the larger phenomenon of pan-ethnic old time music—faces a critical test in the years to come. All of the performers I have mentioned are more than fifty years old. In some cases their children or younger neighbors share their repertoires, but often this is not the case. Born in the post-World War II era, the younger generation, the third generation of immigrants, generally favors electric guitars over accordions; and they prefer contemporary music—be it "modern country" or rock—over earlier forms. This increasing orientation has been exacerbated in recent years by heightened recreational development and the seasonal onslaught of youthful tourists who would rather hear powerfully amplified versions of ol' Waylong's latest than listen to some "hick" alternately pump out "Heartaches by the Number" and "Baruska" on the accordion. At the same time—bolstered by a resurgence of ethnic consciousness, broadcasts of polka-dominated programs like "Chmielewski Fun Time," and frequent live appearances by such youthful ethnic bands as The Northern Stars and The Oulu Hotshots—old-time music may be on the verge of a comeback. Whatever lies ahead, for those who give it an open ear and a long look, the region's music, at once ethnic and American, has a rich sound and a complex history all its own.

NOTES

(Fieldwork for this paper was carried out principally in the summer of 1979 and from September 1980 through August 1981 with funding from the National Endowment for the Arts and Northland College, Ashland, Wisconsin. My thanks also to Matthew Gallmann, who assisted with the fieldwork.)

1. Roderick J. Roberts, "An Introduction to the Study of Northern Country Music," *Journal of Country Music* 6:4 (1978): 23–28; Simon J. Bronner, "The Country Music Tradition in Western New York State," *Journal of Country Music* 6:4 (1978): 30–59; Michael Taft, "That's No More Dollars: Jimmy Linegar's Success with Country Music in Newfoundland," *Folklore Forum* 7 (1974): 99–120; and Michael Taft, *A Regional Discography of Newfoundland and Labrador,* Bibliographic and Special Series No. 1 (St. Johns: Memorial University of Newfoundland Folklore and Language Archive, 1975).

2. Robert B. Klymasz, "Sounds You Never Heard Before: Ukrainian Country Music in Western Canada," *Ethnomusicology* 16:3 (1972): 372–380.

3. See my article "Old Time Music in Northern Wisconsin," *American Music* (Spring 1984): 71–87.

4. Tape-recorded interview, Moquah, March 18, 1981. All interviews were conducted by the author. Tapes, field notes, and tape indexes are deposited in the Vere P. and Rosa N. McDowell Ethnic Heritage Sound Archive and Resource Center, Northland, College, Ashland, Wisconsin.

5. For example, Edward D. Ives, *Joe Scott: The Woodsman-Songmaker* (Urbana: University of Illinois Press, 1978), 371–393; and Robert D. Bethke, *Adirondack Voices, Woodsmen and Woods Lore* (Urbana: University of Illinois Press, 1981).

6. Rickaby, *Ballads and Songs of the Shanty-Boy* (Cambridge, Mass.: Harvard University Press, 1926); see also Daniel W. Greene, " 'Piddle and I,' The Story of Franz Rickaby," *Journal of American Folklore* 81 (1968): 316–336.

7. Tape recorded by Katherine Leary Antenne for the Barron County Historical Society, August 9, 1973; for extensive comparative notes, see Vance Randolph, *Ozark Folksongs,* vol. 1, *British Ballads and Songs* (Columbia University of Missouri Press, 1980), 398.

8. See Edith Fowke, *Lumbering Songs from the Northern Woods,* Publications of the American Folklore Society Memoir Series, No. 55 (Austin: University of Texas Press, 1970), 25–27.

9. From a manuscript collected by Ward Winton for the Washburn County Historical Society, ca. 1954.

10. Interview, Washburn, February 2, 1981.

11. George Russell, interview, Bruce, Wisconsin, June 24, 1975.

12. *Checklist of Recorded Songs in the English Language in the Archive of American Folksong to July 1940,* vol. 3 (Washington, D.C.: Library of Congress, 1942), 138.

13. *Rice Lake Chronotype,* October 14, 1931.

14. This is N-11 in C. Malcolm Laws' classificatory scheme, *American Balladry from British Broadsides* (Philadelphia: American Folklore Society, 1957), 208.

15. Interview, Herbster, January 13, 1981.

16. Interview, Washburn, Wisconsin, March 5, 1981.

17. Interview, Barksdale, Wisconsin, June 22, 1981.

18. See note 9.

19. Jingo Viitala Vachon, *Tall Timber Tales* (L'Anse, Mich.: L'Anse Sentinel, 1973), 2.

20. I examined half a dozen such books and heard of many others.

21. Interview, Moquah, August 2, 1979.

22. *Rice Lake Chronotype,* April 10, 1896, and May 1, 1896.

23. *Ashland Daily Press,* May 2 and 7, 1902: "Saturday evening a minstrel show will play at the opera house, a good house for that company is not questioned."

24. *Ashland Daily Press,* January 12, 1904.

25. *Ashland Daily Press,* January 21, 1904.

26. *Rice Lake Chronotype,* October 16, 1925; April 21, 1926; and September 9, 1929.

27. Richard Hulan, *Teater, Visafton och Bal,* program notes for a national tour of theatre, music, and dance traditions of Swedish America, p. 6; see also Maury Bernstein, "The Man Who Gave Us Nikolina," *Minnesota Earth Journal,* 3 (n.d.).

28. Interview, Ashland, October 23, 1980.

29. *Ashland Daily Press,* March 27, 1925.

30. *Rice Lake Chronotype,* November 8, 1933.

31. *Rice Lake Chronotype,* obituary, August 1975.

32. James F. Evans, *Prairie Farmer and WLS* (Urbana: University of Illinois Press, 1969), chapters 7 and 8.

33. Jingo Viitala Vachon, *Sagas from Sisula* (L'Anse, Mich.: L'Anse Sentinel, 1975).

34. "Thirty Fiddlers Were in Contest," *Rice Lake Chronotype,* March 24, 1926.

35. *Rice Lake Chronotype,* March 2, 1927, and November 2, 1927.

36. Bob Andresen discusses these stations in a lengthier, unpublished version of his ground-breaking "Traditional Music: The Real Story of Ethnic Music and How it Evolved in Minnesota and Wisconsin," *Minnesota Monthly* (October 1978): 9–13.

37. Johnny Lombardo, interview, Ironwood, Michigan, May 1981.

38. Interview, Barksdale, Wisconsin, June 22, 1981.

39. Interview, Trimountain, Michigan, March 23, 1981.

40. Songs and biographical information were recorded from Art in Mass City, Michigan, March 22 and 23, 1981.

Archie Green

Commercial Music Graphics #64: Farewell, Tony

Alonza Elvis "Tony" Alderman, age 83, died on Tuesday, October 25, 1983, in Leonardtown, Maryland. A staff reporter for the nearby Lexington Park *Enterprise,* Joseph Norris, in a well-illustrated obituary ("Fiddler Tony Alderman: The Last of the Hill Billies," November 2, 1983), caught much of the zest and cheer which marked Tony's life. During the 1960s Alderman had helped immensely in my studies of old-time music, and, thereby, in launching this graphics series for the *JEMF Quarterly.* Accordingly, when Harold Closter, a friend at the Smithsonian Institution, telephoned to report Tony's death, I resolved to devote a feature to his memory.

Born on September 10, 1900, at River Hill, Virginia, young Alderman learned the trumpet and French horn from his father—director of the Galax Dixie Concert (brass) Band—and country fiddling from friends and relatives in Grayson and Carroll counties. During January 1925, Tony joined with John Rector and Joe and Al Hopkins to travel to New York for an Okeh recording session. With an anecdote, now embedded in country music history, Tony, in later years, recalled that A&R man Ralph Peer had asked the Blue Ridge mountaineers for their string-band's name. In reply, Al Hopkins identified the performers as a bunch of hillbillies from North Carolina and Virginia. Peer, already acquainted with this word as both a funny and a fighting term, named the group The Hill Billies.

289

The Hill Billies, as sketched for Talking Machine World, *April 15, 1925.*

In time, this band helped denominate Anglo-American old-time music as *hillbilly*. For the past two decades, researchers have elaborated Tony's baptismal account, filled in contextual background, and supplied corroborative detail. As well, one scholar has reported on other pioneer musicians who also used this tag to identify the idiom. (See Wayne Daniel, "George Daniell's Hill Billies: The Band That Named the Music?" *JEMFQ*, no. 70, Summer 1983.) Professor Daniel's article reinforces the necessity for constant revision in our views about American vernacular expression.

The Al Hopkins band, which recorded for Okeh, Brunswick, and Vocalion, did not survive its leader's death in 1932. However, Tony continued to fiddle until the very end. Living in Washington, D.C., for more than four decades, he worked as a dental x-ray technician, where his skill led to several patented inventions. These included a microscopic lens to "peer" into and to photograph the human throat. Learning to fly and obtaining a license, Tony pioneered in aerial photography. He enjoyed telling friends about leaning out of the cockpit, literally, to take landscape photos in the Potomac River area. During Washington years,

Tony played in a local string-band, The Happy Hicks, at times, adding a saw for special effects. I recall an especially happy twilight performance, to which Tony invited me, on a Chesapeake & Ohio Canal mule-drawn boat.

In 1970 Tony retired from formal employment, moving to a little house—including a private darkroom—at Golden Beach on the Pataux-ent River in St. Mary's County, Maryland. His final years were full: music, photography, exchanging tapes, educating grandchildren, crab-bing (pursuing the fabled soft-shelled crab). At Golden Beach he joined with Joe Krahling, Sid Sorrels, Myles Timko, Roy "Speedy" Tolliver, and other local musicians to form the Over the Hill Gang. The Gang played constantly at celebrations such as tobacco auctions and blessing-of-the-fleet rituals. As well, Tony performed for the National Council for Traditional Arts' festivals at Wolf Trap Farm on Washington's outskirts, and for the Smithsonian Institution's Festival of American Folklife on the National Mall. In Alderman's eighth decade, he traveled twice yearly to Washington to fiddle at Fourth of July and Christmas parties at the National Museum of American History. Characteristically, he was en route to a good-will entertainment at the St. Mary's Nursing Home, Leonardtown, when he fell fatally ill.

Tony Alderman enriched the lives of others not only with a lifetime of marvelous fiddling, but also by guiding historians and discographers through the maze of early country music events. Fortunately, we can still hear him in performance on *The Hill Billies* (County 405), an LP reissue in 1974 of twelve classic early tunes. The album, edited by Joe Wilson, holds a delightful four-page illustrated brochure, which permits present-day listeners to see Tony and his fellow entertainers as they appeared in their prime recording/barnstorming years. By a choice set of circum-stances, a few band photos taken by Tony, himself, as well as photos taken by others, have become emblematic of country music origins.

We reproduce a few such pictures here. I open with the very first depic-tion of The Hill Billies to reach any audience. After Ralph Peer selected a name for the Hopkins-Rector-Alderman combination, Okeh publicists needed a visual for their dealers' supplements and related advertise-ments. Although a few dates are imprecise, this sequence of events in 1925 frames the first picture (p. 290):

A) *January 15:* Christening day for The Hill Billies in New York.

B) *February ?:* Okeh dealers' supplement announces release of "Silly Bill"/"Old Time Cinda" (Okeh 40294).

C) *April ?:* Second release, "Cripple Creek"/"Sally Ann" (Okeh 40336).

D) *April 15: The Talking Machine World* uses a lifelike sketch to tout the band.

E) *May?:* Sketch used again in Okeh supplement.

Following key leads supplied by fiddler Charlie Bowman (his letter to Joe Nicholas, *Disc Collector,* January 1961), I first visited Alderman in Washington, D.C. (June 3, 1962). 1 was overwhelmed by his disc and photograph collection, as well as by his kindness and hospitality. More so than many participants, he was conscious of his role as a pathbreaker and, hence, of his responsibility to get knowledge of recorded mountain music into scholarly channels. Accordingly, he was eager to share information and artifacts with all who approached him.

Giving me a set of glossy prints of The Hill Billies, Tony expressed regret that he lacked the first—one he had taken in Galax (February or March, 1925) and mailed to New York. It stood out in his mind because he had used his own tripod-mounted delayed-action camera. This permitted him to pose John Rector (banjo), Al Hopkins (piano), and Joe Hopkins (guitar). Then, triggering the camera, he joined the group, fiddle in hand. After sending the photo to Okeh, he was surprised to see that it was not used directly in publicity material. Rather, a staff artist used it as a model for a drawing in pen-and-ink or pencil.

In my years at the University of Illinois, during the 1960s, I immersed myself in learning about hillbilly music's beginnings. With colleagues who helped form the JEMF, I asked: How did this hybrid music jell and sell? Who named it? What consequences flowed from this act? When did hillbilly, as a label, give way to country-western, bluegrass, and similar neutral terms?

One of my tasks involved reading, page by page, the huge bound volumes of *The Talking Machine World.* To my great joy, I found The Hill Billies sketch in the issue of April 15, 1925. Subsequently, I summed up findings in an article ("Hillbilly Music: Source and Symbol," *Journal of American Folklore,* July 1965). While serving as a faculty advisor to the UI Campus Folksong Club, this group reprinted the *JAF* article. For the pamphlet cover, Professor A. Doyle Moore— a friend, a teacher of graphic arts, a fine printer—reproduced the *TMW* drawing. Upon my sending a reprint copy to Alderman, he enlarged its cover and framed it. Literally, Tony kept this enlarged photo on his living-room wall from 1965 until his death. During April 1984, Tony's heirs and Harold Closter returned the framed photo to me for safekeeping.

The *TMW* drawing contrasts well with subsequent photos of the Hopkins crew. For their first photo all four members wore stylish suits, vests, and ties. Later, they "dressed down" as country bumpkins with overalls and bandannas. Interestingly, the band did not hold together long enough to see mountain musicians turn from dress suits, to overalls, to cowboy togs.

Following the success of its initial Okeh discs, the Hopkins group switched to the linked Brunswick and Vocalion labels, using as names: Al Hopkins and His Buckle Busters for the former, The Hill Billies for the latter. About February 1925, the band made its radio debut on Washington station WRC. In lauding The Hill Billies on the air, *Radio Digest* (March 6, 1926) sagely noted radio's modernizing function in the hill country as well as its role in bringing "the folk music of America" back to the mountains. Washington broadcasts by the Hopkins crew, in turn, led to live engagements from the Carolinas to Ohio and New York. The band members moved readily in many arenas: fiddlers contests, political rallies, school assemblies, vaudeville shows, recording sessions. During a recording trip to New York, the group made a film sound-short for Vitaphone, *The Hill Billies*, released as a trailer with Al Jolson's *The Singing Fool*.

Most histories of country music report the great Depression's Crash of 1929 as a dividing point between old and new styles. Many musicians, embittered by the loss of audience and income, put their instruments aside in the early 1930s, while some accommodated to then-emerging country-western demands. One of Alderman's friends, Ernest "Pop" Stoneman, made an unusual four-decade transition from acoustical to long-play recordings, retaining to the very end his old-time manner. Tony, like "Pop," continued to favor the oldest forms, but never after the Crash did he appear in a recording studio. Fortunately, a few discs holding Tony's fiddling were reissued for new audiences after World War II.

Alan Lomax, in 1947, edited *Mountain Frolic* (Brunswick B-1025), a reissue anthology of five 78-rpm discs by various string-bands. The album included "Cluck Old Hen" and "Black Eyed Susie" by Al Hopkins and His Buckle Busters. This reissue set, and a companion, *Listen to Our Story* (Brunswick B-1024), were both reissued again on 10″ LPs (Brunswick 59000 and 59001) when 78s were phased out by long-playing discs. In time Coral, a Japanese Decca subsidiary, combined cuts from the two 10″ albums into a 12″ LP, *American Folk Classics* (Coral MH 174). Finally, the recent Japanese MCA album *The Fifty-Year History of Country Music* (MCA 3013) included "Black-Eyed Susie." Thus, one of the pieces featuring Tony's fiddling has had an unusually long and wide appeal.

At this juncture, I shall not comment on other LP reissues of The Hill Billies on labels such as Blue Ridge Institute, County, and Vetco. Rather, I shall return to *Mountain Frolic's* cover, reproduced here. Literally, we see, in 1947, a commercial artist's conception of folksong shaped in the New Deal and World War II period. The album's cover shows dancers and musicians as they might have appeared in a Davy Crockett almanac or Daniel Boone memoir. Brunswick executives, assisted by folklorist Lomax, pushed urban listeners back into time to prepare them for mountain music at a war's end—an event which had pulled people out of mountain homes and altered their mores and music.

Today it is easy to note changes in the imagery used by the sound recording industry to promote Alderman and his peers. When Tony photographed himself in "his" band of 1925, he and his buddies donned their very best dress suits. A phonograph record debut called for maximum dignity. Also, Tony was apprehensive that the band's name, The Hill Billies, might trouble some of his Blue Ridge neighbors. Hence, a "proper" picture served as an amulet to ward off bad luck.

A few years later (reaching to the feuding/ moonshining/ high jinks stereotypes of head-of-the-holler pleasure), the troupe donned comic gear. In a sense, in this initial reincarnation, the Hopkins crew visually became white minstrels mimicking their own culture. The Brunswick album cover artist of 1947, in returning to log-cabin days, certified that Tony and his friends represented good times, but times well before backwoods frolics were burlesqued for commercial purposes. Additionally, Brunswick's delineation suggested that The Hill Billies (and fraternal string-band musicians) were as patriotically American as Crockett and Boone. Essentially, *Mountain Frolic*'s album cover bridged New Deal and World War II concerns: as our citizens faced an uncertain future of nuclear energy and imperial world power, they needed constantly to reaffirm a "natural" heritage.

For many pioneer artists we have little memorabilia. All students of country music know the pain in reaching a performer who never felt that his ephemera held value, or in meeting heirs who allowed their parents' "things" to slip away. Fortunately, Alderman kept a trunk full of photos and clippings to mark his personal odyssey. Did he keep the faith in the lean years, hoping that a collector might come along to share his treasures? To the best of my knowledge, no photos or drawings of The Hill Billies were used in print from 1931 until 1966. When Tony presented me with a number of glossy prints, I quickly shared them with fellow researchers. During 1966 Robert Shelton and Burt Goldblatt edited *The Country Music Story,* an early illustrated overview. These compilers used a photo of The Hill Billies on page 29; I believe this to be the first printing of a picture of the Hopkins troupe in historical perspective.

During 1968 the University of Texas Press published Bill C. Malone's *Country Music USA,* a work known to all serious students of the idiom. Here I report only that Malone, in 1968, used two pictures from Tony's collection. In 1969, the Press reissued *Country Music USA* in paperback, retaining the original book's "broadside" cover. However, in 1975, for a second paperback edition, a book designer in Austin selected one picture of The Hill Billies for use on the paperback's cover (reproduced here). Cropping the photo to show a singing trio—Tony (cap on backwards), Joe Hopkins (felt hat), Charlie Bowman (floppy hat and fiddle under

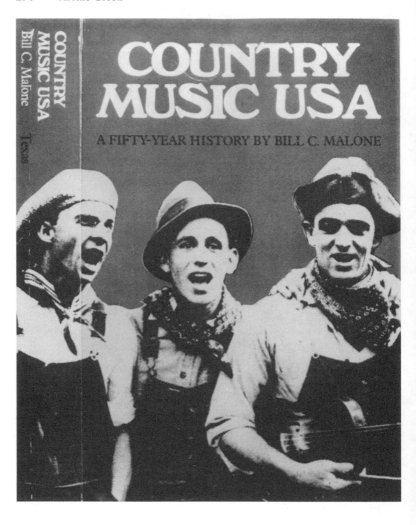

arm)—the designer telegraphed an instant message: this trio personifies country music.

I am pleased that these musicians from Virginia, North Carolina, and Tennessee dominate the cover of an analytic history, published in 1975, by an academic press, and widely distributed in paperback. The University of Texas Press might have decorated Professor Malone's book with Nashville sequins and spangles, or a guns-and-guitar singing cowboy riding down the canyon. Instead, the Press, appropriately, turned back to a

1920s photo, one originally intended to base country music in a past of rural humor.

The kinds of pictures taken by Tony Alderman from 1925–1931, and those taken by others in which he and his fellows play, have been especially useful in displays embellishing old-time music. Hence, I have been able to pay my respects to a friend with but a handful of graphics in which he appears. In this commentary, I have not been impelled to eulogize Tony. Rather, I have called attention to his role as a conservator with a full trunk of pictures and clippings. These archival skills complemented the life of one dedicated to old styles and tested repertoires in mountain music.

To let Tony have the last word I append below one of his early letters to me—an anecdotal document in its own right. When Tony first wrote out his memory of the naming of hillbilly music, he ended his letter by promising to "mend his ways" in order to "answer sooner next time." Those of us who join hands to document vernacular music in its varied manifestations need to mend our ways as we, too, correspond with each other, exchange material, and share experience. Tony Alderman raised high pennants for all who heard his fiddling and shared his wisdom. [ca. 1961]

Dear Mr. Green:

You asked how the Hill Billies got started. Well, my father started me out to play the trumpet like John Philip Sousa, which I enjoyed until I began to hear my uncles and "Pop" Stoneman play for all kinds of gatherings and I decided I just had to join up. So I learned to fiddle. I was working in a barber shop in Galax, Virginia, and one Monday morning along came a man with a guitar. I sent for my fiddle and we started. Friday came along and we were still going strong. I can't remember doing any work.

There lived nearby a man named Henry Whitter who had made some records like "Soldier's Joy," "Little Brown Jug," and others. So we thought anything he could do we could do better. Along came another man by the name of John Rector who had made one record for Victor. He listened for a while and then said, "Would you go to New York if I could get you an appointment?" He got one, and away we went in a 1923 Dodge. Three days later we were in New York.

We played in front of a big horn, banjo ten feet back in the corner. I was fiddling like mad on a fiddle with a horn on it which I couldn't hear. John Rector couldn't hear me either, and no one could hear the guitar. Nobody could hear anybody else, to tell the truth. Victor played the record back to us, and my father could have done better on his Edison! (No reflection on

Victor; it was us.) So we went home a little sad and ashamed that we had not done better.

Not to be outdone, we wrote to Okeh, and they said, "Come on up." This time, no horn, but a microphone 1924 [1/15/25]. We could tell we had made a hit by the way they were grinning. So now we had a record coming out, and no name for the band.

Your account of the conversation between Al Hopkins and Mr. Ralph Peer is correct, word for word (I was there), except for the word "Original," which had not been attached to the Hill Billies as yet, as no other band had called themselves Hill Billies and we had no cause to protect the name at that time. In fact, we were worried because we had agreed with Mr. Peer so readily, for, as you have mentioned, the word "Hill Billies" was not only a funny word, it was a fighting word. To us it meant a back-woods person who knew nothing at all about city life and who hadn't been to school much either. So we were not even sure we wanted to use this name for our band.

But there is a little more to the story than Charlie [Bowman] told you. Two more people had something to do with the name. As we were on our way to New York, a Mr. John Hopkins, Sr. (father of the four Hopkins boys who lived in Washington at the time), asked what brought us to Washington, and we told him that we were on our way to New York to make records. Said he, "What do you hill billies think you can do up there?" After we had made the records in New York, and in the course of conversation, Al said, "We are nothing but a bunch of hill billies." Mr. Peer was pleased with this name, but we sort of wished at the time we had found a more dignified one. So back to Washington where we met up with Ernest "Pop" Stoneman. When we told him what we had called ourselves, he laughed until tears came, and said, "You couldn't have ever got a better name." So it stuck.

I was afraid to go home, as the country people played and sang this type of music and hid their instruments at the sight of a city slicker. And now I had gone to New York and put their music on records and called it a bad name to boot. So I just didn't go home for four years. Things happened so fast that by the time I did get home the name was real dignified. Country people would go into a music store, ask for Hill Billy records, and the salesman would show them all the new country records just out. They just didn't bother with the ritzy kind. The name "Hill Billy" sort of classified them.

We were almost famous when we arrived home from the first trip, as the high school was getting ready for a show which we were to do. We decided that the name "Hill Billies" was being good to us and that we should protect it. We hired a lawyer in Washington to copyright it for us. By the time we got our stock [of records] for sale, we had another call back to New York to make records for Brunswick, and right across the street in the Hippodrome Theater was a bunch of boys who were calling themselves the Ozark Hill Billies. It was just before this time that the "Original Hill Billies" was copyrighted, also under the name of Al Hopkins and his Buckle Busters. So from that day on there were more kinds of Hill Billy bands popping up than you could count, and some of them were so good that we didn't want to stop them anyway.

I think you have the rest of this story on tape.

I shall mend my ways and answer sooner next time.

Regards,
A. E. Alderman

Tony Hilfer

"Wreck on the Highway": Rhetoric and Religion in a Country Song

This essay is for Archie Green (T. H., 1988)
A mistaken premise about the texts and artifacts of popular culture is that they are universally simple and banal, lacking the complexity and resonance of high art.[1] It is self-evident that this is the case for many popular works; if a defense of, say, "Three's Company" is possible, I leave it to someone else. But I intend to demonstrate a complexity and resonance in a classic country song which can be seen on condition only that it be looked for.

The song is "Wreck on the Highway," best known as part of Roy Acuff's repertoire, though composed and originally performed by Dorsey Dixon, a middle-south mill worker. My interest in this text is partly as an illustration of a critical idea—the richness of a popular text— but mostly as an engaging work of art that I want to write about to explain to myself and others why I like it. To put it another way, I did not so much choose this text as it chose me, demanding explication.

My explication will be by way of traditional "close reading" with special emphasis on rhetorical and semiotic analysis since the song has designs on its imputed audience, meaning to persuade that audience to an ideological point of view by constructing a set of oppositions whose sense depends on an inventive interplay of cultural texts.[2] The occasion of "Wreck on the Highway" was a highway crash in the winter of 1938 on U.S. Highway 1 near Rockingham, North Carolina, but the meaning

300

of the song is in its interpretation of this actuality in terms of a Christian, Bible-oriented symbol system.

Dorsey Dixon heard about the wreck while working at a cotton mill near the site of the accident. After work he went to the scene and wrote the song that same night. These are the lyrics, in the well-known version performed by Roy Acuff:[3]

Who did you say it was, brother
Who was it fell by the way?
When whiskey and blood run together,
Did you hear anyone pray?

Chorus:
I didn't hear nobody pray, dear brother,
I didn't hear nobody pray,
I heard the crash on the highway,
But I didn't hear nobody pray.

When I heard the crash on the highway,
I knew what it was from the start,
I went to the scene of destruction,
And a picture was stamped on my heart.

There was whiskey and blood all together,
Mixed with glass where they lay,
Death lay her hand in destruction,
But I didn't hear nobody pray.

(repeat chorus)

I wish I could change this sad story,
That I am now telling you,
But there is no way I can change it,
For somebody's life is now through.

Their soul has been called by the master,
They died in a crash on the way,
And I heard the groans of the dying,
But I didn't hear nobody pray.

(repeat chorus)[4]

Given the rhetorical question that frames the song, the logical starting point for interpretation is the topic of audience—to whom is the song directed and how do its speakers relate to this audience? In a sense, of course, the audience is whoever hears the song, performed live or on various recordings. Among those who have performed "Wreck on the Highway" are Dorsey Dixon himself in more than one version, Roy Acuff in several recordings, and, surprising to me, Jean Ritchie. A particularly interesting recording, as I shall later show, is Acuff's collaboration with the Nitty Gritty Dirt Band on the album *Will the Circle Be Unbroken.*[5] The audience is not homogeneous, as Dixon, Acuff, and the Dirt Band have the different constituencies of folk, country, and rock—although a given individual might cross over. I shall briefly take up the question of the song's various audiences toward the end of this essay, but more immediate and more central is the audience implicitly defined within the song itself and the relation of this audience to the song's meaning.

The song begins with the first speaker's two crucial questions: (1) Who fell by the way and (2) Did they pray? The rest of the song is the second speaker's complex answer to these questions, questions that unite the two speakers and the implied audience in a privileged system of symbols. Indeed, it is only through the shared conventions and code of the speakers and implied audience that the questions are answered, that the argument of the song becomes coherent, that the metaphor of the song is extended. The second question, "Did they pray?," is partially answered, but the answer only has significance within the code. The first question is never explicitly answered. Rather, it is answered in terms of the code, along with the second question: Who were these people? Nonprayers, that's who. (The song is an example of the aesthetics of negativity; what is most important in it is what did not happen.)

The song is framed as the dialogue of two speakers, who are "brothers," that is brothers in the church, in a southern fundamentalist congregation, interested not in the material facts of the event, the journalistic significance (who, what, when, where?) but in the moral and especially eschatological meanings. This is the rhetorical device of the song—its maker's invention to raise an unfortunately commonplace secular event, another highway crash, from journalistic cliche to religious exemplum.

There is a fine logic to this transposition. Car and highway, especially southern highway, have rich mythological associations, associations running directly counter to the ethos of fundamentalist religiosity. The car, as William Faulkner proclaimed, is that to which the American has projected his libido, "our national sex symbol."[6] It was the charger of that cavalier of lowlife middle-south folklore, the moonshine runner, the demigod of Thunder Road. The car is speed, the fast-track life, vitality, sport, and backseat sex.[7]

The highway was a route of adventure and danger interspersed with the delicious temptations of the roadhouse, the highway version of the honky-tonk. James Ross's 1940 novel, *They Don't Dance Much,* has its sordid plot of moonshine, murder, and adultery centered on a North Carolina roadhouse.[8] But Flannery O'Connor's Hazel Motes says the last word on the car as a secular exemplar: "Nobody with a good car needs to be justified."[9] (In fact, the car in *Wise Blood* combines Jonah's ship and whale, being Hazel's failed mode of escape from his religious vocation.)

There are, then, several texts in "Wreck on the Highway": a journalistic text; the text of southern car and highway dreams and wishes; and a religious, homiletic text, itself allusive to the authoritative text of its source of good and bad news, the Bible. Dixon's song is the transposition from the journalistic secular code to that of religious homily. What matters is not who was in the wreck—names, addresses, ages, occupations—but the state of the dead—did they die in grace?

First, however, one secular association of the southern highway can be carried directly over to the religious code, that is, its associations with fatality, sudden death. Have not national and local radio and television news, as the 1920s and 1930s newspaper news did, picked up on the cultural functions of the death's head on the desk, serving as our contemporary *memento mori* to which we make our quotidian observance: "Give us this day our daily dead"? National news gives us assassinations, wars, and large-scale natural disasters; local news, the latest community body count from murders and wrecks on the highway.

Such news casts a kind of bad spell on us, simultaneously arousing and routinizing our terrors, alienating eschatological significance into statistical rationalization and pornographic violence. The pre-Interstate road between Nashville and Louisville, officially the Dixie Highway, was locally known as "the Dixie Dieway," and citizens of Austin, Texas, honor a particularly nasty stretch of highway with stickers reading "Pray for me, I drive Highway 183."

Dorsey Dixon took such material, in its late 1930s form of media pornography and the stuff of appalled and fascinated gossip, and recast it into the providential religious code from which it had originally emerged. He thus dramatically reinvented highway myths as a negative version of the Christian pilgrimage as codified in Matthew 7:13–14:

> Enter ye in at the strait gate; for wide is the gate, and broad is the way, that leadeth to destruction, and many there be that go in thereat; Because strait is the gate, and narrow is the way, which leadeth unto life, and few there be that find it;

and in the many hymns deriving therefrom: "Travelling Onward to the City" ("Treading not the straight and narrow way"); "Savior, Blessed Savior" ("Journeying o'er the road/Worn by saints before us"); "Awake Our Souls, Away Our Fears" ("True, 'tis a strait and narrow road"); etc. The literal southern highway becomes a route traversed by those who "have forsaken the right way and are gone astray" (II Peter 2:15), and those forgetful of "the way of righteousness" (Matthew 21:32). The highway's anagogical meaning is thus its antithesis to "the way, the truth, and the life" (John 14:6) embodied in Christian gospel.

There is, in the seventeenth-century sense of the word, a high wit in this transposition, though Dixon's inventiveness may have been helped along by such mountain spirituals as "Life is Like a Mountain Railroad." In this piece, the Union station which is the traveler's goal is located just the other side of the trestle spanning Jordan's swelling tide, and the Christian engineer has the eschatological charge to "make the run successful, from the cradle to the grave." Dixon, however, not only updates the "way" but builds his song around the tension between traditional and contemporary versions of it.

The word text of "Wreck on the Highway" is rhetorically inventive throughout, especially in the devices of pathos: *enargia, optatio, threnos.*[10] To be sure, all these words, as well as others I have used—semiotic, anagogical, and so on—would have been unfamiliar to Dorsey Dixon. But he uses these devices, uses them with skill, having learned them from the persuasive rhythms of the Bible and from the oral tradition of fundamentalist sermonizing. Of course, Aristotle's great codification of rhetoric is an analysis more of spoken than written discourse, and the devices predate their taxonomy. The song's rhetorical argument is framed by the two initiatory questions in a stanza which also introduces the song's most graphic image ("whiskey and blood run together") and its extended metaphor: the wreck victims as those who "fell by the way," that is, fallen sinners. The graphic image carries on into coding the wreck as an exemplum, a picture stamped on the heart revealing doctrinal truth. This is *enargia,* that is, the rhetoric of vivid description with a vengeance.

There is an intimation of another tension in the conjunction of whiskey and blood. For a fundamentalist temperance advocate, a believer in providence—Dorsey Dixon was all of these—whiskey and violent death on the secular level link naturally with sin and unredeemed death on the religious level, a link directly oppositional to the wine/blood of Christian salvation, two opposed chains of transmutation. (A parallel instance to Dixon's play on symbolic ideas derives from personal experience: many years ago while driving a rural highway in Washington state I came upon a large billboard proclaiming "There's more life in Olympia" controverted by a whitewash message on a rock some thirty yards on, arguing, "The only true [double whitewash underlines] Life is in Jesus Christ." Speaking of intertextuality. . .)

The song throughout is in the rhetorical form of a *threnos,* that is, a form of speech by which the orator laments some person or people for the misery they suffer. It is, in fact, a kind of negative threnody enforced in stanza four by the speaker's *optatio,* that is, a form of speech by which the speaker expresses his desire by wishing to God or Men: "I wish I could change this sad story, that I am now telling you." But providence has foreclosed on their negative vocation: "Their soul has been called by the master." Even the sounds of their death-agony—"I heard the groans of the dying"—gruesomely confirm their choice of the secular, physical life as opposed to the spiritual life expressed in the sound of prayer, a sound emphasized by its absence. The all too apparent groans of the body, then, are antithetical to the unutterable groans of the spirit which St. Paul evokes: "Likewise the Spirit also helped our infirmities; for we know not what we should pray for as we ought; but the spirit itself maketh intercession for us with groanings which cannot be uttered" (Romans 8:26). Perhaps the groans of the victims even preview those of the damned suffering in Hell; this would be a termination fully in keeping with the logic of the song's argument.

Of course, this logic would carry conviction to some audiences more than others, there being two especially appropriate audiences: the "brothers" of a fundamentalist congregation lamenting the fallen, and those backsliders who despite their honky-tonking (or all the more because of it) remain responsive to the religious symbol system of the song and open to its rhetorical persuasion. For both, the song is a kind of sermon, confirming the former group and warning the latter. (I have heard this song in honky-tonks, though I can't say if anyone was converted.) Indeed the Acuff version leaves out two stanzas of the original Dixon song that develop the theme even more explicitly:

Give out the game and stop drinking
For Jesus is pleading with you

It cost him a lot in redeeming
Redeeming a promise for you.

But it'll be too late if tomorrow
In a crash you should fall by the way
With whiskey and blood all around you
And you can't hear nobody pray.[11]

Here the nonprayers seem to be onlookers rather than the victims, implying that if "you," that is, the onlookers and song-audience, fail to recognize the eschatological significance of the wreck by praying for the souls of the dying, this lack of grace will rebound upon you when your time comes. You ought to be in church praying and being prayed for, not boozing at some honky-tonk.

Other audiences will receive other messages, much depending on the setting and style of the performance, the relation between performer and audience. These variables present no obstacle to the analysis in intertextuality since performance-as-spectacle is a text. The performer's relation to audience is enunciated by the tone of the performance; this tone text qualifies the significance of the word text.[12]

Thus, when Jean Ritchie, the folksinger, performed "Wreck on the Highway" before a sophisticated, folk-oriented audience, she distanced herself from the material (though its inclusion in her performance was a sort of tribute) by tonally camping it up a bit.[13] She did this not in the usual fashion of exaggerating and overdoing the emotion but by the opposite method of speeding up the tempo and singing in an efficient, flat tone so that the song comes out sounding rather brisk and informational. In this version the song becomes not an emotional message from the fundamentalist South but a dry comment about its dryness.

However, Roy Acuff, the performer most identified with "Wreck on the Highway," is famous for emphasizing the song's piety and pathos by his literally weepy tonal and visual performance of it. (He cries on stage.) The foregrounded emotionality comes through on Acuff's most culturally interesting performance of the song, that on the extraordinary three-disc album *Will The Circle Be Unbroken,* which was described by the *Nashville Tennessean* as "one of the most important recordings done in the forty-five years of the Nashville music business."[14] The *Tennessean* reporter read the performance text of the album as a bridging of various sociopolitical gaps—youth/age, contemporary/traditional, liberal/conservative—as embodied in the opposition of the Nitty Gritty Dirt Band to various traditionalist country musicians involved in the project: Roy Acuff, Mother Maybelle Carter, and so on.

The suspense of the occasion was whether such an odd cultural conjunction could work, whether the fragmented American consensus of 1971 could be symbolically reaffirmed: "The night before their meeting with Acuff, the members of the Dirt Band seemed as uneasy about uniting with Acuff's conservative traditional mores as he was about joining their hairy liberality. "The point," as the *Tennessean* reporter punned it, "is the way in which the bridge was gulfed with music."

In the recording of "Wreck on the Highway" Roy Acuff is, of course, the lead singer. He is backed by two Dirt Band performers and by four traditional country musicians: Beecher (Bashful Brother Oswald) Kirby of Acuff's own Smoky Mountain Boys, Earl Scruggs, Vassar Clements, and Junior Huskey. (Though Earl Scruggs, influenced by his son, Randy, had already somewhat compromised Nashville traditionalism by playing at peace rallies.) The quality of performance indicated some sort of meeting of the minds, or at the least, talents; no negligible achievement in 1971. The occasion was, so to say, culturally intertextual.

But to the interpretive community of the academic world, such performances are automatically classified as low culture, and this community hates anything low. Unfortunately, they hate it without understanding it in the least. If the basic gist of this song were recast to some pre-automotive form of accident, rewritten in Middle English and claimed as a new manuscript discovery from the fourteenth century, it would be read as the brilliantly inventive play on biblical texts and Christian meanings that it is. But this and other classical works of popular culture are deemed simple because they are read simplemindedly.[15] To cite another biblical text, "Having eyes, see ye not? And having ears, hear ye not?" I hope this essay shows what can be heard and seen in Dorsey Dixon's song.

NOTES

1. See, for instance, Abraham Kaplan, "The Aesthetics of the Popular Arts," in Irving Deer and Harriet A. Deer, eds., *The Popular Arts* (New York: Charles Scribner's Sons, 1967), 315–342, for a superior version of this argument.

2. The song is marvelously exemplary of "intertextuality," "the relation of a particular text to other texts." As Julia Kristeva, whom I am quoting, argues, "Every text takes shape as a mosaic of citations, every text is the absorption and transformation of other texts." Kristeva enjoins the study of the text "as intertex-

tuality considers it . . . within (the text of) society and history." *Desire in Language* (New York: Columbia University Press, 1980), 37.

3. The details about the crash on U.S. 1 come from Archie Green's album notes to the Nancy Dixon, Howard Dixon, Dorsey Dixon record *Babies in the Mill,* Testament Records T3301 (now out of print). For an account of Dorsey Dixon see Archie Green, "Dorsey Dixon: Minstrel of the Mills," *Sing Out* 16:3 (July 1966), 10–13.

4. "Wreck on the Highway." Written by Dorsey Dixon, copyright 1946, renewed 1974, Acuff-Rose Music, Inc. All rights reserved; used by permission.

5. United Artists Records, UAS 9801.

6. William Faulkner, *Intruder in the Dust* (New York: New American Library, 1949), 182.

7. See David L. Lewis, "Sex and the Automobile: From Rumble Seats to Rocking Van," in David L. Lewis and Lawrence Goldstein, eds., *The Automobile in American Culture* (Ann Arbor: University of Michigan Press, 1983), 123–133. Lewis demonstrates the association of automobiles with sex from the teens to the present.

8. (New York: Popular Library, 1976). Originally published 1940.

9. Flannery O'Connor, *Wise Blood,* in *Three by Flannery O'Connor* (New York: New American Library, 1964), 64.

10. For definitions of these rhetorical terms see Sister Miriam Joseph, *Shakespeare's Use of the Arts of Language* (New York: Columbia University Press, 1947), 340.

11. See Dorsey Dixon, "I Didn't Hear Anybody Pray," Bluebird 7449. (Recorded 1938 in Charlotte, North Carolina.)

12. For the distinction of texts within a given singing performance see Nicholas R. Spitzer, " 'Got the World in a Jug': Reputation and Respectability in the Classic Blues," *Folklore Annual of the University Folklore Association,* nos. 7 and 8, University of Texas, Austin, 1977, 54–77. Spitzer distinguishes between word text, tone text, and visual text.

13. See (or rather hear) Jean Ritchie, *Precious Memories,* Folkways Records FA 2427, recorded ca. 1962 in New York City.

14. The *Nashville Tennessean,* Sunday Morning, August 14, 1971. Reproduced on sleeve jacket in *Will the Circle Be Unbroken,* UAS 9801.

15. See Anthony Channel Hilfer, "Inversion and Excess: Texts of Bliss in Popular Culture," *Texas Studies in Literature and Language* 22:2 (Summer 1980), 125–137.

Index

Abner, Buford, 268
Abner, Merle, 268
Abner, Stacy, 267–68
accordianists, 272, 274, 277
Acuff, Roy, 49, 99, 159; songs, 101;
    at WNOX, 263–64; "Wreck on
    the Highway," 101, 300–302,
    305–7
Adams, Derrol, 239
Adcock, Stuart, 260
Addoms, Art, 17
advertising vs. direct sales, 74, 106
Aeolian-Vocalion Company, 202,
    259, 261
"Aggravatin' Papa," 89
"Alabama Girls," 148
"Alabama Jubilee," 219
Albatross label, 238, 247
album covers, 22–23
Alderman, Alonza Elvis "Tony,"
    289–99, *296*
Alexander, "Texas," 90
"Alexander's Ragtime Band," 200
"All I Got is Gone," 243
Allen Brothers, 49
Allen, Eddie, 38
Allen, Rex, 43
Allen, Thornton, 234
Allo, John, 279
Alpine style yodeling, 135–37, 140
Al's Rhythm Rangers, 124
"Amazing Grace," 96
American Folk Classics, 293

American Folklore, 242
American Record Corp., 49
American Vernacular Music, xxiii
Anderson, Bob, 261
Andresen, Bob, 282
Anglin, Jack, 268
"Are You From Dixie?," 219
Arhoolie Records, xvi
Arizona Cowboy, 43
Arizona, Peggy, 282
"Arkansas Traveler," 129, 218
Arkie, the Arkansas Woodchopper,
    39, 281
Arno, Peter, 178
Arnold, Eddie, 23, 140
Arp, Homer, 124
Asch, Moses, 195
Ashley, Clarence, 149
assembly tradition, 162–64, 166
Atcher, Bob, 43, 101
Atkins, Chet, 24, 110, 268, *271*
Atkins, Ray "Duck," 269
Atlas Brothers, 102
Autry, Gene, x, 39, 49, 50; yodeling,
    140
"Avalon Time," 40
"Awake Our Souls, Away Our
    Fears," 304

Babies in the Mill, x
"Back Up and Push," 151
"Back Street Affair," 112
Baez, Joan, 33

Bailey, Blanche H., 144, 145, 146
Bailey Brothers, 269
Bailey, Charlie, 269
Bailey, Clint, 184, 185
Bailey, Danny, 269
Bailey, Marcus, 223
Baird, Maynard, 261
Ballads and Songs of the Shanty-Boy, 274
"Banjo in the Bluegrass," 22
"Banjo in the Hills," 22
"Banjo in the Mountains," 22
banjo techniques, 197–98
"Barbara Allen," 208
Barber, Burk, 98
Barfield, Johnny, 151
Barrett, Pat, 43
Barton, Ralph, 178
Barton, Ward, 137, 141
"Battle of New Orleans," 235
Baxter, Don and Dode, 74–75
"Beautiful Brown Eyes," 283
Beaver Valley Sweethearts, 43
Bechtel, Perry, 205
Belcher, Red, 102
Bell, Cecil, 267
Bell's Hawaiians, 279
Bennett, Bob, 267
Bennett Family, 131
Benton, Thomas Hart, 180
Berry, Chuck, xxi
"The Bible's True," 13
"Big Midnight Special," 110
Biggar, George, 262
Bill Bailey, Won't You Please Come Home, 230, 235
Bill, Edgar L., 36
"Black Draught," 99
"Black Eyed Susie," 293
blackface, 42, 188, 279
Black Hawk Waltz, 220
"Black Jack Davie," 25
black musicians, 48; influence on white musicians, 86–92; interest in

hillbilly music, 89; Jazz Age depictions, 170
black newspapers, 47
"Black Water Blues," 88
black yodelers, 137–39
Blacky Simmons' Famous Blue Jackets, 88
Blake, Blind, 16, 47
Blake, Norman, 244
Blanchard, Lowell, 263–69
"Blessed Jesus, Hold My Hand," 96
Blind Andy. *See* Jenkins, Andrew, Reverend
Bloomquist, Hilda, 279
"Blue Eyes Crying in the Rain," 283
Blue Grass Boys, 92
bluegrass gospel, 20
bluegrass music, 19, 21; development, 28–29; Italian acceptance, 246–47; negative image, 22
Bluegrass Unlimited, 28
Blue Ridge Highballers, 235
Blue Ridge Institute label, 294
Blue Ridge Mountain singers, 207
Blue Ridge Ramblers, 235
Blue Sky Boys, 20–21
blue yodeling, 137–39
Bluestein, Gene, 195
Blythe, James, 87
Bohemian Band, 126
Bolick, Bill, 20, 144, 147
Bolick, Earl, 20
"Bonaparte's Retreat," 235
Bonawitz, Mr., 188
Bond, Johnny, 20
Bonnie Blue Eyes, 101
Bonnie Lou and Buster, 269
Boone, Claude, 269
Booth, Hazel, 87
border stations, 60, 66–75
"Born to Lose," 283
Botkin, B. A., 241
Bowman, Charlie, 292, *296*
Bowman, Euday L., 230

Boyd, Bill, 235
Bracey, Ishmon, Reverend, 138
Bradley, Curley, 282
Brasefield, Rod, 20
Bray Brothers & Red Cravens, 247
Brevak, Vivian Eckholm, 278, 283
Brewster Brothers, 269
Briggs, Bill, 136
Brinkley, John Romulus, 60–71
Britt, Elton, 141
The Broadside Ballad, 15
broadsides, 129
Brockman, Polk, 204
Bromberg, David, 244
Broonzy, Big Bill, 49
Brown, Frank C., 166
Brown, Hylo, 20
Brown, Jim Ed, 239
Brown, John, 38
Brown, Marion "Peanut," "Curly,"
  230
Brown, Quarantine, 124
Brown, Wilbur C. "Bill," 205
Browne, Jackson, 244
Brown's Ferry Four, 25
Brunswick Company, 192, 202, 205,
  261
Brusoe, Leizime, 277
"Bryan's Last Fight," 9–10
Bryant, Boudleaux, 283
Bryant, Slim, 43, 151, 266
Buckeye Buckaroos, 265
Buckle Busters, 293, 299
Buell Kazee Sings and Plays, 195
The Bully of the Town, 220
Bumgarner, Samantha, 164
Burnette, Smiley, 20, 39
Burns, Aytchie, 265
Burns Brothers, 265
Burns, Kenneth (Dude or Jethro),
  265–66
Burr, Henry, 43
"Busted," 239
"The Busted-on Show," 219

Butcher, Dwight, 147, 261
Butcher, Ruth, 80
Buttram, Pat, 43
"Bye Bye Blues," 268
Byrds, 27–28, 244

"Cacklin' Hen," 23
Cajun music, 141
Calhoun, Bill, 267
"The California Pioneers," 15
The Callahan Brothers, 281
"Called to the Foreign Field," 54
Campbell, Alex, 20
Campbell, Archie, 263, 265, 266, 268
Campbell, Glen, 23
Campbell, Guy, 265, 267
campfire songs, 19
Canaan Records, 19
Cannon, Hugh, 220
"Cannonball Blues," xix
Capt. Stubby and the Buccaneers, 43
Caravan, xi, 158
Carlisle, Bill, x, 268, 283
Carlisle Brothers, 49
Carlisle, Cliff, x, xi, 268
Carlisle, Tommy, 268
"Carnival" (radio program), 265
Carol Lee Singers, 110
Carr, Leroy, 49
Carson, Betty, 124
Carson, Fiddlin' John, 16, 164, 218,
  220; "The Cat Came Back," 221;
  fiddle tune adaptations, 225–26; ra-
  dio pioneer, 145, 200; style, 149
Carson, James, 269
Carson, Marge, 124
Carson, Martha, 269
Carson Sisters, 124
Carter, A. P., 74
Carter, Maybelle, 74, 307
Carter, Sara, x, 74, 139
Carter, Wilf, x, 137, 140
Carter Family, 72, 89, *271;* concerts,
  162; discography, xxi; "I'll Be All

Smiles Tonight," 225; influence on citybilly music, 159; "Lonesome Pine Special," 129; at WJJD, 281; on WNOX, 269; XERA broadcasts, 60–61, 75

The Carter Family on Border Radio, xvi

Cartwell, Charles, 220

Caruso, 226

Carver, Bill, 104, 107, 109, 110–13

"Casey Jones," 149

Cash, Johnny, 193, 238, 239

"The Cat Came Back," 221

"Cattle Call," 124, 140, 283

Celebrity label, 26

Center for Popular Music at Middle Tennessee State University, Murfeesboro, xxiii

Chandler, Harry, 62

"Charles Guiteau," 84

Charles, Ray, 23

Chattaway, Thurland, 227

The Cherry Tree Legend, 182

Chicken Reel, 222, 235

Childre, Lew, 20

Childs, Virginia, 147, 150

"Chime Bells," 141

"Chisholm Trail," 283

Chitwood and Landress, 220

"Chmielewski Fun Time," 286

Chmura, Helen, xi

Christeson, R. P., 221

Christine, the Little Swiss Miss yodeler, 43

Chuck Wagon Gang, 95

Chumbler Family, 207

"The Church," 239

citybilly music, 157–58, 159

CKAC, Montreal, 68

Claire, Malcolm, 42

Clark, John, 109

Clark, Luther "Chink," 104

Clark, Old Joe, 269

Clarke, Yodelin' Slim, 141

clawhammer technique, 197

Clements, Vassar, 307

Clifton, Bill, 20

Clinch Mountain Clan, 108, 109, 110

Closter, Harold, 289, 292

"Cluck Old Hen," 293

Cobb, George L., 219

"Cocaine Blues," 23

Cofer, Uncle Jim, 226

Cohen, John, 196, 241

Cohen, Norm, xiv–xxvii, *46,* 215

Cohen, Ron, xxv

Cole, Ab, 103–4, 109

Cole, M. M., 50

"College Lancers," 128

Collins, Arthur, 222, 232

Collins, Jerry, 267

Colorado Mountain Boys, 269

Columbia Records, 108, 110; 15000-D series, 200–216; Corn Licker Still series, 150, 158; distribution patterns, 202, 212–14; field recording, 203–4, 206–7; first hillbilly music, 146; manufacture, 202; out-of-town recording sessions, 149

"Come All Ye Fair and Tender Ladies," 183

"Come Walk with Me," 110

Compton, Mac, 147

Conley, Sherman, 184

Consolidated Films, Inc., 50

Consolidated Royal Chemical Corporation, 73, 74

Continental Radio Co., 262

"Cool Drink of Water Blues," 138

coon songs, 25, 227, 279; elements in, 219–21, 223, 232

Cooper, Carol Lee, 110

Cooper, Dale Troy "Fiddlin'," 97

Cooper, Myrtle, 42

Cooper, Stoney, 94–116

Cooper, Wilma Lee, 94–116

Copas, Cowboy, 20, 24, 268

Cope Brothers, 268

Cope, Charles, 268
Cope, Lester, 268
copper masters, 49–50
Coral label, 293
"Corey," 23
"A Corn Licker Still in Georgia," 208
Corn Licker Still series, 150, 158
Corwine, Tom, 35
Country and Western Spotlight, xi
country jazz, 266
country music, 21; attributes, 283; defined, 159; importance of authenticity, 94; progressive, 244–45; symbols associated with, 15; versatility, 122–23
Country Music, 238
Country Music Foundation *News Letter,* xx
country music industry, 204
Country Music Records: A Discography, 1921–1942, xxvii
Country Music Sources: A Biblio-Discography of Commercially Recorded Traditional Music, xxiv, xxvii
The Country Music Story, 295
Country Music USA, xviii, 295
The Country Music Who's Who, 16
country rock, 244
County label, 244, 246, 294
coupling notices, 202–3, 208
Courtlander, Max, 48
Covarrubias, Miguel, 170, 178, 180, 182
Covington, Tommy, 268
"Cowards Over Pearl Harbor," 101
"Cowboy Jack," 283
cowboy songs, 283
"The Cowboy's Trail," 194
cowboy yodeling, 138, 139–41
Cowles Broadcasting, 122
"Cowpoke," 141
Cox, Bill, xi
Cranford, Bob, 80

"The Crash of the Akron," 202
Cravens, Red, 247
Crawford, Jimmy, 109
Crazy Elmer, 109
Crazy Tennesseans, 263–64
"Cripple Creek," 291
Crockett, Dad, 141
Crook Brothers, 20
Crookson, Samuel, Reverend, 68
Crosby, Stills, Nash & Young, 244
Cross, Hugh, 40, 150, 209, 261
Cross, Roy, 230
Crumit, Frank, xxi
"Cuckoo Song," 136
"Cumberland Gap," 29
Cumberland Ridge Runners, 39–40
Curly Fox and Texas Ruby, 20
"Cyclone at Ryecove," 23

Dabney, Leonard, 269
The Daisy Girl, 230
Daley, Dennis, 277
Dalhart, Vernon, 50, 200; Columbia recordings, 207, 210, 213; copyrights "The Prisoner's Song," 195; image, 16; "The John T. Scopes Trial," 8, 9; singing style, 189
Dalton, Doug, 268
Daly, Joseph M., 222
dance tunes, 272; ethnic, 274, 277
Dandurand, Tommy, 35
Daniel, Wayne, xx, 290
Daniels, Charlie, 244
Dapper Dan, 109
Darby, Tom, xi, 130, 207
Darby and Tarlton, 130, 207
"Darling Nellie Gray," 129
Davenport, "Cow Cow," 87
Davis, Ben W., 54
Davis, Eva, 164
Davis, Karl, 40
Davis, Lynn, 98
"Daybreak in Dixie," 22
Dean, Billy, 123, 124, 126

Dean, Cora, 124
Dean, Eddie, 43, 122, 124
Dean, Jimmy, 43, 124
"Death of Abraham Lincoln," 23
"The Death of Floyd Collins," 12
"The Death of William Jennings
    Bryan," 10–12
Decca label, 110
"Deep Elm," 88
Delmore Brothers, 72, 205–6
Delta blues, 138
DeMare, Bat, 277
"Derby Ran," 276
Design label, 26
"Detroit City," 283
"Devil's Dream," 277
DeZurik Sisters, 43, 140
Dichter, Harry, 15
Dill Pickles, 222, 235
Dillon, Will, 226
"Dinnerbell Time," 40
Diplomat label, 21
direct sales *vs.* advertising, 74, 106
Disc Collector, xi
Dixie Dew Drop, 281
"Dixie Division," 226
The Dixie Jubilee Singers, 279
Dixie Liners, 226
Dixieland Swingsters, 266, 269
Dixon Brothers, x, 243
Dixon, Dorsey, x, 300–305, 307
domestic tradition in folk music, 163
Donigan, Jack, 151
Donnelly Boys, 277
"Don't Make Me Go To Bed And I'll
    Be Good," 101
Doolittle, Jesse, 35
Dorson, Richard, 242
double-thumbing, 197
Douglas, Bob, 230
Downing, Larry, 267
"Down the Center, Cut-off Six," 129
"Down the Old Plank Road," 243
Down Yonder, 151, 222–23, 232

Dr. Demento, xviii
Drawn from the Wood, 178
The Drifter, 281
drop-thumb picking, 197
"Dueling Banjos," 246
Duke of Paducah, 20
Duke, Ray, 104
Dunham, Bert, 123
Dunigan, Jack, 43
Durham, Dave, 266–67
Dutch, the Boy Blues Singer, 63
"The Dying Cowboy," 194

Eagles, 244
Eakins, Thomas, 182
Earle, Gene, xvii, xxv, *46,* 147;
    discographies, xi; work with John
    Edwards collection, xii-xiv
"Earl Scruggs: His Family and
    Friends," 27
"Earl's Breakdown," 29
Early American Sheet Music, 15
Eckholm, Carl, 278
Edwards, Cliff, 210
Edwards, Joe, 110
Edwards, John Kenneth Fielder, ix-
    xiii; Riley Puckett biography,
    143–44, 147, 152; writes for *Cara-
    van,* 158
"Eighth of January," 56
"Eino Maki's Pig," 286
"El Rancho Grande," 283
"Election Day in Kentucky," 194
"Eleven Cent Cotton," 205
Elliott, Jack, 239
Ellis, Red, 20
Emerson, Ralph Waldo, 35
Emery, S. A., 137
EMI label, 238
Emmett, J. K., 136
Epperson, Joe B., 260, 261
Erickon, Knute, 279
ethnic country music, 244–45,
    272–86, 282; on records, 280–81

Evans, Dave, xxvi
"Evolution—Bryan's Last Great
    Fight," 12
Ezell, Will, 86
Ezra, Charles, 264

Faier, Billy, 158–59
falsetto devices, 138, 140–41
family bands, 128
Farkas, Frank, 273
"Farther Along," 96
Faulkner, Roy, 68
Faulkner, William, 302
"Federal March," 15
Federal Radio Commission, 59, 65
Ferrel, Ruth, 261
Festival of American Folklife, Mon-
    treal, 1971, 92
fiddlers, 282
"A Fiddlers' Convention in Georgia,"
    150
fiddle tunes: defined, 219; ethnic,
    276–77; histories, 219–34
field hollers, 138
field recordings, 203–4, 206–7
Fifty Years Ago, 223, 235
*The Fifty-Year History of Country
    Music,* 293
"Fire on the Strings," 22
Fireside Book of Folk Song, 182
"Fisher's Hornpipe," 277
Fitzgerald, F. Scott, 171–72
flappers, 176
Flatt and Scruggs, 109, 159, 269
Flindt, Emil, 233
"Flop-Eared Mule," 151
Floyd, Larry, 234
Flying Fish label, 244
"Foggy Mountain Breakdown," 246
Foley, "Ramblin' Red," 40
folklore: sub-discipline of media stud-
    ies, 1–6; transmission methods,
    2–6; university programs, xiii, xv

folklore scholarship: changing nature,
    1–6; in Italy, 239–40, 242–43
folk music: assembly tradition vs. do-
    mestic tradition, 162–63, 165; de-
    fined, 159; interactions with popu-
    lar music, 130, 225, 235
    relationship to hillbilly music, 157
folk music revival, 158; image, 22;
    Italian analysis, 242
folksongs, art inspired by, 180, 182
Folkways label, 195
"Footwarmer," 89
Ford, Corey, 172
Ford, Oscar, 146, 150, 223–24
Ford and Glenn, 210
Foree, Mel, 107, 268
"Four Walls," 283
Fowler, Wally, 269
Fox, Curly, 235
frailing, 197
Freeman, David, 203, 215
Friedenberg, Edgar J., 30
Friedland, Anatol, 223
Frizzell, "Lefty," 267, 283
Fuller, Blind Boy, 49
Fulton, Buck "Huckleberry," 267

Gabler, Milt, xi
Galax Dixie Concert Band, 289
Galyon, Cotton, 269
Gardner, Robert, 10, 42, 50, 260
Garnich, Will, 279
"The Gateway Home," 56
Gatin, Bill, 230
Geller, James, 178
Gennett label, 48–49, 87, 202
Gentry Family, 13–14
Georgia Camp Meeting, 223–24, 235
Georgia Clodhoppers, 269
Georgia Wildcats, 151, 152, 266
Georgia Yellow Hammers, 224
"Georgia's My Home," 224
German, George B., 123, 125

"The Ghost Walks at Midnight," 109–10
Gibson, Charles Dana, 170
Gibson, Don, 269
Giezendanner, John, 280
Gilbert, Douglas, 225
Gilbert, L. Wolfe, 223, 232
Gilbreth, Frank B., Jr., 170
Gilded Age, 175
Gilpin, Ben, 276
Girls of the Golden West, 43, 140
"Give Me The Roses While I Live," 96
Glosson, Lonnie, 42, 269
Goebel, Georgie, 42
Goldblatt, Burt, 295
Golden, Harry, 232
"Golden Slippers," 129, 218, 277
"The Golden Wedding," 223
Goldsboro, Bobby, 239
Gong, 244
Good, Dolly, 43
Good, Milly, 43
Goodreau, Ed, 35
Gordon, Robert W., 81, 166, 178
gospel music: border station use of, 60, 72; types, 19–20
gospel quartet music, 19–20
"Governor Al Smith," 243
Grace Notes in American History, 15
Grainger, Percy, 194
Gramsci, Antonio, 140
Grand Ole Opry, 110–11
Grandpappy and His Gang, 263, 265, 266, 268
The Grapes of Wrath, 242
Graves, Buck, 109
Gray, A. A., 164
Gray, Ahaz, 227
Grayson, Shannon, 268
The Great Barlow's Minstrels, 279
Greats of the Banjo, 239

Green, Archie, xii, xxiii; publications in *JEMF Quarterly,* xix, xxv-xxvi, 158; work with JEMF, xiii, xvi
"Green, Green Grass of Home," 283
Green Valley Boys, 97–98
Grey Gull Company, 48–49
Griffis, Ken, xvi, xx, 46
Grossman, Stefan, 244
Groves, Paul, 102
guitar picking styles, 147
"Gulf Coast Blues," 89
Gully Jumpers, 142
Gunderson, Carl, 276
Gurney, Chandler "Chan," 119–22
Gurney, D. B., 119, 120
Guthrie, Woody, 238–39, 241, 243

Hagaman, Charlie, 265
Haggard, Merle, 239, 246
half-and-half songs, 284
Hall, Wendell, 137
Hamblen, Stuart, 283
Hamilton, Wyzee, 223
Hand, Wayland, xiv, xxii, xxiii
"Handsome Molly," 23
Handy, W. C., 225, 229
Hankins, Esco, 109
Hansen, Barry, xviii
The Happy Hicks, 291
Hard Cider Boys, 282
Harlan, Byron, 232
harmonica players, 277
Harper Family, 131
Harrell, Kelly, 78–80, 81, 82, 85
Harris, Emmy Lou, 244
Harris, Homer, 269
Hartford, John, xvi
Harvey, Nelly Day, 278
Havana Treaty, 70
Hawaiian guitar music, 130, 223, 280
Hawes, Bess Lomax, 198
Hawkins, Boss, 145

Hawkins, Steve, 282
Hawkins, Ted, 145, 146
Hay, George D., 36–37
Hayden, Palmer, 180
Hayes, Rex, 121, 123
Haynes, Henry (Junior or Homer), 265–66
Hazelrig, Polly, 187
"Heartaches by the Number," 283
Held, John, Jr., 169–82; biography, 176–77; Frankie and Johnny series, 177, 179–80; Gilded Age art, 173, 175, 177, 181; Jazz Age art, 169–73, 176, 181
Held, Uncle Billy, 130
Held's Angels, 170–71
Helen and Toby, 24
"He'll Have to Go," 283
Helms, Bill, 150–51
Hemitt, Dolph, 43
Henderson, Chuck, 109
Hendrickson, Bill, 277
Hendry, Bob, 35
"Henry Clay Beattie," 78–85
Henson, Charlie, 266
Hesitation Blues, 224–25, 235
"He Will Set Your Fields On Fire," 96
Hickory label, 110
The Hill Billies (album), 291
The Hill Billies (film), 293
The Hill Billies (musical group), 289, *290,* 291, 292–95
"Hill Billie Blues," 225
Hill, Delores, 124
Hill, Eddie, 268
"Hillbilly Hit Parade," 24
hillbilly image, 131
hillbilly music: border station use of, 60, 72; defined, 159, 160; early collectors, xii; influences on, 89; name origin, 290, 297–99; Northern tradition, 127–33; origins, 164–65; relationship to folk music,

157–67; selling power, 74; sheet music, 16
Hiller, Tony, xxi
"Hills of Roane County," 103
Hines, Earl, 89
Hines, Pete, 268
Hiram and Henry, 39
Hiser, Rusty, 97–98
Hobbs, Cliff, xi
"The Hobo's Last Ride," 194
Hoeptner, Fred, xiii, 127, 158–59
Hokinson, Helen, 178
Holden, Farley, 269
Holden, George, 220
Holiness Quartet, 54
Holmes, "Salty," 269
"Home on the Range," 239
Homer and Jethro, 43, 265–66
Hometown Boys, 145, 151
"Honey," 239
Honky Tonk cheating songs, 283
Hoosier Hot Shots, 43
The Hoosier Mimic, 42
Hoosier Sod-Busters, 42
Hopkins, Al, 141, 289, 292–93, 298, 299
Hopkins, Doc, 40, 147
Hopkins, Joe, 289, 292, *296*
"Hop-Scotch Polka," 235
Hornsby, Dan, 205–9
Horton, Lewis Henry, 194
Hot Shot Elmer, 268
Houchens, Buck, 267
house dances, 128–29
Housh, Merle, 39
Houston, Cisco, 222
Howard, Don, 72, 73
Howard, Harlan, 239
Howell, Bob, 101
Huckleberry and the Tennessee Mountaineers, 267
Hukkala, Edith, 277
Huron Valley Boys, 20
Huskey, Junior, 307

Husky, Ferlin, 283
Huston, John, 180
Hyland, Bob, 144, 152

"I Ain't Got Nobody," 88
"I Am a Stern Old Bachelor," 37
"I Got Mine," 220
"I Had But Fifty Cents," 129
"I Miss My Swiss (And My Swiss Miss Misses Me)," 141
"I Walk the Line," 283
"I Was Born about Four Thousand Years Ago," 284
"If I Could Hear My Mother Pray Again," 149
I'll Be All Smiles Tonight, 225
"I'll Be With You When the Roses Bloom Again," 283
I'll Meet Her Tonight When the Sun Goes Down, 225–26
"I'm Glad My Wife's in Europe," 226
"I'm Too Old to Cut the Mustard," 283
Indian songs, 223, 227–30
Instituto Ernesto De Martino, 239, 241
instruments, homemade, 88, 184
International Telecommunications Conference, 1932, Atlanta, 69
"In the Garden," 128
"In the Good Ol' Summertime," 129
"In the Jailhouse Now," 16–18
"In the Year of Jubilo," 279
"Irish Washerwoman," 128, 277, 281
Irvin, Rea, 178
"Is Anybody Goin' to San Antone?," 284
Italy, American country music in, 237–47

"Jack of Diamonds," 25
"Jackass Blues," 88
Jackson, George Pullen, 194
James, Bobby, 150
James, Skip, 139

James, Sonny, 239
Jamup and Honey, 269
Jazz Age, 168, 171
Jefferson, Blind Lemon, 47, 86, 88
JEMF Newsletter, xv, xviii-xix
JEMF Quarterly, ix, xv, xvi-xxvii; Commercial Music Graphics series, xix, xxv, xxvi
Jenkins, Andrew, Reverend, 12–13, 165
Jennings, Waylon, 215
Johanik, Phil, 277
Johanik, Tom, 273
John Edwards Memorial Forum, xxii
John Edwards Memorial Foundation, xiii-xvi
"John Hardy," 189
"John Henry," 144
"The John T. Scopes Trial," 8–9, 10
Johnson, Charles L., 222
Johnson, Charlie, 269
Johnson, Earl, 141, 224, 231
Johnson, Gene, 108
Johnson, Herman, 223
Johnson, J. Laurel, 147
Johnson, James Weldon, 178
Johnson, Johnny, 104
Johnson, Lewis, 120
Johnson, Sam, 66
Johnson, Tommy, 138
Johnson, Walt, 284
Johnson, Willie, 269
Johnson Brothers, 269
"The Johnstown Flood," 129
Joker label, 239
Jolly Riggi Boys, 279, 280
Jones, Ada, 223, 229–30
Jones, Coley, 90
Jones, Colon "Red," 150, 152
Jones, George, 24
Jones, Loyal, xx
Jordan, Victor, 110
Journal of American Folklore, xiv
The Journal of Country Music, xx

June Appal Records, 196
"Just Before the Battle Mother," 23

Kactus Kids, 124
Kahn, Ed, xii, xvi, *xviii,* xix; work
    with JEMF, xiii, xiv; writings for
    JEMF Quarterly, xxi, xxvi
Kahn, Gus, 233
Kamplain, Frank, 136
Karnes, Alfred G., 52–57
Karnes Family, 55–56
Katz Agency, 121
Kazee, Abigail Jane, 183–85
Kazee, Allan, 191, 192
Kazee, Buell Hilton, x, 158, 183–98
Kazee, John Franklin, 183–85
Kazee, Lewis Franklin, 196
Kazee, Philip, 191, 192
Keniston, Kenneth, 33
Kentucky Fried Chicken Boys, 245
Kentucky Girls, 43
Kentucky Mountain Boy, 38
Kentucky Slim, 264
Kentucky Travelers, 20, 22
KFKB (radio station), 63, 65–66
KFNF (radio station), 119
KHJ, Los Angeles, 62
Kincaid, Bradley, 38, 41, 284
King Cotton Kinfolk, 269
King, Pee Wee, 20, 266, 267
King Records, 21, 25
King, Wayne, 233
Kirby, Beecher, 307
Kirkpatrick, Floyd, 103
"Kitty Wells," 221
KLCN, Blytheville, 104
Klymasz, Robert, 272
KMA (radio station), 119
KMMJ, Grand Island, Nebraska, 100,
    101
"Knocking at the Door," 78
Knoxville News-Sentinel, 262
Koon, William Henry, xx
KPFK-FM, Los Angeles, xviii

Krahling, Joe, 291
Kreis, "Speedy," 269
KRLD (radio station), 88
KSTP (radio station), 282

Lacy, Rubin, Reverend, 138
Laibly, A. C., 200
Lair, John, 39–40
Lambert, "Yodeling Joe," 103–4
Lanham, Roy, 268
Lanson, Snooky, 24
LaPolla, Francesco, 242
Larkin, Uncle Bob, 63
Lass, Roger, 158
Laterza Publishing Company, 241
Lattimore, Mike, 110
Law, Don, 110
Laws, G. Malcolm, 158
Layne, Bert, 43, 147, 148, 150, 209
*Lead Poison on the Wall, Songs of
    Black Power,* 241, 243
Leake County Revellers, 207, 224,
    227
Leary Family, 95–101
Leary, Gerry, 99
Leary, Jacob, 96, 98, 99
Leary, Peggy, 101
Ledford, Lily Mae, 43
LeMaster, Bate, 184, 185
"Leonard's Waltz," 284
"Let Me Call You Sweetheart," 149
Letko, George, 277
"The Letter Edged in Black," 283
Leverette, Wilbur, 144
Levy, Lester S., 15
Lewis, Sam, 226
Lewis Family, 20, 24
Library of Congress American Folk
    Life Center, xix
Library of Congress Archive of Folk-
    song, 81
"Life is Like a Mountain Railroad,"
    304
Light Crust Doughboys, 86, 88, 89–90

Lilly Brothers, 269
Lind, W. Murdock, 234
Linder, Connie and Bonnie, 43
Lindley, David, 239
Lindsey, Pink, 230
Lindsey, Ray, 230
Listen, Mr. Bilbo, 241
Listen to Our Story, 293
"Listen to the Mocking Bird," 218
"Little Birdie," 23
Little Brown Church of the Air, 38
"Little Brown Jug," 297
The Little Cowboy, 42
"Little Girl and the Dreadful Snake," 23
"Little Glass of Wine," 108
"Little Log Cabin in the Lane," 152
"Little Old Log Cabin in the Lane," 146, 209
"Little Old Sod Shanty on the Claim," 37
Little Robert, 268
"Little Rosewood Casket," 283
"The Little Sod Shanty on the Claim," 283
Little Sunbonnet Girl, 40
Lockwood, Bob, 92
Logan, Tex, 109
Lomax, Alan, 166, 239, 241, 293–94
Lomax, John, 166, 178
"The Lone Pilgrim," 194
Lone Star Saloon, 86
"Lone Star Trail," 140
Lone Pine Ramblers, 131
Lonesome Pine Fiddlers, 20
"Lonesome Pine Special," 139
Loos, Anita, 176
"Lord Thomas and Fair Ellender," 184
Loudermilk, Romaine, 123
Louvin Brothers, 269
Love, Steve, 64
"Low and Lonely," 101
Ludlow, M. J., 225

Lulu Belle and Scotty, 20, 23, 42, 281
lumbercamps, 274, 276–77
"The Lumberjack Song," 285
Lunda, Haiki, 284
Lunn, Robert, 20
Lunsford, Bascom Lamar, 164

Mac and Bob, 10, 42, 50, 260
MacEvoy, Fred, 231–32
MacFarland, Lester, 10, 42, 50, 260
Macon, Uncle Dave, 152, 158, 164, 165, 281; "The Bible's True," 13; "Down the Old Plank Road," 243; early recordings, 259; "Hill Billie Blues," 225; "Peek-a-Boo," 227; singing style, 141
Madden, Edward, 229
Madsen, E. C. "Al," 119, 120
Mahony, Dan, 211
Maki, Einard, 277
Malone, Bill, xi, 127: *Country Music USA,* xviii. 295; edits *Stars of Country Music,* xx
Malone, K. D., 150
Maple City Four, 38
"Margie," 89
Marincel, Tom, 273
"Married by the Bible/Divorced by the Law," 283
Marsh, Reginald, 178
Marshall Tucker Band, 244
Martin, Asa, 147, 148, 165
Martin, Benny, 269
Martin, Emory, 269
Martin, James, 269
Martin, Jimmy, 269
Martin, Zeke, 123
"Mary of the Wild Moor," 23
Massey, Louise, 43, 281
"Matchbox Blues," 88
Matuszka, John, 122, 123, 126
"May Irwin's Bully Song," 220
Maynard, Ken, 140
Mayo, John, 264

McAuliff, Leon, 20
McCann, Mike, 276, 278
McCartt Brothers and Patterson, 147, 150
"McCloud's Reel," 128
McCormack, John, 188
McCormick, Ben, 184
McCuen, Brad, xi
McCulloh, Judith, xx
McFarland, Lester, 260
McFarland, Mac, 42, 50
McGee Brothers, 234
McGee, Gene, 268
McGee, John, 220
McGee, Kirk, 21
McGee, Sam, 21
McGuinn, Roger, 239
"McKinley," xix
McLaughlin's Old Time Melody Makers, 234
McMichen, Clayton, 144, 147, 152; Columbia recordings, 149–50; 207; criticism of Riley Puckett, 146, 148; joins the National Barn Dance, 43; "My Carolina Home," 209; "pop" leanings, 235; at WHAS, 266; on WSB, 145
McMichen-Layne String Orchestra, 140
McMichen's Melody Men, 150–51
McNeil, W. K., xx
McRee Sisters, 63
McTell, Blind Willie, 144
Meade, Douglas, xxiv
Meade, Guthrie T. "Gus," xxiv, xxvii
"Meet Me at the Bars," 232
Melodisc label, 21
"Memories of France," 89
Memphis Minnie, 49
Mercury label, 21
Merkin, Richard, 170, 172, 176
"Merry Widow Waltz," 227
"Midday Merry-Go-Round," 104, 264–67

"Midnight Special," 112
Milanowski, Felix, 277
Miller, Bob, 165, 202, 205–9
Miller, Curly, 266–67
Miller, David, 164
Miller, Frankie, 24
Miller, Harry, 221
Miller, Homer (Slim), 40
Miller, John "Lost," 265
Miller, Roger, 23, 239
Mills, Burrus, 90
Mills, Kerry, 223, 227, 234
Ming, Hoyt, 141
minstrel shows, 279
"Miss McLeod's Reel," 281
"The Mississippi Dip," 200
Mississippi Shieks, 139
"Missouri Valley Barn Dance," 121, 124
Mitchell, Guy, 24
"Mockingbird Hill," 283
Moilanen, Art, 284–85
"Molly O!," 227
"Mom and Dad's Waltz," 283
"Money Musk," 277
Monk and Sam, 266
Monroe, Bill, 27, 107–8, 159
Monroe Brothers, 262, 263
Monroe, Charlie, 20, 23, 267
Montana, Patsy, 43, 140, 281
Montana Slim, 20, 137, 140
Montgomery Ward, 214
Moody, Clyde, 20
Moog synthesizers, 27, 29, 31
Moore, A. Doyle, 292
Moore, Alex "Whistlin'," 90
Moore, Thurston, 16
Moore, "Uncle Tom," 269
Moran and Mack, 210
More Pious Friends and Drunken Companions, 178
Moreland, Peg, 220
Morgan, Carey, 223
Morgan, George, 24

Morris Brothers, 30, 99
Morris, Zeke, 267
Morton, Jelly Roll, 87
Moser Brothers, 279, 280
"Motherless Children," 23
"A Mountain Boy Makes His First
    Record," 194
Mountain Frolic, 292–94, 295
Moye, Claude, 38
Muir, Lewis, 223, 232
"Muleskinner Blues," 283
Mullican, Moon, 20, 25
"Murder in Cohoes," 129
Murphy, Jimmy, 269
Murray, Bill, 229
Muzak, 244
"My Blue Ridge Mountain Home,"
    16
"My Carolina Home," 209
"My Little Girl," 226, 235
"My Lord's Gonna Move This
    Wicked Place," 47
My Nellie's Blue Eyes, 226–27
"My Own Iona," 223
*My Pious Friends and Drunken Com-
    panions,* 178
"My Pretty Quadroon," 221

Nabell, Charles, 10–12, 164
Napier, Simon, 144
Nashville label, 21
National Council for Traditional Arts'
    festivals at Wolf Trap Farm, 291
National Folk Festival (1938), 96
National Museum of American His-
    tory, 291
Nelson, Donald Lee, 144
Nelson, Ed, 276–77
Nelson Family, 124
Nelson, Willie, 215
Nesmith, Michael, 244
"Never Be Lonesome in Heaven," 96
Nevins, Rich, 80
"The New Bully," 220

Newbern, Hambone Willie, 227
New Hillbilly String Band, 245
New Lost City Ramblers, 239
New Yorker, 176–77
Newport Folk Festival (1968), 196,
    198
Newport Folk Foundation, xvi
Nicholas, Joe, 158
Nichols, Bob, 149–50
"Nickety Nackety Now Now Now,"
    37
Nides, Harry, 261
Nitty Gritty Dirt Band, 244, 302,
    306–7
"Nobody Knows What the Good Dea-
    con Does," 227
"Nobody Knows You When You're
    Down and Out," 89
"Nobody's Business," 23
"No More the Moon Shines on
    Lorena," 221
Norfolk Jubilee Quartet, 47
Norman, Ben and Jesse Mae, 100,
    124
Norris, Fate, 148, 149, 150, 207
Norris, Joseph, 289
Norris, Land, 164
North American Regional Broadcast
    Agreement, 60, 71
North and Central American Regional
    Radio Conference, 1933, Mexico
    City, 69
North Carolina Ramblers, 162, 207
The Northern Stars, 286
"Not Turning Backward," x
Novak, Jerry, 276, 279
Novelty Boys, 124

Oaks, Charles O., 10, 259
Oberstein, Eli, 263
O'Connor, Bill, 37–38
O'Connor, Flannery, 303
O'Day, Molly, 20, 98, 102–4, 269
"Oh, Death," 23

O'Keefe, Jimmie, 191
Okeh label, 200, 202, 298
Okkonen, Eino, 277
Old Banjo Brothers, 245
"Old Cabin," 145
"Old Chisolm Trail," 25
"Old Dan Tucker," 218
"The Old Gray Horse Ain't What He Used to Be," 226
"The Old Gray Mare," 279
"The Old Rugged Cross," 128
"Old Shep," 283
"Old Time Cinda," 291
Old Time Music, xx
The Old Timers, 63
Old Timey label, 246
old-time fiddlers contests, 282
old-time music, 16, 272
O'Malley, Happy Jack, 120, 123, 124
O'Neill, Harry, 74
"On Top of Old Smokey," 281
Ordway, John P., 231–32
"Organ Grinder Blues," 87, 88
Original Hill Billies, 299
Osborne, Jimmie, 159
Ossenbrink, Luther, 39
Oswald, Bashful Brother, 20, 307
The Oulu Hotshots, 286
"Our Goodman," 221
"Our Johnny," x
"Out Behind the Barn," 283
Outlaws, 215
Overstake, Eva, 42
Overstake, Evelyn, 42
Overstake, Lucille, 42
Over the Hill Gang, 291
"Over the Waves," 232, 235
Owen, Anita, 230
Owen, Tex, 124
Owen, Tom, 35
Owens, Buck, 239
Ozark Hill Billies, 299

Pact, 244
Painter, Linda L., xxi
Palace label, 21
"Paper of Pins," 99
"Pappy Eatmore's Barn Dance Jubilee," 282
Paramount label, 46–48, 87, 202
Parker, Chubby, 37
Parker, Claudia, 35
Parker, John "Knocky," 86–92
Parker, Linda, 40, 281
Parton, Dolly, 246
Patrick, Ollie, 186
"Paul Bunyan's Ox," 276
Peabody, Eddie, 130
"Peaches Down in Georgia," 224
"Peek-a-Boo," 227
Peer, Ralph S., 74, 178, 200, 204; copyrights "In the Jailhouse Now," 17; field recording methods, 206–7; names hillbilly music, 289, 291, 298
Peerless Quartette, 223
People's Songs, 239
"Performer's Buck," 222
Perkins, Carl, 159
Perry County Music Makers, 139
Perryman, Pat, 151
Peterson, Hjalmar, 279–80
Peterson, Walter, 35
Phipps, Ernest, 54–55
Phipps Family, 20, 21, 25
phonographs, 280
Pickard, Buss, 75
Pickard, Charley, 75, 147
Pickard, Dad, 147
Pickard Family, 72, 75
Pickard, Obed, Jr., 147
"Pickin' the Five String," 22
Pickle, Charlie, 268
"Pick Me Up on Your Way Down," 283
Pierce, Don, 22
Pierson, Willie, 124

Pink Lindsey and His Bluebirds, 230
"Pistol Packin' Mama," 283
Plantation Minstrels, 279
"Plantation Party," 40
Plaza Music, 49
"Polka Dad Used to Play," 284
The Polkateers, 273
Poole, Charlie, 165, 200, 207
Portelli, Alessandro, 243, 244
Powers, Fiddlin', 164
Powis, George, 225
Prairie Bluegrass, 247
Prairie Farmer, 38–41
Prairie Ramblers, 43
"Pray for the Lights to Go Out," 227, 228
Presley, Elvis, 159
Presto cutter, 73
"Pretty Mohee," 191
Prince's Orchestra, 281
"The Prisoner's Song," 23, 195
progressive country music, 244–45
protest songs, 241
Provensen, Alice and Martin, 182
Puckett, George Riley, 47, 164, 165, 220; biography, 143–53; Columbia recordings, 200, 204, 207; yodeling of, 137, 141
"Put on Your Old Gray Bonnet," 279

QRS piano roll company, 48–49, 87
Queen, John, 220

racism among musicians, 86–92
radio: air time purchased by bands, 131; competition with record industry, 58–59, 73, 102, 108–9; effect on Northern rural areas, 281; international agreements regarding, 59–60; as a participatory medium, 125; regulation, 59–60; in the 1920s, 37, 261; signals, 121; syndication, 73; transcribed shows, 59, 73, 75

radio stations: border stations, 60, 66–75; playing ethnic country music, 282; social function, 119, 125–26
"Ragged But Right," 23
ragtime, 89
railroad songs, 283
Rainey Brothers, 264
Rainey, Ma, 47
"Ralph's Banjo Special," 22
Randall, Tex, 123
Randle, Bill, 203
Raney, Wayne, 19, 20
Razaf, Andy, 230
Realm label, 21
Reaves White County Ramblers, 225
record industry: competition with radio, 58–59, 73, 102, 108–9; earliest years, 46–47; manufacturing methods, 49–50
recordings: ethnic, 280–81; influence on musical styles, 163
Rector, John, 289, 292, 297
Rector, Red, 269
"Red Cockin' Chair," 23
Red Fox Chasers, 80
"Red Sails in the Sunset," 149
"Red Wing," 227–29, 277
Reeves, Goebel, x
Rem recording company, 21
Reneau, George, 164, 259
"Renfro Valley Barn Dance," 40, 265
Renfro Valley Boys, 40
Reno and Smiley, 25
Reser, Harry, 130
Reverelli, Mirma, 136
Rice, Hoke, 219
Rich-R-Tone label, 106, 108
Rickaby, Franz, 274
Ridge Runners, 40
Riilta, Dave, 284
Rimrock label, 19, 21

Rindlishbacher Hawaiian Guitar
    Quartet, 280
Rindlishbacher, Otto, 277, 280, 282
"Ring Waltz," 145
"Ringo," 239
Ritchie, Jean, 197, 302, 306
Ritter, Tex, 159
Robbins, C. A., 234
Roberts, Doc, 148, 221
Roberts, Leonard, 195
Robertson, Fiddling Eck, 26, 164
Robinson, J. Russell, 87, 89
Robison, Carson J., 165, 189; "Bar-
    bara Allen," 208; "The John T.
    Scopes Trial," 8–10; "My Blue
    Ridge Mountain Home," 16
rockabilly music, 159
"Rock All Our Babies to Sleep," 137,
    146
Rock Creek Rangers, 43
Rocky Mountain Ol' Time Stompers,
    238–39
Rodgers, Carrie, x, 140
Rodgers, Jimmie, 51, 89; image,
    16–18; yodeling style, 135–37,
    139, 141–42
Rogers, Kenny, 246
"Roll down the Line," 243
"Roll on Buddy," 23
"Roll On, John," 189
Ronstandt, Linda, 244
Rose, Fred, 108
Rose, Wesley, 110
Rosenberg, Neil, xix, 95
Ross, Harold, 174, 176–77
Ross, James, 303
Rounder Records, 196, 246
"The Roving Cowboy," 191
"Roving Gambler," 25
Rowell, Glenn, 36
Royal Hawaiians, 130
"Rufus Blossom," 234
Ruppe, Gene, 40
Rush, Ford, 35, 36

Russell, Mary H., 81, 82, 84
Russell, Tony, xx, xxvii, 227
Rusty Rubens, 131

The Saga of Frankie and Johnny,
    179–80
"Sagebrush Roundup," 102–3
"Sally Ann," 291
Salmoni, Fabrizio, xxi
"Salty Dog," 99
Sammy and Woody, 133
sampler albums, 24
Sandburg, Carl, 178, 181–82
Satherley, Arthur Edward, 45–51, 46,
    108, 110, 200
"Savior, Blessed Savior," 304
Scanlan, William J., 226–27
Schmidt, Elizabeth Blanche, 128–30
Scopes trial songs, 7–14
Scottdale String Band, 223, 235
Scripps-Howard, 262
Scruggs, Earl, 27–33, 109, 159, 269,
    307
Scruggs, Gary, 27, 31
Scruggs, Randy, 27, 29, 30, 31, 307
Sears-Roebuck, 34–44, 50
Sears-Roebuck label, 37
"Seattle Hunch," 87
Seeger, Charles, 157–58, 159
Seeger, Mike, 204, 208
Seeger, Pete, 238–39
"Seeking The Lost," 96
Shahn, Ben, 182
"The Shantyboy's Alphabet," 276
shaped-note singing, 95–96
Shapiro, Elliott, 15
Sharp, Cecil, 161, 162, 166
Shaw, Lee, 158
Shay, Frank, 178–79
Sheafe, M. W., 234
sheet music covers, 15–18
Shehan, Dennis and Louise, 265
Shelton, B. F., 54
Shelton, Jack, 269

Shelton, Robert, 127, 295
Shepard, Leslie, 15
Sherman Family, 131
"The Ship that Never Returned," 129
Short Brothers, 234
The Short but Brilliant Life of Jimmie Rodgers, 16
Shuttleworth, John, 181
Sides, Connie, 164
Sievers, Fiddlin' Bill, 264
Sievers, Mack, 264
Sievers, Willie, 264
"Silly Bill," 291
Silver Bell, 229
Sing Out, 158
"Sinking of the Titanic," 23
"Sitting on Top of the World," 88
"Six Days on the Road," 246
Skidmore, Will, 227
Skillet Lickers, 144, 152; best selling titles, 151; personnel problems, 147–48; popularity, 149, 194; recordings, 194, 200, 205, 207, 213; "Slow Buck," 222
Skinner, Jimmie, 20
Skratthult, Olle i, 279–80
Slayton's Jubilee Singers, 279
"Sleep Baby Sleep," 137
"Slow Buck," 222
Smith, Arthur "Fiddling," 21, 97, 152, 226, 229
Smith, Arthur "Guitar," 20–21
Smith, Arthur Q., 265
Smith, Bessie, xxi, 88
Smith, Bulow, 139
Smith, Fred, 269
Smith, J. T. "The Howling Wolf," 90, 138
Smith Sacred Singers, 207
Smith, Sawmill, 229
Smith, Walter "Kid," 84
Smithsonian Institution's Festival of American Folklife, 291
Smoky Mountain Boys, 307

Smoky Mountain Rose, 267
Snead, Roy, 269
"Snow Deer," 223, 230
Snow, Jimmie Rodgers, Reverend, 110
"Soldier's Joy," 128, 151, 219, 297
"The Soldier's Last Letter," 283
"Songs of the West," 238
Sons of the Pioneers, 19, 72, 159, 239
Sorrels, Sid, 291
Southern Comfort String Band, 245–46
Southern Folklore Collection, xxiv
Southern hillbilly image, 131
"Spanish Flandang," 23
Spareribs, 42
"Sparkling Blue Eyes," 99
Spencer, Len, 223
Spottswood, Dick, xxiv
squaredancing, 277–78
St. Louis Blues, 145, 229, 235
"Standing by the Gate," 226
Stanley, Fred, 147
Stanley, Ralph, 22
Stanley Brothers, 20, 22, 25, 108
Stanley, Roba, 164
Stanton, Jim "Hobart," 106, 108
Starcher, Buddy, 20
Starday Records, 19–26
Stars of Country Music, xx
Stateside label, 21
"Steel A-Going Down," 193
Steele, Harry, 74, 75
Stein, Gertrude, 171–72
Sterchi Brothers' Furniture Company, 259–62
"Stern Old Bachelor," 23
Stewart, Red, 20
Stier, Cliff, 267
Stokes, Lowe, 145, 147, 148; Columbia recordings, 151, 207
Stone Mountain Boys, 152
Stoneman, Ernest "Pop," 47, 164, 165, 293, 298; inspires Tony Alderman, 297; Starday recordings, 20

Story, Carl, 20, 24, 269
Strachwitz, Chris, xvi, xxv
"Strawberries," 137
"The Strawberry Roan," 123
Strictly Instrumental, 29
Stringbean, 20, 21, 25
Stringdusters, 265, 266, 269
Stringer, Lou, 110
Stuart, Am, 259
Stump-Us Gang, 126
"Sugar Hill," 141
"Suicide Blues," 23
Sumner, James, 230
"Sunday Get-Together," 121
Sunshine Boys, 24
Sunshine Sue, 43
Sutter, Smiley "Crazy Elmer," 109
"Swannee River," 239
Swannee River Boys, 110, 267
Swanson, Carl, 280
Swanson, Fritz, 280
"Sweet Bunch of Daisies," 145, 230, 231, 235
Sweetheart Mary, 124
Swiss Yodelers, 279
Sykes, Roosevelt, 87
syndication, 73

"T. B. Blues," 89
Taggart, John "Tiny," 131, *132*
Talent, Skeet, 261
The Talking Machine World, 292
Talmadge, Gene, 205
Tamony, Peter, xv
Tanner, Arthur, 150
Tanner Boys, 150
Tanner, Gid, 149, 150, 152, 164; Columbia recordings, 145–46; correspondence with John Edwards, x, 144; "Down Yonder," 222; in Skillet Lickers, 148, 151, 204
Tanner, Gordon, 151, 152, 218; "Down Yonder," 222
Tarlton, Jimmie, xi, 130, 141, 207

Taylor, Alma, 43
Taylor, Hartford, 40
Taylor, Jo, 43
Taylor, "Pay Cash," 261
Taylor, W. S., 188
Taylor, Webster "Big Road," 139
tearjerkers, 283
"Tennessee Barn Dance," 265, 269
Tennessee Mountain Boys, 268
Tennessee Ramblers, 261, 264
"Tennessee Waltz," 266, 283
Terhune, Max, 42
Terwilliger, Ramson, 131–32
Texas Playboys, 89
"That Silver-Haired Daddy of Mine," 39, 50
"There's a Big Wheel," 110
"There's a Star Spangled Banner Waving Somewhere," 283
They Don't Dance Much, 303
"This Is My Day, My Happy Day," 56
"This Ole House," 283
Thompson, A. P., 80
Thompson, Ernest, 164, 200, 220
Thrasher, M. L., 207
Three Little Maids, 42
Tibbett, Lawrence, 184
Timko, Myles, 291
"Tiptoe through the Tulips," 148
Tolliver, Roy "Speedy," 291
"Tom Joad," 242
trade names, 130
The Trailblazers, 131
"Tramp on the Street," 106, 108
transcribed radio shows, 59, 73, 75
"Travelling Onward to the City," 304
Trevathan, Charles, 221
Triangle Music Publishing Company, 16
Tribe, Ivan, xx
Tronson, Rube, 35
Tropical Islanders, 265
"Trouble in Mind," 152

truck-driving songs, 24
Tubb, Justin, 24
Tucker, Marshall, 244
Tucker, Tanya, 141
Tune Crackers, 126
The Tune Twisters, 131
Tunnah, Renton, 227
"Turkey in the Straw," 218, 277
Turner, "Black Ace," 90
Twelfth Street Rag, 230
"20 Cent Cotton and 90 Cent Meat," 23
"Twenty-One Years," 205
Twenty Original Reels, Jigs, and Hornpipes, 277
Twinkle, Twinkle, Little Stars, 231–32
"Twinkle, Little Star," 218
"Twinkling Stars Are Laughing, Love," 231
Two Black Crows, 210
2001 magazine, 244
"Two White Horses," 88

UCLA Folklore and Mythology Center, xiv, xxii
Ukrainian country music, 272
Ukulele Ike, 210
Uncle Ezra, 43
Uncle Josh, 171
Under the Double Eagle, 232, 235, 283
The Unicorn, 158
union scale, 42
University of North Carolina, xxii, xxiii-xxiv
up-picking style, 197
Utah Slim, 124

Vachon, Jingo Viitala, 278–79, 281, 284, 286
Vaughn Four, 267
Vetco label, 294
Victor label, 297–98
Victor Talking Machine Company, 54, 202, 206

Vocalion, 202, 259, 261
Von Tilzer, Albert, 226

"Wabash Blues," 145
"The Wabash Cannonball," 283
Wagner, J. F., 232
The Wagoner Lad, 194
"Wahoo," 283
"Wait for the Lights to Go Out," 227
Waite, W. W., 282
Waiting for the Robert E. Lee, 223, 232
Walburn and Hethcox, 227
Walker, Frank, 200, 204–12, 214
Walker, T-Bone, 90
"Walking in Jerusalem," 23
Walsh, Dock, 149
Walsh, Mary E., 220
Walsh, William, 225
The Waltz You Saved for Me, 233
Wanderers, 89
Ward, Cecil and Esther, 35
Warmack, Paul, 152
war-tinged songs, 283
Washington and Lee Swing, 234, 235
Watson, Doc, 27, 28, 29, 148
Watson, George P., 136
Watson, Merle, 27
wax masters, 49
"Way down in Georgia," 224
WBAP (radio station), 87, 89
WCCO (radio station), 282
WCHU, Ithaca, 131
WCKY Cincinnati, 20, 22
WDAF (radio station), 64–65
WDBJ, Roanoke, 267
WDGY (radio station), 282
WDOD, Chattanooga, 219
Weaver Brothers and Elviry, 42
"Weave Room Blues," 243
"Wednesday Night Waltz," 56
Weeks, Jack, 218
Weinhardt, Carl J., Jr., 177, 179
Weisberg, Eric, 239

Welk, Lawrence, 122–23
Welling and McGhee, 234
Wells, Kitty, 112, 269
Wells, Patricia Atkinson, xxi
Wells, Paul, xv, xxiii
WELM, Elmira, 131
Wenrich, Percy, 229
WESG, Elmira, 131
West, Irene, 130
Westergaard, Richard, 263
Western music, 159
Western swing, 19, 88, 283
The Westerners, 43
"Westward Ho," 15
WFAA (radio station), 87
WGY, Albany, 131
WHAS, Louisville, 266
Whistling Rufus, 218, 227, 234, 235
White, B. F., 194
White, Clarence, 148
White, Josh, *93*
White, L. E., 110
"The White Pilgrim," 194
"Whitehouse Blues," xix
Whitlock, Ralph, 35
Whitten, Charles, 145
Whitten, Miles, 145
Whitter, Henry, 16, 164
WIBC, Indianapolis, 101
"Wicked Path of Sin," 107–8
The Widow Jones, 220
Wiggins, Gene, xx
The Wild Bunch, 245
"Wild Flow Rag," 88
Wildcats, 43
Wilder, Trulan, 39
Wilgus, D. K., xiii, xiv, 144; death,
    xxiii; doctoral dissertation, 160,
    162; on Southern origin of hillbilly
    music, 127; on the Willis Brothers,
    25
"Will the Weaver," 158
"Willie Taylor," 277
Williams, Baxter, 261

Williams, Bill, 92
Williams, Clarence, 49, 87
Williams, Hank, 135
Williams, Robert Pete, 90, 92
Williams, Roger, 261
Will the Circle Be Unbroken, 302,
    306–7
Willis Brothers, 20, 24, 25
Wills, Bob, 49, 89–90, 159, 235
Wills, Lewis, 147
Wilson, Buddy, 267
Wilson, Conna and Colleen, 43
Wilson, Grace, 35
Wilson, Joe, 291
Wilson, Walter, 72
Wilson and Howard advertising
    agency, 72
"Wings of a Dove," 283
Winsett, R. E., 95
Wisconsin Chair Company, 45–47
Wise Blood, 303
Wise, Chubby, 20
Wiseman, Mac, 269
Wiseman, Scotty, 43
WJJD, Chicago, 39, 101–2
WJMS (radio station), 282
WJR, Detroit, 68
WKRT, Cortland, New York, 131
WLAC, Nashville, 104
WLS Artists Bureau, 41
WLS Family Album, 41
WLS National Barn Dance, 34–44,
    50, 281
WLS Soup Kitchen, 41
WLW, Cincinnati, 40
WMMN (radio station), 97, 102–3
WNAV (radio station), 260
WNAX, Yankton, South Dakota,
    118–26
WNOX, Knoxville, 259–70
Wolfe, Charles, xx, 223, 229, 234, 259
WON, Chicago, 68
Wood, Del, 223
Woodham, Woody, 109

Woodhull, Floyd, 128, 129–30, 131, *132*, 133
Woodhull, Fred, 128, 129, 131, *132*
Woodhull, Herb, 130, 131, *132*
Woodhull, John, 130, 131, *132*
Woodhull's Old Tyme Masters, 127–33
Work, Henry Clay, 279
WRC, Washington, 293
"Wreck of the Old 97," 2, 283
"Wreck on the Highway," x, 101, 300–307
"The Wreck on the Southern Old 97," 16
Wright, Johnnie, 268
WROL, Knoxville, 264
WSB, Atlanta, 68, 144–45
WSM, Nashville, 37, 110
WWNC, Ashville, North Carolina, 104–6
WWVA, Wheeling, 100, 106, 109

XEAC, Tijuana, 71
XEAW, Reynosa, 70
XEG, Monterrey, 71
XELO, Cuidad Juarez, 71, 72
XEMO. Tijuana, 71

XEPN, Piedras Negras, 70
XERA, Del Rio, 60, 70, 72, 73, 74
XERB, Rosarito, 71
XERF, Villa Acuna, 71, 72
XER (radio station), 66–70
XEWT, Nuevo Leon, 71
XFFW, Tampico, 71

"Yankee Doodle," 239
Yankton Old-Time Fiddlers Contest, 120
Yates, Herbert G., 50
Yellen, Jack, 219
"The Yellow Rose of Texas," 221
YMCA College Quartet, 38
yodeling, 135–42, 279, 280
yodeling songs, 283
"You Are My Sunshine," 283
"You Can't Make a Monkey Out of Me," 14
Young, Jess, 205, 230, 235
Young, Mahonri, 176
"Your Cheatin' Heart," 283
"You Will Never Miss Your Mother until She Is Gone," 16

Zimmerman, Harold, 225

About the Editor

Nolan Porterfield has written widely about American music and culture. He is the author of five books, including the acclaimed biography of "the father of country music," *Jimmie Rodgers: The Life and Times of America's Blue Yodeler.* His latest book is *Last Cavalier,* a biography of pioneer folksong collector John Lomax, who produces and hosts a weekly radio program, *Old Scratchy Records,* heard on four NPR stations in Kentucky. A Texas native, Porterfield now lives near Bowling Green, Kentucky.